The People We Were Before

Annabelle Thorpe is a journalist and travel writer for national newspapers and magazines, including *The Times* and *Sunday Times*, and the author of two non-fiction travel books. She has been visiting Croatia for over thirty years.

The People We Were Before is her first novel.

Annabelle THORPE

The People We Were Before

Quercus

First published in Great Britain in 2016 by

Quercus Editions Ltd
Carmelite House
50 Victoria Embankment
London EC4Y 0DZ

An Hachette UK company

A CIP catalogue record for this book is available
from the British Library

PB ISBN 978 1 78429 948 4
EBOOK ISBN 978 1 78429 951 4

10 9 8 7 6 5 4 3 2 1

Typeset by CC Book Production

Printed and bound in Great Britain by Clays Ltd, St Ives plc

For Allan

POST-WAR BALKAN STATES

FORMER
YUGOSLAVIA

ITALY

*
(Serbian Republic
of Krajina 1991-1995)

AUSTRIA

HUNGARY

SLOVENIA

CROATIA

Zagreb

← Krajina* →

Vukovar

BOSNIA

SERBIA

Knin

Sarajevo

Split

MONTENEGRO

Dubrovnik

KONAVLE
REGION

ADRIATIC SEA

ITALY

PART ONE

May 1979–December 1991

CHAPTER 1

Only a fool or a hero will laugh at the man who holds a gun. As I looked at the figure kneeling before me, I wondered which he was. Even on his knees his eyes were almost level with mine: fixed, unblinking, his back ramrod straight, the hint of a smile playing around his lips.

'Go on, shoot him.' Tara nodded towards the kneeling man. 'He wouldn't show you any mercy.'

A short bark of laughter broke the putrid air; anger sparked in me; my index finger tensed hard against the trigger; the clap of the gunshot and the shout of pain came almost together. He fell on his side, hand pressed against his chest, coughed once – and then nothing. I froze. Tara froze. Somewhere in the distance I could hear the rhythmic grind of the factories on the plain below.

'Search him.' Tara's voice was high, a little tight.

I nodded. The sun burned hot on my skin. I re-cocked the gun and stepped forward, sullen grey dust billowing up around my feet. The man didn't move. I kicked at his outstretched leg. Nothing.

And then suddenly an arm shot up, fingers wrapped themselves around my leg and brought me to the floor. The gun slipped through my fingers, my hip banged against the hard earth, his hands were tight around my waist. I opened my mouth to shout to Tara, *Get the gun, get the GUN!* but before I could speak he had pinned me down, knees astride my body, one strong hand holding my arms above my head.

'You thought you had finished me off,' he roared, 'but guns are so old-fashioned, Miro, what are you, a cowboy?' He leered down at me, his face half shadowed from the scorching light. My lungs pumped short, hard breaths into the sticky air; I felt sweat beads begin to pop on my forehead; suddenly he sat back, took his fingers from my arms and waggled his hands at me. 'Death by tickling is the only honourable way for a man to go.'

He pounced before I could move and suddenly his big hands were dancing up my sides and across my stomach until I was giggling and squirming and begging him to stop.

'There was no mercy for me,' he yelled, but before I could reply Tara launched herself at him, knocking them both on to the floor.

'Take that,' she roared, her little fists pounding into his chest. But she was no match for Goran, who simply swivelled round to lay his legs across her body, pinning her down, before reaching back to try to tickle me again.

'I could take the two of you in my sleep,' he laughed as I scrambled away from him. 'You've got to plan your attacks better than this.'

'Get off me,' shrieked Tara. 'You're such a bully.'

'Weren't you the one who wanted me dead?' He lifted his legs off Tara and pulled her to her feet. 'That's a fair excuse for a leg-crush, wouldn't you say?'

He grinned at her and I sidled up to my brother and slipped an arm around his waist. All of the favourite times in my eight-year-old life had been spent with him; I adored Goran, looked up to him, wanted to *be* him. It never seemed to matter that he was twice my age, he always had time: to play with me up at the old fort, to teach me how to dribble a football, to sit on the end of my bed and tell me stories when I couldn't sleep. He hugged me to him for a moment and my face brushed against his chest; his T-shirt smelt of washing powder and sweat and comfort.

'Come on, you two.' I squinted up at Tara; her face fell.

'Do we have to go home already?'

Goran nodded. 'Yes, we do. You know Mother will be cross if we're late for supper, and Tara, your dad will want you home too.'

'He won't notice if I'm there or not,' she muttered.

'Of course he will. Now, shoulders or back? You first, then Tara when we get to town.'

I beamed. 'Back. Then we can run.'

He knelt down and I clambered on, wrapping my arms around his neck, my legs knocking slightly against his hips. He eased himself up, made a noise like a car engine revving furiously and suddenly we were off, down the hill towards the grey streets of Knin, past the vast factory pumping out plumes of dense, mustardy smoke, through the dilapidated churchyard and out on to the dusty main street.

'My turn now,' said Tara firmly, as the low-slung houses and tatty shops rose up around us. I jogged along beside them, Tara bouncing and whooping on Goran's shoulders as we ran past Pa, neatening the vegetables outside his shop, and on down the alley towards our home.

'What have you been *doing*?' scolded Mother, as we tumbled into the tiny yard. Tara slithered down Goran's back and fell in a heap, giggling. 'Tara, it's time you were home – your aunt's been looking for you. Goran, you're not eight *too*. Go and get washed right now. Pa will be home soon and he says he wants us all at the table together. He says he has some news.'

'Go on, trouble.' Goran pushed Tara gently towards the gate, and she raised her hand and wiggled her fingers at me before disappearing back into the alley. 'Now come on, Mother,' he said, putting an arm around her shoulders, 'you forgive us, don't you? Just this once?'

'Once?' But her face had softened and she smiled down at me. 'Let's hope you don't grow up to be as cheeky, Miro; I can't be doing with two like him around the place. Now go and wash your hands – properly, mind. Don't follow your brother's lick-spit example.'

She dropped a kiss on my head but I wriggled away; I didn't want to be the little boy, I wanted to be strong and tall and funny like Goran. I followed him through our cramped kitchen, squeezing past the battered table where we ate our meals and up the steep stairs that dipped slightly in the middle as if every footstep that passed took a minuscule layer of wood with it. The tap in the bathroom creaked and groaned as the rust-coloured water dribbled into the basin and I stared into the mirror hoping – as always – to see a younger version of my brother. But the small face that looked back at me, with nervous dark eyes and a perfectly aligned, freckled nose, bore no relation to his messy features. There was nothing neat about Goran's face; his thick, black hair fell into wide grey eyes and his nose slanted noticeably to the left. 'You should see the other guy,' he would say loftily, when I'd ask him why his nose was bent.

'Come *on*.' Goran appeared behind me in a clean T-shirt and pushed me away from the sink, chasing me down the uneven stairs to the kitchen, where our sister was already sitting at the table.

'Anyone would think you were both children,' she said, as we slid on to the bench opposite her. I liked Cvita, liked it when she took me into town and bought a dinar's worth of sherbet from Mrs Kardovic's shop, but sometimes I didn't really know what to say to her. At eighteen, she already had a boyfriend, Branko, who had a moustache and smelt of cigarettes and talked to me as if I was a baby. I didn't much like him, and I knew Goran didn't either, because when Cvita left the house with Branko he would make a noise, quite an odd noise, almost a growl.

'Do you know what Pa's news is?'

Goran shook his head and reached across the table for a chunk of bread. 'No idea.'

'You'll know soon enough,' said Mother, pulling a huge casserole dish from the oven, almost disappearing behind a great puff of steam. In one seamless movement she laid it on the table and continued to move her right arm so it connected with Goran's just as he was about to take another piece of bread. Their eyes met and a smile moved between them. As if on cue, the door creaked on its hinges and Pa appeared, raising his hand and smiling before disappearing upstairs to wash.

'What's tonight's feast?' he called from the bathroom.

Goran lifted the casserole lid; steam spiralled upwards, the scent of meat and herbs filling the room. '*Lònac*,' he announced, and I licked my lips at the thought of my favourite dinner.

Supper was the highlight of the day in our house; spicy stews and thick meaty casseroles cooked up with whatever was left on the shelves of Pa's shop each evening. Sometimes Mother worked there in the afternoons, and Cvita and I would walk up to help carry home the bags of vegetables and scraps of meat wrapped in newspaper. While she slipped off her overall and pulled her coat from the peg, I'd dip behind the chipped wooden counter, close my eyes and inhale the different smells: smoked sausage and coffee beans and the salty waft of the *kajmak*, a soft cheese spooned into individual paper cups. 'Come on out, rascal boy,' Mother would say, briskly, and I'd look up at her and think how different she looked: a smiling lady in a clean grey jumper with powder on her face, sleeves free of flour and flecks of pastry, hair swept back neatly into a tight bun.

'*Pa*,' said Cvita, as he settled in between us and Mother ladled the stew on to our plates, 'come *on*. We're all desperate to hear the news.'

He smiled, and it took a moment for me to realize that it was a new smile, one I didn't think I'd ever seen before. I watched as he straightened his knife and fork, blue eyes dancing between us. Even I could see that Pa was *excited*.

'And spoil your mother's supper? I don't think so. It's a letter from Ivo; that's all I'm saying.' He winked at me and I smiled a little uncertainly. 'Now eat. *Eat*. And, boys, what have you been doing today?'

Goran grinned. 'I was almost executed,' he said airily. 'By young trouble over there, and little Tara next door. They showed me no mercy whatsoever.'

Pa laughed. 'She's a tough little thing, that one. But then I suppose she's had to be. Glad to hear you showed your brother who's boss though, Miro. Got to keep him in his place.'

I smiled at Pa, unsure quite what to say. I loved my father, but in some ways he was a stranger to me. He left for work before I was awake and by supper I was often tired and we spoke little. Sometimes I fell asleep at the table and he would slip his arms under my legs and I would rest my head on his collarbone, breathing in the lemony scent of the soap he used at night to scrub off the factory fumes and the tang of smoked meats and cheese. I never felt safer than when he carried me slowly upstairs, and I would lock my fingers tightly around his neck so that when he laid me on the bed he would sit with me until I fell asleep.

It wasn't until the plates were cleared and the scent of coffee was twisting through the low-ceilinged kitchen that Cvita tried again.

'Come on, Pa. We've let you eat in peace. What's Ivo's news?'

'Why don't I let *him* tell you,' said Pa, sliding his fingers into the pocket of his cardigan and producing several folded sheets of paper. He pushed his glasses up his nose, peered down at the first sheet and glanced around at each of us. '"*Dear Petar, I hope that . . .*" Oh, this is just family stuff. Hmm, ah, here we go. "*Marjana's father passed away some months ago and the house in Ljeta is now ours. Do you remember it – right on the harbour front? At first we thought we would live there, but Ljeta is changing and tourists are starting to come in bigger numbers. I said to Marjana that it might make a good little business.*"'

I listened as Pa read on, words I didn't understand, about business possibilities and tourist numbers and shared ownership. '"*Would you consider coming to start the business with me? How long have we dreamed of such a thing, to be brothers in business together? And how much better for the children to grow up here, where there is such beauty and now prosperity."'*

'That's enough.' I looked over at Mother; she sounded angry. 'Petar, what are you thinking of, reading this out to the children before we've discussed it?'

Pa laid down the sheets of paper and stared at my mother. 'But it's a wonderful opportunity, Jada, don't you think?'

'No, I don't think –' She stood suddenly, jolting the table as she moved to the window; her coffee cup wobbled and fell, pooling dark liquid across the table. She made no attempt to mop it up. No one spoke. For a moment there was complete silence, then the gentlest hint of a noise. I glanced across at Pa. He was staring at my mother, motionless, just the second finger of his right hand tapping insistently on the sheets of paper.

'How could we possibly move?' Mother turned suddenly, her face was scrunched up and pink, lips pressed together. 'Goran in his last year at school, Miro in his first, the business, our home.'

'We'd have a better business, more money, a bigger home.'

'I don't *want* a bigger home or a better business, I . . .' She looked down at me, as if suddenly remembering I was there. 'Goran, please take Miro upstairs. Cvita, bring the washing in from the yard. *Now*, please.'

Goran pulled me from my seat and I ran up the stairs, but the house was too small and the walls too thin to block out the argument that raged downstairs. I lay on my bed and closed my eyes and tried not to hear the rise and fall of my parents' voices; 'But *why* is it better for Miro to grow up there?' my mother yelled. 'Because there's a better chance of a decent future in Ljeta,' Pa snapped back.

I looked over at Goran. 'Where's Ljeta?'

He pushed open the window, pulled a cigarette packet from his pocket and lit one, blowing the smoke out into the evening air.

'Bloody hundreds of miles away. Down south, on the coast. Near Dubrovnik.'

I had seen pictures of Dubrovnik. It looked like a city in a story-book: hundreds of terracotta roofs all clustered together, surrounded by thick stone walls that towered up above the houses and kept them safe from the wide blue sea beyond. It didn't look real to me; not somewhere people actually lived and went to work and ate their dinner. Not like Knin.

'But we live here.'

'Of course we do. And we're not going anywhere, so don't you worry. I've one more year in school and then I'm joining the police. I'm not swapping that to fold sheets and serve breakfast to tourists. You're settled at school, Cvita won't want to leave Branko . . . and anyway, Mother simply wouldn't have it. She'd never hear of us leaving Knin.'

The next morning it seemed as if Goran was right. Pa had already left for the shop by the time we sat down for breakfast, and the only sign of last night's conversation was a dark stain on the kitchen table.

'Are we staying here?' I asked Mother as she spooned eggs on to my plate.

'Of course we are, it was just a silly idea of Uncle Ivo's.' She patted my head absently and exchanged glances with Goran. They both looked relieved.

'But I like Uncle Ivo,' I said. 'And I'd like to see Dubrovnik.'

'We all like Uncle Ivo,' said Mother. 'And it was a lovely idea. Perhaps we'll go on holiday there this summer; would you like that?'

I nodded, but I couldn't help feeling disappointed. Uncle Ivo didn't come to Knin very often, but whenever he did everything suddenly became more fun. He seemed like a giant in our house – tall and broad with a booming voice that swirled up out of his stomach and filled all the tiny rooms. When he was with us my feet rarely touched the floor; piggyback rides down to Pa's shop, fireman's lifts to take me up to bed. And in the evenings I would sit on his lap and watch the light gleam in the bowl-shaped glasses of Stock he and Pa would drink together, the scent of brandy twisting into the air as I listened to the stories they wove from their childhood.

'What your father doesn't understand,' said Mother, as we sped towards school that morning, her feet matching the pace of her words, 'is that this town has meaning. Growing up in the north, well, of course he doesn't understand, but here . . . it's only thirty-five years since your granddad was fighting against the fathers of our neighbours, Croat against Serb, friend against friend, such violence, such *savagery*. I shouldn't talk of it at your age, but you need to understand – this is the history of our town, and although awful things happened, good has come out of it. Knin – the whole of the Krajina – is proof that we can bury the past, that we can live peacefully alongside those we once fought against. Do you understand?'

'Ye-es.' I didn't understand at all, didn't even know whether we were Croats or Serbs, but it seemed the best way to stop her talking. 'So we're definitely not going?'

She stopped and looked down at me; there were grey smudges under her eyes. 'Not if I have anything to do with it. Your father would jump out of a window if his brother told him to. He might want to live in the south, where the sun always shines and people live silly, shallow lives, but your grandfather didn't fight for our right to live here just so we could go running off to the coast.'

I had never been more glad to get to school. In the days that followed, a strange atmosphere settled over our house, as if all the words that weren't being spoken were cluttering up the air, making it hard to get comfortable or feel relaxed. Dinners were quiet, broken only by brief snippets of chat between Mother and Cvita, or questions from Pa about my day at school. No one mentioned Uncle Ivo, or

Dubrovnik, and I felt sad for my father, who had been so excited by the letter and the new life it promised.

'I'm glad you're not going.' Tara's foot pushed against my shoulder and I looked up at her, sat on a branch of the ash tree above me, sucking on an ice pop. 'Who would I play with?'

I considered her question for a moment. 'Martina? Elena?'

'They're both *wet*.' She jumped down from the tree. 'I wish I had a twin. Then there'd always be someone. I'd never be on my own.'

I said nothing. Tara and I never really talked about what went on at her house, but I knew her mother was dead and that she often appeared at our back door at just about the time supper was being served up.

'I think it'd be weird. It'd be like there were two of you, only the other person would be someone different.'

She wrinkled her nose. 'That doesn't make sense.'

I shrugged.

She stood silently for a moment, sucking her ice pop so hard that the strawberry colour seeped into her mouth, leaving just a faded shard of ice. 'Look –' she stuck out a scarlet tongue and laughed. 'I'm bored. Let's go and get your brother and go up to the fort.'

'OK. But he might be busy.'

'He'll find time. I like Goran. Maybe I should marry him – when I'm older. Then we'd be family, like twins. What do you think of that?'

Before I could answer she broke into a sprint; I picked up the ice-pop wrappers and ran after her, almost tripping over a broken paving stone, twisting through the huddles of grey-haired women who stood on the street corner talking, their voices scratching like the chickens in the next-door yard.

'Goran?' She pushed open the door to our house to find my brother sat in the armchair, half-hidden behind *Večernji List*. 'Stop reading the paper, we want to go up to the fort. Come with us?'

'I'm busy.' He lowered the newspaper, turned a page, winked at me and lifted it again so that his face was entirely hidden.

'You're not busy. You're reading the paper.'

'Incorrect, Little Miss Imperious –' he lowered the paper again – 'I *am* busy. Reading the paper. Go and have a kick around or something.'

'*Please*, Goran.' She sidled up to him and laid a hand on his arm. 'It's always so much more fun with you, and it's ages since we all went up there.'

'It was only . . .' He smiled and shook his head. 'Oh, all right. But I want to finish reading this article. You go on and I'll catch you up – my legs are twice as long as yours so I'll be there in half the time.'

'But . . .'

I shook my head at Tara; Goran never took kindly to being nagged.

I followed her out of the kitchen and we broke into a run as we headed down the street, skipping over piles of dusty crates and bags of rubbish. 'Where's Goran?' called Pa, as we sprinted past.

'He's coming,' I yelled back, trying to keep time with Tara's scuffed green plimsolls as she jogged up the hill ahead of me.

'Let's hide,' she said, turning suddenly. 'Then Goran won't be able to find us. Let's climb up on to the walls and watch him. It'll be so funny.'

'But you can't get up the walls. There's no stairs.'

'There are at the back. There's an old stone staircase that goes right to the top – over there, see?'

I squinted at where she was pointing; on the far side of the hillside I could just make out a crumbling set of steps built into the only remaining tower.

'But Goran always says not to go that way.'

'That's exactly why he'll never find us,' said Tara, grinning. 'Come on.'

'I don't think we should.'

'Don't be such a *girl*. Come on, I'll race you.'

She set off, her plimsolls thudding down on to the dusty grass, slower now, winded a little by the steep climb up the hill. I fell behind, my eyes dropped to the ground and then suddenly something happened, something otherworldly: a thunderclap from beneath the ground, the earth spewing up like a fountain, Tara in the air, on the grass, screaming, writhing. Something hit me in the face and I opened my mouth to shout but nothing came; only Tara's noise, sharp spikes of sound like I had never heard. I tried to move towards her, but my legs were frozen. I closed my eyes, couldn't look, not at her, not at *that*.

And then the world went black.

CHAPTER 2

'Miro. *Miro.* Christ. Miro, wake up!'

Goran. I opened my eyes to find my brother's face staring down at me. 'Thank Christ. Are you OK? Are you hurt?'

'I'm all right,' I said. My voice sounded small and tight. 'I . . .'

'Christ. Tara. Oh Jesus.' The hand he had wrapped around mine slipped away, and I turned my head slightly so I could see him; he pulled off his T-shirt and knelt beside her, ripping it into two and winding a length of torn white material around her leg. It instantly turned red. She was crying now, gasping and gulping. It sounded like she was drowning.

'Tara, it's Goran . . . you're OK, darling, I'm here, I've got you.' He kept one hand over the material around her foot and pressed the other piece against her left hand. I stared at something small and pink in the grass. It looked odd, out of place. Suddenly I realized what it was. I felt sick.

'Miro? You're OK, right? Tell me you're OK?'

He didn't turn around, kept his focus on Tara. I began to cry; I wanted Goran to be looking after me; my cheek throbbed and my knee hurt and every time I breathed in a minuscule wave of dust got sucked into my mouth and coated my tongue.

'Miro.'

'I'm all right. But I'm scared. What happened?'

'I don't know.' His voice was oddly thick, as if he was choking. 'But we have to get Tara to hospital. Tara, sweetheart, I'm going to lift you up. I'm going to carry you to the hospital ... It's going to hurt though.'

'Nooooo.' Tara's wails grew louder and I watched as my brother slipped an arm under her shoulders and carefully sat her up.

'I have to, Tara. I have to get you to the doctor. You're going to be fine. Nothing is going to happen. Are you ready? Hold on to me, sweetheart, hold on as tightly as you like. I've got you. All right? I've got you.'

She screamed again as he tucked his arm under her legs and stood up, slightly unsteadily. He looked down at me, and although he tried to smile, the skin seemed to be stretched too tightly across his bones.

'Miro, I need you to be very brave and help me. We need to keep Tara's leg up, keep it straight. Can you do that?'

I stood up slowly and nodded. My knee was bleeding, but Goran didn't seem to notice.

'Come on then. The quicker we can get Tara to hospital, the better.'

I tried not to think about how much I wanted him to be carrying me, and instead I slipped my fingers under Tara's legs and lifted them so they were parallel with the rest of her body. She was almost rigid in Goran's arms, her body vibrating as the breath ripped in and out of her mouth, faster and faster, mixed with bursts of wailing that sounded horribly like the foxes I sometimes heard at night. I bit my lip and told myself not to cry as we staggered down the hill towards Knin.

'Pa!' Goran's voice was harsh and loud and my father heard it even though we were right at the top of the street. As he came towards us my face wobbled, I couldn't hold it in any more. Tara wouldn't stop sobbing and the blood from her leg was starting to leech on to my fingers.

'Oh my God, what happened? Miro, are you all right?' I almost fell into him, crying with relief at the scratchy feel of his work shirt and the smell of the shop that seeped off his skin.

'Take the van.' I heard the jangle of keys. 'I'll tell her aunt. Or her father, if I can find him. Get Mika to go with you; he's in the shop. He can drive you. You need to keep that leg straight. Go. *Go*.'

I watched over Pa's shoulder as Goran disappeared down the street, Tara still wailing into his shoulder. He pulled back a little from me, and just the sight of his familiar craggy face made me start crying again.

'My boy –' he kissed me roughly on the cheek – 'let's get you home.'

By the morning of the next day I still didn't understand what had happened to Tara and me. When Pa carried me through the door, Mother had been her usual practical self; ran a hot bath, made me drink sweet tea and carefully cleaned up the scratch on my face and my bloodied kneecaps. Then she sat me on the sofa, wrapped in a blanket, and fed me thick slices of home-made bread and beef and tomato soup.

'What happened?' I asked, when she came back into the room with a bowl of stewed plums and a huge dollop of cream. 'Is Tara going to die?'

She smiled. 'No, my rascal boy, Tara is not going to die. But she is hurt. Maybe we'll go and see her in the hospital in a day or two. But right now, you need to rest.'

In the end it was Goran who explained, who sat on the corner of my bed and told me about the silent silver discs that lay mutely beneath the dusty grass: sleeping killers, waiting for an unsuspecting foot to wake them.

'I thought it was the devil,' I said. 'It was like he was coming up from hell.'

Goran ruffled my hair. 'What have they been teaching you at school?'

I broke off a piece from the huge bar of chocolate he had brought me and thought about what he was saying. 'But if these mines have been there since the war, how come no one has come and dug them all up? How come we didn't know they were there?'

'No one knew – everyone thought they'd all been removed. In the war, there were a lot of mines in this area, but afterwards soldiers came and cleared them. When I was growing up it was a big thing; Knin was safe, kids could play anywhere. But Mother never liked me going to the back of the fort, although she'd never say why. People don't talk about things in this town, Miro. That's part of the problem. But we never go the back way up to the fort – what on earth were you doing around there anyway?'

'Tara thought it would be fun to hide from you. She said . . .' Tears stung the back of my eyes and I swallowed hard. 'She was hurt really badly, wasn't she?'

Goran looked down at his hands. 'This is my fault,' he muttered. 'I should have been with you.'

'Goran, is Tara . . . ?'

'She's going to be OK, I promise. She's having an operation today and the doctor said she'll be able to walk again after a while, although she'll need a special shoe. He said she'd been very lucky.'

'Because she could have died?'

Goran put his head in his hands. 'Yes.'

'Boys?' Mother appeared from the kitchen, frowning anxiously. 'Come on now. No point in talking about it endlessly. Miro, I think you should go back to school tomorrow. Goran, don't you have some homework to do? Pa's going in to see Tara later; he'll be able to tell us how she is at dinner. Sitting around worrying won't help anyone.'

Goran passed me back the comic I had been reading and followed Mother out of the room. 'I keep thinking it could have been him in that hospital,' I heard him say in a low voice. 'Why didn't I go with them? Why?' And then there was silence, a lot of sniffing, the sound of a kiss. I hoped Mother wasn't crying.

Their voices started again, but although I strained to listen I could only catch the gist; they were talking about Uncle Ivo and Ljeta and the letter he had sent Pa. Suddenly it seemed it was all anyone could talk about; I had overheard Mother and Pa in the yard the night before, although I couldn't work out whether they were cross with each other or not. 'This is what you mean by the past being buried, is it?' I heard my father say. I wondered if it was a joke, but neither of them laughed.

When Pa came home that night I hugged him and slipped on to his lap. 'Is Tara OK?' I asked, as he bent down to kiss me.

'She was asleep when I went in. But the doctor said the operation went well. She won't be home for a few days, but she's going to be fine. Nothing for you to worry about, my boy. Nothing for you to worry about.'

But I *was* worried. Where else were these landmines buried? What if I stepped on one next time – or Goran, or Mother? How did the whole town just go on about its business with the threat of suddenly being blown up hanging over everyone? I didn't understand, and I didn't like it.

'I'm scared,' I said suddenly, when we were all sat around the kitchen table. 'I don't want to live here any more. I want to go to Ljeta.' To my fury, I found myself crying, tears streaming down my face. Cvita drew me to her and Pa put his hand gently on my arm.

'Do you, Miro? Is that really what you want?'

I nodded; I wanted to get away from all of it: from the horrible images of Tara that flashed up in my mind every night before I went to sleep, from the sad expression on my brother's face, from a place where flat silver devils slept beneath the ground, waiting to explode at any moment.

'Well, your mother and I have been talking, and we feel that perhaps it is a good idea to move,' said Pa slowly. 'After what's happened, you deserve . . . an adventure. Because that's what it would be, Miro, a real adventure. Wouldn't it, Jada?'

Mother smiled, but there was something odd about it; it didn't quite reach her eyes. 'Yes,' she said brightly. 'An adventure.'

'For all of us,' I said, beaming at Goran.

'Not quite.' He coughed awkwardly. 'Look, well, the thing is, my exams are soon and also, well, Tara's going to need a lot of looking after and I'm not sure her father's quite up to it. And Cvita doesn't want to leave Branko.'

'You're not *coming*?' I stared at Goran. 'But we're a *family*. You can't . . . I mean, we can't . . .' But I couldn't find the words, and I pushed back my chair and ran out of the room. As I climbed the stairs to my bedroom I heard Pa's voice, angry and sharp: 'You see? I *told* you it would break his heart. As if he hasn't been through enough. You think only of yourself, Goran. Only of yourself.'

It took just three weeks for Pa to pack up our lives. Another envelope came from Ivo, and Pa took out a handful of notes and bought a rusting yellow truck that screeched like a donkey every time he put his foot on the brake. Mother spent her days piling books and crockery into the cardboard boxes that Pa brought back from the shop, stopping regularly to take out the tissue she kept tucked into the sleeve of her cardigan. After school one afternoon I sat at the kitchen table and watched her wrap the china; one piece at a time fetched down from the cupboard, placed in the centre of a sheet of newspaper that she tucked slowly and carefully around the cup. There was a rhythm to it, but it wasn't a happy rhythm.

'Tara's home.' Pa's voice broke the silence, and I ran out into the yard to see Goran with my friend in his arms. My stomach twisted at the sight of her; her right cheek was covered by a square of plaster, her left hand and right foot were entirely hidden by thick white bandages.

'Hey, Miro,' she said, grinning. 'How are you? Guess you might finally be able to beat me at football now I've got this.' She waved the bandaged foot at me and I laughed.

'Can she stay for tea, Mother?'

'Not tonight. Maybe tomorrow. Her aunt's staying for a few nights to settle her in and I know she wants her home. Tara darling, why don't you come for dinner tomorrow?'

Goran nodded, and Tara waved as they disappeared back through the yard and into the alley. Mother walked back into the kitchen and Pa smiled down at me.

'You look different,' I said, as I followed him to where the yellow truck was parked. 'You look like Goran.'

'It's amazing what the thought of an adventure can do. A few weeks in Ljeta and you'll look different too, mark my words.' He wrapped an arm around my shoulders, pointing at the grimy, low-slung cottages stretching away down the street. 'Remember all this. Look at the sky, at the mountains – everything is grey or brown, the streets are dusty and dirty. Where are the colours, Miro, the blue sky and the green hills? In Ljeta the mountains are covered in pine trees, the sunsets are pink and gold, the sea is full of fish. What an adventure we're going to have.'

And when I was with Pa it felt like an adventure to be escaping Knin, to be travelling to this other world he talked of. But as the day of our departure grew closer I felt increasingly panicked at the thought of leaving my home and my brother, Cvita and Tara. When the last morning came, I didn't want to let go of Goran, squeezed up close to him while we ate a silent breakfast, and let him carry me into the street, my face buried in his shoulder.

'How many weeks till I see you?' He set me down on the street and smiled down at me. 'Come on, Miro, be a man. How many weeks till your birthday?'

'Six,' I mumbled.

'And they'll go by really quickly,' said Cvita, ruffling my hair. 'You'll have so many new things to do you won't notice the time go by. Will he, Mother?'

I looked at Mother; there were tears running down her cheeks. My stomach went funny. I held on to Goran more tightly.

'Come on, Jada,' said Pa. 'No crying now. You'll upset the boy. It's a big enough day for him.'

'For all of us,' she said, thinly. 'I'm saying goodbye to my children, Petar. I think some tears are allowed, don't you?'

Pa smiled awkwardly and drew Cvita towards him, dropping a kiss on her hair. Behind them, I saw Tara walking slowly up the road with her aunt; she had crutches under her arms, her still-bandaged foot hanging limply between them.

'You're going then?' She poked at me with one of her crutches.

I nodded. 'I'm sorry.'

'Just don't lose your dribbling skills while you're away. When you visit I'm going to be just as good at football as I always was. Which is better than you. Goran's going to coach me – aren't you?'

Goran smiled. 'I certainly am. Every day after school. I'm a tough coach, Little Miss Hopalong. Don't expect me to go easy on you.'

'See you in six weeks, son.' Pa turned to Goran and for a moment it was as if neither of them knew what to do. Finally Pa put out his hand and Goran shook it. I waited for my brother to say something else, but he simply stared at Pa, his face set and closed. Pa stood for a minute, then nodded slightly and moved towards the truck. 'Come on, you,' he said, taking my hand. 'Let's get you in.'

I scrambled up into the cab of the truck and looked behind the seats at the stacked cardboard boxes. Poking out of the nearest box was Pa's old camera; I reached over and took it out, sliding back the lens cover and lifting it to my face. There they were, perfectly framed: my brother and sister, my mother, my damaged best friend.

'Smile.' They looked over and the button clicked beneath my

finger. A feeling of relief surged through me, as if I had somehow taken a small part of them and stored it away. Goran raised his hand and I took another, just of him, pointing the camera straight at his dark, asymmetrical face.

'Take some photos and send them to me,' called Cvita. 'Then we'll know what you're up to.'

'Look after your sister,' Pa said to Goran, as Mother opened the door and slipped in beside me.

'Look after your mother,' Goran called back, pointing to me and smiling.

'Who's going to look after me?' I said, raising my hands, and to my delight he laughed and even Mother smiled and suddenly the engine was running and we were pulling away. I turned round to look and there they were, three of the people I loved most in the world, growing smaller and smaller until they disappeared completely and there was nothing to do but turn around and look forward, into a world I had yet to recognize.

The journey from Knin was the longest day I had ever known, sat between Mother and Pa on the peeling leather seat, staring through the windscreen. The scrub-faced mountains of the Krajina gradually softened into tufted hills, dotted with clutches of whitewashed houses; square church spires peering out over the trees. As the land grew flatter the road stretched ahead of us, punctuated with battered yellow signs bearing unfamiliar village names that told of countless lives in places I didn't know and would never visit. When we pulled up at a petrol station and Mother went in with Pa to buy tissues, it occurred to me that the world was a very big place indeed. I was glad when they got back in the truck.

'Are we nearly there?' I asked Pa, as gleaming shops and neat rows of brick-built houses began to rise up on either side of us. 'Is this Dubrovnik?'

Pa laughed. 'We've a long way to go yet, son. But look, over there, between those buildings. Do you see it?'

I followed his gaze to where a wide swathe of blue shimmered and sparkled on the horizon. 'Is that the *sea*?'

'It certainly is. But it's going to be a while before we reach it. Maybe try and have a sleep?'

'I'm not going to *sleep*. This is way too exciting.'

But the gentle motion of the truck and the long, slow roads gradually caused my eyelids to droop. Eventually I must have fallen properly asleep because the next thing I knew, Pa's hand was on my shoulder and the truck had stopped moving.

'We're here,' he whispered. 'Look, Miro. Welcome to Ljeta.'

Mother opened the door and climbed down; I took her hand and scrambled out on to the warm road. Even after all Pa's excited words, my first glimpse of Ljeta didn't disappoint; the sky was a colour I had never seen before: sherbet pink, shot through with streaks of gold and long white feathers that he later explained to me were aeroplane trails. In front of us the sea shimmered in the evening light; two small islands glowed purple in the haze, behind a cluster of terra-cotta-roofed houses standing neatly together along a small, low hill.

'Smell that air,' Pa said, and I sniffed obediently. It was nothing like Knin: salty and fresh and slightly sweet. 'The sea and pine trees and good living. Eh, Jada? Isn't it beautiful?'

'Where will we find Ivo and Marjana?' she said, briskly. 'It's been a long day for Miro, he needs tea and bed.'

Pa took my hand and we walked away from the truck, skirting a low white barrier that separated the road from the harbour front. A line of palm trees fringed the waterfront, while neat rows of tables and rattan chairs criss-crossed the cobbled street, spreading out from a handful of cafes and restaurants, painted in crisp yellows, pale pinks and blues. We walked past glass cabinets filled with wide-eyed fish, a small shop with a rack of tattered newspapers in languages

I didn't recognize; a glass-fronted *slastičarna*, where the tubs of brightly-coloured ice cream made my tummy rumble with anticipation. But none of it felt real, the air full of noises I didn't know – music that lilted to unfamiliar rhythms, a dozen different laughs at once, women with blonde hair and men in brightly coloured T-shirts drinking beer and eating pizza with their fingers.

'*Petar*.' My father's name echoed through the evening air. His face broke into a huge grin and I watched as the vast figure of Uncle Ivo wove through the cafe tables, arms outstretched, with Aunt Marjana bustling behind him. Within moments I was scooped up and smothered in kisses, held tightly in unfamiliar but strangely comforting arms.

'But this can't be Miro,' boomed Ivo. 'When did you get so big? Welcome to your new home, my boy. You're going to be so happy here. Now tell me, do you swim? Fish?'

I shook my head.

'Oh, Ivo, don't be ridiculous,' scolded his wife. 'Of course the boy doesn't swim – there's no sea in Knin. Although,' she added hurriedly, taking a look at my mother's expression, 'there's lovely mountains of course.'

'And you probably won't remember Cata,' Uncle Ivo said, drawing forward a small girl who had been hiding behind my aunt. 'Cata, this is Miro, your cousin.'

She stared at me solemnly, wide dark eyes framed by jet-black hair cut into a neat bob, with a fringe high above her eyebrows. She looked like a doll.

'You can't swim?'

I shook my head again, blushing furiously.

'Well, tomorrow we'll teach you,' said Uncle Ivo hurriedly. 'And then you and I will take the boat out and catch some fish and the women can cook them for our supper. What do you think, Miro? Will that do for your first day?'

CHAPTER 3

My first weeks in the village were something of a blur. Pa had been right, it *was* an adventure, and every day brought new experiences. Some days we would go out on Uncle Ivo's boat, silver-scaled fish dangling from a thin wire between his fingers, Cata teasing me from the water, calling to me to jump in. On others I would go with Pa and my uncle to buy furniture for the pension, watching as they lashed down chairs and folding tables on to the back of the truck, helping carry boxes of glasses and clear plastic bags filled with cutlery and candleholders. Within two weeks I could swim, after three I could dive, and every evening Cata and I would run down to the jetty that led off a small bay around the corner from the harbour and hurl ourselves into the cool, clear water. And at night there would be four kisses rather than two: Mother and Pa, then Ivo and finally Marjana, a warm hug infused with her lavender scent, which I could smell on my pyjamas if I woke up in the night.

After a month school began, and life in Knin became even more of a distant memory, replaced by sunlit mornings in a hot classroom and long afternoons with my new friends, Josip and Pavle, and my tomboy of a cousin. The only cloud over those happy days was when a letter arrived two days before my birthday from Goran: he was sorry but he could not get away from police training, he would not be here for my birthday. I tried not to let my disappointment show, and my new group of friends proved an excellent substitute. As the last warm autumn days melted away into winter the four of us became inseparable, and when Goran came at last, just before Christmas, I told him stories of our adventures up in the pine woods and out on the water with Uncle Ivo in his boat.

'Well, it obviously suits you down here,' he said, laughing, as we sat in the *slastičarna* one evening and I gobbled down the banana split he had bought me. 'You've grown about a foot since the summer.'

'That's because you haven't seen me for so long,' I grumbled. 'How long are you staying? How's Tara? And why didn't Cvita come? Why don't you just move down here too?'

'One question at a time,' he said, laughing. 'I know it's been a long time but I'm working now – you can't be a policeman and say, Oh, I fancy going to the seaside for a week.' He poked me in the ribs. 'I'm far too important. But I'm staying till after New Year. Cvita didn't come because she wanted to spend it with Branko's family. Tara's doing really well – I've got a letter for you somewhere. And I can't move down here because, as I say, I'm just far too important.'

I giggled. Suddenly, without any warning, I felt someone's hands over my eyes and the spoon chinked in my ice-cream bowl. 'Get off,' I yelled, pushing the fingers away to find Josip standing behind me and Pavle sat next to Goran, tucking into my banana split.

'Going up to the woods,' he said, licking the spoon and grinning. 'Fancy coming?'

Goran leaned in and removed the bowl and spoon from Pavle's hands. 'I don't believe this was bought for you,' he said crisply. 'I'm Goran. Miro's brother. And you are?'

Pavle squirmed a little. 'I'm Josip.'

'Oi. *I'm* Josip.' I laughed in spite of Goran's cross face; Josip pulled up the spare chair and threw himself into it. 'Goran, it's nice to meet you. We've heard a lot about you. I'm Josip and this *idiot* is Pavle. Sorry about his manners. We don't let him out much.'

Goran smiled and I felt a wave of relief; even my brother wasn't immune to Josip's charm. 'So you three all go to school together?'

We all groaned. 'When we have to,' said Pavle. 'If there's nothing better to do.'

'Well,' said Goran, picking up his cigarettes and pushing his chair back. 'I think I'll leave you three to do whatever it is you do. Miro, don't be late for dinner. Josip –' he paused – 'Pavle, nice to have met you.'

We watched as he walked away, the pale winter sunlight throwing a long, slim shadow across the cobbles. 'Bit bloody scary, your brother,' said Pavle.

I smiled. 'He can seem like that, I s'pose, but he's not really.'

'How come he doesn't live here?' asked Josip. 'I've never really understood why your brother and sister are somewhere else. Why did you get to move and not them? They must be pretty unhappy about it.'

'Not really.' I shifted a little in my chair. I'd never told Josip or Pavle about what happened in Knin, or the reason why my family had been split apart. I didn't want to tell them that I was the reason; it was hard enough to think without actually saying it. 'I thought we were going up to the woods?'

The moment soon passed, and by the time I was sat next to Goran at dinner, all thoughts of what had happened in Knin had disappeared. That Christmas was the happiest I could remember; the badnjak that Pa and I had cut from a tree up in the pine woods burning on the crackling fire, the polished boots I had put on the windowsill filled with sweets, all of us sat around a table groaning with roasted meats, and heaped bowls of stuffed cabbage and mliñci, Mother's delicious home-made noodles. 'It's a feast,' roared Uncle Ivo, his face flushed with pleasure. 'A veritable feast. Your first Christmas in Ljeta, Miro. Pretty good, eh?'

'Oh yes,' I beamed, wrapping my fingers around the new camera that had been my present from my parents and uncle and aunt. 'My best Christmas *ever*.' Goran grinned, Ivo slung an arm around his shoulders, and as their glasses chinked together I clicked the shutter and felt a rush of warmth that in a week or two I would be able to open a packet of pictures and see this moment all over again.

But in spite of the happiness I felt all day, Knin invaded my dreams that night. I was back at the fort with Tara and somehow I could see beneath the grass; it was dotted with big silver coins with sharp, angular faces. They were nice faces, smiley ones, but every so often one of them would screw itself up and burst out of the ground, mud and grass and flecks of blood belching from its mouth. I woke up sweating, my heart thumping, and I knew I had to get out of my tiny room and into the fresh air, where the first glimmers of sunlight could chase the devils away.

'Pavle?' As I walked out on to the harbour I saw my friend sitting on the wall, his eyes closed against the creeping light. 'Pavle? You OK?'

'Miro? What are you doing up?'

'What are *you* doing up?'

'Couldn't sleep,' he said briefly. 'Huge row in my house last night. Christmas is always difficult. Mum wants to go back to Belgrade, see her family; Dad wants to stay here.'

'Why can't your mum's family come here?'

He shook his head. 'Land of the Croats, that's what they call it. Reckon they wouldn't make it out alive.'

'Sounds like the sort of thing people say in Knin, only there it's all about the Krajina belonging to the Serbs. Who cares anyway?'

'What *are* you doing up?'

'I had a nightmare. Really horrible.'

'About?'

I looked at Pavle. 'Something that happened back in Knin. There was . . . an accident. A friend of mine got hurt. I was with her. That's why we moved away.'

'What sort of accident?'

'She stepped on a landmine.' The words were out before I even realized I was going to say them.

Pavle let out a long, low whistle. 'Holy crap. Was she . . . ?'

'She's OK. Her foot, hand, they're both . . . well, she limps a bit. I was OK, but what I saw . . .' I covered my face with my hands. 'It seems as if it's gone away, you know? I forget about it for weeks, months even. And then something . . . and having Goran here; it's so great, but it kind of makes me remember . . . and they're all talking about my sister's wedding – we'll have to go back to Knin for that, and I don't want to. I *really* don't want to.'

'Didn't you know there were mines?'

I shook my head. 'Goran said everyone thought they'd all been cleared.'

'But why were they there anyway?'

'From the war, I s'pose. I think of them like little silver devils. Just waiting to explode.'

'Will you have to go back for the wedding?'

I nodded slowly. 'It's going to be a huge thing, a big party. Mother keeps saying how lovely it will be to be back, to all be together. I feel sick just thinking about it.'

But somehow, when it came to going back, there wasn't time to be worried. Cvita had chosen May for her wedding, and as the day drew closer I would come home from school to find the pension in uproar – the small lounge floor freckled with scraps of pink satin and yards of ribbon, Ivo and Pa packing up glasses and plates and loading them into the truck, along with crates of wine and boxes of beer. Mother gave me some money to buy two new film cartridges for my camera, and I slipped them into my bag carefully, next to the neatly folded suit and brand-new shoes we had gone to Dubrovnik to buy. Cata and I were delighted at having two days off school, and as we pulled away in Ivo's car, Mother and Pa driving the truck in front of us, I felt a rising sense of excitement at seeing my brother and sister again.

The journey seemed to take forever, but by the time we were all squeezed in around the familiar table in our cramped kitchen in Knin, I could barely keep my eyes open. Goran was wedged in next to me, and I slumped a little against him, comforted just by the feel of his arm against mine.

'We must have a toast,' said Pa, when we had finished eating. 'To Cvita. May tomorrow be the start of the happiest days of your life.'

Goran leaned across the table and poured a little of the beer in his glass into the empty beaker in front of my plate. Tara's eyes widened jealously. 'Well, of course, now Cvita's going to be married off, there's a bit of a job vacancy.' He winked at me and pulled gently on Tara's dark ponytail. 'How do you feel about a spot of cooking and cleaning?'

Tara punched him on the arm and he pulled a face. 'You've got to learn to fend for yourself,' Cvita said, laughing. 'The man can't even boil an egg.'

'But you can?' Goran sipped his beer and his eyes sparkled with mischief. 'I think I'd better have a word with that bridegroom of yours about some of your . . . er, culinary disasters over the last few months.'

'Don't you dare . . .'

'Now come on,' said Mother, squeezing out of her seat and beginning to clear the table. 'There's no time for bickering. Ivo, all the glasses need polishing. Petar, Goran – there's still about a hundred jobs to be done.'

'And me?' I looked across at Pa, the slightly bitter taste of the beer fizzing on my tongue.

'Bed for you, young man. Cata went up an hour ago. And Tara, you should go home, sweetheart. You can come back as early as you like tomorrow.'

Tara slipped obediently from the table, kissed my mother good-night and began to put her coat on. I had been shocked to see that she still couldn't walk properly – that for all her talk of playing football again, her smashed-up foot hadn't truly recovered. I had never asked Goran or Pa about how badly she had been injured; always assumed she would simply get better and be exactly the way she had always been. The sight of the scar on her chin, the thick black shoes she wore and the way she kept her left hand firmly in her pocket made me want to treat her differently, like one of the china cups Mother kept in the glass cupboard but never actually used.

'I don't *want* to go to bed,' I said sulkily. I thought of the thick, ominous darkness in the small bedroom where I had lain awake in the nights after Tara had been hurt, Goran close enough to touch but lost to me, far away in his own dreams.

'Well, I can't have my official photographer being all tired tomor-row,' said Cvita, picking up my camera and passing it to me. 'Let's have a picture of my last night as a Denković, and then I'll take you up.'

'Shouldn't Miro be in it too?' said Aunt Marjana, as they all gath-ered around Cvita. 'Perhaps Tara could . . .'

'No, I'll take it,' I said, hurriedly. Tara reddened slightly and looked down; we both knew she wouldn't be able to hold the camera and take the picture with her damaged hand.

'Hurry up,' said Goran, his face split by a slightly manic grin. 'Before I get stuck like this.'

I snapped the six of them, felt the reassuring click of the button beneath my finger and smiled at Cvita as she handed me the camera case. 'Thank you, darling,' she said. 'And now it's time for you to escort the bride up to bed. It's quite a responsibility, Miro. Are you up to it?'

I felt Mother's eyes on me and nodded reluctantly. Once I had brushed my teeth, and Cvita had tucked the sheets around me, she sat on the edge of the bed and took my hand.

'Are you all right?' she said, softly. 'Bit strange for you being back, I expect.'

'I didn't think Tara . . . I thought she'd be OK.'

Cvita leaned in and stroked my hair out of my eyes. 'She is OK, sweetheart. You should see her with Goran, riding around on his back, playing football.'

'Really?'

'Well, sit-down football. She sits on the field and kicks the ball and he runs around after it. Really, Miro, she's doing brilliantly at school, and she lives with her aunt now, so she's much better looked after – although she wasn't happy about that. She didn't want to move further away from Goran; she just adores him.'

'It's just . . .' I bit my lip. Everything was so jumbled and confused; when I thought of how badly Tara had been hurt I felt sick and guilty, but also relieved and lucky that it wasn't me who walked with a limp and had to keep my hand in my pocket. I missed Tara but I was jealous of her too, of all the time she got to spend with Goran, and I worried that somehow she would replace me, that he would start to forget his little brother, hundreds of miles away by the sea. I wanted to try and explain to Cvita, she always made things better, but when I looked into my sister's face I saw the same expression Goran wore in the days after the mine had exploded. I didn't want her to look like that, not on the night before her wedding.

'It's nothing. I'm fine.' I smiled and she looked relieved. The tight feeling in my chest loosened a little.

'All right, darling. Give me a hug.' She leaned in and her soft curls fell against my face. 'Night-night.'

When the light clicked off I tried not to remember what I had seen when Tara was lying in the grass. I tried not to think about whether it hurt every time she walked and what was so wrong with her hand that she never took it out of her jeans pocket. I touched my finger to the tiny scar on my cheek and remembered the feel of the earth against my face, lying so still, watching Goran bend over my screaming friend. Yet in spite of the shadows that crept across my bed, I must have fallen asleep, because the next thing I was aware of was daylight streaming in through the gap between the curtains and Goran sitting on the bed opposite, his face dark.

'Are you OK?'

He stared at me and shook his head.

I sat up, my stomach bubbling a little with worry. 'What's wrong?'

'Tito died.'

'The president?'

'That's right.'

'Oh.' I had no idea what to say. When Goran said the president's name I almost laughed with relief; he had looked so serious I thought something awful had happened again, someone else injured like Tara.

'You know who he is, right?'

'Of course I do,' I said indignantly. It was impossible not to know Josip Broz Tito; he watched me in class each day, frowning down from above my teacher's desk, stern and scary with slick black hair and a soldier's uniform.

'Tito's dead, y'know,' announced Cata, strolling into our bedroom, already dressed in a blue satin frock, her hair tied back with cream ribbon. 'Everyone's talking about it downstairs. Uncle Petar says it's going to be cat-errr-stroff-ic.' She beamed proudly. 'Goran, what does that mean?'

'Never you mind,' he said, pulling on a T-shirt and heading out of the room. I looked at Cata.

'Did you have breakfast already?'

'No. I *told* you – they're all just sitting around talking. I don't under-stand – you'd think it was someone they knew. Come downstairs, maybe if your mother sees you she'll actually make something to eat.'

I picked up my camera and followed her down the stairs. '. . . no one will be able to keep the bloody Serbs in line like he did,' I heard Goran say as we walked into the kitchen. 'Why didn't he pick a successor? He knew this day would come – did he *want* everything he's achieved to just fall apart as soon as he's dead?'

'Goran.' Mother raised her eyebrows and tilted her head slightly to where Cata and I were standing. 'Come on, we must get the day started. Where's that bride? Cata, go and get your cousin out of bed. Lena is coming to do her hair in an hour and we need a good breakfast. Miro, lay the table. Petar, Ivo – stop looking like the world has ended. This is Cvita's day, and no one – not even Tito himself – is going to spoil it.'

I had never been to a wedding before, and from what Josip and Pavle had told me, I expected the day to be little more than a boring adults' party. But from the moment Branko and his best man knocked at the front door of our house, it felt as if something extraordinary was happening. Cvita appeared in a beautiful white dress that sparkled like the sea in Ljeta, and Uncle Ivo swung me up on to his shoulders so that when I turned my head I could see dozens of people walking behind us. Knin's main street – with the shops closed for the afternoon and paper lights hanging from the trees – seemed unrecognizable; instead of cars jolting over the uneven tarmac, couples strolled arm in arm, white-haired ladies in crumpled black lace were helped along by their grandsons, Branko's friends were jigging around to the folk-songs played by the band who strolled alongside. I took picture after picture, trying not to mind that there was another man there with a bigger camera, who took lots of photographs too.

By the end of the afternoon it felt as if hundreds of people were in the town square, sitting at long trestle tables that glinted with glasses and plates of half-eaten *kolači*, or dancing to the folk songs that Uncle Ivo was playing on the *tamburitza*. But however much Mother would have wished it not to be, Tito was the word I heard more than any other that day. As the sun drifted across the sky, men who had appeared outside our house that morning in ironed shirts and shiny shoes pulled off their ties and undid their collars and banged their glasses of Stock on the tables as they talked of the president's death.

'I feel sick.' I turned round to find Tara had slid into the chair next to me. 'I've had six lollies and three slices of cake. What have you eaten?'

Cata, on my other side, raised her eyebrows. They didn't seem to like each other very much, although I couldn't understand why.

'More than that,' I said loftily. 'And I've had some prosecco. We found some half-drunk glasses, didn't we, Catz?' I didn't add that my head was aching and I felt more than a little sick myself.

'Dance?' Cata asked suddenly. I looked at Tara, awkwardness flooding through me.

'Go on,' she said, smiling. 'Goran's promised to whizz me around the floor when your uncle plays something fast. Don't worry, I'm fine, really.'

'All right then,' I said, longing to get in among the outstretched arms and stamping feet that were whirling around the square.

Cata pulled me up towards the dancers just as Uncle Ivo began to play a song Mother used to sing to me when I was little. Other voices began drunkenly to sing along and I joined in, whispering the words to myself, swinging Cata around, our hands locked, the world beginning to spin. Tara stood up and edged around the dancing bodies, clearly looking for Goran. The song picked up speed and we spun faster, the night grew thick with shouts and laughter and then suddenly, unexpectedly, there was a terrible, discordant crash. Cata stopped moving and I smacked into her, almost sending both of us to the floor.

'Look,' she hissed. I turned to see a man lying in the middle of a table, surrounded by broken glass and scattered bits of cake.

'You Serbian scum.' A man I recognized as Tara's father launched himself at the man on the table, pulling him up and punching him hard in the face. 'You would knock over my daughter? A cripple?'

Silence rolled in like a mist, deadening the strains of the tamburitza and the warm twists of laughter. People froze where they stood. I stared for a minute and then remembered I had my camera in my pocket. I pulled it out, clicked on the flash and pointed it at the two men.

'I didn't knock her over,' shouted the stranger, raising his hand to feel around his mouth. 'I just bumped into her. It was an accident, I was dancing . . . I'm sorry, sweetheart.'

Tara blushed and said nothing.

'Accident? You ploughed into her. But then that's how you people treat cripples, you filthy Serb *dog*.'

'Better a dog than a *Ustaše* drunkard who can't even care for his own child. And whose fault is it that she's crippled anyway? Who—'

'Fuck *you*.' The aggression in his voice ripped through the air and Tara's father hurled himself at the man, knocking him to the floor. Shrieks began to echo across the square. Goran and Branko plunged towards the two men, pulling at arms, hands sliding off the enmeshed bodies, the air thick with violence. Cata shivered and I tightened my grip around her waist. Eventually the men were pulled apart and the stranger staggered away into the night. Tara's father lurched towards his daughter, his face bruised and bleeding.

'Are you all right, Tara?'

'Go away.'

'Tara.'

'She said go away.' Goran had appeared by her side, his face black with anger.

'What's it to do with you? And when did you become such a hypocrite? Drinking with a Serb.'

'This is my sister's *wedding*,' Goran said, and I noticed his voice shook a little. 'This isn't the place, Korda. You're drunk. Go home.'

Korda struggled free of Goran's grip, stared at him for a moment and then spat heavily on the floor. 'You disappoint me, brother,' he said, wiping the blood from his lip and shaking his head. 'I thought—'

'Well, you thought *wrong*,' said Goran, slamming his hands into Korda's arms and pushing him backwards. 'Now go on, fuck *off*. Haven't you done enough to ruin things?'

'How dare he behave like that?' said Pa, watching Korda stagger away into the darkness. 'He brings shame upon himself.'

'You think so?' Goran's voice was low and quiet.

'You're defending him? You saw what happened – it was just an accident. And that man – whoever he was – barely touched Tara. Korda was just spoiling for a fight.'

Goran met my father's gaze. 'Well, I stopped him, didn't I? But only because this is family. You've forgotten how people feel up here, forgotten what matters, Christ, you even let Miro run around with some snotty-nosed little—'

'*Shut up!*' Pa hissed, but it was too late. I knew he was talking about Pavle. I just didn't know why.

'Have it your way,' Goran said sullenly. 'Go back down to your safe little enclave in the sun. You might not want to remember, Pa, but this is the Krajina. Here, we never forget.'

CHAPTER 4

The atmosphere at breakfast the next morning was quiet and strange. Branko and Cvita had left for their honeymoon in Zadar, while Goran had disappeared from the house before I'd even woken up. Cata was yet to surface, having thrown up in the night – 'a mixture of general overexcitement and too many strawberry lollies,' Aunt Marjana said wearily, when she appeared in the kitchen with an armful of balled-up sheets. Pa and Uncle Ivo sipped coffee and closed their eyes when Mother laid poached eggs on toast in front of them. And no one mentioned the fight; not over breakfast or the following day, when we packed up the cars and began the long journey back to Ljeta.

In the weeks after we returned from the wedding, the first visitors of the summer began to appear at the pension. Mother gave me a string of jobs, starting with the trip to the baker's in the early morning light. I used to grumble when she woke me, but once awake I loved the silent run through the streets, the first rays of sunlight creeping up the cobbles, swathes of violet bougainvillea against the clear blue sky, the village still slumbering beneath terracotta roofs. Once the warm loaves were in my hands I'd walk slowly back, munching on a pastry that Sara, the baker's wife, would often slip in the bag when her husband wasn't looking.

'Are you paying the boy?' Uncle Ivo asked one morning, as I stood at the counter, clumsily sawing the bread into misshapen slices.

Mother looked at him, astonished, but that night when Pa kissed me goodnight he slipped a handful of dinars into my hand, and when I was alone in my room I slotted each one into the silver can Goran had made me and listened to the satisfying chink as it fell inside.

It wasn't until several weeks later that Mother added picking up the packets of wedding photos to my list of things to do. I waited in Drogan's hot, dark shop while he sorted through the thick green packages, Pavle and Josip loitering outside impatiently, bickering about what flavour ice creams they would buy from the *slastičarna*.

'God, weddings must be so *boring*,' said Josip, as we walked towards the beach, his lips slightly green from the pistachio ice. 'All that endless love stuff.' Pavle laughed, but I was too busy flicking through the photos to react: Cvita and Branko, Mother laughing with Ivo, a neat line of Pa, Goran, Branko, Ivo and me, all with slightly awkward expressions on our faces. Suddenly Pavle pulled a picture out of my hands. 'What was going on *here*?'

I looked at the picture: Korda and Goran glowering at each other. 'Oh,' I said, trying to sound nonchalant, 'there was a bit of a fight.'

'Your brother got into a fight at your sister's wedding? That's so *cool*. What was it about? Did they roll around on the floor like in the movies?'

I laughed. 'It wasn't Goran – he was trying to break it up. It was, I don't know. This guy –' I pointed at the photo, 'got really angry with a man who had nearly knocked his daughter over, called him Serbian scum . . . Then the other guy called him an *Ustaše* drunkard . . .'

'What's *Ustaše*?' Josip threw his towel on to the rocks and pulled his T-shirt over his head.

I shrugged my shoulders.

'Why did he call him Serbian scum?' asked Pavle.

I shrugged again. 'I don't know. It's different up there. It's like – they all care who's Serbian and who isn't. People pretend they're friends, but they're not really. They're always on about *what happened in the past.*' I glanced at Pavle but he didn't look up. My cheeks burned a little at the memory of Goran snarling about the 'snotty-nosed kid' I chose to run around with.

'Oh, who cares anyway?' said Josip, taking the photos and slipping them back into the packet. 'Come on – aren't we going to swim?'

But I knew, as I walked back to the pension later, that Mother and Pa would care very much. I meant to take those photos out of the packet, but I left them on the side while I went to wash my hands, and when I walked back into the kitchen Pa was looking through the pictures. He didn't hear me come in and I watched as he sifted out four or five photos, quietly opened the lid of the bin and slipped them in. I stepped back so he couldn't see me, but once he'd taken some bottles of beer from the fridge and walked back into the sunlight, I lifted the lid and took the pictures back out of the rubbish.

'Miro?' I turned round to see Mother in the doorway. 'What *are* you doing?'

Before I could answer she had taken the photos out of my hand. Her lips compressed into a thin line as she looked at them. 'Did you throw these away?'

'No. Pa did.'

'Who took them?'

'I did.'

She walked to the table and sat down, holding a hand out for me to come and join her. She put the four pictures in a neat line on the table and smiled up at me. 'These are amazing pictures for you to have taken,' she said. 'So clear, so focused; you're right there in the moment.'

'I thought you'd be cross. I think that's why Pa put them in the rubbish.'

'I am cross, Miro, but with *them* – it could have spoiled the whole day. But that doesn't mean we should pretend it never happened. These photos aren't easy to look at, but they tell the story – the truth of what happened. You shouldn't hide from that, or people get hurt.'

'Like Tara?'

She laid her palm against my cheek. 'Yes, darling. Like Tara.'

'Mother, why didn't . . . ? I mean, no one told me about the mines and stuff.'

An expression I didn't recognize crossed her face; her eyes dropped and it was as if the skin sagged across her bones. 'Sometimes it's complicated,' she said slowly. 'We were told years ago that Knin was mine-free – the soldiers came with their machines and trucks and assured us that every one had been cleared.'

'But you always said not to go to the back of the fort.'

'That was just . . . superstition, I suppose. My mother knew some-one who was killed by a mine there during the war, and it always felt like a bad place to me. And I didn't tell you . . .' She stopped and took my hands in hers. 'The thing is, Miro, those mines, they were put there by our soldiers, Croatian soldiers. In the war. It's a hard thing to admit to, that your own people can do things like that. So we didn't talk about it. And I thought it was the best way – leave the past behind, try and live together with people who had been our enemies. And then . . . and then poor Tara.' She pulled me to her, kissed the top of my head.

'So you didn't mind moving here?'

She drew back and smiled. 'I look at you – all happy and healthy and strong from all that swimming, and I know it's the best thing we could have done. Look at this.' She picked out a photo of Josip, Pavle and me with our arms around each other, all laughing. 'This is what I want for you. It doesn't matter to you, does it, that Josip's Croatian and Pavle is a Serb? You're just friends.'

'It matters to Goran.'

'Well, you mustn't worry about that. Look at that photo, Miro, what story does that tell?'

'That we're friends? That we'll always be friends.'

She looked at the picture and smiled. 'I hope so, my rascal boy.'

That summer was the year the business really took off. The six bedrooms in our pension were filled with an ever-changing mix of visitors: British and German in the early weeks of the season, Italians and French when the sun was at its hottest, and even the occasional American or Australian, who seemed wildly exotic to me. Cata and I spent our evenings weaving between the tables with baskets of bread and saucers of plump green olives, and when Goran came to visit, at the height of the season, even he ended up carrying plates and opening beers for our visitors.

'Not a bad life, is it, son?' Pa would say to me on the occasional afternoons we spent together, swimming in the clear salty sea, or fishing off the back of Ivo's boat. 'How lucky we are that this is our home. We have much to thank your uncle for.'

And I did feel lucky. As the months stretched into years, life fell into a pattern; sleepy winters when school took up most of my attention and rainy skies and a chill wind kept us from the pine woods and the white-tipped sea. But as the days grew longer, it was as if the village came alive again; the first unfamiliar faces brought with them the promise of another long, busy summer that peaked with my birthday, when Goran and Cvita, often with Tara in tow, would come for a few days of September sunshine.

During the crisp, bright days of our fourth winter, Pa and Uncle Ivo worked on converting what had been our bedrooms into three additional guestrooms, stopping only once to drink copious amounts of beer and toast the arrival of the newest member of our family, Cvita's daughter, Emilja. We moved into a small stone house on a quiet street that led from the harbour up the hill, and the following autumn Goran came for my thirteenth birthday and stayed on until the season had finished, to help us strip out the kitchen and re-pave the terrace.

Mother had plans for a slicker, more sophisticated restaurant. 'I can't keep serving up *lònac* and omelette while they're doing steak au poivre next door,' she said to Pa, when he complained about the cost of the new cooker. 'It'll pay for itself in the end, Petar.'

As I grew older, I knew enough to understand that she had made her peace with the village she now called home. She worked long hours: up early preparing breakfast, still in the kitchen late in the evening, stirring vast pans of mussels and chasing George, the useless Albanian boy, into finishing the washing-up. But our guests were always happy; 'You have such a beautiful country,' they would say, hugging her goodbye, and Pa would slip his arm around their shoulders and say, 'Same time next year?' And he would wink at me and grin, and I'd know what he was thinking, because I thought it too: how incredibly lucky we were.

CHAPTER 5

By the time I was fourteen, Ljeta was no longer the centre of my world. The summer had passed in a whirl of waiting tables in Mother's new restaurant and helping Ivo and Marjana with the constant stream of visitors that filled up our rooms each week. At the end of August, Cvita came to stay with her tiny new son, Ante, and I had little time to worry about the change that was coming. Josip, Pavle and I would no longer walk to the village school each day; instead two of us would board the bus to the high school in Dubrovnik, while Pavle helped open up his uncle's workshop and began 'the much more worthwhile business of learning a trade', according to his father.

Within days of being in the city, I discovered I loved being somewhere so much bigger, so *different*. On the second day Josip and I took our sandwiches up on to the city walls and gazed down on the square-eyed mansions, topped with neat rows of burnt-orange tiles and slim attic windows that told of tucked-away secrets and histories buried in the dark. 'City of adventures,' Josip said, beaming and nodding his head towards the harbour, where gleaming white yachts sidled up to each other on the waves. 'This is where it all begins, Miro. This is where it all begins.'

Josip was right, it did feel like a new beginning. As the bus drove away each morning I felt an unexpected sense of escape, and each time we walked through the wide arch of the Pile Gate and on to the gleaming marble of the Stradun, I felt as though a part of me was coming alive, a part I hadn't even known existed. By the spring term we had grown confident enough to occasionally miss the bus home, and settle in at a cafe table on the harbour front, smoking cigarettes and drinking tiny cups of coffee so strong it made my tongue curl slightly against the roof of my mouth. 'Look at the girls, man,' Josip would breathe, as British and American women in skimpy dresses or tiny shorts walked past. But I was interested in only one girl: the one who sat in front of me in class with the long dark plait, and rendered it impossible for me to concentrate whenever she was near.

'You're such a pair of sad schoolboys,' Pavle said, when we gathered outside Tomas's cafe in the evenings to tell him our stories of the city. 'I never see you any more. You're always off with what's-her-name –' he pointed at Josip – 'and it's all I can do to get *you* –' he poked me in the ribs – 'to take your nose out of your books. You should both get a real job, like me.'

'Her *name* is Tatiana.' Josip grinned. 'Come on – have you seen her? If you had to choose between spending time with her or with you two losers . . .'

'Thanks very much.' I flicked the back of my spoon at Josip and flecks of chocolate appeared on his T-shirt.

'Brilliant,' he said, brushing at his chest and smearing the chocolate across a wider area. 'Anyway, it's not like I'm the only one.' He fixed his eyes on me and smiled. 'Am I, Miro?'

'What's this?' Pavle's long face sparkled with interest. 'Not you too?'

'No.'

'*Yes.*' Josip prodded me with his spoon. 'Oh, he doesn't think I know. And it's not like he's actually *talked* to her or anything. He just stares at her. On the bus on the way to school, then in class – she sits in front of him – then on the bus on the way home. He's like a puppy, Pavle, it's embarrassing to watch.'

'You just . . . stare?' Pavle grinned. 'Interesting technique, Miro. How about, you know, actually speaking to her?'

'It's not difficult,' chimed in Josip. 'Ask her her name . . . if she wants to have lunch with you.'

'Ask her if she fancies a swim!' Pavle snorted with laughter. 'That way you get to see her with her clothes off.'

'Shut up.' I blushed furiously. 'Look, I just think she's pretty, that's all. I'm not going to go up and introduce myself to a complete stranger. She'll think I'm crazy.'

'Well, you are,' said Josip, giggling. 'Crazy in love.'

'Oh ha ha,' I said crossly. 'Grow up, Josip. You don't know what you're talking about.'

'There's a new girl at the *slastičarna*,' Cata announced one afternoon as we carried piles of linen up into the bedrooms. 'Very pretty. I don't know where she's sprung from.'

'*Miro.*' Josip's voice floated up, followed by the sound of heavy footsteps thumping up the stairs. 'Miro – oh, hi, Cata – Miro, you'll never guess what.'

'There's a new girl at the *slastičarna*?'

Josip's face fell. 'Oh. Well, yes. But do you know who it is?'

I shook my head.

'It's her. *Her*. You know, the girl you spent months staring at, the one you were heartbroken that you wouldn't see again until September? She's here – she's got a summer job at Mij's. It's like a sign or something. Come on, come *now*. Get an ice cream. It's the perfect excuse to talk to her.'

I stared at him. Ever since Pavle and Josip had teased me about the girl with the plait, I'd tried to stop looking at her, but I endlessly rehearsed lines in my head that I knew Josip would have said without the slightest hesitation. They remained unsaid.

'Er, we've got work to do?' Cata stood with her hands on her hips, an unimpressed expression on her face. Josip slung an arm around her shoulders and planted a long kiss on her cheek.

'Go on, gorgeous. Let him go – you know how long he's been mooning after her.'

'Oh, all right. But come straight back. I'm not doing these beds all on my own.'

'Now just be cool,' said Josip, as we walked towards the glass-fronted shop. As we drew nearer I could see her through the window – long dark hair drawn back in the plait she always wore, a checked apron over a pink T-shirt, her face bent over the brightly coloured tubs of ice cream.

'What the hell am I going to say?' I hissed at Josip as we walked into the shop. He pushed me forward and she looked up as I stumbled towards the counter, her wide hazel eyes dancing with amusement.

'Hello.' Her voice was low and sweet. 'What would you like?'

I stared at the bewildering array of flavours; my mind had gone utterly blank.

'Rum and raisin, please.' Josip smiled as she picked up the metal scoop and dug it into one of the containers.

She passed the cone across and beamed at him. My stomach flipped. 'And for you?'

'Hello.' I stared at her; one strand of dark hair had escaped from under the white cap she was wearing and she raised her hand to push it aside. My palms went sweaty.

'Hello.'

I stared at the coloured tubs. 'You get on our bus,' I mumbled. 'We see you . . .'

'I know.' The voice was a little quieter. 'I recognize you both. Now, what flavour would you like?'

'Coffee?'

'Coffee?'

'No, would you like to have coffee? With me?'

'I'm working.'

'No, I mean after—'

'Dina.' We both turned to see Mij, the owner of the *slastičarna*, standing in the doorway, an irritated expression on his face. 'Dina, there are customers waiting. This isn't a job where you can talk to your friends all day.'

'No, Mr Listović, of course. Coffee?'

'Um, yes, thank you.' She handed me the cone and I passed over the money, aware of Mij's eyes boring into the back of my head. 'It was nice to—'

'Next, please.' Her voice was firm. I backed out of the shop, tripped over the step and almost knocked over a knickerbocker-glory glass on one of the tables. Mij tutted and Josip giggled. I could feel my face was scarlet.

'Well, I think we can say that was a complete disaster,' I said, as we went to sit on the harbour wall. 'She's going to think I'm a total idiot, and I've probably lost her her job.'

'Don't be daft,' said Josip easily. 'You know Mij is all bark and no bite. And at least now you've spoken to her. Just make sure you're there when the shop closes. Then you can just carry on the conversation.'

But the fates were against me; the restaurant was having one of its busiest nights of the summer and by the time I had finished running out plates of steak au poivre and clearing empty mussel bowls, the lights on the *slastičarna* had gone out and the doors were closed. Dina was nowhere to be seen.

'Hello.'

I knew who it was before I even looked up from my book. *Dina*. In the week since we had spoken at the *slastičarna* I had got no further; whenever I strolled past there was always a queue of customers, and I never saw her arrive or leave. I had taken to sitting on the harbour wall whenever I had free time from the restaurant, hoping to catch her on a break. I never imagined she would catch *me*.

'Hello.' I squinted up at her through the sunlight; she was wearing a simple yellow sundress that hung perfectly from her slim shoulders and seemed to flow into her long, honey-brown legs.

'Can I sit with you?'

I brushed my hand across the dusty wall. 'Of course. It's a bit dirty.'

'Don't worry about that.' She dropped her bag, settled in next to me and laughed. 'I'm used to it.'

'I'm sorry about . . . I mean . . .' I paused and tried to think what I was attempting to say. 'I hope we didn't get you into trouble on Friday night. With Mij?'

She shook her head. 'He was fine. I just have to be a bit careful – he's not that keen on having a girl working for him. My brother, Bobo, got me the job – told him about my dad, that we couldn't afford the school books. He was determined for me to go to high school; he just kept going on at Mij until he gave in.'

'Is your dad . . . ?'

'He died,' she said simply. 'It's just me and my mum and my brother. And Mum, she isn't always very well. She finds it hard, without a man. That's why Bobo was so keen for me to go to school. I need to be able to rely on myself, he says. He's so wonderful, does everything for us. But he's moving away soon, going to Split to be a lawyer. I'm going to miss him so much.'

'I've got an older brother too,' I said, trying not to notice how close her hand was to mine. 'He lives up in the north. I used to miss him all the time, but you get used to it.'

'Why does he live up there? Is he a farmer?'

I laughed. 'I can't imagine anyone less like a farmer. But he lives there because, well, we all used to live there. And then me, Mother and Pa moved down here to start a business with Pa's brother. And Goran – that's my brother – and Cvita – my sister – stayed in Knin.'

'Oh.' She looked at me, frowning slightly. 'That's a bit weird. Why?'

The muscles in my chest tightened. She bent down and pulled a foil-wrapped packet out of her bag; I found myself staring at the long, smooth curve of her neck.

'What's in your sandwich?' I blushed at the inanity of my question, but I was desperate to change the subject away from the reason we moved from Knin. I had dreamed of this moment for so long, and now Dina was actually sitting so close, an almost tangible scent of her lilting towards me on the breeze. I didn't want to spoil it with memories I spent my life trying to avoid.

'Pršut, tomatoes and cheese,' she said. 'My grandpa makes it – it's the best you'll ever taste. And tomatoes from the garden. I grew them myself.' She reached into her bag and retrieved the other half of her sandwich. 'Go on, try it. I always make too much just for me.'

I bit into the sandwich carefully, but a whole strip of pršut slid from between the bread and I had to push it quickly into my mouth. She giggled again, and I found myself entranced by the way her eyes sparkled when she laughed, her skin creasing tiny freckles into clusters across her cheeks and nose. Somehow in among my clumsiness and her laughter, any awkwardness melted away, and I began to tell her about my life in the village, the pension we ran and my surprise at finding her behind the counter in the slastičarna.

'When Josip told me you were working here, I was so pleased. I've been wanting to talk to you for so long.'

'I know.' She pressed her lips together in a half-smile; cheeky, cute. It made me want to kiss her so badly I could barely think.

'What do you mean, you know?'

'All that staring at me in school – what, you think I didn't notice?'

'Oh.' I felt foolish suddenly.

'You're blushing.'

'No, I'm not.' The words came out more crossly than I meant them to.

'Well, I have to get back.' She screwed up the sandwich wrapper and stood up, brushing down her dress.

'Already? I was just joking.'

She smiled. 'I know. But Mij is very strict about breaks, and it took a lot of effort to get me this job. Bobo was really determined. I can't let him down.'

'Can I see you again?'

She looked down at me, a mischievous expression in her eyes. 'OK then. I finish tomorrow about seven. I'll tell Bobo I'm finishing at eight and then you can take me for that coffee or something. How's that?'

'That,' I said, hardly daring to breathe, 'is just about perfect.'

As it happened, the evening was far from perfect. Dina got out half an hour late, because Mij had been watching the news and wouldn't come down to close up until the report was over. There were no free tables at the cafe and we ended up walking into the woods just as the gathering clouds gave in and the rain cascaded down through the pine needles on to our skin. But none of it mattered. We sheltered beneath thick, fringed branches and the rain's steady patter framed our words, a soft, warm murmur that carried us effortlessly from one subject to the next.

The conversation we began so easily that night flowed into the next evening, and the one after that, and through the whole school year that followed it felt as if we never stopped talking, that there was always so much more to say. She told me of her home in Morsać and her frail, heartbroken mother, and I shared tales of the tourists who slept in our beds and ate at our tables, the cities they called home, the foreign words they taught me, the exotic, alien world they seemed to inhabit. I took photos of her among the olive trees and barefoot in the sea, and told her of my dreams to take pictures for a living. One night, when the moon was full and the world was silent, I even told her about what happened in Knin.

'And what will you do with all this education?' I asked one afternoon, as we sat on the bus coming home from school. 'Are you going to be a lawyer like your brother?'

She shook her head and laughed. 'Me? In an office? I'm an outdoor girl. I shall have my babies first . . .'

I raised my eyebrows. 'Oh, really? How many?'

'Two. A girl first – she'll be called Irina. And then a boy. And then I'll open my restaurant, up in the countryside near Morsać, and I'll grow all my own vegetables and buy my meat from the farmers and seafood from the local fisherman. I will make my grandma's recipes famous – *pašticada* and *janjeća čorba* and *fritule* – and all my guests will say they never tasted such succulent beef, such tender lamb, such light, sweet pastries as Dina makes.'

'The Konavle Kitchen,' I said, smiling at her. 'I can just see you, tables in a garden, flowers everywhere.'

'That's what I'll call it.' She clapped her hands and beamed at me. 'And you can be out front and take the orders and talk to the tourists and I'll make all the food.'

'Ah, but I might be off on assignment for *Večernji List*,' I said, lifting my camera and laughing. 'Or maybe the BBC? Maybe I'll become a cameraman and we can travel the world together.'

'Well, you can go off on assignments as long as you're back on the weekends, because the restaurant will be busy,' she said, bringing her face up to mine for a kiss. 'I'll need you to—'

'Marry me.' I said suddenly, catching her in my arms and swinging her around. 'Marry me, Dina. Not yet, but one day. When we've left school, as soon as we've left school, the *day* we leave school.'

'Marry you?' Dina looked startled. 'I'm only fifteen!'

'Oh. No . . . of course . . .'

'I'm just teasing you.' She laughed, and I kissed her, my heart thumping so hard I thought I might burst. 'Of *course* I'll marry you. Oh my God, how exciting. I'm going to be your *wife*.'

CHAPTER 6

The next two years were the happiest of my life. Suddenly everything I did had more of a purpose; I worked harder at school, saved my wages from the restaurant, and on the cold winter evenings that followed our promise to each other, Dina and I made ever more detailed plans for our life together. When the warmer days came, and school finished for the summer, we became inseparable; each morning I waited impatiently for the last guests to leave their tables so that I could jump on the rackety old scooter Uncle Ivo let me borrow and revel in the breeze against my skin as I sped through the countryside to Morsać.

'He's obsessed with that Dina,' I heard Mother say to Pa one morning, and she was right; at night I dreamed of my beautiful girl with the long plait and the lemon-yellow dress, and in the morning I counted the minutes until we could be together in the Konavle woods, kissing until our lips were sore. On the first anniversary of our secret engagement, I slipped the clothes from her suntanned skin and we became lovers, and even though I was only sixteen, I knew that was the day I joined the adult world, that I left all childish things behind.

'Can't we get married *now*?' Dina said, her naked body curled around mine. 'I love you, Miro. I know everyone will say we're too young, but . . .'

I let my fingers drift across the soft, velvety skin of her back, bent my head to kiss her. 'And have to share you with everyone else? This is our time, my love, they'll all be involved in our lives soon enough – your mother, Bobo, my family. Let's keep our little world secret just a while longer.'

'Let's tell them on my seventeenth birthday,' said Dina, smiling. 'Mum was eighteen when she got married, so she can't say anything . . .'

'Another year of this?' I pulled back the rug and began to kiss her neck, my hands moving down over her body. 'I think I can live with that.'

But things began to change in the months that followed. Dina and I remained blissfully happy, but I was dimly aware of darkening clouds over my country. Pa and Ivo increasingly spent their evenings glued to the news, shaking their heads and tut-tutting about the policies of the new Serbian leader, Slobodan Milošević, debating what was happening in Belgrade over large glasses of brandy. I was too much in love with Dina to care deeply about anything else, but at times I felt a nagging sense of anxiety that events were unfolding that I should have been more aware of.

'You're engaged?' Mother said, when we finally stood in front of my parents, hand in hand, and told them of our plans to marry. 'But that's wonderful! Some good news is just what we need. We must have a party, don't you agree, Petar? Get that brother and sister of yours here, have a real celebration.'

Two weeks later everyone I loved most in the world was in Ljeta: Pavle and Josip laughing with Uncle Ivo, Cvita holding a wriggling Ante while Goran tickled his nephew's feet, Mother and Marjana laying the tables that had been spread across the cobbled harbour front.

'And you must be Tara?' Dina pulled my old school friend towards her and I felt the familiar twist of guilt as she awkwardly returned the hug with just one arm, the other staying firmly by her side, her right hand tucked, as always, into her skirt pocket.

'Who is *that*?'

I turned to see Cata standing behind me, clutching a bottle of prosecco and a handful of glasses, staring at a man who was slowly sauntering towards us dressed in an elegant navy linen suit, open-necked shirt and dark sunglasses that framed his tanned, angular face. Before I could answer, Dina squealed with delight and ran across the cobbles; he scooped her up and swung her around like a child.

'Wow,' said Tara.

'That's Bobo,' I said casually. 'Her brother.'

'He's *gorgeous*.' Cata set the bottle and glasses down and stared at the two of them. 'How come you never told me about him?'

'I've only met him once or twice; he's studying in Split. To be honest –' I lowered my voice as they walked towards us – 'I've always found him a bit stand-offish.'

'Well, I'm not meeting him looking like this – my hair's a complete mess. But make sure I'm sitting next to him at lunch, will you?'

Before I could reply she was walking away back to the kitchen, and I raised my eyebrows at Tara and forced my features into a smile.

'Miro.' Bobo pushed the sunglasses on to the top of his head, revealing the same hazel eyes as Dina, only cooler, more distant. Somehow he always made me feel like a slightly grubby schoolboy, an annoying adolescent who wouldn't stop pestering his sister. 'Good to see you again. And congratulations of course.'

I rubbed my palm against my jeans and held out my hand. 'Thank you. And thank you for allowing me to marry your wonderful sister.'

'Can I leave you two to get to know each other a little better?' said Dina, beaming. 'Maybe Tara and I should go and help your mother – Marjana, well, she's not always the most *useful* in the kitchen, is she? And I love the thought of my two favourite men being together.'

She kissed Bobo on the cheek, planted another on my lips and we both watched her walk away, slowing her pace a little to match Tara's limp. 'It means the world to her you're here,' I said. 'She looks up to you so much. I know that, after your dad . . .'

'It was hard for her,' he said brusquely. 'Of course I tried to fill the gap to some extent, but every girl needs her father. It's good to see her so happy, although I hadn't imagined her marrying so young. She's a bright girl, that's why I fought so hard to get her to go to high school. But I hear you have big plans – you want to be a cameraman?' I nodded and squirmed; it was something Dina and I had talked about in the early days, when I was desperate to impress her. Now the words sounded unrealistic, even to me.

'Ideally. When I leave school.'

'Then you'll have to come to Split; I can help you with that. Or maybe Zagreb. It will do Dina good to see a little more of the world.'

I stared at him, wondering if he knew his sister at all. To suggest moving to Split or Zagreb to Dina would be like suggesting moving to the moon. It was the only hint of concern I ever felt about our relationship: marrying Dina closed the door on any thoughts of discovering the world beyond Ljeta.

'I'm sure you're right,' I muttered.

'Well, I'm pleased she's met someone who has a curiosity about the world, who knows there's more out there than –' he waved an arm dismissively – 'just this. And I know you'll do everything you can to make her happy. Won't you?'

There was something in the final two words, almost the hint of a threat; imperceptible but definitely there. I swallowed, straightened my back and looked directly into his elegant, arrogant face. 'Of course. Dina's happiness is the most important thing in the world to me.'

'Well, you must be Dina's brother.' Goran's words cut through the slight chill and I felt a wave of relief at the sight of his rough-hewn face. 'I'm Miro's – Goran. Good to meet you.' I watched as he wrapped his long fingers around Bobo's hand and held them there for just a moment longer than necessary. Their eyes met. 'What a great day this is, don't you think? Your charming sister and my clever brother. Shall we get a drink?'

He began to steer us over to the long line of tables, decked out with flowers and Mother's best glasses, extracting information I already knew; that Bobo was in his final year of a law degree in Split and planning to move to Dubrovnik to work as a solicitor. Cata appeared from nowhere and slotted into the spare seat next to Bobo, grinning.

'I couldn't move back here,' Bobo said crisply. 'Surrounded by idiot tourists who spend all day with their faces in their towels and learn nothing about the country they've come to visit.'

'And I suppose the people who work for the idiot tourists, they're idiots too?' Goran's voice was pleasant but there was an edge.

'Are we interrupting?' An English voice cut through the slight air of tension, and we turned to see Mark and Sarah, two of our most regular guests, standing in the sunlight, jointly holding a large box. 'We wanted to say congratulations; your dad told us about your engagement.'

'Come and join us,' I said, delighted to be able to show off my English in front of Bobo. 'This is my brother, Goran, and Dina's brother, Bobo.'

Goran grinned and stood up to shake their hands. Sarah beamed at me and placed the box on the table.

'Miro, we have something for you,' she said, smiling. 'Go on, open it.'

'Really? Shouldn't I wait for Dina?'

'Well, it's really more a present for you,' said Mark. 'In fact you might recognize it. But you and your family have always made us feel so welcome, Ljeta feels like our second home. So it's a thank-you for that too.'

I tore back the tape, opened up the box and peered in to see Mark's video camera, packed carefully in polystyrene pieces. 'I can't accept this,' I said. 'It's so kind, but—'

'Don't be daft,' he said. 'Of course you can. I treated myself to a brand-new one a few weeks back, half the size of this one. Fabulous bit of kit. But this still works perfectly well and there's no point in it sitting up in the loft gathering dust. You're a natural with a camera, Miro, you always have been. Now you've got one of your own.'

'I don't know what to say.' I lifted the camera out of the box; it fitted into my hands perfectly. 'It's so generous of you.'

'It's our pleasure,' said Mark. 'And if it helps you along the road to making some sort of career out of it, then we'll be chuffed to bits.'

Mark and Sarah's present made the day even more unforgettable. I loved knowing the celebration wouldn't be over when the party drew to a close, that there were moments stored on the camera we could watch over and over again. I wanted to tell the story of our day and so I captured little vignettes of all those who came to celebrate with us: Uncle Ivo spinning Tara across the cobbles, Pavle flirting with Aunt Marjana while she blushed and giggled like a girl twenty years younger, Josip and Goran with huge slabs of cake, competing to see who could shove the biggest slice into their mouths. When they weren't looking I filmed a few seconds of Bobo and Cata strolling away from the party, her face upturned towards his, shadows lengthening behind them as they headed towards the pine woods on the headland.

Only when I focused in on Mother, Goran and Tara, sat at the end of the tables, far away from everyone else, did I take the camera away from my eye. They were deep in conversation, utterly divorced from the festivities, wrapped up in whatever secrets they were sharing. As I began to walk towards them, Goran noticed me, broke off from what he was saying and stood up, his face breaking into a huge smile.

'Put that camera down,' he said, slinging an arm around my shoulders. 'It's time to dance, Miro. Every bridegroom-to-be should know how to dance. All you need is the right partner –' he grinned down at Tara – 'but in the absence of one, I suppose you'll have to do.'

'*Goran.*' Mother shook her head but Tara just laughed.

'I'm used to it, Mrs Denković,' she said, standing up slowly. 'I just humour him. Someone has to.' Goran bowed with fake gallantry and she slipped her arm through his. 'Come on then, old man – let's show these soft southerners how to really dance.'

I watched them walk slowly away, and for the rest of the evening I kept my brother in sight. He was the life and soul of the party, whirling Tara around, soothing Emilja when she started crying and even sharing a beer with Bobo. But I knew my brother, and I knew something was wrong.

'So what was all that about last night?' I asked, nodding a thank-you at Tomas as he laid two beers on the table between us. 'You and Mother, you looked as if you were at a funeral rather than a party. Is there something I should know? Is something wrong?'

Goran sighed and took a long sip of beer. 'Nothing's wrong, Miro. Nothing for you to worry about.'

Something in his tone annoyed me, a dismissiveness I had never heard from him before. 'Don't treat me like a child. I'm eighteen and I'll be married before you are.'

He laughed, a discordant, unpleasant sound. 'Married? Christ, with everything that's going on right now, you'll be lucky if there even *is* a wedding. How can you sit there and ask me what's wrong? Don't you read the papers? Or are you so blinded by the eternal bloody sunshine down here that you can't see what's happening in your own country? Have you even heard of Milošević?'

'The Serbian guy? Of course I've bloody heard of him.'

'Yes, the Serbian *guy*.' Goran raised his eyebrows wearily. 'You know, the one who's intent on redrawing the map of our country. Haven't you seen the rallies? "Meetings of truth", they're calling them, saying that after fifty years of suppression, the Serbian race is finally free to speak. Hundreds of thousands of people come to hear that man rant and rave – and not just in Belgrade, but in Kosovo and Vojvodina and Montenegro. Don't you see what he's trying to do? Those little independent states – he wants to absorb them into Serbia. And when he's done it, when he's whipped all those stupid fuckers up and we've got a Greater Serbia, what the hell do you think that's going to mean for the rest of us?'

'But it's all just noise and posturing, surely? Everyone in Kosovo is Albanian. They're not Serbs.'

'Not everyone.'

'Oh, come on – their bloody president is Albanian. He's not going to just cave in to Milošević, is he?'

'If he survives,' said Goran darkly. 'That's Milošević's plan – don't you see? Get rid of leaders who don't support him, put puppets in their place, and hey presto, suddenly you've got more power and control than the rest of Yugoslavia put together. I'm not exaggerating, Miro; you should hear them talk in Knin. It's like he's the second bloody coming.'

'But that doesn't affect us, does it? I mean, it's Serbia's problem.'

'Don't be so stupid. If his plan is to create a Greater Serbia, he's going to want the Krajina – more than half the population in and around Knin are Serbs. There's already talk of it – old grievances are coming back. He's stirring up memories from half a century ago to propel his people into another war. And he's not going to stop until he gets one.'

'But it won't come here.'

'And that makes it OK, does it? Thousands of Croatian people – including me if I choose to stay in Knin, and why shouldn't I as it's my bloody home – will be forced to live in an independent Serbia or, more likely, forced out altogether. But, hey, as long as it doesn't happen down here in the land of the tourist dollar, then everything's fine. Is that really what you're saying?'

'No. I mean, I don't know.'

'Well, you should bloody know. Everyone should. Honestly, Miro, I'd expect better from you.'

I'd never been on the receiving end of my brother's contempt before, and I had a horrible sense that I'd disappointed him. The very next day, after we waved him and Tara off, I went to Drogan's shop and bought two newspapers, one Serb, one Croat.

'You don't want to read that dross,' Drogan said, as he handed over my change. 'It's all propaganda.'

But I did want to read it; I wanted to know everything I had been trying to ignore, too wrapped up in Dina to care about what was happening elsewhere in my country. As I turned the pages I saw that everything Goran had said was true: images of vast crowds with raised arms and wide banners daubed with slogans – *Vojvodina is Serbia*, *Kosovo is Serbia*, *Together We Are Stronger*. As I read the columns of print – so guarded in *Večernji List*, the Croatian paper, so hyperbolic in *Večernje Novosti*, the Serbian equivalent – I kept seeing the disappointment on my brother's face that I didn't know what was happening in my own country; even worse, I didn't care.

'Makes for uncomfortable reading, doesn't it?' I looked up to find Ivo had settled himself on the bench next to me.

'Are you worried?'

'Yes and no.' He lit a cigarette, passed one to me. I smiled; Mother and Pa didn't even know I smoked. 'What Milošević wants is an independent Serbia, that's clear. But he doesn't have enough power to make that happen. *Yet.* It's what everyone else does now that matters. He needs controlling.'

'Goran made me feel like an idiot because I didn't know much about it,' I admitted. 'It's just . . . maybe it matters more to him because there are so many Serbs in Knin. And, you know, Dina, exams . . .'

'You don't have to worry about it. Nothing's going to happen here.'

'That's what I said. But Goran said – and he's right – where's next on Milošević's list? If he wants a Greater Serbia, he's going to go for the Krajina, isn't he? So I should care. I *should* be interested. My family are there.'

'Your family are here too.'

'Yes, and we all know whose fault that is, don't we?'

'Miro –' Ivo laid a plump hand on my arm – 'is that what you think? Moving here has been nothing but good for your family. It's made a man of Goran, Cvita is married and you and your parents have a better life here than you could ever have had in Knin.'

'Maybe. But what's happening up there, it *was* my home. And it's still Goran's and Cvita's and Tara's. I've been so busy with school and Dina and making breakfasts for bloody tourists that I haven't really connected with any of it. And I should, you know? After what happened to Tara ... I know I was just a kid, but God, if anyone knows how important it is to be aware of what's happening, it's me.'

Ivo turned to look at me. 'Aren't you happy in Ljeta?'

'Of course I am. How could I not be? I'm so grateful to you, and working with tourists is fun, but I read all this and listen to Goran talk and I realize I've been burying my head in the sand. I don't want to do that any more, Ivo, I don't want to pretend everything's all right, because it *isn't*.' I picked up the open newspaper. 'These pictures make me realize there's a whole world out there and I don't know about any of it. I used to think I'd be a photographer, do you remember? Christ, I even used to say to Dina that one day I'd be a cameraman, that I'd work for a paper, or even the BBC. But now, I don't know. In a few months I'll have finished my exams, and then what?'

Ivo said nothing; stretched his legs out from the bench and tipped his head back so that his face was covered in sunshine. 'Read all of *Večernji List* today, have we?' he asked.

'Most of it.'

'Well, read it again,' he said. 'There's a story, page twenty-four or twenty-five or somewhere around there. I think it might interest you.'

I picked up the paper and flicked through the pages, intrigued. As I reached page twenty-five, a small headline in the top right-hand corner caught my eye. Under 'Expansion of Zagreb TV' the article noted that a new outpost of the Croatian state broadcaster was to open up in Dubrovnik. I read the words several times, and for a moment I imagined myself out on the streets of the city, a camera on my shoulder, the lens heavy against my face. What would Goran say to me then? And Bobo? If things were as bad as my brother said, there were only two choices: get involved and play a part, or continue to do what I had been doing all year and keep my head buried in the sand. Suddenly that no longer seemed an option.

'Bloody hell.' I glanced across at Ivo. 'Do you think, I mean . . . ?'

'Bloody hell indeed,' he said. 'Chances like this don't come along very often.'

I laughed. 'A chance for what though? I hardly think they're going to hire me as a cameraman – I've no experience, no knowledge of TV.'

'You'll have no chance at all if you don't go along and see what's what,' Ivo said firmly. 'If this is really what you're interested in, then you have to grab an opportunity like this with both hands. Time to dust off that suit of yours, don't you think?'

'Thank you for coming by, but I'm afraid we're fully staffed.' The woman behind the desk looked at me, her kohl-rimmed eyes unsympathetic. 'And when it comes to cameramen, we do tend to look for people who have a bit more experience than family parties.'

'Right,' I said. My face felt hot as I shifted from one foot to the other. I glanced across at the television flickering silently in the corner; it was showing pictures of the Kosovan president being hustled out of the parliament building. 'Perhaps I could leave my details?'

'There really wouldn't be any point. As I said, we're fully staffed.'

'Katja?' I turned to see a tall, bulky man standing in a doorway that had previously been closed. He wore a crumpled beige shirt, sleeves rolled up, and a brown striped tie hung limply from the left-hand side of his collar. His face was framed by a messy black-grey beard, but his eyes were sharp and clear and the air seemed to crackle around him. 'Who are you abusing now?'

The woman behind the desk sat up straighter and her bright red lips twisted up into a smile. 'This young man was just asking about opportunities for work as a cameraman. I was telling him we were fully staffed. He was just leaving.'

'Actually I wasn't,' I said quickly. 'I was going to say to . . . Katja, that I'd do anything. I wouldn't expect you to put me behind a camera straight away.'

'Well, that's good of you.' His lips twitched behind his beard.

'I mean, look, I'll make coffee, open the post.'

'I do that,' Katja snapped.

'Then I'll sweep up in the cutting room. I'll print off the newswires. Anything. I'll work for nothing. I just want a foot in the door. And I am good behind the camera; I don't know why, but I understand what makes a good story. And with what's happening, what might happen . . .' I thought of Goran again, saw the disappointment in his face. 'I know about the riots in Belgrade and Kosovo. There are a lot of stories that need telling. I want to be part of that.'

There was a pause and then the man gestured to the open door behind him. 'Nice speech. That buys you two minutes of my time. Come through.'

I sucked in a deep breath and followed him into his office. Before I could speak the phone rang and I listened as he barked instructions, taking in the huge desk crammed with stacks of newspapers, magazines, notepads covered in scribbles, four coffee mugs and an ashtray overflowing with half-smoked cigarettes.

'Name?'

'Miro. Miro Denković. I'm from Ljeta. I—'

He held up his hand. 'Enough with the speeches. Heard what you said out there. Liked it. You're right, things are happening, that's why we've opened up down here – nearer to Kosovo, to Montenegro. Bloody pain in the arse getting crews down there and back all the time. But it's not a picnic. No heroics. Not much fun. So why do you want to be part of it?'

'Because . . .' I took a deep breath. 'Because if I don't, I'm going to leave school and work in my parents' pension, fixing breakfasts for tourists and mixing gin and tonics. I've done it since I was a kid, but it's not enough. Not with everything that's happening right now.'

He looked at me for a moment and then shook his head slowly. 'I don't think—'

'When I was eight I saw my best friend get blown up by a landmine. We lived in Knin, we went out to play . . . it just happened. Right in front of me.' I ran my fingers through my hair and tried to keep my voice steady. 'We didn't know. People need to *know*, don't they? They have to be told the truth. I want to be—'

The phone rang suddenly. He lifted the receiver without looking at it and crashed it back down on to the cradle. 'Did he die? Your friend?'

I shivered. 'She. Tara. No, she was lucky. She lost part of her left foot and hand. But she can walk. But we didn't know, I can't . . . I want to *do* something.'

'Journalism isn't about personal crusades.'

'It's not just about that,' I looked down at my hands for a moment and tried to keep my voice calm. 'I'm *good*. I understand what makes a good image, how a single expression on someone's face can explain a whole conversation. I know that where everyone else is looking, that's not the place to look. Give me a chance. Please.'

'You really do want to work here, don't you?' He let out a short, throaty laugh. 'Haven't even introduced myself, have I? Damir Blašić, head of the studios. Such as it is. Been in this business longer than I care to remember. Never seen the like of these rallies. Worrying.' He tailed off for a moment and I wasn't sure whether I was supposed to speak. 'You know what my years have taught me? Confidence – not too much, just enough – is key. And you've got it.'

'I'm a hard worker too.'

He waved his hand dismissively. 'Anyone who works for me works hard. Or they get their arse kicked all the way to Zagreb – or wherever you come from.' Another long drag on his cigarette. 'All right then. When do you finish school?'

'June.'

'Then come in on the first Monday in July. And yes, you will be running errands and getting my lunch and when – and if – I have a few spare minutes I'll take a look at what you can do. No promises though. I'll give you a month. Paid, but no guarantees. If at the end of that month I'm not happy, or you're not happy, no hard feelings. My word is final. Agreed?'

'Mr Blašić, I don't know what to—'

'Good, right, see you in July.' He picked up the phone and started dialling. I realized my presence was no longer required.

'Oh, and Miro?'

I turned; the phone was hooked between his ear and shoulder and he was already lighting another cigarette. 'It's Damir. We don't do Mr's around here. No time. Just no bloody time.'

CHAPTER 7

By the end of my first week at Zagreb TV, the world looked a very different place. I caught the same bus to Dubrovnik that I always had, but the similarity ended there; no Josip or Dina, no familiar classrooms, no exams to worry about. I did little in those first weeks but run errands: sent out into the sweltering August sunshine for new typewriter ribbon and batteries, packets of cigarettes and pocket-sized paper cups of steaming espresso from the Italian cafe on the corner of the street. But I listened too: to the television that was constantly on, with images of reporters in Knin and Vojvodina and Belgrade, to the roared telephone conversations between Damir and the Zagreb office. As the months rolled past I grew used to the frenetic pace of the studio, to days shaped by whatever came in on the newswires, to the sharply barked instructions to crews departing for Kosovo and Montenegro that inevitably ended with 'and just don't fucking get yourselves killed'.

'There's no chance of that, is there?' Dina asked me, one cold January evening, when she came to meet me off the bus. 'I mean – they're not in any real danger? And you won't have to go, will you?'

I laughed. 'No chance of that. I barely get out of the post room. Don't worry, sweetheart,' I pulled her to me, and kissed her. 'Now, tell me where we're up to with the wedding.'

She beamed and I felt a small wave of relief. I never shared with Dina what I learned during my working days, and as the storm clouds darkened over so much of my country, what was left of the sun seemed to shine ever more brightly on our small corner. Pa and Ivo spent the winter redecorating the pension, ready for the start of another busy season, and Dina had agreed to work in the restaurant, fulfilling the role I knew my father had hoped would be mine.

'I think there are going to be over two hundred people,' she said. 'Your parents seem to know everyone in Ljeta, and Mother has invited the whole of Morsać. I think Bobo's bringing half of Split.'

'No girls, I hope, or Cata won't be pleased.'

Dina shrugged; she was less than enthusiastic about her brother's on-off relationship with my cousin. 'Who knows? You know Bobo. If Cata thinks she's the only one, she's a fool.'

I listened as she chattered away about various relations I had never met, but there was really only one person I was concerned about coming: Goran, still holding out in Knin, while hundreds of other Croats, including Cvita and Branko, Tara and her aunt, packed up their lives and moved away to cities and islands free from the steady rise of Serbian nationalism. Every morning I scanned the newswires for anything from Knin and the Krajina, counting down the days until my wedding, when I would see my brother and do everything I could to persuade him against going back.

It was a conversation that never happened. I'd hoped to meet Goran off the bus on my own, but Mother insisted on coming too, hopping impatiently from foot to foot and craning her neck every time there was a sound of an engine coming around the bend in the road. 'At *last*,' she sighed, when the familiar blue and grey frontage finally appeared around the corner. 'There's still *so* much to do.'

I watched as Goran stepped off the bus, sweeping his hair out of his eyes with one hand, the other outstretched to Mother. He winked at me as she hugged him and I just smiled, a huge, grateful smile that my brother was here, that he was safe and that when I married the woman I loved, he was going to be standing right beside me.

'Dinner first,' said Mother, as we walked back to the pension, 'and then I'm sorry, but it's all hands to the pump. Goran, I thought you might go up to Morsać with your father – pick up the meat and the wine. He'll only forget something if he goes by himself.'

I barely got to speak to Goran at dinner, and the next day disappeared in a haze of last-minute errands and endless unexpected tasks: mending wobbly legs on the trestle tables, threading fairy lights through the vines above the terrace, and a last-minute dash to Dubrovnik to get a new shirt for Ivo, after Marjana discovered he could no longer make the buttons meet the buttonholes on the one he had been intending to wear. It wasn't until the morning of the wedding, when we were stood together in my bedroom waiting for Josip to arrive, that I finally had a chance to ask about the dangers of life in Knin.

'Right now, what's happening up there doesn't matter,' he said, straightening my tie. 'All that's important today is that you get to marry that gorgeous girl and we can all get drunk and celebrate.'

'But—'

'But nothing. Today the world is a place where good things happen.' He put an arm around my shoulders and for a brief moment I was my nine-year-old self, reassured by his strength and solidity.

'It's a shame Tara couldn't be here.'

'She wanted to come. But getting from Krpać – it's two ferries before she'd even reach the mainland. That island is bloody miles from anywhere – I think she's bored stiff.'

'She sounds it in her letters.'

'I'm still glad she's there. She's much better off.'

'Because it's dangerous in Knin? Please don't go back Goran. Stay here.'

'We're here for the condemned man.' Josip's voice floated up from the street below, accompanied by an insistent hammering on the front door.

Goran grinned. 'Your *barjàktārs* are here. Are you ready?'

I thought of Dina, waiting at Marjana's house. I could picture the exact colour of the flush on her cheeks, the way her eyes would be sparkling, how her words would be slightly running into each other in her excitement. My skin prickled a little at the sheer pleasure of being able to call her my wife.

'Having second thoughts, are we?'

I pushed open the window and looked down to where Josip was standing, smarter than I had ever seen him, in a dark grey suit. Pavle stood behind him, his tie slightly askew, a cigarette at his lips. 'Not for a second. Hold on – we're coming down.'

Ljeta had never looked more beautiful than on that morning. Josip, Pavle, Goran and I walked along the harbour, Pa and Uncle Ivo behind, Tomas and Mij and Branko falling into step alongside them. Other men joined the procession; old women sweeping their door-steps stopped to applaud as we passed, little girls in sparkly frocks and small boys in smart suits wove between the adults, shrieking and giggling to each other. Yet none of it seemed real until the door to Ivo's house opened and Dina came slowly down the stairs, her dark hair swept up, studded with minute flowers, her body swathed in white silk, eyes sparkling with happiness.

'You look beautiful,' I whispered. 'Ready to be my wife?'

She grinned and slipped her arm into mine. 'Miro Denković, I was ready before I even met you.'

The first months of our marriage were suffused with a blissful sense of contentment. In the mornings, I would often wake first, and it would take a moment to realize Dina was lying next to me, that simply by moving my body a few inches I could take her in my arms and kiss her, feel her soft skin under my lips, her body start to wake at my touch. Sometimes I would be like a child, impatient for her to wake so I could slip inside her and know a closeness with another human being I had never even dreamed of. On other mornings I simply listened to her soft breath twisting out on to the pillow, watched the silvery morning light filtering through the blinds, and felt the same sense of calm happiness that I had felt on the morning of my wedding.

Winter came early that year. An unseasonable chill settled across the village less than a month after we were married, and instead of bright winter sunshine, I battled back and forth to Dubrovnik through vicious winds and rain that seemed to drive into my skin. None of it mattered. Each night I came home to find my wife at the stove, our home filled with the scent of thick *gulaš* soup or rich *lònac*. Sometimes the dinner burnt a little, or never got eaten; we would be upstairs in the cream-walled bedroom, lost in each other's bodies, limbs happily entangled beneath the crisp white sheets. On other nights she would show me the changes she was making to the little stone-walled cottage Ivo had bestowed on us as a wedding present. 'Nothing a lick of paint won't fix,' he had said a little awkwardly, as the floorboards creaked beneath our feet in the lounge and Dina ran her fingers over a dusty old range in the small kitchen.

'I love it,' she told him, and she did. That winter she transformed our home: a kitchen table restored and painted, crisp clean curtains in our bedroom, the garden slowly tamed until what had once been a mess of nettles and weeds was a freshly seeded lawn and neatly hoed beds, waiting for my wife to grow her first batch of fruit and vegetables.

In some ways I envied Dina the simplicity of her days, but working with Damir was addictive. The moment I walked through the glass doors each morning I felt a surge of adrenalin – the studios pulsating with conflicting opinions and unanticipated stories, cigarette smoke mingling with the smell of half-eaten sandwiches left after a late night in the editing suite, the newswires constantly spewing out the latest words from Belgrade. 'The man's a monster,' Damir would roar regularly, whenever Milošević appeared on screen, but as the weeks passed it was a new face that preoccupied all of us: Franjo Tuđman, the fiercely nationalistic leader of the new HDZ party, a beak-nosed, bespectacled politician, who promised to realize the dream of a free, independent Croatia and who swiftly became our chief combatant in the slow break-up of my country.

My world became divided between those who supported Tuđman and those who feared he was little better than the Serbian leader. I listened to Pa and Ivo debate the rights and wrongs of his speeches, to Damir boom on about how he was 'the only man with the balls to stand up to Milošević', to Mother's quietly spoken concerns about what our new breed of nationalism would mean up in Knin, where the cracks that had appeared between the Serb and Croat communities were growing ever wider.

'I don't know what to think,' I admitted to Dina, as we lay in bed together one night, her body tucked perfectly around mine. 'An independent Croatia, my love – can you imagine not being a part of Yugoslavia any more?'

'But at what cost?' she asked sadly, propping her head up on one arm. 'People aren't going to want to come on holiday to a country where there's fighting.'

'I don't think it will actually happen,' I said, with more certainty than I felt. 'It's just politics, just noise and posturing. When it comes to it, we're stronger together than as little countries on our own. They'll see that in the end.'

But even as I spoke the words, I knew my prophecy was wrong. Within weeks a date had been set for our first free election, and on the day itself Damir was so convinced of Tuđman's victory he opened several bottles of champagne to toast the result even before the polls had closed.

'This is a great day,' he said, handing out glasses and beaming with palpable excitement. 'A great day.'

'And what about the days to come?' Stefan, the station's main cameraman, whose job I coveted on a daily basis, shook his head and refused to take the glass Damir was offering him. 'What do you think they're going to hold?'

'A free Croatia,' Damir said, raising his glass and ignoring Stefan completely. 'I never thought I'd see the day. Drink to it, Miro. Stefan, come *on*. We're on our way now, we really are. Finally, *finally*, Croatia's time has come.'

I was too excited to take the bus home that evening, fired up by Damir's ebullient words and the taste of champagne sharp on my lips. Instead I sat on the wooden ferry and watched the first pinprick stars suddenly spark in the lilac sky, flecks of light from the water-front villages of Priska and Tulić start to twinkle through the dusk. I thought of the families in each of the houses, eating their suppers, talking of what tomorrow would bring, and for a moment I could almost feel it: a whole country teetering on the brink of spectacular, unforeseen change. As Ljeta came into view I lit a cigarette and felt a shiver of pride. *We're on our way now*, Damir had said. We were on our way, and I was part of it.

'You've been *celebrating*?' said Mother, when I arrived at the restaurant to find Dina sat with my parents and uncle and aunt, an open bottle of Stock on the table. 'The results won't even be announced until tomorrow morning.'

'Well, everyone knows Tuđman's going to win,' said Dina, as I bent down to kiss her. 'And that's got to be good news, right?'

'You think so?' Mother's tone was sharp. 'What about that speech he made last week, justifying what the *Ustaše* did in the Second World War? To a Serb, that's like trying to justify the Nazis to the Jews.'

Suddenly celebrating with Damir seemed a very long time ago. 'But that's all history, Mother,' I said. 'Don't you think it's better to look forward?'

'Try telling that to Tara,' she snapped. 'What happened to her happened to thousands and thousands of Serbs at the hands of the *Ustaše* – and much, much worse. "Kill a third, expel a third, convert a third" – that was their slogan. Just by *saying* the word, Tuđman is raising ghosts, disturbing the dead. You know what Goran told us last time he was down, the speeches going on up there – what's his name? Babić – ranting on about how the Serbs must fight before they suffer the same fate as fifty years ago? And there's thousands like him, who think that Tuđman means the rebirth of the *Ustaše*, and everything we tried to do up there – Serbs and Croats living side by side – it'll all be destroyed.'

'But isn't an independent Croatia the best way? The way to move on from all this fighting? Two separate countries.'

'It's not that simple,' said Ivo gravely. 'How do you draw borders when whole regions are shared by both races? These things can't be achieved without bloodshed. And your mother's right, the Krajina – Knin – will be the flashpoint . . . That will be where it starts.'

I looked at Mother; her face was pale and her lips were pressed together so hard they had almost disappeared. 'He'll be all right,' I said, slipping an arm around her shoulders. 'Goran's not stupid. He'll get out if the risks become too great.'

'You don't know that,' she whispered, and her eyes blurred a little. 'None of us knows anything any more. Everything's starting to break apart, to go wrong . . . When was the last time you saw Pavle, apart from the wedding? You two used to be inseparable.'

'What do you mean? There's no problem with me and Pavle – we're both just busy. If I asked him for a beer, he'd come. I just haven't had time recently.'

'All right, Miro. If you say so.'

'I do. In fact I'm going to go and find him right now.'

'You won't have any luck,' said Pa. 'He's gone to his cousin's for a few days, I saw him getting the bus.'

'Well I'll see him when he gets back then.' I pushed my chair back and walked away, irritated by my mother's words, but they stayed with me through the following days and I grew impatient for Pavle to return so that I could prove her wrong. By the end of the week I decided to drop in on him on my way home from work, but as I approached the lock-up where he spent many of his evenings, tinkering on boats for extra cash, I began to feel a little uncertain. I had told myself it was just because I was busy that I hadn't spent any time with Pavle recently; our lives had diverged, we were doing different things. It occurred to me suddenly that I still spent plenty of time with Josip.

'Pavle?' I slid back the heavy metal door and heard the rhythmic rasp of sandpaper on wood. 'Pavle?'

The rasping stopped. He appeared suddenly from behind the wooden hull of a fishing boat, his long face flecked with dirt. 'Miro. Hey. What are you doing here?'

'Just wondered if you fancied a beer. It's been a while.'

He smiled. 'Yes. Yes, it has. How's the world of TV? Bit different from taking breakfast orders and making up beds.'

I nodded. 'It is. It's . . . depressing and, God, just fascinating.'

'Bad times are coming, yeah?'

'Maybe. Never mind that. Come and have a beer.'

'Got to finish this.'

'Tomorrow then. Day after. Next week. Come on, mate. What's happening, it doesn't have to affect us, right?'

He stared at me, wiped his hands on a cloth and beckoned me outside. 'Look up,' he said. 'What do you see?'

I looked where he was pointing, to the flagpole above our tiny police station. Flying from it, for the first time, was the new Croatian flag.

'The Šahovnica,' Pavle said. 'Your man, that Tuđman, gets elected and the first thing he does is bring back the flag of the Ustaše. How do you think that makes people like me feel? My grandfather was killed by the Ustaše – you should hear my father talk.'

'I'm sorry.' Awkwardness spread through me. 'I don't—'

'The Sovereign State of the Croatian Nation. Isn't that what Tuđman has created? And where am I in this? The Sovereign State of the Croatian Nation and, oh, a few Serbs too? Not even that.'

'But that doesn't have to affect us, you and me and Josip.'

'Oh, Miro, you're so naïve. God knows how, with what you must see in that TV station all day. And with your brother where he is.'

'Don't bring Goran into this.'

'Why not? He's me, isn't he? Up there, surrounded by Serbs? And I'm here, surrounded by Croats. Maybe we should just swap lives, what do you think? That'd be an answer, wouldn't it, everyone just swap. But it's not going to be that simple, is it?'

'Don't be fucking cross with me,' I said, beginning to get angry. 'I don't want any of this.'

His face softened suddenly. 'You're right, let's have a drink. But maybe here's better. I've got a bottle of Stock out the back.' I followed him into the lock-up and watched as he disappeared through a door and came back with a dusty bottle of brandy and two mugs.

'You don't want to be seen out with me?'

He laughed but didn't answer, his face turned away to the table where he was sloshing brandy into the mugs.

'What shall we drink to?'

'To the past.' He threw back a gulp of brandy and reached into his pockets for a cigarette, striking a match along the table to light it. I felt the old stab of envy I had felt as a kid; Pavle could light a match on anything – wall, pavement, tabletop. It was one of the things that made him so cool.

'To sticking together,' I said firmly. 'We can always be friends, can't we? Whatever happens.'

'I'm going away.'

'What do you mean?'

He sighed and took a long pull on his cigarette. 'I'm joining the army, Miro. Oh, don't look at me like that. What do you expect me to do? Just sit around and wait to be thrown out of a country that doesn't want me?'

'It's not like that.'

'Not for you maybe, but I don't belong here any more. I love this village, but it's changing; people are changing. Remember when we were kids, we couldn't understand why it mattered who was Serbian and who was Croatian? Well, it matters now, and it's only going to get worse. And that makes me so angry, Miro, so bloody angry.'

'I'm sorry.'

'Don't feel sorry. Feel lucky. You win this one; you have your wife, your family, a life. But what's happening to me here is exactly the same as what's happening to your brother up in Knin. He'll have to go sooner or later – and sooner if he's got any sense.'

I wanted to snap at him not to talk about Goran, that I couldn't bear to think of the risks he was taking, but I knew the conversation was on a knife-edge. I took a deep breath and lifted my glass: 'To the past, then?'

He nodded. 'To the past.'

A week later he was gone. 'Gone to fight for our future,' his mother said, when I stopped by to ask her if Pavle had left Ljeta. She had looked at me unsmilingly, moved away before I had time to respond, and as I watched her I remembered the day she had bandaged my knee when I had fallen out of the almond tree in their garden, and all the times I had eaten supper at their table.

In the weeks that followed Pavle's departure, life began to change in our small, sunlit corner of the world. The boat that carried me back and forth to Dubrovnik was no longer crammed with tourists, and as I walked home through the thick August heat each evening, many of the tables outside the harbour restaurants sat empty and silent. 'If Tuđman is a force for good, why is my restaurant dead?'

Pa would whisper to me, when I joined him and Ivo for a cold beer before heading home to Dina. It was a question I couldn't answer.

Dina and I tried not to let the summer's gloom taint our world, but it was impossible to remain unaware of what was happening. 'The pension's doing badly too,' she told me as we lay in bed together on a sweltering Saturday night, stickily humid air flowing in through the open window. 'Only three rooms taken this week, and all anyone wants to talk about is whether there's going to be a war. It used to be times of the boat to Dubrovnik and walking trails in Konavle and what your mum puts in her *buzara* sauce. Now it's what do I think of Milošević? Is Ljeta safe? And I smile and tell them that there's nothing to worry about, that the only place where there's any problem is up in the mountains, hundreds of miles away.'

'Where Goran is.'

'I know.' She leaned in to kiss me and I felt a pull of desire just at the scent of her skin.

'It's Mother I feel sorry for,' I said, brusquely. 'If this is how I feel, God knows how she even sleeps. And if the pension is quiet, that's not good.'

'She needs to hear some good news. Maybe—'

'She needs to hear from Goran.'

'Well, I can't make that happen, but maybe if I told her she was going to be a grandmother again?'

I stared up at her, not quite able to believe the meaning of her words. The curtain lifted a little in the breeze and a shaft of moonlight flooded in, lighting her face.

'You're pregnant?'

'Five weeks. You're going to be a father, my love. We're going to have a baby.'

Dina's announcement was a rare moment of joy in a world that was growing ever darker, and the time we spent together in our small, quiet cottage was the only tranquillity I knew. We had decided that, once inside, we wouldn't talk about what was happening in our country, an attempt to recreate the blissful private world we had known as teenagers. But every day at work I listened to stories of sinister deals with Eastern Bloc countries and caches of guns smuggled over the border, and it seemed obvious – although it never made it on to the air – that we were arming for war. I began to wonder more and more what sort of a man we had elected to lead our country, and even Damir's belligerent rhetoric began to sound hollow.

The months rolled by and it began to feel as if we were in some kind of unspoken holding pattern: waiting for the baby, waiting for news of Goran, waiting to see what stroke of madness struck Tuđman or Milošević next. I took the boat each morning to Dubrovnik with a growing sense of discomfort at being away from my heavily pregnant wife, and each night she was waiting for me on the jetty, hair pulled back in the long dark plait, skin glowing, eyes dancing as she pulled me to her for a kiss.

'I wish you'd stop coming to meet me,' I said as I clambered off the boat one warm April evening. 'You need to take it easy, put your feet up. Don't want you having our baby on the beach.'

'If I put my feet up any more I'll lose the use of my legs,' she laughed. 'Anyway, I had to come tonight, I couldn't wait. We've heard from him, darling. From Goran. He's safe. He's OK.'

'Oh my God, really? Did you speak to him?'

'Your mother did. Just briefly. She picked the phone up and just screamed – we thought it was bad news. But it was just his voice . . . she couldn't believe it was really his voice. He was calling from the police station in a village called Krno. There are lots of Croats there apparently; it's become a bit of an outpost. But he's well. Unhurt.'

'Oh my darling.' I wrapped my arms around her and kissed her, not quite able to believe what she was telling me.

'Come on, we must get back. Your mother's made a huge *lònac* to celebrate, and Cata and Bobo have come for the weekend. It's like a party, like old times.'

As soon as I walked through the door I could see the change Goran's phone call had made; my mother's eyes were red and puffy, but her face was alight, Pa and Ivo were laughing with Bobo, Cata and Marjana were stirring a huge pot of lònac – more life than our kitchen had seen in months.

'I always knew your brother was more than a match for a few jumped-up Serbs,' said Cata, grinning.

'Hope he took a few down on his way out,' said Bobo. Pa caught my eye and raised his eyebrows, but even my brother-in-law's belligerent tone couldn't sour the evening.

'I've got some news too,' I said. 'It'll be on the news tonight, but, well, Tuđman and Milošević met today at Tito's old villa, and it seems they reached an agreement. The news agencies have quoted Milošević as saying that the creation of a Greater Serbia allows for a more powerful Croatia, so maybe . . .'

'Really?' Pa's voice was grave. 'That sounds like a deal with the devil, if ever I heard one. Someone's going to have to pay, somewhere.'

'Oh, come on, Petar,' said Marjana happily. 'Don't get all political. Come and sit down. This lònac is just about ready.'

'She's right,' Ivo boomed. 'Let's be positive, drink a toast. To Goran, to Tuđman, perhaps even to Milošević. Perhaps he's not such a monster after all.'

I raised my glass, but Pa's words had left me with a slightly sick feeling. 'There goes Bosnia,' Stefan had said, when I had read out the newswire report of the meeting between the two leaders. 'A Greater Serbia and a more powerful Croatia? The only way that's possible is if they carve up Bosnia between them.'

But as the wine flowed, any concerns began to fade. Dina was right, it did feel like old times: Cata and I bickering across the table, Marjana fussing around Dina, plumping cushions and bringing her tea. Pa even sang a little, Uncle Ivo on the *tamburitza*, and our kitchen rang with laughter, with relief, until Dina returned from the bathroom with an expression on her face I had never seen before. 'Miro, get the bag.' I felt my stomach lurch. 'We need to go to the hospital. The baby's on its way.'

CHAPTER 8

The drive to Dubrovnik was one of the most unreal of my life, Dina moaning with pain in the seat beside me, Pa driving so carefully that I had to stop myself from yelling at him to speed up. As soon as we drew up at the hospital, Dina was whisked away, with only Mother allowed to follow. As the swing doors closed behind them, I looked at Pa.

'Nothing to do now but wait, son,' he said. 'Best go outside, I think.'

He led me out into the gathering dusk and we sat on a low wall, the brickwork rough against my legs. He talked, but I barely listened, his low voice meshing into the rhythmic scraping of the cicadas in the plane trees and the occasional yell of pain that ricocheted out of the windows above us into the cool night air.

'Our baby is going to be born into a war,' I said suddenly, unable to bear my thoughts any longer. 'What if I can't protect them, Pa? What if something happens?'

He laid his hand on mine. 'Nothing bad is going to happen, Miro. It's natural to be scared at a time like this, but you have to keep your head. There may not be a war. And even if there is, the baby won't know anything about it. All it will know is you and Dina, and the love you show it. And we'll all help, you know that.'

I was just about to speak when a nurse appeared in the doorway, waving and smiling. 'Congratulations, Mr Denković,' she called. 'You've a beautiful baby girl.'

Nothing could have prepared me for the first sight of my daughter. 'Isn't she gorgeous?' Dina whispered, after I had kissed her, straightened her pillows, tried to do something, anything, to make her more comfortable.

'Oh, stop fussing around the girl,' Mother said, as she left the room. I smiled, but I felt the most overwhelming sense of uselessness; that Dina had produced a miracle while I had done nothing but sit outside with Pa, smoking cigarettes.

'Say hello to your daughter,' Dina said, passing up a tiny, woollen-wrapped bundle. I tucked her into the crook of my arm and looked down at the small face; two dark lines fringed with lashes, a neat snub nose, and lips that were Dina's in perfect miniature. Something tightened in my chest.

'Welcome to the world, little one,' I whispered. 'I'm your dad.' Even as I said the words, it didn't seem believable, that this fragile warm little body could be mine. I bent to dust her forehead with my lips, and in the cool, quiet room I thanked God for delivering her to us safely.

'She looks like an Irina,' I said, smiling down at Dina.

'You remembered.'

'Of course. Irina Jadranka? I think Mother would like that.'

She nodded sleepily. 'All right, Daddy. I think I can live with that.'

Two days later we drove back to Ljeta as a family, and when all the well-wishers had gone, we closed the door and tried to remember how our home had felt before this small, perfect creature came to join us. When night fell we put her in the crib at the bottom of our bed and as her cries began to ebb away I put my arm around Dina and we watched as our daughter slowly succumbed to sleep, arms raised either side of her head as if in some silent celebration at the end of her long bewildering journey.

But if we had hoped for some peace and quiet to adjust to our new life, we were almost immediately disappointed. Before she was a week old the first deaths had been reported, tourists caught up in gunfire, rocket-propelled grenades shattering the tranquillity of the Plitvice National Park. I watched the images on the news, looked across to where Dina was feeding our baby and made a decision: work didn't matter, Zagreb TV didn't matter, nothing mattered apart from my baby girl and her mother. Irina had changed everything; it was as if becoming her father had finally made a man of me, or perhaps the sense of responsibility I felt towards her meant I finally became *Croatian*. Whatever ambivalence I felt was no longer relevant; all that mattered was keeping my family safe, and if Tuđman could promise that, I no longer cared how he achieved it.

But it wasn't long before my lack of focus on my job became noticed. One morning I arrived at the office to find Damir barking orders with a ferocity that seemed explosive, even for him. Dina and I had been up half the night with Irina and I had had no time to buy a paper on the way in. As Damir beckoned me into his office he held up *Večernji List* and I stared at the newspaper's front page. The picture was shocking in its simplicity: a road, trees, blue sky and three blackened bodies, their faces barely discernible.

I sat down. Damir continued to bellow into the phone. The air thickened as I stretched my hand to turn the pages. 'TWELVE DEAD,' screamed the headline. Inside there were more photographs of the bodies beneath the words 'HOLIDAY MASSACRE'. A sudden crash snapped my attention away from the newspaper and I looked up to see Damir had slammed the receiver down so hard it had cracked the face of the dial.

'You see this?' he yelled, ripping the newspaper out of my hand and throwing it on the desk. 'See it? Twelve dead. More injured. Drove straight into a fucking Serb ambush.'

'What ambush?' I asked, confused. 'Why?'

'You don't know. You. Don't. *Know?* You're supposed to be a fucking newsman and you don't know anything about this?'

I shook my head mutely.

'They're *dead*.' He jabbed at the newspaper with his finger. 'Dead for trying to replace the Yugoslavian flag with the *Šahovnica*. Bit of a stunt it was, four young guys in the local police force – bit drunk probably, thought the town was unguarded. But guess what?'

I stared at him miserably. 'It wasn't?'

'Well, well, well. So you do know something. But I'm guessing you don't know that two of the four were wounded and taken prisoner by Serb militia. And you also don't know that when a bus-load of their colleagues went in to rescue them the next day, those Chetnik fuckers were waiting for them – in huge numbers. They gunned them down, Miro, like some fucking fairground attraction. But you don't know any of this, do you? And you work in a newsroom, *my* newsroom. Is your head all the way up your fucking arse?'

'I'm sorry. The baby . . . we were up all night. I know that's no excuse.' I looked at Damir, his scarlet face gleaming with sweat. 'I'm really sorry. It won't happen again.'

'You're damn right it won't.' He ran a hand across the top of his head and looked at me. 'I don't envy you, Miro. You're a young man. Everything you know is being thrown upside down and you've just got yourself a new baby. That's change enough, without everything else that's going on. If this isn't the right place for you, then walk away. No hard feelings. I need people around me who are absolutely dedicated to what we do, now more than ever.'

Panic shot through me. 'This is the right place, Damir, really. It's just quite an adjustment. The baby . . . but look, like I say, that's no excuse. I got it wrong today. I know that. I won't get it wrong again.'

Damir sat down heavily in his wide leather chair and his face softened. 'You're not a bad kid. And you don't need to tell me about the havoc a baby can wreak on your life. I remember the first day you came in here, all bright and bolshie; *I'm good*, you said, and you are. Good with a camera. But you need to pick up the pace a bit, understand what we're part of, our role in what's happening.' He paused. 'Come to the Ragusa tonight. They're all there – CNN, the BBC, reporters from dozens of different countries. You'll learn more about the job we do from an evening with these people than a month in our little set-up.'

The surprise must have registered on my face.

'What? You think I don't know the difference? I'm proud of what we do, but we can't compete with the Brits or the Americans – CNN broadcasts news bloody twenty-four hours a day. We're part of a global industry, and right now those reporters at the hotel are telling the same stories as us, but with the kind of technology you've never seen. Our reports go into homes in Konavle and Split, theirs reach London, New York, Berlin. But they won't be here for long – a bigger story will break somewhere else and they'll move on. It's a circus, Miro, a real circus. And you need to see it before it's gone.'

We set off in the early-evening haze, weaving through the crowds on the Stradun and leaving the imposing walls of the old town shimmering behind us. I had been unable to concentrate all day, excited just by the prospect of setting foot in the Ragusa. It was Dubrovnik's most luxurious hotel, and in the old days it had hosted presidents and movie stars and *Večernji List* regularly ran pictures of glittering parties. 'We'll sit at that bar one day,' Josip used to say, as we pored over the photographs of women in their low-cut dresses, dripping with jewellery, cocktail glasses to hand. Not for one second did either of us believe it would happen.

'Ready?' asked Damir, as we approached the gleaming, gilt-edged doors. I nodded and followed him through.

'Bloody hell.' The lobby was heaving with people; groups of soldiers in army fatigues, pale-faced men in crisp white shirts with 'UN' stitched on to the arm, knots of grim-faced men clutching glasses to their chests, voices raised, fingers pointing. One or two of the faces were familiar from the foreign news reports that were beamed into our office.

'UN, hacks, military, Yanks,' said Damir, pointing to the different groups in turn. 'Life in all its colours, eh, Miro?' He gestured towards the bar and I followed him, through air that was thick with cigarette smoke and a strange visceral energy that seemed to pump out of everyone who spoke.

'I'll get us a drink,' he said. 'See you on the terrace. It's sweltering in here.'

As I began to weave my way between the groups of people towards the wide French doors I suddenly felt clumsy and horribly, hopelessly young. Everyone looked glossy and smart and they all talked at an astonishing speed, short sentences, finished by others, as if their shared experiences ran so deep they knew each other's thoughts. As I stared into the mêlée I realized Bobo was standing talking to a group of soldiers. He looked over and I began to walk towards him but he simply raised his beer glass nonchalantly and smiled, before turning back to his conversation. I stopped in the middle of the terrace, unsure whether to continue towards him or turn round. Humiliation flooded through me.

'And you are . . . ?'

I recognized the voice instantly: Marian Wiseman, the BBC's most famous female war reporter, chic, immaculate and seemingly fearless. I had watched her in Belgrade, in Zagreb, even on the road up to Knin, cool and unmoved in a crisp white shirt, straight blonde hair pulled back in a neat ponytail. Stung by Bobo's dismissive behaviour, I ignored the nervousness that was creeping through me and looked her squarely in the face.

'I'm Miro Denković. Cameraman at Zagreb TV here in Dubrovnik. Do you know Damir Blašić? He runs the station. And you're Marian Wiseman, of course. I'm a huge fan of yours; it's an honour to meet you.'

'Don't be ridiculous,' she said, raising an arm and gesturing to someone I couldn't see. 'Everyone's equal here. In fact you guys have got the run on all of us – it's your country after all. At least you can make some sense of what's going on.'

Out of nowhere a man appeared with two bottles of beer. 'Meet Miro, he's from Zagreb TV,' she said, taking one of the bottles and handing it to me. 'This is Friedrich from RTL.' The German put out his hand and I shook it, clammy from holding the beers.

'It's like the UN in here most nights,' Marian said, laughing. 'Over there, that's Jean-Claude from TF1, and she –' her voice grew a little thin – 'is Elena Morcello from RAI Uno.'

'*Et moi?*'

I looked round to see a short, grey-haired man dressed entirely in black. His jeans sagged a little and the shirt bunched up above the waistband, creased and messy.

'And this is Nic Richaud, also from TF1,' said Marian.

'When I feel like it,' he said. 'Sometimes TF1, sometimes CNN, mostly whoever'll pay the most.' The Frenchman looked at me, intense blue eyes gleaming beneath messy grey hair that fell forward into his unshaven face. 'I'm freelance, work for who I please. And this, Marian, who's this? You and your eye for a pretty local.'

'Fuck off, Nicolas,' she said sharply. 'Show some respect. This is Miro. He works for Zagreb TV with Damir.'

'Ah, the ebullient Damir.' Nic laughed. 'Is he here? I could do with a little fun. I have a great joke to tell him about a Serb, a Croat and a Slovene at a party. He'll love it. *Excusez-moi.*'

'Ignore him,' said Marian, her voice an odd mix of amusement and distaste. 'He's a law unto himself. Complete arse in lots of ways. But he's the man you want with you in a sticky situation.'

'What's his secret?'

'Total lack of fear. I'd like to say it's just bravado, that he's scared shitless inside, but I honestly don't think he is. He actively seeks out the most dangerous places, gets a kick out of the risk. And he *loves* basking in all the adoration when he comes back with footage no one else had the guts to go looking for. He's carved out quite a reputation.'

'And you? Do you get scared?'

She shook her head. 'Not really. You can't afford to. In this game fear just increases your risk of getting hurt. Hesitation, indecision – a moment can make all the difference. Every so often you have a bad day, but it passes. Not that I've ever seen Nic have one. I was with him in the Gulf and he was exactly the same every day. I actually think he's got a slight screw loose.'

I frowned. 'Screw loose?'

'Sorry. It means . . . not quite right in the head. Not mad, just a bit unbalanced. It's like he doesn't calculate the risks like everyone else does.'

'Why do you do it?' I asked, a little mesmerized by the way her blue-grey eyes were resting on my face as if I was the only person in the room. 'This isn't your country, it's not your fight – and it's pretty bloody dangerous.'

'Why do *you* do it?'

'Because I want to tell the stories. Like today. We were shooting at the hotels in Lapad, there's so many refugees, just pouring in. What's happened to them, what's happening in their villages . . . people need to know.'

'I completely agree,' she said crisply. 'Don't assume that I find what's happening here any less shocking or unbelievable than you do. You're right, people need to know, they need to be informed. It's not a comfortable job but, well, I've never been very good at comfortable. We're here because—'

'Because your fucking governments won't step up to the plate and help us out of this mess?' Damir appeared, his rumpled appearance making her look even more elegant. 'So your country will send journalists but not troops, you'll film our battles but not stop them, eh?'

'Damir.' Marian leaned in and kissed him on both cheeks. 'Always with the small talk. Why don't you try talking about something serious for once?'

'It's not a joke, Marian. Can't you people get your politicians to listen? We're dying here, literally. We need your help. You go charging into the Middle East at the drop of a hat, but you won't help people in your own backyard? What's that about? Do you honestly think it's right that none of our closest neighbours is coming to our aid?'

I stepped back a little; it was a discussion I had with Damir most days and I was more than willing to let someone else take up the debate. Snatches of other conversations drifted through the night air: a gun battle in Iraq, oil fires in Kuwait, countries I had never even heard of were talked about in the way Josip and I might talk of Korčula or Split.

'Don't you *see*?' Damir's voice broke into my thoughts, louder suddenly, filled with frustration. 'That *massacre* in Moreñi Trpać – it's all part of Milošević's plan. They're done for, those poor fuckers up in the Krajina. Anyone with any sense has fled – they're here in the bloody hotels or in Split or Zadar. But the others, the ones who've stayed put because . . . because the land *belongs* to them, well, they're going to be the first mass martyrs of this bastard fucking war.'

There was a pause. 'Oh, come now, *mon ami*,' Nic's voice, instantly recognizable. 'Aren't you being a little *mélodramatique*? Slovenia will go first, and they'll pave the way for your independence. Why should it be any more difficult for you? And after all, haven't you just, um –' he paused theatrically – 'pulled back from the brink?'

Suddenly everyone on the terrace burst out laughing. It was as if the Frenchman had told the funniest joke in the world; they held their sides, sank back into the wide rattan sofas; the air felt hot and sour with the slight mania of their laughter. I looked at Marian, bemused as to what had just happened.

'It's known as the "Croatian catchphrase",' she said, lighting a cigarette. 'You lot have got so close to war and pulled back from it so many times that we've all lost count of how often we've used that phrase. I think Friedrich is running a book on who's said "back from the brink" most times on camera.'

I stared at her. 'So, forgive me, this is all just a big joke? You people find what's happening in my country *funny*?'

She met my gaze; her blue eyes were cool and amused. 'Of course we don't think it's funny. But you do this job for long enough, you soon realize that a sense of humour – and this –' she raised her bottle of beer – 'are the only two things that stand between you and complete insanity. Grow up, Miro. Most people here won't go back to nice comfortable lives after this is over. They'll be on to the next war or famine or whatever bloody crisis the world throws up. There has to be some *relief*. We have to be able to laugh at things.'

'Well, my fucking brother is up in the Krajina,' I said, the words hurtling out with such fury I could almost taste the anger. 'So why don't you laugh about *that*?' I turned away and began to push through the crowds towards the lobby.

'You're going?' Damir caught my arm. 'Already?'

I looked behind him to Marian and Friedrich and Nic; suddenly it was as if their masks had slipped and instead of the sleek, sophisticated creatures I had first encountered, all I could see was a bunch of dysfunctional men and women who travelled the world as a pack, smelting down human misery into snide jokes at the expense of people whose suffering they didn't understand.

'I'm going,' I said roughly. 'I wish I'd never come.'

I didn't tell Dina about my visit to the Ragusa, but then I increasingly told her very little about how I spent my days in Dubrovnik.

By the time I reached home she was tired, and once we had eaten I would often wheel Irina around to see my parents to give her a break. There I could talk to Pa and Ivo about what was happening: Slovenia's announcement of independence, the ten days of fighting that followed, the extraordinary withdrawal of the army with only a small number of lives lost. I had none of those conversations with my wife; we kept rigidly to our embargo on talking about the war inside our house, almost as if we didn't want to poison the air Irina breathed with talk of the horrors that were happening further north.

But everything was changing. Ljeta was unnaturally quiet, cafe tables bereft of customers, the beaches empty of towels and sunhats and laughing couples in the sea. In Dubrovnik, the hotels replaced tourists with hundreds, then thousands, of hollow-eyed refugees, who had fled the increasingly Serb-dominated interior with whatever they could carry. Stefan and I spent our days among the hungry and the desperate, listening to stories of lives destroyed, all hope gone, and when I got home I wrapped my arms around my wife, felt the soft breath of my baby daughter against my skin and thanked God I had this other world, so different from the drama that characterized my days.

But the separation of the two couldn't last. I came home one night to find Dina on her knees in our lounge, surrounded by sheets and blankets, and a small heap of clothes that had been presents for Irina, some of which she had never even worn.

'Why didn't you tell me?' she snapped, as I came through the door. 'How could all this be going on on my doorstep and me not know anything about it?'

'What are you talking about?' I asked, utterly confused. 'Where's the baby? What's going on?'

'She's asleep. How could you not tell me, Miro? The hotels in Dubrovnik? The refugees? I saw Karena today – she's organizing a collection of clothes and blankets, said I must know all about it, what with you filming there. Why didn't you tell me?'

'But, darling, we agreed . . . and anyway, it's been in all the papers.'

'I don't have time to read the papers,' she snapped. 'And I know we said we wouldn't talk about the war, but this is different. This is –' She swallowed and I realized she was on the point of tears. 'This is our home. It's happening here, where we went to school, on the streets we used to walk when I came and met you from work. It's not hundreds of miles away any more and I can't, it isn't . . .'

She broke down and I pulled her to me, feeling her body curl into mine. I kissed her, smoothed her tears away with my hands, felt the wonderful sense of escape as her body responded to mine. It was the first time we had made love since Irina was born and it felt as if something was re-forged between us, a mutual reassurance that nothing could touch the intimacy we shared.

'We'll take the clothes along tomorrow. I'll come with you,' I said, as we lay on the couch, her body still entwined around mine.

'You have to work,' she whispered.

'It's Saturday tomorrow.'

'God, so it is. I don't even know what day of the week it is any more.'

The following morning we walked to the harbour with Irina asleep in the pram, a bagful of clothes and linens carried between us. As we came in sight of the boat, there was an odd, noiseless explosion; a burst of colour shot into the air and landed on the cobbles, accompanied by high, angry voices. As we drew nearer I could make out a mustard-yellow blouse lying in the street; a few feet away a fawn blanket was flapping lazily over the harbour wall.

'We don't want anything from you.' Karena's voice was high with anger, loud enough for everyone to hear. 'Take your dirty clothes and go. They would rather freeze to death than be clothed in the charity of a Serb.' I tried to make out who she was snarling at; an old woman whose face I couldn't see. My stomach lurched as I recognized Pavle's father fighting his way through the crowd.

'You see?' he yelled, pulling her away from the group. 'You *see*? I told you.'

Pavle's mother looked up at me as they walked past, her face gaunt and tear-stained. 'I'm sorry,' I mouthed, but she looked away as I spoke and I felt ashamed suddenly, as if somehow we were all guilty of bullying a frightened old woman who had only been trying to help.

I left Dina with Karena and wheeled Irina over to the pension. Ivo appeared, pulled up a chair and laid his coffee cup on the table. It smelt strongly of brandy, and as I watched him take a large gulp I realized the tables weren't even set for breakfast.

'What would be the point?' he said, following my gaze. 'No one will come now.'

'No bookings at all?'

'None. Finished. Last month three rooms were taken, last week one, this week none. Would *you* take your holiday here? Would you even *be* here if you could be somewhere else? Slovenia was one thing – it's the other end of the country. But these pictures of the refugees in Dubrovnik . . . It's over, Miro. No one's coming here on holiday any more.'

'What are you going to do?'

He shrugged and drained his cup. 'What is there to do? We've money enough to survive for a while, but how do we fill our days? It's your mother I worry about; all that work kept her from thinking about Goran. I've never known a woman find such solace in cooking and cleaning. Now there's little of either to be done.'

I thought about my mother as I lay in bed that night, of all the years she had spent in the kitchen, her heart yearning to be somewhere else.

'I'll never make you live anywhere you don't want to,' I whispered to Dina as she lay curled up beside me. 'We never have to leave Konavle. I don't ever want to make you unhappy.'

Before she could answer there was a loud bang on the front door.

Dina's eyes grew wide and as I ran down the stairs I heard her feet rush across the boards to Irina's cot.

When I opened the door I felt a jolt of fear. A man stood in front of me, his face disfigured by blood and bruising, one eye purple and swollen, a deep cut running from cheekbone to chin. He leaned against the door frame, his right arm hanging limply in such an awkward position that I knew the bones were fractured. I looked into the blackened, swollen face, and as the first wave of fear started to dissipate I felt a sense of utter disbelief.

'Hello, Miro.'

The voice rasped with pain and exhaustion but I knew, knew before the first word had melted into the night. My throat grew tight with love and relief as I held out my arms to support him and he half stepped, half fell through the door. Goran had come home.

CHAPTER 9

'Goran.' My brother's name fell from Dina's lips as she froze halfway down the stairs. For a moment none of us moved; my arm tightened around Goran's waist and I felt his hipbone through the skin. Dirt flaked off his shabby coat, blood oozed from a blistered split in his lower lip, a sweet rancid smell seeped from his clothes and mouth. I half carried, half dragged him to a chair and he collapsed on to it, hunched like a child, swollen eyes looking up at me through matted, bloodied hair. A sudden shriek from Irina's room split the silence and his whole body jolted at the noise.

'Go and settle her.' Dina's voice was calm and authoritative and almost unconsciously I did as she said; climbed the stairs, crept into my daughter's room and tucked her small body under the blanket. As I bent in to kiss her, a conversation began in the room below; Dina's unmistakeable lilt and then a deep, quiet murmur. Although the words weren't clear, something happened when I heard Goran's voice – it was as if I suddenly woke up to the fact he was here, in my house, *alive*.

I came down to find she had begun to work her magic; a towel lay in the sink, stained with blood and dirt from my brother's face. She must have slipped the coat from his shoulders and unwrapped the scarf, but I sensed he couldn't bear to bring his arms above his head, because the filthy clothes remained on his body. Dina was at the stove, warming what was left of the casserole we had eaten for supper; on the table lay a bottle of Stock, two glasses poured, neither touched.

'I can't believe you're here,' I said, sitting down next to him. 'How did you . . . when . . . ?'

Goran shook his head, raising a finger to point at the brandy. I passed him a glass and he winced as he lifted it to his lips, the silence only broken by Dina, spooning chicken and vegetables on to a plate and bringing the tray of food to where we sat.

'First you must eat,' she said, and he picked up the spoon, drew it across the plate and tried to move it to his mouth. The movement was clearly too painful; his eyes closed, breath whistled through his lips, after a moment he simply laid the spoon back on the table. Dina moved closer, tucked a napkin into the neck of his jumper and began to feed him. After three mouthfuls she sat back, looked at Goran and grinned. 'There's not really much point in this is there,' she said, pulling the napkin away to reveal the filthy jumper.

Goran tried to smile. 'I don't know,' he said, hoarsely. 'First time I come for dinner and I haven't even had a bath. Mother'd say I've no manners.'

'Well if you can't make an effort, we shan't ask you again,' I said, and suddenly the awkwardness passed and it was just my brother and my wife and I around our kitchen table. I laid my hand on Goran's arm, watched Dina lift the glass of Stock to his lips and in that moment I realized everyone I loved most was within the same four walls and I was filled with an urge to lock the doors and bolt the windows and never let them out.

'More?' Dina lifted a napkin to his face and carefully mopped the skin around his dry, blistered lips.

Goran shook his head. I lit two cigarettes and passed him one.

'Thank you,' he said. 'I will . . . I'll tell you, but not tonight. There's so much . . . I don't know. I need, I need . . .' he looked at Dina, as if hoping she could provide the answer.

'To sleep? A bath first?'

'The baby,' he said. 'I'd like to see the baby.'

I waited for Dina to say she was asleep, that he could see her in the morning, but instead she simply walked upstairs and returned moments later with a barely-awake Irina, placing her carefully in Goran's lap, tucking a cushion behind her to offer the support his limp arm couldn't. I expected Irina to cry, angry or frightened by this strange new face. Instead she wrapped her small pink fingers around Goran's dirty thumb, looked up at him and chuckled.

'Hello, little one,' he whispered, staring down at the small face that seemed so delighted to see him. 'I'm your Uncle Goran.' He bent his head to kiss her, staying bowed for what seemed like minutes. When he slowly straightened up, my stomach twisted to see his face was streaked with tears.

'Goran . . .'

'Miro, please.' There was real desperation in his voice and I realized that for tonight at least, I had become the older brother. Dina scooped Irina off his lap and he raised himself up, pushing my hands away, climbing the stairs to our bedroom painfully slowly.

'Where will you two sleep?' he asked, but his words were blurring with exhaustion. I slipped off his boots, undid the buckle on his belt and helped him lie back, tucking the covers around him just as I had done with Irina. Before I switched off the light he was asleep.

'We must tell Mother and Pa,' I said as I came back down the stairs.

'Not tonight,' said Dina. 'They'll want to come now and he needs rest. And while he looks like this, it'll be so hard for your mother. The first person he needs to see is Dr Mesić.'

'OK, but I'm not moving him to a hospital, whatever Mesić says. We'll look after him here. He needs his family now.'

Fortunately Goran's injuries were less serious than they appeared. 'Complete rest and lots of it,' said Dr Mesić, once he had examined my brother and was sat at our kitchen table, sipping tea. 'The arm isn't badly broken, he can manage without a cast, but he must keep it in that sling. Do your parents know he's here?'

I shook my head.

'I'd keep it that way for a few days if you can. I know how worried your mother is, but what Goran needs more than anything is sleep, food and peace. I don't expect he's had enough of any of those in months. He's young and strong and he'll be fine. But I think just you two, if you can manage it.'

'Whatever he needs,' I said. 'We'll do whatever he needs.'

It was the evening before Goran surfaced, appearing suddenly on the stairs, bleary-eyed, clad in my dressing gown. He said little, devoured three platefuls of beef and vegetables and went upstairs to sleep again. By the time I returned from work the following evening he was just getting out of bed, and he spent the next couple of days in the same way, Dina popping in and out of our bedroom with water and tea for the brief moments he woke, while I watched the clock at Zagreb TV and longed to be home with my brother. On the fourth evening, I came home to find him sitting in the garden with Dina, Irina gurgling softly in her pram.

'You can tell Mother now,' he said simply, and I nodded, trying not to show my shock at his emaciated frame. We had burned the clothes he had been wearing on the garden fire, watching the sparks leap into the scented evening air, and my dressing gown had hidden the worst of the changes to his body. But even though I was smaller than my brother, my T-shirt clung to his concave chest and the shorts flapped around his thin, bruised legs.

I wouldn't tell my parents why I needed to see them so urgently, and when they arrived I led them silently to the back door and pointed to the garden, where Goran sat beneath the almond tree, playing with Irina.

'He came home.'

For a moment Mother didn't speak, raised her hands to her face and watched as Goran cradled my daughter on his lap. 'Oh my son,' she whispered, 'you're *here*.' Her voice broke on the words, but she steadied herself and somehow Goran must have sensed them because he looked over and waved easily and Mother ran out into the sunlight and wrapped her arms around him.

'Leave them, my love,' said Dina, as I went to follow Pa into the garden. 'We had that first, joyous moment when we realized he was home and safe. Let Mother and Pa have that too. This time belongs to them.'

A week passed, and Goran grew fitter and stronger each day, although he still refused to tell us what had happened in Krno, or how he had got to Ljeta. Although he protested, Mother insisted there should be a big family dinner to celebrate his safe return to us. Bobo and Cata came from Dubrovnik; Josip, Mij and Tomas were invited to join the party, and although I had warned Goran she was bound to go to town, as we turned the corner on to the harbour and saw two big tables outside the restaurant, neatly laid with plates and glasses and mounds of bread and salad, I heard him groan.

'Jesus, has she invited the whole bloody village?'

'You know what she's like,' I said, smiling nervously at Dina. 'She wants to spoil you.'

A cry went up suddenly from the harbour wall and Josip bounded towards us, throwing his arms around my brother, in spite of his neatly bandaged arm.

'Steady on, he's a bit frail,' I said, as Goran winced.

'I'm not a bloody invalid,' he snapped. 'And I'm certainly not frail. Josip, it's good to see you. You never were one to miss a party, were you? Tell me you're not married too? There must be a few girls left in Dubrovnik you haven't got round to yet?'

'Not many.' Josip laughed as we walked slowly towards the restaurant. 'Blimey, how many is your mother feeding? The whole village?'

'God knows,' said Goran roughly. 'And everyone's going to ask me the same questions, and what am I supposed to say? I mean, they don't really want to hear what's happening up there.'

'Get over yourself,' said Josip. 'There's free food and beer. What makes you think anyone's here for you?'

Goran burst out laughing and slung his good arm around Josip's shoulders. 'Free food and beer? Then what are we waiting for? Let the party begin.'

'We can go whenever you want to,' I said. 'Just say the word. Mother will understand.'

Goran stood it for as long as he could: questions from Marjana about his bandaged arm, from Mother as to how long he would stay, opinions sought by Ivo and Pa as to what the future held for the few Croats still living in the Krajina. I tried to listen as Cata talked to me of her work in Dubrovnik's hospital, but snatches of Goran's conversation with Bobo kept floating across, and something about it chilled me, mutual fury lingering beneath the politely chosen words.

'Get me away,' he murmured, as the dessert plates were cleared and Uncle Ivo began to tune his *tamburitza*. 'The only person I can talk to at this table is your brother-in-law; he's the only one who has any grasp on reality. If Marjana asks me again if it's been tough, I'm going to tell her what I've seen, what I've done. And then there'll be no more party and I'll have ruined Mother's day. I need to go, really.'

I looked across at Dina and nodded; she scooped Irina out of the pram and passed her to my mother, knowing this was the best way to distract her attention. I steadied my brother as he rose from the chair and we slipped away along the harbour and on to the path that led into the pine woods. Goran said nothing, his breath coming in short, staccato puffs, and as the trees closed in around us and the path grew steeper he pointed to a wooden seat, lowered himself on to it like an old man and produced a bottle of Stock from his pocket.

'No one has any idea, do they? Only Bobo – and I never thought

I'd hear myself say much good about him. But he understands what's happening. What needs to be done. And you must, right? There were cameramen up there, even if they're from Belgrade TV. You get to see that footage, don't you?'

I nodded. I had seen Serbian soldiers waving guns and leering into the camera, shooting at trucks with food and supplies attempting to reach the blockaded Croatian villages; houses on fire, shops looted, bodies lying unclaimed in the streets. I had looked and not looked, tried not to see, terrified I would recognize one of the corpses as my own brother.

'Even that, it doesn't come close, it doesn't give any real *idea* of what they're doing to people.' Goran took a long swig of brandy. 'You couldn't show it, what I've seen.'

'Do you have to go back?'

He shook his head. 'I can't get back into the Krajina. But it's happening in the regions further north too; the Serbs want to claim them as their own. It has to be stopped, Miro. We have to stop it.'

'But can we? I mean, we don't have an army.'

'We're growing, growing all the time. People are—'

'But you don't have to—'

'Do you know what *čišćenji terena* means?' His words cut across mine, hurtling out as if he had been waiting to say them all day.

'Of course. I've heard Milošević's speeches.'

'But do you know what he means by it?'

'To clean the earth.'

'To clean the earth,' Goran repeated slowly. 'Sounds good, doesn't it, like some noble aim. But Milošević doesn't want to make the earth clean, he wants it bloodstained and rotting and empty, empty of us, empty of all of us. He wants us dead, mutilated, raped, obliterated, until there are none of us left. *Etničko čišćenje.* Ethnic cleansing. That's why they levelled Krno, why they looted shops and burned houses and laughed as they beat old men and violated their wives in front of them when they were too weak to look away. *Čiščenji terena.* Cleansing the earth *of us.*'

'Was it—'

'Worse. It was worse than you can possibly imagine. Whatever you've seen, whatever footage . . .' Goran closed his eyes but almost immediately they flicked open as if he couldn't bear the images he saw. 'I couldn't make you understand even if I tried. We were the last outpost, Miro, the last village left, an enclave within an enclave. We held out for as long as we could, but when the bombardment started it quickly became clear that they meant to leave nothing. Utter destruction. We'd been hiding out in a cellar, a group of us, waiting for it to stop, until we realized it wasn't going to, that they were going to go on and on and on until everyone was dead. And so we ran, some of us, and there were other people coming up out of their cellars, running from houses already on fire . . . One man was covered in flames. I tried to beat them with my coat, but his face, it shrivelled in the heat, melted away from the bones. He was screaming, no, not screaming, a different noise, like an animal, like I'd never heard before.'

'You don't have to tell me,' I said, 'if it's too hard.'

'I've got to tell *someone* or I'll go crazy. I keep seeing it, seeing them, hearing them . . . so many people, so much noise. One woman was sitting in the road, holding her son, she was covered in blood and screaming and when I got nearer I saw . . . his legs . . . blown away. It was obvious he was dead but she kept calling his name – Carlo, Carlo. I can hear her, Miro, sobbing and screaming, I just keep *seeing her* . . . and the boy.'

'I still see Tara.'

'Tara?'

'That day. Up at the fort. I saw . . . her foot. And hand. Never told anyone. Pretended I hadn't.'

He looked at me for a moment and I felt anxious at what he was going to say. That it was nothing to what he had seen? That it couldn't compare? 'Then you'll know,' he said simply, and relief flooded through me. 'Just seeing . . . Christ, Miro, and you were just a child. I didn't think—'

'I didn't have the words, not then. Not now really. Her finger . . . I could have stretched out and touched it.'

'Franka's arm,' said Goran suddenly. 'This sweet old couple, Tibor and Franka, they were determined to stay in their house, but when we realized what was happening I went to get them. Neither of them could walk very well – "Go where?" they asked me whenever I tried to persuade them to leave. "Where should we go?" But in the end even they realized there was no choice. I'd gone to help them; Franka was bending down tying Tibor's shoelaces – he had arthritis in his fingers – when . . .' He shook his head. 'I don't know. Mortar fire, bomb. Something. A huge roar and then . . .'

'Fuck. You could have been killed.'

'I thought I had been. When I came round, all I could see was Tibor's neatly tied shoes, his legs and then . . . just bricks. Crushed to death in his own home. I was pinned down under something, a cupboard, I think, but I managed to push it off me. I could barely see or breathe, but there was light, I started crawling, and then my fingers brushed against something warm. Warm and sticky.' He ran his fingers through his hair and looked at me; something in his eyes made me go cold; there was an emptiness, a stare without sight. 'Franka's arm. Just her arm. Wedding ring on the finger, tatters of blouse, then skin, bone, blood. So much fucking blood.'

'Jesus.'

'No. He wasn't there.' I looked at Goran to see if he was making a joke, but his face was unmoving. 'Mother keeps saying God must have been looking after me, but anyone who's seen what I've seen knows there's no God. Life's nothing but chance, Miro. If I'd been standing where Tibor and Franka were, that party today would have been my funeral. It's just fucking luck, that's all. That's all it is for any of us.'

CHAPTER 10

Goran stayed for another two weeks, but it wasn't until his last night that he finally told Pa and me how he got to Dubrovnik from Krno. We sat, the three of us, in my small lounge and listened while he spoke of lying in Tibor's house for hours, playing dead, praying the soldiers wouldn't see the minuscule rivulets of air whispering in and out of his lungs. As he talked, I searched his bruised face for the man who had feigned death for me all those years ago up in the fortress at Knin. He caught my gaze and smiled and suddenly there he was, the lanky teenager in the crumpled T-shirt, who never tired of playing with me and always kept me safe. My eyes stung, my throat tightened and I had to stand up and walk away, just for a moment, until I could compose myself.

'You'd think I'd have been happy to see Dubrovnik, but the hotel was just as bad in its own way,' he said. 'I got brought in on the back of a truck with a load of others, people who'd never seen the sea or even a city before. There was such fear . . . and it wasn't like Krno, where people feared for their children or their homes or their possessions. All that had gone. They'd already lost everything they owned. Their fear was of the future. That they didn't have one.'

There was silence. 'Will it come here?' Pa asked. 'The war? To Ljeta?'

Goran nodded. 'I think so. Milošević will grow tired of limiting his attacks to where there are Serbs to "liberate". The man is insane. The more he takes, the more he'll want, and sooner or later it will be the coast; he'll want Greater Serbia to have ports, access to the sea. Maybe Zadar and Split first. But Dubrovnik will be the ultimate prize.'

'How?' I asked. 'It's a walled city. You can't exactly get tanks along the Stradun.'

'They'll bomb the walls, destroy the city gates and there *will* be tanks on that street,' he said. 'Milošević won't be able to help himself. They'll come here, Miro, however much you wish it otherwise. And they'll come soon.'

He was up early the next morning, as I knew he would be, hoping to leave without goodbyes. But I wasn't going to let him simply disappear, and when he walked into the garden with his bag on his back, I was already sitting in the sunshine with my daughter dozing in her pram.

'I have to go,' he said. 'I know it's dangerous, but I can't just stand by and watch. What happened in Krno, it's happening in other places now. I've got to be there. You do understand?'

I nodded. 'To have you here . . .'

His slow, warm smile spread across his dark features. 'You brought me back to life, my brother.' He reached into his pocket and held out his hand. 'I want you to have this.'

I looked down to see a small St Christopher charm on a slim gold chain. 'Did Mother give this to you?'

He shook his head. 'Tara. Before she left for Krpać. She tried and tried to persuade me to leave too – she was so angry that I wouldn't – and then when she left she gave me this. It was her grandfather's – she told me he survived the war, that it kept him safe. She wanted it to do the same for me.'

'Well, you've got to keep it then. I can't take it – Tara meant it for you.'

'I know,' he said wistfully. 'But nothing can keep me out of danger.

Nothing. But you, you and Dina and that adorable little girl – I know what I said about luck, I know nothing can keep you safe either but . . . I just like the thought of you having this. Please. I couldn't bear to lose it and if you have it . . .'

I pulled him towards me, tightened my arms around his thin, familiar frame. 'Don't go,' I muttered. 'Stay here, stay with us.'

He pulled back, kept a hand on my shoulder. 'You know I can't do that.' He bent down to the pram and my throat tightened as I watched him put his finger to his lips and touch Irina's sleeping face. 'Bye-bye, gorgeous girl.'

'Keep in touch, Goran. Please.'

'I'll do my best.' He looked up at the bedroom where Dina was still sleeping, and smiled suddenly. 'You're really loved, you know that? Treasure it. Keep it safe.'

'You're really loved too, you know.'

'Oh fuck off,' he said, pushing me gently. 'But look after Mother. She understands, but there'll be times . . . and when there are, you must help her.'

My brother's departure took away the last distraction we had from the reality of our situation. The country was now at war. The destruction of Krno was quickly overshadowed by what was happening in the northern town of Vukovar; every morning there was new footage, some of it smuggled out, some of it from Belgrade TV, all of it horrifying. I watched mutely, Goran's words echoing through my mind, my thumb and forefinger pressing the cold metal of the St Christopher between them.

'It's fucking carnage,' Damir bellowed, as we looked at images of deserted streets and houses blown apart. 'Like the end of the fucking world. And watch this, Miro; I want you to pay close attention to this bit.'

I sat in silence as the camera panned across: rubble, smoke, a loud explosion and then an odd sharp sound. Someone spoke, almost spoke, more like a gulp and then the image slipped, blurred and refocused. It took a moment to understand that I was looking at a close-up of the muddy street, filmed at eye level.

'Shot by a sniper,' said Damir, switching off the monitor. 'Dino Salević. Slovenian guy. Lovely. Met him once. Accredited press he was. Would have said it on his jacket.'

'But they shot him anyway?'

'They don't fucking care who they shoot. Kids, women, the elderly – anyone who isn't a Serb is fair game.'

'My brother says it could happen here.'

'Could? It's happening already.' Damir lit a cigarette. 'I got reports this morning of skirmishes on the border between us and Montenegro. How far is that from Ljeta? Forty-five minutes' drive? An hour at most. And there's talk that they're going to blockade Mlić. So that's troops to the north and the south of us; we're hemmed in, sitting ducks. They're massing all around us, Miro, and there's nothing we can do. It's going to be a fucking bloodbath.'

'But my wife's mother lives in Morsać; it's barely fifteen minutes from the border. She's not safe.'

'No one's safe. But you want to get her to Ljeta. That's all we can do: prepare. Go home tonight to your wife and family and tell them . . . and I think perhaps you shouldn't come in for a few days. If the worst does happen and you can't get home, I'll never forgive myself.'

'But I have to be here; it's my job. If this is really happening, then I want to . . .'

Damir got up and flicked the monitor back on; the grainy image of the Vukovar street flickered on to the screen. 'There'll be more like Dino. And I won't let you be one of them. Not at your age. There's no rhyme or reason to it, Miro; you can't stay safe. One morning you go out with your camera, just like all the other mornings, and it's dangerous but you feel OK, and you get some good pictures and you're coming back to the office, and then *bang*. It's over. And it's your footage we're watching and your funeral we're going to. I can't let that happen.'

'But—'

'Go home. If things stay calm you can come back. But for now –' his voice dropped and he looked old suddenly, old and tired – 'just go home.'

There was an added poignancy to my journey back to Ljeta that day. I stood on the harbour and watched a fisherman slowly pull apart his tangled nets, rich autumn sunshine glinting off the sky-blue hull of his battered boat. The air was sweet and still, broken only by the excited shrieks of a group of small boys hurling themselves off the end of the jetty into the water. As the boat pulled away, I remembered how it felt to *be* them: hot wooden planks beneath my feet as I ran, sun on my face, the moment of pure exhilaration between air and sea, the smack of the cold salty water as it wrapped itself around my body.

'Look,' said a man sitting opposite me. I followed his gaze out to sea; silhouetted against the purple-hued islands, three warships sat in a line, dark and menacing. 'The devil is with us,' he muttered.

I stared at the three shadows, immobile against the waves. 'How will it happen?'

He shrugged. 'We will know. When it does, we'll know.' He passed me a cigarette; I shielded his match from the breeze and felt the nicotine hit my system. There seemed nothing else to say.

But the tension was everywhere. When I reached Ljeta the streets were eerily quiet. Even the dogs had stopped barking. Only when I reached my house was the stillness broken; I could hear Marjana's raised voice before I had even slipped my key in the lock.

'If it wasn't for your bloody brother, she'd be here now,' I heard her say as I stepped into the lounge. 'If anything happens to her . . .' She brushed past me out of the house and I raised my eyebrows at Dina.

'Cata's not coming home,' she said. 'And Mother's gone. Bobo came today to take her from Morsać – she's going to stay with Auntie Clara on Mgrañi. He told us that Cata wants to stay in Dubrovnik with him and keep working at the hospital – she feels she'll be more use there. She's right, and it's admirable, but your aunt's heartbroken. She wants her home obviously – no one knows what's going to happen. But it isn't Bobo's fault.'

I put my arms around my wife and kissed her hair. 'Cata will have made up her own mind,' I said. 'And if she wants to stay, I admire her.' I thought of my conversation with Damir, and how a part of me had longed to remain in the city and play a role in whatever was to come. 'Bobo will look after her, and at least we know your mother's safe.'

'But I'm worried about him too, about you, about Irina – what's going to happen to us?' Her voice cracked, and when I lifted her face towards me I saw she was crying. The same cold anger I had felt when Goran told me about Krno spread through me, a frustrated, undefined fury I could do nothing with.

'We're going to be fine, I promise. I'm never going to let anything happen to you, or to Irina.'

I wouldn't let go of Dina that night, and we took Irina out of her cot and let her sleep between us, needing to be as close as we could. I slept fitfully, aware of her warm little body nestled into mine, and as a slim line of dawn began to filter between the curtain and the window, I realized the silence was starting to fracture; a car engine, a door slamming, voices, someone running, another car, suddenly it was if the day had begun, but everything was speeded up, happening too fast, noise piled on top of noise until I threw back the sheets and ran down to see what was happening.

Outside, in the half-light, a man in a dressing gown was sitting on the bonnet of his car holding a cat; across the road, two women in raincoats and nightgowns were standing as if frozen, arms around each other. Further along the street I could see more people, clambering out of cars, shaking themselves, all of them oddly dressed in hats and slippers, scarves and pyjamas. Another car drove past, then a motorbike with a man and woman squeezed on to it, a small boy between them.

'They're coming.' I turned to see two women standing behind me, their faces taut with fear. 'They're in Konavle, they've torched Morsać, the houses – they're on fire, not everyone got out . . . they couldn't. We just got in Marko's car, he drove, he drove so fast.'

'People are dead,' said the other woman, and her voice began to rise. 'People are *dead*.'

Her final word was almost a scream and I pulled her into me, holding her tightly against my body. 'It's all right,' I said. 'You're safe now. You're safe.'

'Son?'

I looked up and saw my parents, their faces white and strained. 'They're in Konavle,' I said, and saw Pa's arm tighten around my mother's shoulders. 'Soldiers came over the border in the night. Morsać is on fire.'

'Morsać is *burning*,' cried the first woman. 'The whole valley will burn . . . we must pray.' She clawed at Mother's arm, pulling her down to kneel on the grass. '*Zdravo Marijo, milosti puna, Gospodin s tobom*.' She stopped and looked up towards Pa and me. 'Pray. To a merciful God. You must pray.'

To my amazement, Pa closed his eyes and joined in with the words; along the street men and women stopped their conversations and fell in with the rhythm of the prayer. I realized Dina was standing on the doorstep of our house, her cheek against Irina's head, eyes closed, her voice joining the others. I opened my mouth but the words wouldn't come and instead all I could think of was Goran on the wooden seat beside me in the pine woods, talking of a world where there was no God, a world he had seen and experienced.

'What the hell's going on here?' I opened my eyes to see Josip standing at my gate, flanked by Tomas, Mij, Dina's friend Karena and Slobodan, her husband. 'There's no time to *pray*. We've got to get out there. Someone's got to stop those bastards before they get any further. Now. Who's with us?'

Pa walked over to Josip. 'Don't be a fool,' he snapped. 'Fight them with what? Invisible tanks? Toy guns? We've nothing to fight with. You go into Konavle now, and none of you will come back. *None.*'

'We have to do something,' Josip protested. 'We can't just sit here and wait for them to arrive.'

'That's exactly what we have to do,' said Ivo, detaching himself from a group of men and approaching Pa and Josip. 'Petar is right. We have no choice.'

'Then let's go. Get in our cars and go. All of us. Before they get here. My parents live on Tršt. We can go there.'

I stared at Josip in astonishment; his usual sangfroid had completely deserted him. 'We can't go anywhere,' I said. 'We're cut off. There's troops north of Dubrovnik and the port will be blockaded. Apart from driving into Bosnia – which makes no sense – there's nowhere to go. Anyway, I'm not leaving Ljeta so they can come in and destroy it. It's my home. I'm not running away. And neither should you.'

'Well said,' said Mother, rising to her feet and looking contemptuously at Josip. 'No one is going to run. For one thing, there's too much work to be done. Look at all these people – they need food and blankets, they'll need to sleep somewhere. And more will come, maybe hundreds more, and they'll all need our help. Come to the pension, come, everyone. We'll have coffee and eggs and think what to do, and who can help.'

'Tower of strength, your mother,' Uncle Ivo whispered, as we walked down to the harbour. 'Those wet-nosed little bastards won't have a chance against her.'

'How long do you think we've got?' I asked, anxiety churning in my stomach.

'A day, maybe two. There's nothing to stop them just charging straight through. Everyone in those villages, if they don't run . . .'

'Where are our bloody soldiers? People knew Milošević was after Dubrovnik. Sticking a handful of kids on the border is a fucking joke.'

'No one thought they'd come from the south though,' Ivo said. 'I thought they'd come over the mountains and aim squarely for the city.'

He stopped and none of us spoke. I looked around for Dina, drew her into me, felt Irina's tiny hand on my chest and we stood for a moment, looking along the harbour to the small row of shops and cafes, the sweep of green pines stretching to the sea beyond. How small it looked suddenly, how vulnerable, a neat cluster of houses and business and lives just waiting to be overrun. People were already gathering outside the restaurant, huddling around tables. I could see Tomas bringing up chairs from the cafe and Mother bustling in and out with cups and plates.

I joined her in the kitchen, and in some strange way it felt like old times again, running out trays of eggs and coffee and baskets of rolls. But instead of the soft hum of tourists' chatter, a grim, heavy silence smothered the tables, broken only by the clatter of a knife on a plate or the brief whirr-click of a cigarette lighter.

'Who's in charge here?' I looked up to see a tall bulky man wearing jeans and a navy blue jacket with *Armani* written in small letters across the chest.

'I am,' said Mother, appearing behind me. 'Well, we are,' she gestured to Pa, pouring coffee at the next table.

'Good work you're doing,' he said, slightly condescendingly. 'I'd like to help. The hotels – the Dubrovnik, the Croatia – they're mine.'

'You're Mr Kardović?'

The man nodded. 'I am. And I wanted to say, the hotels – I'm reopening them this morning. For the refugees. I'm not sure how long we can feed them, but at least it's shelter. We'll fill the Croatia first, and then we'll see if we need to use the Dubrovnik as well.'

'I'm afraid we probably will,' said Pa, walking over to shake hands.

'More people are coming all the time. This is very good of you, Mr Kardović, but shouldn't you be talking to the mayor?'

'Can't be doing with that power-mad little upstart,' he said, and for a moment he reminded me of Damir. 'Wanted to talk to the people actually doing something. That seems to be you. The mayor will hear. You know how this town is for talk. Now I must get up to the hotels. Give me an hour or two . . . but anyone who needs to come is welcome.'

He turned on his heel and walked away, leaving Mother and Pa staring as he disappeared along the harbour. 'Well, I've seen everything now,' she said, looking at Pa. 'That man has never come to this restaurant in all the years we've lived here; didn't think he ever left that mansion of his.'

'Perhaps war brings out the best in some people as well as the worst,' I said, lifting a stack of plates and following her into the kitchen.

'Perhaps,' said Mother. 'We should start a collection – they'll need clean clothes, toiletries, toys for the kids. We can get people to bring things here, and then maybe we can take everything up tomorrow morning. Will you come?'

I looked at her for a moment, apron around her waist, coffee grounds on her cheek, already thinking, planning, fighting for a village she had never really called home. 'Of course,' I said, and found myself thinking, not for the first time, what an amazing woman my mother was.

CHAPTER 11

'It was dark. Dark and I was sleeping, but not really sleeping, you know? Illya had locked the back door, put a chair in front of it, under the handle. We sat up late, drinking brandy, talking to our neighbours. Some of them said they'd sleep in our lounge, somehow we felt safer, all being together.' She paused, looked down at the floor; I took the camera off my shoulder.

'Are you OK to go on?'

She nodded. 'Will you show this? I want people to see . . . maybe someone will know what happened to Illya. Maybe he's in Dubrovnik, maybe someone found him.'

'My son will try,' Mother said, stretching out to take the woman's hand in hers. 'But it may not be possible. Getting to Dubrovnik is dangerous now. But what you're saying, what you're telling us, we will keep the tape safely. And one day people will know. One day they'll hear you, hear what happened.'

'We'd been saving, all of us . . . Illya will be fifty next month.' She resumed speaking without warning and I lifted the camera back on to my shoulder. 'For thirty years he's worked at the airport, loading bags, unloading bags. All those planes and he's never been inside one, can you imagine? Never flown. So we bought him a ticket to go to Zagreb. He has a brother there. I have it here.' She dug into her bag and pulled out a slim white envelope with *Aviogenex* printed on the outside. 'You see?'

I nodded. 'Tanya, when did you last see Illya? How did you get separated, can you remember?'

'It all happened so fast,' she said, and tears began to tip over on to her cheeks. 'First we heard cracks, sharp noises, bang bang bang.'

'Gunshots?'

She nodded. 'And then a much bigger noise, like a huge crash, and then another, and I could hear . . . people started screaming. Straight away it was obvious that staying in our house was the wrong idea. Illya pulled the chair away from the door and we ran on to the street, people were out in the darkness, crying, screaming, there was heat, this strange unexpected heat and then I realized the house along from us was on fire, a woman was screaming from the upstairs window, people were calling to her to jump but she was too scared.'

'Were there soldiers in the village?'

'We didn't see any on our streets, but we could hear the guns so we knew they were close. Our neighbour, Milan, had a car; he was shouting to us, but it was full already – his wife and his sister and their two children. "We can take you," he said. "Get in, get in," and the children squeezed up, but there was just a tiny space in the back, not really big enough for either of us. "Go," Illya said, "get in," but I wouldn't and I clung to him and Milan was calling that they were leaving, but I didn't want to go, and Illya said he'd come, that there'd be another car, and I had my arms around his neck and he was trying to prise my fingers apart, bending them back so I would let go. It was hurting, I was crying, but he was begging me, "Please, Tanya, please go. I'll come for you. I'll find you."'

'And so you got in the car?'

She nodded. '"There are worse things they can do to a man than kill him," Illya said. And then he kissed me, and I knew, I knew what he meant, what those soldiers do to the wives, and so I got in the car and he slammed the door before I could even say goodbye, and Milan drove so fast.'

'And could you see what was happening?'

'I could see *nothing*,' she wailed, beginning to sob. 'I saw nothing but Illya. I left him . . . I left him.'

I put the camera down; I had learned to recognize when an interviewee had said all they had to say. I took her hands in mine. 'Thank you, Tanya,' I said. 'I think you're incredibly brave. And if I was Illya . . . If it had been my wife, I would have wanted her in that car.'

'Thank you,' she whispered. 'Thank you.'

I nodded at Mother and we stood up and moved away. 'We should get back,' she said. 'We've been much longer than we said. They'll be worried.'

'What time is it?'

'Gone four. It'll be getting dark soon.'

'Then we must go. I said to Dina we'd only be a couple of hours. She'll have been expecting us since lunchtime.'

But part of me didn't want to go; I wanted to stay and record more of the stories of those who had fled their villages in the night. After Mr Kardović's unexpected announcement at the restaurant, the big tourist hotels that lay five minutes' walk from the village had reopened their doors, and bedrooms that had once hosted foreign families and over-excited children became a temporary home to the dispossessed and the terrified.

'He's dead, isn't he?' I said as we walked out of the gleaming marble lobby and into the fading light.

'Who? Her Illya?'

I nodded. 'But I'd have done the same thing, you know. She was right to—'

'*Pavle?*' I stopped and stared at my mother. 'Look,' she hissed. 'It is, it's Pavle.'

I peered through the gathering gloom. A figure was walking

towards us, a soldier, clad in military fatigues, holding something in his hand. As he drew nearer I realized two things, neither of which seemed believable: firstly, that it *was* Pavle; secondly, in his left hand was a shiny black service revolver. And it was pointing straight at us.

'What are you doing here? Why are you not in your homes?' The voice was unmistakable but there was little else I recognized; his head was shaved, his face thinner, dark shadows beneath his eyes.

'Pavle? How, I mean . . . what are *you* doing here?'

'I am here as part of the occupying forces of the Yugoslav National Army,' he said sharply. 'As of this afternoon, a curfew has been imposed. All residents must be off the streets by dusk or face arrest.'

'What? When? I mean . . .' I looked at Mother; she was staring at Pavle in disbelief. We'd known the army was coming; everyone in Ljeta knew it was when not if, and the village had existed in a state of muted panic for days. I'd pictured tanks rolling in, women screaming, barricading ourselves into our homes – and now it seemed the whole thing had taken place without my even having been aware it was happening.

'Didn't you hear me?' Pavle gestured towards the village with his gun.

'Who the hell do you think you are?' Mother said, and there was real fury in her voice. 'You practically grew up in my house. Speak to me with some respect, Pavle Nikolić.'

His eyes dropped for a moment and he tucked the gun into the waistband of his trousers. 'Mrs Denković, I don't mean to disrespect you. I remember your many kindnesses. But that is the past.'

'Didn't we drink to the past not so long ago?' I asked, scarcely able to believe what was happening. 'Don't you remember?'

'Please don't make this any more difficult than it already is,' he said. 'I could arrest you now, but instead I will escort you home. Is that enough respect?'

'What bloody curfew anyway,' I said. 'Since when?'

'Occupation began at 14.00 hours. Where have you been that you were unaware of this?'

'At the Hotel Dubrovnik, trying to help. There are hundreds of refugees from Konavle there.' A thought struck me. 'Were you a part of . . . of what happened up there?'

His shoulders stiffened. 'We assumed the hotels were empty. Thank you for informing me they're not. We will send troops immediately.'

'They've seen enough of your troops,' said Mother icily. 'They've seen—'

'Please just walk, Mrs Denković.'

I slipped my arm around my mother's shoulders and we turned towards the village; the slap of her sandals and the sharp click of Pavle's boots alternating in the silence.

'Shocking, what Tanya was saying,' Mother said suddenly, in a loud, clear voice. 'I mean, not knowing if someone you love is dead or alive . . . It must be the worst thing, Miro, don't you think?'

'And that story about the airline ticket . . . Things like that really make you see people as individuals, don't they?' I said, making sure Pavle could hear every word. 'Every one of those people: someone's brother or sister or mother or wife, all with their own stories.'

'What could we say to her? That the airport's been destroyed and her husband is probably lying dead in a field somewhere.'

'Be quiet.'

'It came across on camera very powerfully,' I said, my anger making me reckless. 'When people see what was done in Konavle, what happened there—'

'I said, *BE QUIET*.' The lights of my house came into view and we stopped outside the front gate. Pavle pointed to the camera case with his gun. 'Open it. Give me the tape.'

'No. It's my property.'

I felt a hand on my arm and watched, almost entirely detached, as Mother took the camera case, placed it on the ground and snapped open the catches. She lifted out the camera and held it in front of me. 'Give him the tape, Miro. Do as he says.'

I looked at Pavle, his face closed and expressionless, and in that moment I realized I had no idea what he was capable of. I kept my eyes on his face as I pushed the small red button and a slot on the side of the camera opened. Pavle dropped the tape on the ground and ground his heel into the black casing, before leaning down to pick it up, handing it to me with a contemptuous smile. 'Always a camera, never a gun, eh, Miro? See how worthwhile your work is?'

Mother's hand tightened around mine. 'May God forgive you,' she said.

'God has no business here,' he said, and disappeared into the night.

'Miro, Jada, where've you been? My God, we've been so worried.' Pa pulled us into the house, closing the door swiftly, and as I stepped inside Dina threw her arms around me and I felt her body shudder against mine.

'Do you know what's happened?'

I nodded. 'The army—'

'You've been *hours*,' said Dina. 'I expected you at lunchtime. When you didn't come I thought, we all thought . . .'

'Darling, I'm here, I'm safe, we're both safe. But I think we could use a drink. Did you know Pavle is here?'

'*Him*,' Josip appeared out of the kitchen, clutching a large glass of Stock. 'Thinks he can come here, tell us what to do – how dare he? What kind of sick joke is it to send him here? I'm telling you, if he lays a finger on anyone in this village, I'll kill him with my bare hands.'

'And what will that achieve?' asked Mother wearily. 'You being arrested? Killed? Another grave to dig? You can't think like that, Josip. They've already shown in Konavle they have no humanity.'

'Why were you so long?' asked Dina. 'You said you were just going to take up some toys and blankets.'

'A lot of people wanted to talk once they saw the camera. They were desperate someone should know what happened to them.' I tailed off as I remembered Pavle stamping on the tape, carelessly destroying the words of people who had already lost everything. 'But what the hell happened? When we set off this morning everything was calm, and now suddenly we're under occupation?'

'What happened was that no one stood up to them,' roared Josip. 'They just rolled up, three trucks, maybe four, full of soldiers . . . no warning. It wasn't like the villages, we didn't hear explosions or gunshots first; they just appeared. People started screaming, most ran to their homes, but your uncle, your dad and I, we stood and watched them.'

'After what we'd heard from the villagers, we were waiting for the shooting to begin,' said Pa. 'But it didn't. They simply sat in their trucks, waiting. They looked at us; we looked at them.'

'We did *nothing*,' snarled Josip. 'We all just stood there.'

'We *know* what you think,' boomed Ivo. 'But you saw their guns, boy. Just because they weren't pointing them at us doesn't mean they wouldn't have used them if we'd made a move. And what did we have? Old shooting pistols that probably can't even fire straight any more.'

'And then suddenly there was Pavle,' said Pa. 'He roared up in a Jeep, with a huge man next to him, obviously his superior. He went straight into the police station and brought poor Ristović out at gunpoint. The man was nearly in tears. Then he and the big man took the rest of the troops into the police station and nothing happened for half an hour or so, until Pavle reappeared. He drove along the harbour in his Jeep, announcing through a loudhailer that Ljeta was under occupation, that Major Argović had imposed a curfew, that if people abided by the laws of occupation there would be no violence. And there hasn't been.'

'Yet,' said Josip. 'But I'll bet . . .'

A knock at the door made us all freeze. Anxiety was etched across Ivo and Pa's faces, fury on Josip's, Mother and Dina looked terrified. In that moment I realized a seismic change had occurred in all our lives; the outside world had become something to fear.

'It's me.' I recognized Tomas's whispered tones and opened the door to find him clutching a bottle of Stock and a round of cheese. 'I thought I'd find you all here. Planning a counter-coup?'

That night there were eight of us around the table for supper, squeezed into our tiny kitchen. As the brandy flowed the air grew thick with anger and resentment: at the army, at Pavle, at the Western powers who seemed content to leave our country to slowly implode. The following night Karena and Slobodan joined us, the night after Tomas bought Jelena and Mij and slowly our house morphed from unremarkable family home into the headquarters of some sort of low-key resistance movement.

'Tomorrow I'm going to reopen the post office,' said Jelena, after nearly a week of occupation. 'It's *my* post office and no jumped-up Serb is going to tell me when I can and can't open. Communication is a basic human right, about one of the only ones we have left. If they want to shut the post office down, they'll have to do it over my dead body.'

Tomas nodded and took Jelena's small wrinkled hand in his own. 'You're right. And tomorrow I will reopen my cafe. Come, all of you, and tell everyone. We will eat *pršut* and drink *travarica* and toast Croatia. We'll show those who occupy our town that they may be able to control us physically but they can't crush our *spirit*.' He picked up Jelena's coat and wrapped it around her shoulders. 'Make sure everyone knows,' he said firmly. 'Tomorrow, from midday.'

I let Jelena and Tomas out of the back door and within seconds they had disappeared into the night, heads covered in black scarves, plimsolled feet silent on the grass. I stood for a moment on the back step. With the village in darkness the sky was ablaze with stars and the moonlight picked out the silvery olive groves and the tall thin tower of the church. It looked as it always had, but somehow it felt different, as if the village was no longer ours.

'Miro?'

I turned to see Dina behind me, and in the moonlight, with her face upturned to mine, she looked like the schoolgirl I had met years before, when life was simple and we had no concept of what the future might hold. Her fingers were twisting the end of her plait; her wide hazel eyes were cloudy with worry and fear. I slipped an arm around her waist and drew her to me, kissing her, gently at first, then harder, pressing into her, feeling her hands slip under my shirt, knowing we were both desperate for each other, to escape to the safety of the world that only we shared, far away from this new reality none of us wanted to face.

'I want you,' I whispered.

'I know. Me too. But we can't, not with everyone here. And you need to come – Josip and your father, you need to calm it down. Josip is so *angry*.'

I kissed her again, more tenderly this time, and followed her back into the lounge. 'Having lunch and sending letters is hardly the great rebellion though, is it?' Josip was pacing up and down in front of the fireplace. 'After what they did in Konavle, it's not right.'

Before I could speak, Mother was on her feet, her face ablaze with anger. 'Right? *Right?* Listen to yourself, Josip, and stop being such a *child*. This is war, we are *at war*. There's no right or wrong any more, there are no rules, all there is is power – who has it and who doesn't. Right now the only power we have is in acquiescence: to choose to stay alive. That might seem like cowardice to you, but you haven't seen the alternative, you haven't watched people dragged from their homes, killings in the streets; you don't know, you don't *know*. Because if you did, if you'd ever seen . . .' she stopped suddenly, exhaustion shadowing her face. 'I was six years old when the war came to Knin. All my life I've tried to forget the things I saw as a child. Don't wish for them, Josip. Don't wish for them.'

The next day it seemed the whole village had heard of Tomas's invitation; the tables outside the cafe were packed with families and the atmosphere was almost celebratory. Through the lens of my camera it looked as if I was filming a movie that had already been carefully lit and edited; the autumn light spun gold tints and long shadows across the tables, while beyond the harbour wall the sea basked beneath a flawless blue sky.

'Here come your parents,' said Tomas, pouring beer into a glass and beaming down at Irina. 'Look, Miro. Your mother came to see me this morning, told me what she was planning.'

I turned to look as Mother and Pa walked slowly towards us, carrying a vast platter of mussels between them. As they drew closer, people stopped their conversations and slowly applause began to ring out. Dina rose to her feet, then Karena, Jelena, soon everyone was standing, clapping my parents, who were both clothed in traditional Konavle dress. Before I could speak, Dina passed me the baby and disappeared along the street, others following. I knew where they were going, back to their homes, to open their wardrobes and take out the pinafore dress edged with scarlet and gold, the ornate tapestry collar, the cherry-red hat.

'You look amazing,' I said, as Mother laid the platter on the table. 'I didn't think . . .'

'Don't make a fuss,' she said, and ladled mussels on to my plate. 'Just make sure you get all this on that camera of yours. Today will be something to remember, I think. There may be times when we need to remember it.'

She was right, the day was quite something. The camera ate up the scenes that drifted by: Mother fending off compliments in her dress, Pa pouring glasses of *slivovitz*, the local plum brandy, and clinking them noisily with anyone who would drink with him, Josip and Tomas competing to see who could carve the thinnest slices of *pršut* from the bone. And then Dina, lifting Irina out of her pram, shafts of sunshine filtering through the fronds of the palm trees, lighting up my daughter's sleepy face. 'I love you,' she mouthed at me, and I felt such a rush of love for them, felt so bloody *lucky*, that I laid down my camera and walked through the tables to take my girls in my arms.

The afternoon ended with an uproarious sing-song of traditional Konavle folk-songs, watched uneasily by clusters of soldiers at either end of the harbour. A combination of beer and bravado enabled us to ignore them at first, but as the sun started to dip behind the rooftops, families began to drift away, keen to be home before the curfew.

'Time to get that little one home,' Pa said, nodding at my sleepy-eyed daughter. 'Time we were all indoors.'

Josip tutted loudly in disgust and lit a cigarette, placing his feet on a chair opposite.

'Don't sit there and tut, boy,' said Pa wearily. 'Today was a good day. Today we've shown that we're proud to be Croatian, that we won't give in to those who try to crush us. Today we won. And that might not happen again for a long time.'

'You think there won't be trouble because of this?' Josip said, rising to his feet and staring at Pa with an expression I didn't like. 'You don't know him like Miro and I do. Pavle won't let this go, you mark my words. Someone's going to pay for what we did here today.'

CHAPTER 12

It didn't take long for Josip to be proved right. The following morning Dina and I took an early walk with Irina, to discover the village was dotted with posters: pinned to trees, taped to windows, even one stuck to the post-office door.

'You've seen these?' asked Jelena, as she marched past us, swinging her keys. 'I won't stand for it.' She looked across to where Pavle was sitting with two other soldiers, pulled herself up straighter, ripped the poster off and screwed it into a ball. 'That's what I think of *their* rules,' she said, unlocking the door and striding into the tiny office.

Dina and I watched nervously as Pavle said something to the soldier sitting beside him. He went into the police station, came out with another poster, walked to the post office and taped it on to the door. Within seconds, Jelena appeared, ripped the second poster off, threw it contemptuously on to the ground and stalked back inside.

By now, people had stopped to look; Tomas and Mij were standing outside the *slastičarna*, Ivo and Pa had begun to walk up from the pension. Pavle lit a cigarette and muttered to the second soldier, who went back to the police station, reappeared with another poster and began to walk towards the post office.

'Bastard.' I turned to see Josip standing behind me, watching as Pavle moved his cigarette back and forth between his lips, letting small twists of smoke ripple through the warm air. Suddenly he moved fast, deliberate, disappearing into the post office. Within seconds he emerged, his hand wrapped tightly around Jelena's arm. He pointed to the soldier.

'Lieutenant Božić is going to put this poster up *again*. This time it will stay up. You will not tear it down. If you do, I will close your post office for good. Do you understand me?'

It was as if the entire village had fallen silent. Out of the corner of my eye I could see Josip, standing with his hands on his hips, face taut with fury. Jelena pulled her arm out of Pavle's grasp and looked at him in disgust.

'Pavle Nikolić, I've known you since you were a boy in short trousers. You used to sneak into my garden and try to steal my tomatoes – I gave you such a smack on your legs once, do you remember? Don't think because you're wearing that idiotic uniform and carrying that ridiculous gun I won't do it again.'

Nobody moved. I remembered the day she spoke of clearly; we had feasted on the small tomatoes he had produced from his pockets and teased him about the bright red finger marks on the back of his legs.

Suddenly, unexpectedly, he laughed. 'You stupid old woman,' he said loudly. 'You? You would slap me? Your filthy *Ustaše* hands are not worthy of touching my skin.'

But the word *Ustaše* was too much for Jelena. She drew herself up, paused dramatically and spat at Pavle, a shot of white liquid landing on the collar of his fatigues. For a moment he stood as if frozen and then, without warning, his arm lifted and sunlight shot across his palm just before it connected with Jelena's face – a sharp, heavy slap that sent her sprawling on to the street.

'You *fucking bastard*.' Josip lunged past me towards Pavle, pushing him to the ground, smacking fists into his body. Some of the men began to cheer as my two friends rolled in the dirt, kicking and pulling and tearing at each other. Suddenly I was shoved aside by two soldiers who wrapped their hands around Josip's flailing limbs and pulled him away, one pinning his arms behind his back while the other punched him viciously in the stomach.

Pavle staggered to his feet, his lip bleeding, uniform ripped and muddy. For a moment he said nothing; ran a hand across his head, pulled down his jacket, his breath audible in the calcified air.

'Apologize.' Ivo's voice was thunderous. Jelena was tucked under his arm; she looked almost birdlike next to his bulky frame. One side of her face was raised and scarlet. 'What sort of a man are you?'

Pavle took a step towards them, but when Jelena raised her eyes to him he stopped. 'I am ...' His voice faded. He sucked in a breath and stiffened his shoulders. 'This will not happen again.' The words were crisper now, deliberately controlled. 'There will be no violence here, from *either* side. Do as you are told and you can live peacefully. But take notice of these posters; any group of more than four people meeting together will be seen as seditious and there will be arrests. You will not meet at Tomas's cafe again. You will not meet at Miro's house. Do not imagine *for one moment* I will show anyone here any special consideration.'

'No violence?' muttered Tomas, his face pink with fury. 'No violence – apart from knocking an old woman to the ground. You Chetnik bastard. To think you were once one of us.'

Pavle turned, walked across to Tomas and stood in front of him, leaning in until their faces were almost touching. 'I was never one of you,' he said, and there was real venom in his voice. He turned to look at Josip. 'Bring him,' he snapped, and I watched, mutely, as he strode off towards the police station, the two soldiers hauling Josip along behind.

It was a week before I saw my friend again. Seven long days, when we came to realize the realities of occupation and how isolated we were from the outside world. Food was already in short supply, and the feasting that had taken place at Tomas's began to seem like an act of idiocy. Although we suspected Josip was being held in the tiny cells at the back of the police station, Pavle refused to be drawn on what had happened to him, and in the cold hours of the night, when Irina wouldn't settle and Dina slept beside me, I found myself obsessing over my friend's fate. On the morning of the eighth day I decided to face down Pavle and demand to know what had been done with him, but I was barely out of the house before I recognized the tall, rangy figure heading towards me, wearing the same dirty shorts and T-shirt he had been dragged away in.

'Hello,' said Josip, his face tired but unbruised. 'They let me go then.'

I threw my arms around him. 'Thank God. I had visions of you languishing in some dungeon up in the hills. Are you OK?'

He nodded and followed me into the house. 'I've just sat on my arse all week in one of the cells. Don't know what it was supposed to prove. In the end I got chatting to the soldier who was bringing me meals, if you can call them that. And d'you know what? He's not even Serbian. He's fucking Montenegrin. And not very sure about all this either, I can tell you.'

'Well, I expect he thought he was joining the Yugoslav army, not the bloody army of Greater Serbia.'

'Fucking wake-up call he's had. He was as appalled as we were at what happened with Jelena. But what can he do? Try to leave and he'll probably get shot. *Probably* by Pavle. It won't be Argović – all that fat fucker does is drink Stock and sleep behind the desk.' He sighed heavily. 'God, I need a cigarette. Got any left?'

I shook my head. I had smoked my last cigarette three days ago, and coffee and sugar had also disappeared from my life.

'Can't even get a fucking smoke. Funny how *they* weren't short of anything.' Josip ran his fingers through his hair, and I watched as he began to pace up and down the room. He seemed deflated, as if the anger that had been sustaining him had dissipated, replaced by something I didn't recognize, a coolness, almost resignation.

'Well, I had plenty of time to think in there, and you know what?' He flung himself down in the chair and stared up at me. 'I'm gone. I've had it with this war, this fucking pointless fight. Yugoslav or Croatian, call me what you like, I just don't bloody care any more.'

'You'd care if someone called you a Serb.'

'You think? We're all the same, man; don't fall for that political crap. They believe the same things we do: their land, their right to it. I'm not saying I agree with them; I'm just saying, what's the difference? I'm sick of this whole bloody country, it's all fucked, no one cares – the world doesn't care, Carrington and Vance and Kohl and all those bloody European politicians – they'll all dance with Milošević if it suits them. What's the point in fighting? I tell you we're fucked, all of us.'

'So what's your answer then?'

'I'm going.'

'Don't be ridiculous. Going where? How?' Josip was beginning to worry me; when he set his mind to something he usually made it happen. 'You don't know what you're saying. You've been in a cell for a week. You want to let Pavle win? Because if you give up, if you run, that's what it means. He's won.'

'Oh, Miro, you don't get it, do you? I don't *care*. I'm beyond it. I can't stay here any more. I mean it, one morning I just won't be here, and you won't know how or when I left or where I've gone. And that'll be the best way, because he'll ask you. My God, he'll ask you.'

'You're being ridiculous. You can't just walk out of the village.'

Josip produced a thick wad of dinars from the back pocket of his shorts. 'Who says I'll need to walk?'

Before I could speak, the front door opened and Dina wheeled the pram into the hallway. She looked as if she had been crying, but when she saw Josip she gave a shaky smile.

'They let you go.' She hugged him, stood back, took his face in her hands. 'Let me look at you. Are you all right?'

'I'm fine, but you look—'

'It's Vukovar. It's over. The city's fallen.' She turned to look at me. 'Mother got a letter from Cvita; what the papers are saying, it's just horrific.'

'You see?' said Josip. 'All those people, they fought, they held on. Christ, wasn't Goran up there? And what good has it done? What do you think's happened to him – to all of them?'

I stared at Josip in disbelief. I thought of the last letter we had had from Goran, a hastily scribbled note that he had joined the fledgling Croatian National Guard and was on his way to Vukovar, a border city under vicious, relentless bombardment. Each day I prayed for his safety, touched the charm around my neck, thought of Tara, evacuated to an island I had never even heard of. I knew the situation in Vukovar was worsening by the day, and sometimes I tried to persuade myself that Goran would have escaped across the moonlit cornfields with the handful of others who made it out to tell their nightmarish tales. But I knew my brother too well; deep down I knew he would stay in the city until the end came.

'I don't know what's happened to him,' I said coldly. 'But I'll tell you this: he won't have fucking run away when things got tough.'

'I'm sorry. I shouldn't have said that. Come on, man, you know Goran – he's got nine lives.'

'I think you should go.'

'What?' He stared at me. 'Come on, Miro, I was only saying—'

'Josip.' Dina walked to the front door and opened it. There was no mistaking her message and he shrugged and walked out of our house.

'Miro. I've been waiting for you. We need to have a little chat.'

I looked at Pavle, sitting on the wall outside my house, smoke twisting out of his mouth, and my heart sank. I was exhausted; Irina had been violently sick in the night and neither Dina nor I had got any sleep. In desperation we had wheeled her around to Mother and Pa's, where she had promptly fallen asleep, and over breakfast the conversation had turned to Josip. I hadn't spoken to him since we had fallen out over Goran, and it seemed no one had seen him for days. Now, suddenly, Pavle was waiting outside my house. It was unlikely to be a coincidence.

'You know why I'm here?'

'I never know why you do anything,' I said. 'Dina, take the baby into the house. I'll deal with this.'

'Josip is missing,' he barked. 'Major Argović released him on condition he reported to him daily at 3 p.m.. Today he didn't come. I have been to his house. He's not there. Where is he, Miro? I know he'd have told you.'

'I don't know where he is. He told me he was going to go, the day he got out of jail. I didn't believe him. You know Josip, always the talk.' It felt odd suddenly, to be trading on shared knowledge of a man who had once been our mutual best friend. Pavle must have felt it too because he dropped his eyes from my face and shifted his feet awkwardly. I took a breath. 'He told me then he wouldn't give me any details – because he knew you'd come straight to me. He was protecting me. Because of our friendship – do you remember that word?'

'You're lying.'

'I'm not. He didn't want me to know. But I'll come with you if you like. Argović can ask me. You can ask me. Milošević himself can ask me. And you'll all get the same answer. I. Don't. Know.'

Pavle looked at me, his eyes searching my face. 'If you're lying . . .'

'You'll what? Slap me about like you did Jelena? Fuck off. I don't know where he is, and I'm glad I don't know. I don't *want* to know. Christ, what have we become? He's a coward, you're a bully.'

'And you?' His voice was ice. 'You, Miro? What have you become? A man who does nothing, who simply watches. Who *takes pictures*. You are a joke, a—'

'*Miro. MIRO!*' Dina's screams broke through the air and even Pavle's eyes widened at the palpable fear in her voice. I ran inside and up the stairs, my stomach twisting as she called my name again and again. I pushed open the bathroom door and found her rocking on the floor, Irina held tightly in her arms, tears streaming down her face.

'Oh my God, oh my God,' the words hurtled out of her, mixed with sobs and short, hard breaths. 'I don't know what happened, I don't . . . I lay her on the towel to change her nappy and she just started twitching. It was awful, like convulsions.'

'It's all right, darling, she's all right.' I looked at my daughter, crying angrily in Dina's arms, and bent down to take her. 'Come to Daddy,' I said, smiling into her crumpled red face. 'Now what have you been doing to make Mummy cry?'

'I couldn't stop it. I didn't know what to do.' Dina stood up shakily and sat on the edge of the bath. 'It was like a current going through her body, and then it just stopped . . . and she's so hot.'

I felt Irina's forehead. 'She is hot, but it might just be because she's got herself into a state. She looks fine to me.'

'You weren't *here*. It was terrifying. I thought she was going to die. We have to take her to see Mesić; we have to take her now.'

'Miro? Dina?' My mother's voice floated up towards us and I walked on to the landing to find her halfway up the stairs. 'I saw Pavle. He said . . . Is everything all right? Is Irina OK?' She looked at her granddaughter, wailing in my arms. 'Well, baby girl, and what's wrong with you?'

'We don't know,' I said, as Irina's cries grew louder. The first pinpricks of fear started to feather their way up my arms. 'Dina said . . . she thinks, well, that she had some sort of fit.'

Mother took Irina and looked into her face. 'Convulsions in small children aren't rare; it's probably just a virus. But you should take her to see Mesić all the same.'

I held Irina while Mother slipped on her coat and Dina gently slid the pink woollen hat on to her head. She had stopped crying and stared at me solemnly while they dressed her, wrapping her fingers around the small gold disc that hung around my neck. For some reason I couldn't seem to let go of her, and instead of putting her in the pram I carried her to Mesić's house, my scarf wrapping her small body to mine, binding us together.

We walked in silence, the cold December air spiteful against our skin. The village was silent, no one about apart from occasional pairs of soldiers, loitering, smoking, looking bored. When we reached Mesić's house I tried to smile at Dina, but her eyes filled with tears and she looked away.

'Dina, Miro – this is a surprise.' The elderly doctor ushered us inside and listened while Dina explained what happened. He peered down at Irina and suggested we go through to the surgery, but as soon as we entered the brightly lit room, my daughter began to shriek. I thought I knew all of her cries: flat and whiny when she was tired, sharp and insistent when she was hungry. But this was something different; discordant, almost inhuman, and we both stood in silence and watched as Dr Mesić shone a tiny light into her eyes, took her temperature and peered into her mouth. He seemed to do everything in slow motion, and as the seconds ticked by I had to fight the urge to yell at him to do something – anything – to relieve my daughter's distress.

'Dina, Miro –' He paused, and I knew he was struggling to find the right words. 'Irina, well, I'm sorry, but your daughter is very poorly. Of course it may be a simple viral infection, but when you put together the high temperature, the vomiting and the convulsions, my diagnosis is that she has meningitis. Her reaction to the bright lights in here is a classic symptom.'

'Meningitis?' The word hung in the air, stared at by all three of us. Dina scooped Irina up off the mat and clutched her tightly. 'Oh my God.'

'Dina, the lights are upsetting Irina. Why don't you take her out to the waiting room and I'll have a word with Miro about what to do next.'

She nodded mutely, and once the door had closed I looked straight at Mesić. 'Are you sure?'

'Pretty sure. And if it is, then it's essential she gets the right antibiotics. The problem is, I've run out of everything. To get them, you'll have to go to the hospital in Dubrovnik. A convoy reached the city last month – mostly a publicity stunt of course – but the Red Cross did bring in some supplies. The hospital will definitely have Cefotaxime, which is what your daughter needs. It helps combat the types of illnesses – bacterial infections and suchlike – that are rife in the city just now.'

'But I can't get to Dubrovnik,' I said, sinking into the chair beside Mesić's desk. 'No one leaves the village, and now Josip's disappeared it's going to be even more impossible.'

'Yes, I heard about that,' he said absently. 'Disappointed in the boy. Quite disappointed. But anyway, that's irrelevant. You can get to Dubrovnik – a boat goes daily from up by the Hotel Croatia; it's safer by water than by road. It takes UN personnel, humanitarian workers . . .'

'Neither of which I am.'

'Calm down a minute and just listen. It's not just for UN staff. I've been on it. I go across to the hospital to help when I can. Sometimes they take locals – mothers to see their sons in hospital, that sort of thing. It's at the discretion of Argović, or rather Pavle. But if you have a cast-iron reason to go, they will sign the papers. The only proviso is that you have to come back the same day, otherwise you're seen as defying the curfew. Come back after that and it's instant arrest. They keep it quiet, but I think after what happened in Konavle they feel the need to try and generate a little goodwill.'

'You don't understand. He's sure I know where Josip is. He'll think—'

'Well, you must convince him,' said Mesić, banging his hand down on the desk. 'Come on, Miro. Beg, plead, fight – do whatever is necessary. Get down on your knees if that's what his ego requires. You must make him understand how ill Irina is, and that you have a prescription from me for the medicine. If he doesn't believe you, tell him to come here. He'll hear it from me. Many years ago, Pavle's mother was seriously ill and not expected to survive. Under my care, she did. That buys me a little leeway.'

'What are her chances?' The question sounded unreal, almost ludicrous. 'She's so little, Mesić, she's barely nine months old. Will she be strong enough to—'

'Get the medicine,' said Mesić, standing up. 'Bring it to me, and I will make your daughter well.'

I shook his hand, took a deep breath, and walked outside to where Dina was sitting, rocking Irina gently in her arms. 'Right,' she said, and her voice was low and even, 'tell me *exactly* what Mesić said. Don't keep anything from me. I have to know the truth.'

And so we sat together in the waiting room, the grey December light pooling dimly on the walls and I tried to find the words to explain to my exhausted wife that our tiny daughter's best hope of survival was for me to travel to a city under siege, to a hospital decimated by war, and bring back the medicine she so desperately needed.

'It's too dangerous,' she said in a small voice. 'If anything was to happen to you, if anything . . . I couldn't bear it.'

I tipped her face up towards me and kissed her. 'We don't have any choice, my love. And I promise, nothing is going to happen to me. I'm going to get on that boat, reach the hospital and bring the medicine home again. That's all. Nothing will happen, I promise.'

CHAPTER 13

'Dubrovnik? You've got to go to Dubrovnik?' Marjana's voice, shrill and panicked, cut through the silence. 'That's insanity. There must be another way.'

I looked around the room; no one else spoke. Pa had slipped his arm around Mother's shoulders, while Ivo had turned to the window, staring speechlessly out across the hills.

'There is no other way. She needs medicine, Mesić doesn't have it, the hospital does. I have to go and see Pavle now, get a pass for the boat.'

'Petar can go,' said Mother suddenly. 'Your place is here, with Dina and the baby. It's ridiculous for you to risk your life as well.'

'Yes,' said Dina, with relief. 'Yes, of course. It doesn't have to be Miro that goes. I couldn't bear it if anything happened to him. Not that, I mean . . . if you went, Petar—'

'Pa's not going. I am. This is my job, my responsibility.'

'Tell him, Petar,' said Mother impatiently. 'Tell him you'll go.'

'Don't be stupid, woman.' Ivo turned round, his face ashen. 'Petar's an old man. Anything could happen. Miro is young, quick on his feet.'

'This isn't your business, Ivo,' said Mother coldly. 'This concerns my husband and my son. Petar, say something, tell him.'

Pa stood up and walked over to where Ivo stood. 'Actually, this concerns Miro and his daughter and his wife. Of course I'll go if he wants me to. But I don't think you do, do you, son?'

I shook my head. 'Dina, I'm sorry. But I have to do this. I can't trust it to anyone else. Do you understand?' She looked at me, tears forming in her eyes.

'Yes.' She slipped an arm around my waist and kissed me softly on the cheek. 'I suppose I do.'

'Well, I *don't*,' snapped Mother. 'I just can't believe you, Petar. That you would let your son walk into danger.'

'*Mother*, you're not *listening*. This is my decision, my daughter. Dina, pass me my coat. I have to go and see Pavle.'

'If you get to the hospital, will you see if you can find Cata?'

Dina rounded on Marjana. 'No, he won't. He's going there for one reason, and one reason only. How can you ask him that? How can you ask him to do anything but get our daughter's medicine?'

'I was only—'

'I'm going,' I said, desperate to get away from the fraying tempers and sudden acrimony that seemed to be developing within my own family. 'I've got to get Pavle's permission now, or I won't get on that boat tomorrow. Dina, I'll be as quick as I can.'

It was a relief to be out in the night air. The village was hushed and dark and the thick, ominous silence left no sound but the drumming in my head, unspeakable thoughts of what the next hours might hold. I walked the familiar route to the harbour as if in a dream, sickness rising with every footstep.

'Out past the curfew again?'

Pavle appeared out of the shadows, a bottle of beer in his hand. He was wrapped in a grey military coat that buttoned under his chin. He looked older, more official.

'I was coming to see you. I have to talk to you.'

'Tomorrow morning. You know the curfew.' I didn't move. 'Go home, Miro. Be sensible. Whatever it is can wait till tomorrow.'

'No,' I said, trying to speak calmly, 'it can't. That's the point. It can't wait until tomorrow. It's Irina … she's ill, really ill. I have to get to Dubrovnik. I have a prescription from Mesić but he doesn't have the drugs. I have to get to the hospital; he says there's a boat.'

'Tomorrow.' The word hung in the air as Pavle began to walk away, and as I thought about what tomorrow might bring, the possibilities were so awful that fear and adrenalin catapulted through my system and before I knew what I'd done I had grasped the collar of Pavle's coat and thrown him against the wall. He groaned as his body hit the brickwork, the right side of his face slammed up against it. I leaned in to him and pinned his hands behind his back, trembling with the white-hot fury I had first felt for the foreign reporters at the Ragusa.

'No,' I yelled, 'not tomorrow. *Now*. Because the boat goes at 8 a.m. and I have to be on it. I can't risk you not being around in the morning to sign the papers. I have to get the medicine. Don't you understand? Without it, she might die, my daughter might die. Do you want that on your conscience? Do you?'

Unexpectedly Pavle lurched backwards, almost knocking me off my feet. 'This is about Josip,' he snarled. 'You're going to join him. Do you really think I'm that stupid?'

'Yes!' I screamed. 'Yes, if you really think this is some lie I made up just so I could run off and join Josip. You stupid bastard, don't you have a soul? She's my daughter and she might be dying. If you don't believe me, go and see Mesić. Here's the prescription; you know his handwriting.' I waved the piece of paper in front of him. 'Please, Pavle, I'm begging you. If that's what you want, I'll get down on and my knees and beg.'

Pavle flicked open his lighter and glanced at the paper. 'Come with me,' he said. I followed him in silence, watched him unlock the door to the police station, cross the tiled floor, open a second door and walk behind the desk. He clicked on a lamp, pulled out a pen and began to scribble on a sheet of paper.

'The boat goes at 8 a.m. from the jetty outside the Hotel Croatia. It will not wait. It will leave Dubrovnik at 1 p.m.. It will not wait. There is no other boat. There is no other way back. If you miss it, if you don't come back tomorrow, we will find you.' He looked up at me, his face blank and unmoving. 'I mean it, Miro. Argović is convinced that Josip bribed the ferry captain to get away. It was all I could do to keep the boat running and keep the captain out of prison, but if you disappear too, I can't . . . Some things are beyond my control.' He tailed off and the skin above his collar began to flush bright red. He handed me the piece of paper. 'This will get you to Dubrovnik and back. There'll be a soldier waiting on the jetty; you sign in with him when you board the boat, and sign again when you come back. Argović sees that form every night, and if your name isn't on it . . .'

I nodded, my thoughts already racing ahead; what if Irina grew more sick in the coming hours? What if she awoke in the night, hot and distressed, and there was nothing we could do to soothe her pain? I looked at Pavle. 'Thank you,' I said, and walked out of the office without waiting for a reply.

My two girls were both asleep when I arrived back at the house. I sat on the corner of the bed and looked at them; Irina's small face framed with wisps of dark, curly hair, one tiny hand resting on Dina's stomach. My wife slept with her face turned towards our daughter, her body rising and falling as sleep drifted through her. For a moment I thought of getting my camera, of filming this perfect, silent moment, and then I realized why: because some part of me believed this might be the last time I would see them like this. Fear rippled through me and I bent in to kiss them gently, desperate to touch and yet not wanting to disturb their peace.

'I sent Marjana home,' said Mother as I walked into the kitchen. 'Sleep's the best thing for them both, I think. I've made supper, but I can go if you'd rather be on your own.'

'Stay. We can eat.'

'You don't have to eat it. Just . . . I'd always rather be *doing* something, you know? I can't just sit.'

'I know.' I put an arm around her shoulders; she felt small suddenly, almost frail. 'You do understand why I couldn't let Pa go for me, don't you?'

'I suppose. I just wish sometimes he, oh, never mind. But with Goran where he is, Cvita so far away, at least I have you, at least you're here.' Her eyes began to swim and my stomach twisted.

'I'll be back before you know I've gone.'

'I know, I know,' she said, wiping her face roughly and squeezing me tightly. 'You don't need my tears. And you're doing everything you can; you must take some peace from that. Travelling to Dubrovnik is a brave thing to do.'

'It's not brave,' I said. 'I'd do anything for Dina, for Irina, you know that. I'd go anywhere. Bravery is about doing something you're afraid of, overcoming your fears. I'm not scared of going to Dubrovnik. It's what might happen if I don't go that terrifies me.'

'It *is* brave,' she insisted. 'Why are you always so hard on yourself? I know you've always compared yourself to your brother, but his is just one type of courage. Can't you see that so much of what you've done in your life has been immensely brave: to marry so young, raise your daughter, to find – and make a success – of a job that is far beyond anything your father and I would have expected.'

'I'm not fighting for my country though, am I? Not like him.'

'Oh, my rascal boy,' she said, laying her palm against my cheek. 'We're all fighting for our country now, don't you understand? And your way is just as valuable as Goran's. Those refugees up at the hotel – look at what it meant to them to think that someone, somewhere would hear what had happened to them. You're born to tell stories. Remember those pictures you took at Cvita's wedding? Remember how cross your father was? It's because he couldn't see what you saw. The way your little hands just knew what to do with a camera. I always knew you would do something extraordinary, and we're both so proud. And certainly no prouder of Goran than of you.'

A creak of the floorboards upstairs signalled Dina was awake, and my mother smiled. 'Go to them,' she said. 'And in the morning go to Dubrovnik and know we'll all be thinking of you, counting the minutes until you're safely back home.' I hugged her, felt her arms tighten around my waist, and just for a moment I was a boy again, scooped up after a fall, comforted by the very essence of her, the first body that had ever held me close.

The pale December dawn came too soon that morning. Dina and I lay silently facing each other, her hand in mine, feet tangled together, aware of nothing but the small, overly-warm body asleep between us. And then Irina stirred, and as she woke she began to cry and it was the discordant wail again, the one that scared us both. We did everything Mesić had told us; laid cold compresses against her forehead, massaged her tiny limbs, and as the sun broke through the grey wisps of dawn I took her in my arms and my heart ached at the soft skin of a life barely started.

'Goodbye, my darling,' I said, as I kissed her. 'Daddy will be back soon and then you'll feel much better.' I unwrapped her tiny fingers from around my thumb and as I passed her to Dina she stretched her small arm out towards me. 'Daddy loves you so much.'

'Oh, my love.' Dina looked up at me, but I shook my head and bit hard on my lip.

'I'll just be gone a few hours. No big deal, OK? Please. I can't bear it.'

She nodded. 'We'll be here,' she said, and gave a small, sad smile. I took one last look at the two of them wrapped up in our bed, blew a kiss to my beloved daughter and walked out of the room, my heart so full it ached.

'Papers?' I unfolded the sheet Pavle had given me and stared at the soldier while he scanned it and wordlessly handed me the form to sign. I scribbled my name, walked along the jetty and climbed aboard the travel agency ferry, glancing at my fellow passengers. Opposite sat two elderly women, while on my side sat three men in navy-blue jackets with UN stitched on to the chest. One of them smiled and leaned over to offer a cigarette; I took it, lit up and inhaled. The unfamiliar hit of nicotine made my stomach lurch.

'Been over before?' he asked. 'Since, well, you know.'

I shook my head.

'It's a mess,' he said simply. 'An absolute bloody mess.'

'Is the hospital still functioning?'

'Just about. Is that where you're going?'

'Yes.' He waited for me to say more. 'You?'

'Oh, you know,' he said vaguely. The engine began to throb more loudly and I watched the boy on the jetty untie the rope. 'We're observers, that sort of thing. Report back on the general state of affairs.'

'Doesn't seem as if anyone listens,' I said, and instantly realized how rude I sounded. 'Sorry, that was . . . things on my mind.'

'No, you're right,' he said mildly, shifting away slightly as if sensing the possibility of an argument.

I lifted the cigarette to my lips and felt my heart rate quicken as Ljeta began to shrink away into the mountains. I wondered how many hundreds of times the captain had plied these waters, taking tourists in their floppy hats and strappy dresses, skin pink from the unaccustomed sun. How carefree this boat must have felt, how lightly it must have glided through the water. Now it seemed to shudder as it moved, weighed down by the anxieties of those who had boarded her. I shivered; the wind coming off the mountains was bitter, and I turned my face to the sunlight, where the city walls made a thick grey line that shimmered in the haze.

'See the smoke?' said one of the women, and I looked in the direction she was pointing, to where grey plumes were beginning to billow up from the rooftops of the city.

'More shelling,' said the other. She looked at me. 'Your first time?'
I nodded.

'Keep close into the walls and your eyes on the ground. If you don't,
you'll be over in seconds; the streets are like an obstacle course.'

'It's like nothing you've ever seen,' added the first one. 'Like the
end of the world.'

As we drew closer to the harbour I could see the women were not
exaggerating. Burnt-out fishing boats lay dead in the water, scraps of
blackened wood and twisted aluminium glinting in the sunlight. I
stepped off the boat and stared for a moment at the vast walls that
had kept the city safe for hundreds of years. They seemed bowed,
almost vulnerable, scorched and pockmarked, chunks of blue sea
visible through the gaps that had been blasted by the Serbian rocket
launchers up on Mount Srđ. I walked through the crumbling Pile Gate
and on to the Stradun, the wide pedestrian boulevard that bisected
the city. For a moment it seemed impossible this was the same
place that I had worked, where Josip and I had come as schoolboys
to watch the tourists eat their ice creams and listen to the man
outside St Peter's Church who sang arias by Verdi and Toscanini.
Now there was nothing but filth, mess and silence. The polished
marble slabs that had once gleamed beneath the feet of chattering
tourists were littered with rubble and glass, shopfronts oozed empty
postcard stands, scattered costumed dolls and broken cassettes of
classic Croatian folk-songs. Disfigured buildings lined each side of
the street; roofs sagged into walls, glassless windows gaped at open-
mouthed doorways and everywhere there was dirt and litter, plastic
bags flapping lazily in pools of greeny-yellow liquid, rusty cans and
broken bottles whisked along by the cold, unforgiving wind.

I began to walk, broken glass crunching under my feet. A man
appeared out of an alley, swathed in a long, grimy coat stretching to
his feet. He looked at me as he passed, and in his fleeting glance I
saw a depth of exhaustion that made me almost feel guilty for how

easy life remained in Ljeta. Fear coloured the air here; it permeated the walls and seeped into every new crack and gash. A distant explosion made me focus and I remembered the women's advice; drew closer to the wall, kept my eyes on where I placed my feet, my shoes growing filthy with splashes of mud and shit and urine. The sour stench, mixed in with the smell of burning rubber and wood, grew worse in the alleyways. I turned a corner and tripped over something soft; a long-dead cat, slowly decomposing and encrusted with flies.

After the empty city streets, the flurry and noise of the hospital seemed deafening. The corridors rang with shouted orders, screams of pain, doors banging, trolleys screeching and above it all lay a sense of barely controlled panic, that there simply wasn't enough of anything: of staff or beds or medicine, heat, light or water. A nurse walked by and I grabbed her arm and asked where I could find Dr Petrovać, the man Mesić had told me to see.

She frowned. 'He's busy. Why do you want to see him? If you've got a sick child—'

'I do, but she's not here. She's in Ljeta. She has meningitis. We don't have the drugs she needs.' Her face remained unchanged and I realized one more sick child meant little to her, already surrounded by dozens of small bodies she was powerless to help. I pulled the prescription out of my pocket and held it close to her face. 'Please? Please help me.'

As she looked at the prescription her face softened. 'This is from Dr Mesić? Jorg Mesić? Why didn't you say? Wait here.' She disappeared through the swing doors and within moments they swung open again and a tall bearded man stood in front of me, his face white with exhaustion.

'Jorg Mesić sent you? How is he? That man's a godsend. When he's here, he seems to do the work of five men. Please tell him that Mario – a boy he treated last week – is doing well. We tell him not to come, that it's too risky, but—'

'Please, Doctor. Do you have the medicine? I need to get back to the boat.'

He nodded. 'Liza is getting it for you.'

I thought suddenly of Marjana. 'Do you know Cata? Cata Denković? She's a nurse – my cousin. Is she working?'

He shook his head. 'You've just missed her. Her shift finished half an hour ago.'

'But she's OK?'

'Depends what you mean. She's dead on her feet like the rest of us, but she's OK. Managing.' He looked over as the nurse reappeared with two small bags. 'This is what your daughter needs,' he said, handing me the first one, 'and these are a few supplies for Mesić. Antibiotics, insulin, aspirin. I know he has nothing in his surgery.'

I tucked the bags carefully into my jacket pocket and held out my hand. 'Thank you, Doctor.'

'No need. Get back to your daughter, I hope she recovers. But go, now. This is not a place to be unless you have to.'

Outside the hospital, relief flooded through my body with such force I had to stop, lean against a wall and breathe slowly in and out. I checked my watch: midday. I would be back at the harbour in twenty minutes, and all I had to do was sit and wait on the boat until it carried me back to Ljeta.

Suddenly a discordant shriek split the silence, followed by a roar that made the ground shake beneath my feet. My heart raced and I ran as another mechanical scream rent the air, followed by a huge, splintering explosion. I quickened my pace, tripped over rubble, grazed my shoulder on the corner of a building as I cut too close. Two women stumbled past me, their breath jagged on the air as they hurried on. I clutched my jacket pocket with my right hand and began to run down alleys that were menacingly empty, as if I was the only man left alive in the city.

Finally I turned the corner on to the Stradun, but just as the Pile

Gate came into sight, a different noise rang out above the rumbling explosions; a high-pitched wail, broken by sobs. The tears rose into screams and the skin on my arms went cold. For a moment all I could see was Tara lying on the grass, her foot a mass of torn skin and exposed bone, scarlet blood leeching into the dusty yellow glass. Another wail – '*Mamaaa*' – and I swallowed down my fear and ran back up the alley, almost falling over a small girl in a heap on the stones.

'Are you hurt?' I found myself staring at her legs and hands, praying inwardly: Please let her be OK, don't let her be injured, not now, not *again*.

'*Mama*,' she wailed, looking up at me. I bent down, slipped an arm underneath her and helped her stand. She clung to me, wrapped her arms around my neck and I remembered the feel of Tara's legs heavy on my arms, the blood from her foot dripping stickily on to my skin.

'Where is your mama?' I asked, but she shook her head and sobbed. Another explosion ripped through the air and she tightened her arms around my neck. 'We have to get you out of here,' I said, drawing back and tilting her face so that her eyes met mine. 'It's OK. I'm not going to leave you.'

Her lower lip trembled. She didn't speak. Her eyes were pink and swollen, there was dirt on her cheek, her chin was grazed. I knew I would never forgive myself if I simply left her on the street.

'Where's the shelter?' I asked, but she didn't speak. 'When the bombs come, the big noises, where do you go? Come on darling, it's OK. Just tell me.'

She frowned. 'Fish.'

'Fish?'

'To see the fish. In their house.'

I stared at her for a moment, unable to think what she meant. Then I remembered that one of the two big fortresses in the walls was home to an aquarium. I scooped her up and ran, back down to the Stradun and up the hill to the vast, thick-walled building.

'There.' She pointed to a huge wooden door and I set her down and pushed it open. The sight that met my eyes was overwhelming: hundreds of bodies huddled together, children bundled in blankets, old men staring into the darkness. As I walked in a woman looked up and I led the girl towards her.

'I found her in the street. Can I leave her? I'm not from here.'

The woman nodded and extended her hands. She showed no interest in asking where I had found the girl or who I was. I was unsurprised; one morning in this dying city had shown me that normal forms of interaction had long since broken down. I backed away, waved at the girl and hurried back down to the Stradun just as another shell shrieked overhead. For the hundredth time I checked the bags of pills in my pocket and looked at my watch: still only twelve thirty.

But when I passed through the Pile Gate, it was like walking into a thick fog; great plumes of acrid smoke were rising from the water, flames licking along the sea, oil slicks glinting in the water. A gust of wind blew, the air cleared a little, three yachts were on fire at the far end of the harbour. I ran past the dismembered fishing boats and suddenly stopped, frozen. Where the boat should have been there was just an empty space, grey water crusted with ash and wood. I looked around wildly. Suddenly a man appeared out of the smoke, and with a surge of relief I recognized him as the UN observer from the boat.

'Where's the boat?' I yelled. 'Do you know where the boat is?'

He looked at me, confused, shook his head.

'Where is it?' I shouted again, pointing at the space where the boat should have been. '*Where's the fucking—*'

A huge explosion cut across my words, water shot into the sky, raining down on us, knocking me off my feet. My arm smacked hard against concrete, pain sheared through my body and a strange, odd thud began to pulse against my forehead. I staggered to my feet, turned to look for the man beside me, and as I did the wind suddenly gusted and the smoke lifted and I realized he was standing a few yards away, his arm outstretched, pointing out to sea. And I knew, before I even looked, what he was pointing at; pain and fear and panic spiralled up through my system as I followed his gaze, and the last thing I saw before the world went dark was the travel agency boat, rolling slightly in the angry waves, slipping away beyond the harbour wall, back to Ljeta, where my beloved wife and daughter were waiting for me.

PART TWO

December 1991–July 1993

CHAPTER 14

'What are you doing here?'

I looked around for a minute, trying to work out where I was. A long wooden counter swung into view, behind which I could see glass jars filled with coffee beans and the wire rack for the cones of *kajmak*. What the hell was I doing in Pa's shop?

I realized it was Goran who was speaking; he looked older, bearded, done up in a greatcoat like Pavle's. 'You told me to come,' I said, slowly. 'You said to bring her here.'

'Not *here*.' He stared at me contemptuously. 'I said take her to the *hospital*. Look at her, Miro. Can't you see the state she's in?'

I looked to where he was pointing to see Tara, leaning against the counter, tears running down her face. There was something odd about her, something wrong. At first I couldn't work out what it was, but as I walked towards her my stomach lurched horribly. Her left arm was missing, blown away just below the elbow.

'Jesus Christ.'

'It's here,' Goran said, walking towards me. 'Take it, it's here.'

I knew what he was holding, but I couldn't bear to look. 'Don't,' I shuddered, backing away. 'Don't . . .'

'Come on, Miro,' he wheedled, and suddenly his hands were around my arms and he was shaking me. 'Be a man for once. Come on . . .'

My eyes flicked open. Goran took his hands off my arms and

I squinted through the gloom, up to a face I didn't recognize. Bewildered, I looked beyond into a darkness that was studded with pale twists of light filtering through small, slit-shaped windows. The air was thick with cigarette smoke and the ripe smell of human bodies.

'Where am I?' The words rasped out; my throat was dry and sore and my head throbbed with pain.

'Dubrovnik. In a shelter. You were shouting out . . . bad dreams.' The man turned and pointed to a figure hunched up against the opposite wall, apparently asleep. 'My colleague brought you here. Don't you remember?'

I tried to think. As my eyes adjusted to the darkness I could see I was in some sort of church; stone walls and floors, long wooden pews, the flag of St Peter hanging from a tall wooden pole. I stood up slowly and inched along the wall in the half-light; damp plaster clung to my fingers. In spite of the silence, the space was crammed with bodies: women wrapped in blankets clutching children on their laps, old men huddled together, young boys playing noughts and crosses in the dirt. I looked across as the man who had brought me in stretched and groaned, and suddenly I remembered: the child in the alley, the hospital, my sick baby girl. Reality crashed over me; I hadn't got back. *I hadn't got back.*

'So you're awake?' The man stirred and raised his hand. 'You've slept for many hours, my friend.'

'You were on the harbour with me?'

He nodded. 'You hit your head when the shell exploded. We were both very lucky.'

'What time is it?'

'Midnight.'

'*Midnight?* Jesus Christ, I've got to get back to Ljeta, now, right now. My daughter's ill. I came to get medicine – without it she might, she might . . . You have to help me. Please.'

'There's nothing I can do,' he said. I looked down and realized I was grasping his shirt, thin cotton against my damp palms. I let my hands fall to my sides. 'I'm so sorry. There's no way, not tonight. If you go out now you'll be the only person on the streets and the snipers will pick you off in seconds. I'm supposed to be in Montenegro, but there's nothing to be done but wait it out.'

'I can't wait, I can't. There must be a way.'

'There isn't.' The finality in his tone made my skin prickle. 'I don't know what's happened, but obviously the latest ceasefire has failed. If you go out now, you will be arrested or killed. How will that help your daughter?'

'But my wife, she won't know where I am, what will they think? They'll be so worried.' I sunk my head into my hands and pictured Mother and Pa stood by the jetty, watching the boat come closer and closer, straining to see me, persuading themselves I was there, that I must be there, counting the passengers off, waiting, disbelief starting to creep into their thoughts. How had they found the words to tell Dina I hadn't come back, that there was no medicine for Irina, that Daddy had disappeared and left her to struggle alone?

My throat tightened so fiercely I could barely breathe. 'Is there any water?'

'None that's fresh.' A woman's voice, strangely gentle against the harsh surroundings. 'You can use this. Don't drink it, but if you want to wash . . .' She reached below her and pulled a bucket from under the pew, half full of greyish water with a thick layer of white scum clouding the top. I nodded gratefully, plunged my hands into the bucket and rubbed them across my face. It smelt of rotting flowers and overripe tomatoes but the wetness against my skin helped bring me round. If I couldn't go now, I would go at first light – when most of the soldiers would be asleep at their posts. Somehow I would find a boat, steal a car, anything to get back to Ljeta. I tried not to think of Pavle, waiting to arrest me the moment I set foot in the village. I would deal with him when the time came.

I sat back against the wall, my hand on the pocket of my coat where the pills were stored. The hours passed in a strange, semi-conscious muddle of sleep and anxiety, my eyes straining up to the tiny windows, waiting for the first hint of grey dawn to slip in through the darkness. When it came, when the early glimmers of day began to flicker on to the wall above me, I rose carefully, stepped across the sleeping bodies and out into the silence. The city lay cowed and mute beneath an opaque sky, and as the Pile Gate came into sight I felt an overwhelming sense of relief at having escaped the shelter. 'I'm coming home, my loves,' I said out loud, optimism rising within me at the sight of the sea shimmering in the distance.

Suddenly the silence was ripped apart by a huge crash that thundered towards me like a vast, discordant wave. The road shuddered beneath my feet and I froze, waiting for the moment to pass, but as the explosion died away another took its place, then another, until my ears were ringing with the sound of buildings collapsing and the air was pierced with screams and wails and strange distorted shouts. I tried to keep moving but my legs began to shake. *You will be arrested or killed. How will that help your daughter?* The air splintered again, the loudest explosion yet, and I found myself running back to the shelter, hurling myself through the door and collapsing on to a pew, breath searing my lungs.

'Is it bad?' The woman who had offered me the water looked up, her face taut and white. For the first time I noticed the small girl lying next to her, face buried in her lap.

'It's just non-stop. One then another, deafening. I could hear people . . .'

Tears began to slide down her cheeks. 'My parents, they won't come to the shelter. They're in a cellar.' She closed her eyes and the little girl stirred slightly and stretched out her legs. My heart twisted.

'What's your daughter's name?'

She dropped a kiss on the sleeping child's head. 'Marta.'

'I have a daughter too. Her name—' A metallic scream burst through the air, cutting off my words; a huge roar shook the wall next to us. Dust fell. I felt her hand on mine. In an attempt to comfort us both, I put my arm around her shoulders and felt her thin, tense body rigid against my own.

'We're going to die.'

I pulled back a little and tucked my finger under her chin, tilting her face up to mine. 'What's your name?'

'Ella.'

'Ella, I'm Miro. I came here to get medicine for my daughter. She's very sick and I have to get back to Ljeta with it. So I'm not going to die. And neither are you, or Marta. You're not going to die, Ella, I promise you.'

'You're very certain. I like that.'

I nodded, hoping she couldn't see how entirely uncertain I was. Marta sat up and moved on to her mother's lap, her battered shoes resting against my legs. I closed my eyes and tried to pretend the woman and child in my arms were the two who belonged to me and that I was keeping them safe, that I would always keep them safe.

Minutes passed, then hours, and as the explosions grew louder, the silence in between became thicker, almost impenetrable. It was as if each of us was slowly withdrawing to our own individual world, that if this was the moment of our death, we would spend it with those we loved. I closed my eyes and let my mind roam through the sunlit years of my childhood: playing in the fortress with Goran, walks with Dina up in the Konavle hills, Pa and Ivo sharing brandies late in the evening, when the last tourists had gone to bed and the cicadas sang in the trees above them. I thought of my mother, my brave, unselfish mother, slipping her hand into mine as she walked me to school, of coming home to find her baking, watching her face grow older as the long days in the sweltering kitchen at the pension gradually took their toll. And finally my baby girl, the way she clung to me when she woke, her tiny heart beating against my chest, the feel of her soft hand slowly exploring my face.

When the silence came, no one knew quite what to do. For six hours we had felt the ground shudder and moan beneath our feet. With every shriek and whine we had readied ourselves to be catapulted into a world of chaos and darkness. But the moment never came. We sat, unmoving, buried in our damp, candlelit hiding place while beyond the ancient walls the world went noisily crazy. And then, quite suddenly, it stopped.

'Is it over?' Ella lifted her head from my shoulder. The words hung in the dust-clogged air and slowly people stirred and began to move. Men stood and stretched, children started to wail; in the far corner a tall boy who reminded me of Josip rose gingerly to his feet. He was looking down at himself, and even in the half-light I could feel his humiliation. One trouser leg was darker than the other; the long hours of fear had caused him to wet himself.

'I don't know. It must be about ten minutes since the last shell.'

'It's been twelve.' It was the man who had brought me here. He stood up and walked to the middle of the aisle. 'If we get to fifteen, it's probably safe to assume this is a ceasefire.'

'You don't know that,' said a man's voice, and there was murmured agreement from the pews behind.

'I do actually. I know how negotiations with the JNA work, it's my job.' He looked around and clasped his hands together. 'If we get to fifteen, I'm going out there. There's going to be a lot of casualties. Who's with me?'

What was left of my youth disappeared forever on that cold December afternoon. When we first reached the Stradun, I simply couldn't comprehend what I was seeing; it was as if the earth had surged up from below, breaking buildings apart, billowing through shops and restaurants, scattering door frames and roof tiles and street signs, while churches groaned and houses swayed at the injuries they had sustained. In the immediacy of the horror I forgot everything but what was around me, ripping off doors and heaving masonry aside to reach those who screamed and wept below, lifting warm, limp bodies covered in plaster and ash, hurling water at buildings shimmering with flames.

'Who could do this?' cried Christoph, one of the men from the shelter, as we walked back down to the Stradun from the hospital. His face was blackened, his coat smeared with blood from the man we had half dragged, half carried to the hospital. 'Don't they have mothers? Daughters? If they could see—'

'They don't have to see, do they? That's how war is.'

'Well, someone needs to fucking see . . .' We turned the corner on to the Stradun and he broke into a roar of anger. 'What the *fuck* do you think you're doing? Get away! Don't you have any respect?' He ran towards a man who was filming in the street, his lens focused on a woman sitting by the side of the road. She was sobbing openly, her hands outstretched towards the camera as if trying to push it away. The man shoved the reporter hard and he stumbled backwards. 'What's wrong with you, man? Leave her alone. Leave her *alone*. Have you no shame?'

'Just trying to do my job,' the man with the camera replied. 'You said someone needs to fucking see this – what do you think I'm doing?'

'Not *NOW*,' roared Christoph. 'Now there are people dying. Put the fucking camera down and help us.'

'I *am* helping you, you stupid man. *Mon Dieu.*' Nic Richaud. I couldn't believe I hadn't recognized him instantly.

'You,' he said, pointing at me. 'Tell your friend, yeah? Get him off my back. I am doing a job. You understand that, don't you?'

'Don't film her,' I said. 'She doesn't want you to.'

'She won't even remember.'

'I said, don't film her.' I walked closer to him, and his face changed. 'You? I know you. Where do I know you from?'

'The Ragusa. I work with Damir.'

'Of course. Then you understand – it's my job. Without me, no one will know this fucking shitstorm has even happened. Now, let's stop fucking arguing, and I'll do my job and you can get on with yours.'

'You bastard.' Christoph began to harangue Nic, but I was no longer listening. Further along the street, helping shift a broken door that was blocking the entrance to a house, I suddenly saw my brother-in-law.

'BOBO. BOBO!' I yelled his name and he turned, peered through the gloom and raised his arms in obvious surprise.

'Miro,' he exclaimed, as I ran towards him. 'What the hell are you doing here?'

'Christ, Bobo, thank God. Irina's ill . . . meningitis.' I explained as fast as I could. 'You must know someone, someone with a boat. I'll pay anything, whatever it takes. I have to get back or she might . . . she might not . . .'

'Jesus.' He looked genuinely shocked. 'My God, poor Dina. I'm so sorry.'

'Don't be sorry. I don't want your pity, I need your help. Come on – you must know someone.'

He lifted a hand as if to hold me where I stood and ran back to the group of men. I watched as he pointed towards me, felt my heart thud frantically against my ribcage. If anyone could get me back, it would be Bobo. Cata was always telling me he knew everyone in Dubrovnik, and I felt sure the siege would have strengthened his allegiances within the city.

'OK.' As he walked towards me his face was clear and sharp. 'I can help, but it'll have to be tonight. And you'll have to row; the patrol boats will hear an engine. Can you do that? Row all the way back to Ljeta?'

I nodded, trying not to think of the extra patrols set up in the waters around the village since Josip's disappearance. 'Of course. I'll do anything.'

'Right.' He glanced around and lit a cigarette. 'This is how it'll work. Leave the shelter at eleven forty precisely. There's a shift change on the harbour at eleven forty-five, so they'll be distracted. You'll have to swim from the harbour around to the small beach beneath the Ragusa hotel. At the far end there's a small cave; if I can get the boat, that's where it'll be. To move the boat to the water, try to lift it; you must make as little noise as possible. If you're fortunate there'll be noise from the Ragusa terrace, but in these temperatures it's unlikely anyone will be outside. Don't just drag it across the stones. And if they catch you, if they ask you . . .'

'I stole it from the harbour,' I said quickly. 'I wouldn't tell them anything, Bobo, you know that.'

He nodded quickly. 'I must get back. There's so much . . .' A look of exhaustion crossed his face. 'It's just carnage. Utter carnage.' He turned to leave.

'Bobo? How's Cata?' He turned, and to my surprise his face darkened. He paused for a moment, shrugged and then turned on his heel and walked away.

Once I had seen Bobo, I slipped guiltily back to the shelter, desperate to salvage whatever strength I had left for the journey back to Ljeta. I calculated it would take me around four hours of solid rowing, and my arms already ached from the lifting and carrying of rubble and bodies.

When the time finally came, I rose quietly and headed for the door. As my fingers closed around the handle, I felt a hand on my arm and turned to find myself looking into the blue eyes of the man who had saved me on the harbour.

'Don't do it. I know you need to get back, but it's too dangerous.'

'I've no choice,' I said curtly, and then remembered that I quite possibly owed this man my life. 'But I should thank you. I haven't thanked you. You saved me.'

'No need. At least I've felt . . . well, these past couple of days I've been of some use.'

I looked at him, neat blond hair, expensive khaki trousers now stained with blood and dirt. 'I don't even know your name,' I said.

He smiled. 'Johann. Johann Sauber. From Germany. Military strategist with the UN.'

'Do you have a wife, Johann? Children?'

His smile grew wider, a little wistful. 'Yes. A girl and a boy.'

I laid a hand on his arm. 'They'll sleep safely tonight. You know that. That's how you can be here, even though it's not where you're supposed to be. But my daughter does not sleep safely and so I must get home to her. You're a father – you must understand.'

For a moment he looked beyond me and I knew what he was seeing; a small blond boy and a sweet-faced girl, tucked up beneath soft clean duvets. His eyes blurred a little and he leaned past me to pull open the heavy oak door. 'Good luck, my friend,' he said. 'Godspeed.'

I stepped into the night. A wall of sharp, cold air smacked against me, but as I began to walk the feelings of exhaustion gave way to an almost manic sense of purpose. I moved carefully, ensuring each step avoided the broken glass or rubble that would crunch beneath my foot and push a finger on to a trigger somewhere high on the walls above me. By the time I reached the sea my breathing was shallow and fast; the icy water tightened like a band around my legs and chest as I waded in. I swam furiously, forcing my arms and legs through the water, desperate to keep them below the surface to avoid any sound of splashing. My laboured breathing sounded deafeningly loud, but if I tried to quieten it my head began to spin and my chest constricted with pain. Finally the terrace of the Ragusa came into view and I dragged myself up on to the stones and crept along in the inky darkness.

Bobo had been as good as his word. Inside the cave lay a small, weather-beaten boat, with two oars, a blanket and a small package tucked beneath the seat. Barely breathing, I took everything out of the boat and hoisted it over my head, arms almost buckling at the weight, legs wobbling on the uneven beach. Suddenly, a light from a patrol boat swept along the beach. I froze. It barrelled past me and back again and then all was darkness. I lowered the boat into the water, ran back for the blanket, the package and the oars and waded into the sea. Desperate to get away from the shore, I plunged both oars into the water and pulled as smoothly as I could, pausing only when the lights of the Ragusa had become a blurred glimmer in the distance.

I turned to look towards Ljeta, but only the dimmest flecks of light were visible. It was as if the village didn't exist; the curve of the bay and the mountains behind rose up like some silent, mono-lithic barricade, walling in the great rolling wastes of the sea. Fear and some kind of strange hyper-consciousness washed over me; I felt completely overwhelmed, swallowed up by an infinite sky that seemed bereft of moonlight or the warm glow of stars. Everywhere was darkness, above and below, and I felt the strongest urge to plunge into the water, that to be absorbed into the vast inky void would bring with it a wonderful sense of calm, of giving in.

'Irina,' I said out loud. The sound of my voice made me jump and my knee brushed against the package Bobo had left for me. Inside lay slices of bread and ham and a bottle of wine; I devoured the food, shoving it into my mouth like an animal, then unscrewed the bottle and took a long grateful swig. I massaged my aching shoulders a little and as I did my fingers brushed against Goran's St Christopher. My brother's face flashed up in my mind like a talisman and I took another gulp of wine, felt the alcohol rip its way into my bloodstream.

'Thank you, Bobo,' I said, and this time the sound of my voice reassured me; I began to row again with renewed determination, closing my eyes as the pain burned in my arms and shoulders, pulling myself through the water back to my girls.

It took three more hours before I reached the headland. My body was shaking, the muscles in my upper arms were on fire with pain. I half clambered, half fell into the water, crawled on to the stones and lay there, my legs locked and frozen, heart pounding in my chest. I couldn't move. The boat rocked a little against the waves I had created and then began to drift out to sea. The patrol would see it before long. I didn't care. I lay on the hard stones, looked up at the darkness and felt my thumping heart begin to slow. I'd made it. I was home.

CHAPTER 15

The house lay in darkness. I slipped my key into the lock and closed the door, barely daring to breathe. They would be asleep upstairs, I told myself, just as I had left them. I slipped off my shoes and began to creep across the lounge. And then I saw her, sat at the table with her back to me; head bowed, hands in her lap, body utterly still.

'Dina?'

She made a sound, a sound I had never heard before, breath sucked in, hard and fast, a tiny, high-pitched gasp that broke as it hit the air. She raised herself slowly, fingertips pressing down on the table to steady herself. When she turned, what I saw – even in the half-light – made my stomach plunge with shock. This was not my Dina, this was a different woman; one with swollen eyes, skin raised and sore, who shook a little as she stood.

'*Miro?*' Just the sound of her voice was enough; I stumbled towards her, gathered her body into my arms, kissed her, smelt her skin.

'Oh my darling, I'm so sorry, so sorry. Irina, how is she, where is she?'

Dina froze at my words, her body rigid against mine. And I knew then, knew what I had known from the moment I had woken up in the shelter, a reality I had tried to deny on the streets of Dubrovnik, in the boat, even as I unlocked my own front door. I buried my face in her shoulder, pressing down, trying to grind my skin into her body, to hide from the building wave of horror that was roaring towards me.

'No,' I whispered. 'Please, God, no.' As I spoke she began to sob. I couldn't think, couldn't feel anything, tightened my grip around her, but in my mind all I could see was my daughter's solemn face, asleep in our bed, where I had left her.

'When?'

'Last night.' Her voice was so quiet I could barely hear. 'It was quiet, so quiet. The day had been difficult, Mesić had come, he'd said to prepare. But then she just grew so peaceful, and . . .' She pulled away and looked up at me. 'Where were you? WHERE WERE YOU?' She began to sob again and I took her hands in mine, tried to unlock her fingers, but they were clenched around something.

'Please.' She let her hands fall apart. In her palms lay a tiny pink cardigan. I remembered how Irina would frown at me when I clumsily tried to wrestle her arms into the sleeves, wriggle as I did up the tiny flower-shaped buttons. I took it out of Dina's hands, laid it against my cheek and in its fibres I could smell the soft, sweet scent of my tiny daughter.

'Where were you?' Dina whispered again. There was such desperation in her voice that I fought back my tears and began to explain what had happened in Dubrovnik. She sat still at first, curled into me like a child, but when I told her about stopping to help the little girl she suddenly pulled away and stood up, her face dark and angry.

'So that's why you missed the boat? *That's* why you didn't get back in time to save our daughter?'

'No,' I said, horrified at hearing Dina voice the thought I had been desperately trying to avoid. 'I had *time*. I got back to the boat twenty minutes before it was supposed to leave, but it had left early.'

'I don't care, I DON'T CARE.' Her words hurtled towards me, angry and a little out of control. 'You went to Dubrovnik for one reason, Miro, just one reason. To get the medicine for our daughter. But you put that other child first – how could you, how *could* you? How could *anything* have been more important to you?'

'It wasn't like that, it wasn't . . . What else could I have done? Just leave her there with bombs going off? She was terrified. Anyone would have done the same thing. And I *had time* – I'd never have helped her if there wasn't enough time.'

'But there *wasn't*,' she screamed. 'There wasn't, was there? You took a risk, gambled with our daughter's life. How could you do that? How could saving someone else's child be more important than saving our own?'

'How can you say that?' My own voice started to rise, guilt and grief threatening to overwhelm me. 'I would never have risked Irina's life, never.'

'Well, she's DEAD.' The word stopped us both. I thought of the bodies I had seen on the streets of Dubrovnik, there but not there, gone but still present. That couldn't be my daughter. Not another lifeless, cold corpse.

'Dina . . .'

'Oh, just get out. I can't bear to look at you, can't bear that you've done this. Get out. GET OUT.'

I reached out to touch her, but she backed away, collided with the table. Pain shot across her face. 'Get away from me,' she shrieked, and I knew she was in danger of losing control completely. 'I can't . . . just get out, *please*.'

For a moment I couldn't move. Nothing seemed real, not Dina's uncontrollable fury, or the small empty cot upstairs or the sick sense of guilt that was beginning to embed itself in my stomach. 'I love you,' I said, praying she would soften. But she was somewhere else, lost to her grief, and I knew that right now there was nothing I could do but slip on my shoes, wrap my scarf around my neck and walk back out into the night.

It wasn't until the first slug of brandy hit my system that I even realized where I was. Somehow, without conscious thought, I had got myself to the pension, unlocked the door and reached behind the reception desk for the bottle of Stock Ivo always kept there. I raised it to my lips and the alcohol burned further into my mind, allowing me a gut-wrenching moment of clarity. My daughter was dead. My wife blamed me. I tipped the bottle up again and this time the realization gave way to a wave of rage and I staggered back into the street and slammed my fists against a table, hurled the brandy bottle against the wall, anger roaring up from my lungs. I began kicking furiously at an upturned wooden chair until a leg came free, picked it up and smashed it against the table, harder and harder, frenzied, out of control.

'Miro.' Unseen hands whipped my arms behind my back and I fell to my knees. I knew without turning who it was.

'She's dead,' I shouted, but the words were choked with sobs and sharp twists of air so cold it burned my throat. 'She's dead, Pavle. My little girl.'

For a moment there was silence. 'I'm so sorry.'

I tried to speak but no words would come, just an oddly strangled wail.

'Try and stand up.' His voice was brisk but gentle, and I felt his arms loop around my torso and drag me to my feet. 'And be quiet. Stop the noise. You'll wake the whole village.'

'I don't care. You're going to arrest me anyway, aren't you? Go on, fuck it, there's nothing you can do to me, nothing worse.'

'Yes, I am arresting you,' said Pavle, and his voice was oddly loud. 'You know how this has to be. I gave you passage on the boat and you didn't come back as you should. You leave me no choice.'

By the time we reached the police station I was numb. I followed Pavle into the building and up the stairs at the back of the room, barely wondering why he didn't put me straight in a cell. He flicked a light switch to reveal a bare-walled flat with an unmade bed, dirty stove and faded sofa. Even in my distressed state I could see there was something terribly lonely about the small unkempt room.

He pointed at the sofa and I fell on to it, watching him pull a blanket from the cupboard and take a pillow from the bed. 'You need to sleep,' he said. 'We'll talk in the morning.'

I didn't move. My legs were leaden and even the movement required to shift from a sitting position seemed too much. Pavle placed the pillow at one end of the sofa and before I understood what was happening he had knelt down, unlaced my shoes and slipped them off. 'Come on,' he said, lifting my legs on to the sofa, and gently turning my body so I could lie flat. I was asleep before he had laid the coarse, woollen blanket on top of me.

I slept fitfully that night, Pavle's thick, rasping breaths filling the room. I dreamed I was on a boat in a wonderfully starlit sea and Irina was swimming beside me, her splashes caught up in the moonlight, a tiny beacon in the velvety darkness. 'You can't swim,' I called to her, but she just giggled and began to float away. I tried to row after her, my arms burning, but however hard I rowed I never got any closer. 'Stay with Daddy,' I cried, 'stay with Daddy,' but I could no longer see her and her laughter was turning to long, drawn-out breaths, deep and ragged, too big for her tiny lungs, and I knew it was because they were filling with water as she slowly slipped beneath the waves.

'You're awake?' Pavle's voice cut through the gloom.

'Yes.'

'Then go and shower,' he said. 'I've put some clean clothes in there. Make yourself presentable, then we'll talk.'

I nodded, stumbled into the bathroom and stood motionless as tiny darts of freezing water stung my skin. My arms were too painful to raise and hung limply by my sides; I stared as the droplets slid from my shoulder down past my elbow to my wrist. I could have stood there watching them for hours, days, but Pavle banged on the door and I clambered out, dried myself roughly and pulled on the jeans and jumper that lay, neatly folded, on a stool beside the bath.

'We'll eat while we talk,' he said, and pointed to a small camping table with coffee, rolls and two plates of scrambled egg and a pile of *sremska*, the crispy sausages I had eaten at his mother's table more times than I could remember. I wasn't interested in eating, but as I watched Pavle shovel the food into his mouth, it seemed easier to copy his movements rather than try to think of my own.

'So,' he said, laying down his coffee cup, 'you came back. Nearly thirty-six hours late. What the hell happened? The boat came back – how come you weren't on it? They were waiting on the harbour, your mum and dad, Dina and Ivo and Marjana back at the house – it felt as if half the village was holding its breath. And how in God's name *did* you get back last night?'

I closed my eyes, tried not to think of Dina's face. 'There was a girl,' I began, and I realized I was desperate to tell him, to hear a reaction that might undo a little of the guilt. He listened as I told him of my race to the shelter with the child in my arms, the shelling of the harbour, the gut-wrenching sight of the boat disappearing out to sea.

'I couldn't have left her there on the street, could I? She was terrified, she was a little girl. What would you have done?'

He ignored my question. 'So you got to the harbour too late?'

'NO.' I slammed my fist down on the table, scattering crumbs and cigarette ash. 'I had time, there was *plenty* of time. I'd never have helped the girl if I wasn't sure I'd be able to make the boat with time to spare. But it went early.'

'You're wrong. It didn't go *early*, it just went when it went. Timetables don't count, there are no schedules or routines any more – haven't you learned that yet? Of course you had to help the girl; I'd have done the same thing. And if the boat had left at 1 o'clock you'd have been a hero. But it didn't – the shelling started so it left. That's how life is now: unpredictable, chaotic. Don't you know that?'

'Obviously not. Not all of us find a state of war so easy to adjust to.'

He flinched. 'Very few people find it easy. Perhaps some are just better at hiding their difficulties.'

'Oh, spare me the sympathy vote. Difficulty? You seem to have made the transition with ease.'

'Why haven't I arrested you then?' he said unexpectedly.

'I thought you did. I might have been drunk, but I distinctly remember you saying—'

'You heard me *say* it,' he said, and there was an odd note of triumph in his voice, 'as did anyone else who might have been listening. But are you in a cell? Did I write out any paperwork?'

'So you're not going to . . . ?'

'I don't know yet. It depends if anyone saw you, if anyone else knows you're back. If they do, you're done for.' He looked at me and suddenly his face softened. 'This isn't good for either of us, but, Christ, you think I don't understand how awful this is for you? For Dina? You were like family to me . . . I'm so, *so* sorry about Irina.'

'Don't.' I stared at the half-eaten food on my plate. 'Please. I can't . . .'

'Don't think . . .' he tailed off, stared at the table. 'All those years, don't think they don't mean anything to me. What I did, joining the army, I believed him, you know, Milošević. We all did. It felt like I had to make a choice, it seemed to *matter* so much. And now, being here like this, it does still matter, but other things matter too.'

I looked at him and suddenly he was Pavle again, my Pavle, who taught me to backflip and stole tomatoes and mimicked Aunt Marjana's way of walking, mincing along behind her when she wasn't looking. 'I killed her,' I said, desperate to say the words that spun crazily in my brain. 'I killed my own daughter.'

'Don't be ridiculous. Irina was seriously ill – truth is, even if you'd got back with the medicine she probably wouldn't have recovered. I saw Mesić that afternoon and he was in a dreadful state, said that with something as virulent as meningitis the odds were never on her side. I think he felt he'd sent you with false hope, that in some way he'd caused Dina to lose you as well as the baby.'

'I haven't even seen her,' I muttered, 'to say goodbye. I need to, before the burial.'

He stood up suddenly. 'Miro, there's no easy way to say this. The burial was yesterday – there was no choice. Nowhere to keep her. It was what Dina wanted, up in Konavle.'

'Jesus.' I covered my face with my hands, this new piece of information was too much to bear. 'How . . . ?'

'Shhh.' Pavle put his finger to his lips as the door below creaked open. He disappeared down the stairs and I clenched my fists and listened to Argović hurl his anger at Pavle; where was I? First Josip and now me – was he in on it? Didn't we all used to be friends?

'I don't know anything, I've told you,' I heard Pavle say. 'I'll talk to the wife and parents this morning.' The door slammed shut and the stairs creaked beneath his feet.

'Miro, we're going to have to get you out of here. You can't be in Ljeta.' He ran his fingers through his hair and even in my current state I could see he was seriously rattled. 'Argović is still furious about Josip's disappearance, and he can be a sadistic bastard when he feels like it. You know the penalty for not coming back is prison.'

'But I *am* back. I came back as soon as I could. And I'm not going anywhere. If it means a couple of weeks behind bars . . .'

'You're not *listening*. It won't be a couple of weeks, and it won't be those nice cosy cells downstairs. Argović got a royal bollocking when Josip disappeared, and when he saw the form and that your signature wasn't on it . . .'

'I'll talk to him. I'll explain.' I stood up, but Pavle pushed me back into my seat.

'Miro, I'm serious. If he sees you, you'll be in a Jeep to some godforsaken prison camp in the back end of nowhere so fast, and you'll be in there for months, maybe years. And it won't end there. Argović will make life hell for your parents, for Dina . . . you've got no idea what he's capable of. You don't have a choice.'

'I think you'll find I have. You think I'm leaving Dina at a time like this? She's angry now, but in a few days . . . And I have to visit Irina's grave. I have to.'

His face was impassive. 'I'm sorry. You don't have a few days. If you hide you'll be found. Then questions will be asked: did I know? Was I protecting you? I'll help you, but I won't choose your life over mine. And that *is* what it'll come to, believe me.'

'I'm. Not. Going.' I looked at Pavle, and all the warmth between us had gone. 'You can't make me.'

He stood up. 'Perhaps not. But there are others who will.'

It was Mother who came first. While Pavle questioned my father in the office below, one of his lieutenants at the desk opposite, I sat with her on the grubby yellow sofa and told her in the softest of whispers what had happened in Dubrovnik. My guilt multiplied when I saw the grief and sleeplessness in her eyes, and as I told her what had happened in the city, her face grew pale and she wrapped her fingers around mine.

'When Pavle told us you were here, I couldn't believe it,' she whispered. 'I'm so sorry.'

I shook my head. 'Not here. I can't . . . We have to think of something, Mother. Pavle says I have to leave Ljeta, that if I stay I'll be arrested, that it will be bad for Dina too.'

'But that's ludicrous.' Her voice was starting to rise and I laid a finger on her lips.

'I know. But he says if I stay, Argović will find me, that he's going to put all his men on it. That it's a matter of pride for him after Josip. Pavle says I have to go, but I've told him I can't, that I *won't*.'

'Of course you can't,' she agreed. 'We'll hide you. How long can this situation last anyway? If you want to protect Dina, we can keep you at our house, or Ivo's. But you mustn't go away, Miro, not now, not after . . .'

She fell silent at the sound of footsteps on the stairs. I looked up and saw Pa in the doorway, anger written across his face. 'Jada,' he said loudly, 'Captain Nikolić wants to question you now. I'll wait for you here.' He moved aside to let Mother reach the stairs; seemed to deliberately draw back as if to avoid touching her.

'Your mother's wrong,' he said, as he sat next to me. 'I'm sorry, but she is. If Pavle says you have no choice, then you have no choice. You'll have to go. This is the reality of occupation: one side imposes, the other submits. And there are worse things than separation, even at a time like this.'

'How can you say that?' I hissed. 'We've lost our daughter. Don't you care?'

His eyes misted a little. 'How can you ask that? I adored that little girl, you know that. But it's all very well for your mother to say we'll hide you, or Ivo will hide you, but she doesn't think things through. They'll search for you, really search. And when they find you, they'll take you away along with whoever was hiding you, and anyone they think might have known about it. Including Dina. Is that what you want for her, Miro? If you love her, you have to go. It's the only way you can keep her safe.'

'I can't *go*. Don't you understand?'

'It's you that doesn't understand, Miro. I wish there was another way. But if you stay, it will bring more pain to Dina, not less.'

I looked at Pa, desperately fighting the realization that he was right. I couldn't bear the thought of leaving Dina, but if I stayed I was risking prison, or worse, for both of us. 'This is a nightmare,' I muttered.

'Yes,' said Pa simply. 'But I genuinely don't think you have a choice.'

'You should be ashamed, Petar.' Mother's voice was loud and angry as she stood at the top of the steps. 'Don't worry – they've both gone out, I don't know where. Pavle said to wait for him. Don't listen to your father, Miro; he's weak and scared.'

'I am *not*!' thundered Pa. 'I'm a realist. You think this is some game, Jada, where we can outsmart our enemies.'

'How dare you? If anyone understands it's not a game, it's me.'

'Then stop putting ideas into the boy's head that will get him killed. Because that's what'll happen if you don't accept that we have to abide by the rules imposed on us.'

'Pathetic,' snapped Mother. 'To think . . .'

'For God's sake, stop it, both of you.' I stood up and turned away from my parents. 'How is this helping? I need to think what to do.'

'Sorry, son.' Pa came and stood beside me. 'I can't imagine how hard this is for you. We just want to help.'

I bent down and picked up Pavle's cigarettes, lighting two and passing one to Pa. 'I don't think you can,' I said, watching the smoke twist up into the stale air. I stared out of the window and the minutes drifted by until suddenly the door slammed below, and we heard footsteps crossing the room below and coming up the stairs.

'Has he seen sense yet?' Pavle's face was flushed and he looked agitated. 'Have you made him understand? I'll drive him to Dubrovnik, but we have to go *now*. I can't hold Argović off much longer. I've been to see Dina. I've explained . . .'

'You've been to see *Dina*? Is she coming here? Will she see me?'

He shook his head. 'I'm sorry. She's still very angry, but I wanted her to know you're leaving only because I'm insisting on it. And you'll need . . .' I suddenly noticed the bag at his feet and my heart lurched at the thought of Dina folding my clothes, laying them neatly inside. 'I don't want . . . I think . . .' He stopped and looked down at his hands. 'There has been enough pain, I think.'

I looked at Pa. There seemed to be nothing else to say. If Dina wouldn't even come to say goodbye, it felt as if there was nothing left to fight for. I hugged Mother, felt the mix of desperation and fury in her body, tried to ignore the uncomfortable sense that in some way I was letting her down.

'Be strong, son,' said Pa, his eyes ablaze with an intensity designed to exclude Pavle from our farewell. 'Be strong and you'll be home soon.'

'Tell Dina I love her so much. And Ivo and Marjana too. Look after her for me, Pa. Keep her safe.'

He nodded mutely and turned, steering Mother firmly towards the stairs. He stopped and looked at Pavle. 'There has been enough pain, I think,' he said slowly, repeating his words. 'How right you are, *boy*.' The final word was laced with a vitriol I had never heard from his lips, and as he pushed dismissively past, my old friend closed his eyes, as if to shield himself from my father's contempt.

'So . . .' Pavle said to me, when the door had closed, 'we go then. Are you ready?'

CHAPTER 16

I didn't see the rooftops of Ljeta fade into the distance as we drove away in Pavle's JNA Jeep. Instead there was only darkness, my face pressed against the peeling leather seats, his greatcoat thrown over my body. With every jolt and turn of the wheel my head banged painfully against the door, and I felt sick at the thought of leaving Dina to return to a city that was dying on its feet. Fibres from the blanket started to catch in my mouth, my forehead ran with sweat and I sat up suddenly, the sharp winter light scorching my eyes.

'Get down.'

'I can't breathe. I need to think where to go, I can't go back to the shelter.' I thought suddenly of Damir. 'Take me to Lapad. The peninsula.'

'If I can get there. Now get back down. There's a roadblock in a minute.'

I did as he said, lay frozen beneath the blanket as the Jeep slowed to a halt. A window creaked open, papers rustled, a quick burst of laughter filtered down to me. Every muscle in my body was rigid, and then the engine fired up again and my forehead smacked against the door as we jolted away. I tried to remember where my boss's house was; somewhere on the shore in Lapad, close to the big hotels. Relief surged through me just at the thought of him. I knew Damir would be unchanged by what was happening, he would be thriving on it, the biggest story of his career.

The car stopped. 'Get out now. Quickly.'

I stepped on to the street, heard the door slam, a screech of tyres and Pavle was gone. I stood for a moment, looking around. Lapad had been a wealthy residential and smart tourist area: elegant villas draped in hibiscus and bougainvillea, gleaming hotels that stepped neatly down the rocky cliffs to the sea. Now it looked like what it was, a war zone, the street a mess of glass and brick and random objects. A broken chair poked out of a hedge on the street corner, across the road a television lay upended in a gutter.

'Dinars, dinars.' A gaggle of small, dirty-faced boys appeared behind me, skinny arms outstretched. 'Dinars, dinars.' In another life they would have been the boys outside the *slastičarna* in school shorts and crumpled shirts, counting up their pennies for ice cream. I reached into my pocket and pulled out a few coins; they whooped with delight and scampered away across the rubble-strewn street.

Damir's villa was barely recognizable. Several of the neat green shutters hung limply off their hinges, the terracotta roof tiles that had dovetailed so perfectly lay blackened and messy. I walked up the empty steps that had once bloomed with pots of jasmine and geraniums and knocked loudly at the door, trying to ready myself for the appearance of my boss.

But it wasn't Damir who opened the door. Instead a gaunt woman with pink-rimmed eyes and hair scraped back into a tight bun appeared. It took a moment for me to recognize her as Serenja, Damir's elegant wife. Last time I had seen her had been at a dinner for a visiting academic; her gleaming blonde hair had perfectly framed a face that sparkled with radiance and wit. Now her features were blank and free of make-up, dark roots exposed at her scalp.

'Miro? It is Miro, isn't it? What are you doing here? Come in, for God's sake, don't just stand on the street, it's too dangerous.'

I followed her into the hall and was instantly surrounded by the high-pitched tones of children bickering, a woman's voice trying to calm them. 'My sister,' said Serenja, with a half-smile. 'They lived in Zacjňan – when the troops came they had to flee. They just appeared, with nothing but the clothes they were wearing.'

'It happened with my brother,' I said, remembering Goran's sudden arrival on my doorstep, the joy of seeing his face. 'He got out of Krno.'

'In one piece?'

I nodded. 'Just about.'

'Lucky man.'

She gestured into the lounge and I followed her, taking in the bare walls, the mattresses by the fire, all the other furniture pushed to one side. 'Like what we've done with the place? Every time a shell hit nearby, something would fall off the walls, so in the end I stripped them bare. And we have no heating so we all sleep together for warmth. We live between here and the kitchen. The rest of the house . . .' She raised her palms and smiled weakly.

She pulled a chair out from a group stacked against the wall and I sat down while she wrestled another free for herself. 'So, my unexpected guest, how do you find yourself here?'

I told her as briefly as I could, trying to rush the words out so there was no time for images of Irina to fire up in my mind. As I faltered over the words she laid her hand on my arm and I sensed the compassion in her eyes, but I couldn't look up, didn't stop. 'If I'd stayed in Ljeta and they found me, they would have arrested my wife and my parents . . . I didn't know where else to go. I hope you don't mind me coming here. I hope Damir . . .' A thought struck me suddenly. 'Where *is* Damir? Is he OK?'

Serenja stretched into her pocket and produced a packet of cigarettes, lit one and passed them to me. 'Oh, Damir is OK, more than OK. He's at the Ragusa mostly, having the time of his life.'

I shifted awkwardly in my seat.

'I'm sorry, that's unfair. Of course he doesn't want any of this to be happening. But he's a newsman and one of the world's biggest stories is happening right on his doorstep. He's at the Ragusa more than here; it's dangerous to move between the two. He's obsessed by the idea that what's happening in Dubrovnik could finally provoke some action from the Germans or the Brits – that it's the story that will finally make the EU *act*. But I worry for him. At this rate it won't be a sniper that gets him, it'll be overwork.'

'Well, if he's not here, maybe I should go there.'

She shook her head. 'Don't be ridiculous. You're exhausted, in shock. You need to catch up with yourself. And there's plenty of room. We all sleep down here, but you can get warm in front of the fire, wrap yourself in blankets and take the smallest room upstairs. I'm not taking no for an answer. You'll stay here until I'm sure you're not going to collapse at any moment. I'm not having you on my conscience as well as my husband.'

I stayed at Serenja's house for three weeks. The first ten days slipped by almost unnoticed; after one night I fell ill, brought low, she said, by grief and exhaustion. By the time I was better it was Christmas and Damir finally came home from the Ragusa, thinner and greyer than I remembered, but otherwise unchanged and full of stories of the foreign reporters and their hard-drinking, uncompromising ways. We spent New Year's Eve sitting alone in his kitchen, and while I told him what had happened in Ljeta, he smoked and tut-tutted, pouring the wine that was easier to find in the city than clean water.

'Well, there's only one thing for you, my boy,' he said, when the bottle was empty and my throat was sore from talking. 'You're coming back to the Ragusa with me. We need to put you to work. Make 1992 a better year for you, eh?'

Damir wasn't joking when he talked of putting me to work. From the moment I set foot in the hotel, he made sure my days were full: using the English I had learned over the years in my father's restaurant to translate interviews, guiding new reporters through the back streets of Dubrovnik, even doing a little filming with Stefan when Krystof, his regular cameraman, sprained his knee running from a shell. The days shot past in a blur of barked orders from Damir and confused questions from the foreign crews who seemed endlessly bewildered by the racial mix in my country and even more so by the growing problems in neighbouring Bosnia. As the weeks rolled by it was the word on everybody's lips; first the Bosnian president, Izetbegović, declared independence, then the Bosnian Serbs declared their own Serbian Republic within the country.

'It's a ticking bomb,' Stefan told us, when he and Krystof came back from a foray across the border. 'Entire villages are on alert; you go out at night and there are old men on patrol with antique hunting pistols and shotguns and weird bits of farm equipment. Christ knows how they think they're going to stand up to real soldiers when they come. And they will come; it's when, not if. It's a place right on the brink.'

The phrase echoed horribly in my mind, reminding me of the very first evening I had stepped through the doors of the Ragusa. How long ago that seemed, and yet there was a terrible sense of history repeating itself, of Bosnia falling headlong into the abyss that had swallowed up my country.

But if my days were busy, at night the ghosts surrounded me. Irina haunted my dreams and thoughts of Dina proved impossible to keep at bay. I couldn't bring myself to join the drinking and grandstanding that went on in the bar; talk of piled-up corpses and gun-toting soldiers rampaging through villages made my constant fears for Goran even more real. Instead I spent hours in the makeshift editing room, watching endless uncut footage in an attempt to black out the scenes that played over and over in my head: Dina lowering our daughter's body into the ground, sitting alone in our house, Argović questioning her, again and again – Where was I? Where had I gone? Didn't she know? She must know, she MUST.

But one evening, as the first whispers of spring were beginning to rise from the winter darkness, I couldn't face sitting alone in the editing suite yet again. To my surprise the bar was almost empty; I laid down some of the deutschmarks I'd been paid for a translating job and took a bottle of Stock and a glass to a table in the darkest corner of the room. Tonight I was going to allow myself to think of Irina; I closed my eyes and instantly she was before me, wispy dark curls framing wide eyes that stared so trustingly into mine. But within seconds a loud, clattering noise caused my eyes to flick open and I watched, with a sinking heart, as Nic Richaud threw himself down in the chair opposite.

'*Mon Dieu*, what a day. May I?' He reached for the bottle of Stock and poured himself a huge measure of brandy. 'You're a bunch of ruthless fuckers. I mean, hats off, you guys really know how to play the game.'

I said nothing, hoping he would get the message and go off to harangue a more receptive audience.

He looked at me. 'Haven't you heard the rumours?'

I shook my head, interested in spite of myself.

'The meetings? Between your lot and the Serbs? Secret discussions, talking about how to carve up Bosnia between you. No one's supposed to know, but old Damir's got a mate with an ear to the ground. He reckons these negotiations have been going on for months, that Tuđman and Milošević have always seen splitting Bosnia between them as the endgame. Pretty nasty, if you ask me.'

I remembered the first time I had heard the rumour: when the two men met at Tito's villa almost a year ago, and came away promising both a Greater Serbia and a Greater Croatia. A deal with the devil, Pa had called it; the last words anyone had spoken before Dina arrived back in the kitchen and announced the baby was on its way. Something tightened around my heart at the memory of that extraordinary night, and I leaned forward, poured myself more brandy and tipped it back in one gulp. Nic stared at me.

'Didn't think you drank. Clearly I was wrong. Don't normally see you in the bar. Special occasion, is it?'

'Birthday.'

'*Félicitations*.' He grinned and tossed a packet of Marlboro Red on to the table. 'How old are you? Eighteen?'

I shook my head. 'Oh no. No. It's not *my* birthday. It's my daughter's. My. Beautiful. Daughter.' I flicked the lighter with each word, watching the flame shoot up into the murky air.

Nic leaned in to light a cigarette. 'I didn't know you had a daughter. How old?'

'One. She'd be one today. But she died. So I was told.'

He stared at me.

I stared back, locking eyes with him, daring him to say something callous or inappropriate; anything that would give me the excuse to take the rage and grief that was piling up inside me and smack my fist into his face.

'You were *told*?'

Suddenly it stopped being a good idea, this plan to goad Nic into saying something stupid so I could thump him. It stopped being a good idea and it started to hurt.

'I wasn't . . .' I closed my eyes and took a breath. 'Meningitis. I had to come here, get the medicine she needed. It was December, you know? The day the shelling was really bad? I saw you on the street. But I couldn't get back in time. Too late.'

To my astonishment Nic laid a hand on my arm and an expression crossed his face that looked like genuine sorrow.

'I have a daughter,' he said. 'Claire. She'll be . . . fourteen next month.'

'You've a daughter? Are you married?'

'I was. Stunning woman. Valérie. She was a model. For a while there it was . . . but, well, let's just say ours was a crowded marriage. We separated when Claire was six. They live in Switzerland now. I barely see her. But I write to her. Every week.'

'Does she write back?'

He smiled. 'When she feels like it. But such letters. She'll write wonderful novels when she's older. I try to get to Geneva a few times a year and we spend a little time together. In winter we ice-skate – she's wonderful, and even her old dad can stumble around on the ice with her.' He fumbled in his wallet and pulled out a picture. 'Here. Isn't she gorgeous?'

I looked at the photo. A slim, auburn-haired girl looked back at me, cheeky smile on an open face, and when I glanced across at Nic there was a longing in his eyes that was no less powerful than my own.

'She's lovely. You're lucky.'

'To you perhaps. To you, who's lost a daughter.' He looked down into his glass for a moment. 'That's a terrible thing I can't begin to imagine . . . But the truth is I've lost Claire as well. To her I'm some character she wants to put in one of her books, an exotic figure who appears occasionally but has little connection to her life. I don't even know what colour her school uniform is, does she like pain au chocolat or brioche?'

'Well, try harder, spend more time with her.'

'She has another father,' said Nic slowly. 'The man Valérie married. He knows whether to give her brioche, and what lessons she has on Wednesdays and who her friends are. You can't have two people fulfil this role in your life. And so I must be something different, something extraordinary, unique. She'll be proud of her old dad at least, even if she doesn't really know him.'

'I had no idea.' And I didn't. I knew nothing about Nic, or any of the other reporters I worked with, nothing beyond the characters they had created for themselves in the strange microcosm we all inhabited. Life started afresh each morning, with thick heads and short memories. Gratification was fast; if you got the story it was a good day, if someone else got it, bad. There was no life beyond that, no backstories, and that suited me just fine. I wondered who else knew about the broken marriage and the lost daughter, and how much it played into his recklessness, the careless front he shared with the world.

'Remember her,' he said suddenly. 'Your daughter. Fix on a few specific memories and remember them each day. Otherwise you'll start to forget. Think them through over and over again and gradually they'll imprint themselves on your mind. That way you'll always have . . . What was her name?'

I swallowed hard, stubbed out my cigarette and lit another. 'Irina.'

'Lovely name.' He sloshed more brandy into my glass and poured himself a slug, lifting his glass towards me. 'To Irina, on her first birthday.'

I felt my throat tighten. 'To Irina.'

Our eyes met and he tossed his brandy back, ran his fingers through his hair and stood up. 'Now come on, you lazy fucker. Stop sitting here feeling sorry for yourself. Jakob's heading back to Poland tomorrow and we've got some serious drinking to do before he goes.'

After that night, Nic seemed to befriend me. We never again spoke of Irina or Claire, but I spent fewer evenings alone in the editing suite and more time in the bar with him and the other reporters, although I was often aware of Damir watching me with slight concern in his eyes. Sometimes Nic would ask me to accompany him on trips into Bosnia, paying me to talk our way through checkpoints, explain the racial issues that were threatening to engulf the tiny country, how they differed from village to village, town to town.

'You're all crazy,' he said to me one afternoon as we walked back to the Ragusa in the warm spring sunshine. 'All of you. Decades of everyone managing to get along and coexist and now some mega-lomaniac makes a few good speeches and the whole world fucking explodes. Not that your guy is any better. You're all just as bad as each other. You fight for your own country, but you think nothing of carving up somewhere else for your own needs.'

I said nothing, but Nic's brutal honesty made me feel uncomfortable. Rumours were flying about the army pulling out of Dubrovnik, that Tuđman had negotiated the withdrawal in return for Croatian troops leaving Bosnia. If true, it meant the siege would finally be over, and if Dubrovnik was freed it wouldn't be long before the troops fled Ljeta as well. Quite what it meant for Bosnia, suddenly bereft of any force who could adequately engage with the Serbs, didn't bear thinking about.

'Don't brand us as all the same,' I said hotly. 'That's just fucking lazy. We're only interested in fighting for land we actually have a right to. Why is the army here in the first place? The Serbs never had any claim to Dubrovnik; everyone's Croatian down here.'

'Well, if the rumours are true they'll be gone by the end of the week.'

'Don't underestimate them. They'll go when they're ready, and they won't go without some sort of final showdown. You guys make me laugh. You think it's all about Bosnia now, but the story's not finished here. You really think they're just going to climb in their tanks and drive away?'

I had no idea how prescient our conversation was to prove; within days the city streets shuddered beneath falling shells, doubly shocking after the weeks of relative peace. Reporters began to flock back to the Ragusa, and I walked in one afternoon to find the lobby in chaos and two badly injured men on the floor.

'Are you a doctor?' A man pulled me by the arm and I shook my head.

'No, no, I'm sorry. What happened?'

'Some scuffle at the checkpoint on the Ljeta road. They're BBC.

He'll be OK, I think, but the other one . . .' I looked down. One of the men had pulled himself into a sitting position and was staring across the lobby, his eyes dazed and blank. The other lay slumped on the floor, apparently unconscious, while a woman knelt next to him, pressing a balled-up cloth against his ripped, bloodied shirt.

'They're here.' The doors crashed open and four men walked in carrying a dirty stretcher; one of them crouched down next to the woman.

'Just him?'

She turned towards the man hunched against the wall. 'Jim?' He opened his eyes slowly. 'Are you buggered, really buggered, or *Christ, I think I might die if I don't go to hospital* buggered?'

He shifted slightly. 'Really buggered, I think. Sorry, Marian. It's my leg.'

'Two,' she said. 'Jesus, I'm fucked.'

Marian Wiseman. I suddenly remembered the conversation we had shared all those months ago on the very first night Damir bought me to the Ragusa. I watched as two of the medics lifted the unconscious man on to the stretcher, while the other two carefully levered Jim to his feet.

'Call my wife,' he said. 'Tell her I'm fine.'

'Of course.' Her voice was unexpectedly soft. 'I'll be in to see you later.'

The doors swung back to let them through and within seconds a surge of people filled the space where the men had been lying.

'Are you OK? Were you with them?' I laid a hand on Marian's arm and she looked up, surprised.

'God, yes, I'm fine. Not a scratch.' She looked at me, clear blue eyes examining my face. 'Have we met?'

'Months ago. Miro Denković – Zagreb TV. I was a cameraman. Now, well, I'm kind of freelancing.'

She raised her eyebrows, gestured towards the bar. 'Have a drink with me.' It was an instruction, not an invitation. I followed her into the dimly lit space and sank into a chair, watching as she walked to a nearby table, picked up a bottle of whisky and poured two glasses, batting away the good-natured complaints.

'I'd heard there was a spare camera guy hanging around,' she said, passing me a glass and tipping hers back in one go. 'You might be the very answer to my prayers. That was my cameraman who just went out the door on a stretcher. Hit by a sniper at the bloody Ljeta checkpoint, can you believe it? Weeks in Sarajevo, where the hotel's actually on Sniper Alley, and he gets shot here. Great bloke. Nasty wound. Anyway, point is I need a replacement. Now.'

'Do you mean me?'

Her face twitched with annoyance. 'No, I mean the sodding barman. Of course I mean you.'

'You want me to work for you? I mean, you're the BBC. How do you know I'm good enough? Don't you want to see some footage or something?'

'Christ almighty,' she banged down her glass and frowned at me. 'D'you think I've got time for showreels and references? My camera-man just got *shot*. This is a war, not fucking human resources, and I don't have time . . . What's happening here is happening now, right now. When the army withdraws it's going to be an utter humilia-tion for Milošević, and if my coverage isn't shit-hot then, well, then I'm fucked. Do you know what they'll say, my bosses in their nice comfy offices in London? Why the hell didn't you get Jim off his stretcher – he's not fucking dead, is he? I've got to file a story today and tomorrow, and they've got to be good, better than good, because I'm not one of the boys, because . . .' She tailed off, took a breath. 'Anyway, that's beside the point. But don't sit there all wide-eyed and ask me if I need to see examples of your work. What I need is a cameraman. And you clearly need a job. So what do you say? Want to work for the best news network on the planet?'

CHAPTER 17

I had forgotten how good a benevolent sun could feel against my skin. Blades of grass tickled my knees, beads of sweat slipped from my forehead down the sides of my neck, somewhere along my lower arm an insect was doing its feathery dance. I didn't raise my hand to sweep it away. I didn't move. I just lay like a dead man in the sunshine, lulled by the gentle rushing of the river that surged beneath the bridge and the silence that drifted past on the warm breeze.

'Time to go.' I opened my eyes and squinted up at Marian. She had appeared silently and was sat above me on the wall of the bridge, sunglasses on top of her head, shirtsleeves rolled up. 'It's heavenly here though, isn't it? Almost as if the war isn't happening.'

I sat up slowly, brushing the grass from my arms and trousers. 'I know. Just over those hills . . .' I didn't need to finish my sentence. We both knew what lay beyond the quiet valley we had come to. 'So, did it work?'

We fell into step as we walked back to the van. 'Kind of. It's not really the story I'd hoped for. It might look like everyone is still managing to get along here, but scratch the surface and it's all very different. Ana – the Muslim lady – she told me all about how her father had been killed by Serbian death squads in the Second World War. Then Javor and Senka, their parents lost the family farm to the Ustaše, so they hate the Croats. And Kristina and Duško, the Bosnian

Croats, well, they'd cross the road to avoid Javor and Senka – purely because they're Serbian.'

'So the whole multiracial street idea?'

'All we've done is show a time bomb waiting to go off. But what's really horrifying is that none of them could hold a candle to your lot. I got talking to some men in the *kafana*, Croatian guys who had fought in your war, up near Knin. You'd have thought—'

'Was he one of them?' I pulled out my wallet and took out the small photo of Goran I kept alongside a picture of Dina and Irina that I could never bring myself to look at.

Marian peered at the image and shook her head. 'Nope. Sorry. Is that . . . ?'

'My brother. It's stupid, I know. No chance it would be him. He was in Vukovar, he probably isn't even . . .' I couldn't finish the sentence, brushed the smooth metal of the St Christopher that hung around my neck, remembered him suddenly in my garden; *You're so loved.* Was I? Still?

'Don't,' Marian passed me back the picture and her fingers tightened around my wrist. 'If I've learned anything in this job, it's never assume . . . not the worst, nor the best. Until you *know*, until there's proof, nothing is ever certain. And d'you know what, Miro? I'd be glad that your brother wasn't one of those men – they were so angry and bitter, talking about how the JNA – or the army of Greater Serbia as they called it – had stolen parts of their country, and how they weren't going to let it happen again in Bosnia. It's not even their war, you know? But they were so vicious.'

I said nothing as we climbed into the car and began the slow, tortuous journey back to Dubrovnik. We had come to Jaradić, a Bosnian town not far from the border with Croatia, famous for its mixed population, where Muslims, Croats and Serbs were continuing to live side by side on the same streets. It was a story worth telling, Marian had said, a story that disproved Milošević's wild rhetoric about the genocide of Serbs in Bosnia, that proved coexistence was possible. She had wanted to do the story in Sarajevo, a city that prided itself on its multiracial population and the equanimity with which Serbs lived next to Croats, Muslims alongside Jews. But in recent weeks the place had exploded, barricades had gone up, and Sarajevans were more concerned with surviving than with talking to reporters about how they once lived.

As the walls of Dubrovnik came into view a deep, pulsating roar rumbled up the hill towards us and smoke billowed from the rooftops.

'They're shelling again,' said Marian. 'You were right, Miro, those bastards aren't going to go quietly. Bojan, put your bloody foot down. I want to get in there while it's happening, show that it isn't over here, not by a long way.'

'Are you crazy?' I leaned forward to try and see her face. 'We'll be hugely exposed down there.'

She turned to look at me. 'Well, I'm not filming from the terrace of the bloody Ragusa. I want to do it in front of the Pile Gate, with all that smoke and shit behind me.'

'It's too dangerous.'

'Which is exactly why people will watch. I'm sick of this city being off people's radar. If they won't watch because they don't care what's happening here, then maybe they'll watch to see if I get shot.'

'Aren't you making yourself the story?' I said, only half-joking. 'Isn't that what you said about Nic? That there's no story that fascinates him as much as his own?'

Marian shook her head and smiled and I knew there was nothing either of us could say to dissuade her. Over the weeks we had been working together I'd come to realize that once she made a decision she became unstoppable, determined to manoeuvre her way to the very front of wherever the action was. I respected her for it, understood she was driven by a need to prove herself as fearless as the men who surrounded her in the bar each evening. But there was

something more – a much-distilled version of Nic's recklessness –
and I was never quite sure just how far she was prepared to go to
get her story.

'I'll take you there,' growled Bojan. 'But I'm not waiting around.
I'm not going to be a sitting duck, waiting for a fucking shell to
land right on my head. You can walk back, or run. Crazy fuckers,
the pair of you.'

'Fine.' Marian's face was set, implacable. None of us spoke as the
Jeep juddered past the Ragusa and on down towards the harbour.
Just as I was lifting my camera out of the car, the sky split with a
shriek that bottomed out into a great shuddering roar. I raised my
eyebrows at Marian, but she simply slammed the car door and began
to walk down the steps that led to the Pile Gate.

'You're going to get us both killed,' I shouted. 'You don't have to
do this.'

'Just get it running,' she said. I flicked the switch and lifted the
camera to my shoulder. Short snaps of sniper fire ricocheted off the
walls; a woman's screams twisted up into the air and were abruptly
cut short.

'Terror is back on the streets of Dubrovnik today, as an army that was
supposed to be departing the city has instead begun to . . .'

Another huge crash rocked the spot where we were standing and
bits of shattered brick and masonry showered down at our feet.

'Don't stop filming,' she yelled, and I tightened my grip around
the camera as she continued to speak, her voice calm and clear above
the constant rumble of explosions.

'Did you get it?'

I nodded. Another shell screamed overhead, exploding nearby. I
felt a sudden spike of adrenalin, a thrill at being so exposed and yet
remaining untouched.

'Then let's go.' A third shell shrieked above us. 'Come on, Miro,
we'd better move.'

She grabbed my hand and we ran back up the steps in the direction of the hotel, keeping close to the walls, brickwork grazing my elbow, until I felt the skin tear away and the soft ooze of blood against my shirt. Another explosion, nearer this time; the noise ricocheted into my brain and I pulled her into a doorway.

'Shit, that was close.'

'Jesus.'

The sky split again, and as the noise rumbled around us she buried her head in my shoulder, both of us tight against the wall. The ground shuddered beneath my feet, my heart thudded against hers, it felt unbelievable we had been out there, standing around while rockets and shells hurtled towards us, missing us by inches as we ran for cover. I felt a strange desire to laugh, to mock the Serbs for the futility of what they were trying to do. Hadn't we outrun death? Weren't we invincible? The walls shook as another vast crash exploded nearby and Marian tightened her arms around me.

When I felt her press into me, it was as if the world began to shrink; I could almost see us from above, two bodies locked together in a tiny corner of a city that was shattering around them. All my senses felt heightened; her skin smelt warm and sweet, the fingers of my right hand burned against the waistband of her trousers. Without meaning to, without conscious thought, I found myself imagining undoing them, slipping her trousers off, exploring what lay beneath.

Once the thought had begun to seep into my mind, I couldn't think of anything else. Her breasts pressed against my ribs, the outline of her bra bit tantalizingly into my skin. I stared straight ahead, trying to read a faded poster that was in the window of a shop; a rock concert, where to buy tickets, who was the singer, did I remember him? Anything to drag my thoughts away from the strange, uncontrollable longing that was building up inside me.

'Miro,' she drew back suddenly, looked up at me. I couldn't stop staring at her lips, desperate to kiss them; I wanted to force my tongue into her mouth, feel her push me back against the wall, tear off her clothes, smother her skin with mine. My body felt on fire with energy and fear and adrenalin; I wanted – needed – to do something with it, kiss her, be inside her, feel something *real.*

I looked into her face and something inside me twisted with a mix of excitement and terror; it was in her eyes too, a strange, manic longing, *Come on, let's do it, fuck me here right now, I need you to, I want you to.*

'Serb maniacs.' A man ran past, carrying a woman in his arms. His words snapped me back into reality and I realized the explosions had stopped, the world was quiet again. Marian pulled away slightly, ran her fingers through her hair and gave a short, nervous laugh.

'Well. Seems like things have quietened down. Shall we make a run for it?'

I nodded, unsure of what to say. Had the whole moment been just in my head? And if so, what had I nearly done? What about Dina? If that man hadn't walked past at exactly that moment, would I be kissing her now, up against the wall, hands everywhere, totally out of control?

'Let's go,' I said, unable to meet her eyes. As we began to run, I turned my head to glance back at the doorway, telling myself it was a moment of madness, nothing more.

'Heard of the Bureau for Population Exchange?'

'Afternoon, Marian.' I pulled up a chair and allowed myself a half-smile; she never had time for pleasantries, always straight to the facts. 'Have you been here all day?' The table was stacked with papers and notebooks, half-drunk glasses of water and a coffee cup full of cigarette ends. Energy sparked off her.

'I'm serious. Do you know what it is?' She stared at me and I felt a slight shiver at the memory of what had so nearly happened in that shop doorway, a week earlier. Guilt and shame flooded my system every time I thought about it, along with bewilderment at how this cool, blonde Englishwoman had provoked such ferocious, uncontrollable desire.

'No, Marian,' I said obediently. 'I don't know what it is.'

'Well, I had a call from an old mate on the *Chronicle* this morning. He's up in northern Bosnia, and d'you know what's going on up there? Forget the usual stuff – rape and torture – these guys are much more *civilized*. If you're Muslim or Croat, and you want to flee the town where you live – probably to avoid being raped or tortured – you have to go to this Bureau and basically sign documents that give away everything – your house, car, business premises, everything. Then you can leave. With nothing.'

'They can't do that.'

'I think you'll find they can. And they are. And d'you know why they're getting away with it? Because everyone's looking the other way, everyone's looking at Sarajevo. Half the world's news media is in that city – politicians, peacekeepers, journalists – and everyone is so focused on what's going on there that we're all missing what's happening in the rest of the country. There's a genocide going on up there; it's like the fucking Second World War.'

'So Goran was right.'

'Goran?'

'My brother, the one in the picture. He was in the Krajina when the Serbs first overran the villages up there. He told me . . . *čišćenji terena*. Cleansing the earth. He saw it first, knew what it meant.'

'Well, don't take this the wrong way, but from what I hear, what's happening up there makes the Krajina look like a kids' tea party. Did you see the TF1 footage last night?'

I nodded. We had all watched it, and I had thought of Nic behind the camera, filming the long trail of refugees leaving the villages, haunted faces, bodies bruised and dirty. Every so often one of them would gabble into the camera, fingers clenched, voice high and raised, and an unseen voice would calmly translate words that barely seemed credible: 'They came into our village, dragged away the women, we could hear them screaming, they made boys run into the woods like animals while they shot at them and laughed . . .'

'I'm going up there,' she said. 'To Burjska. At the end of the week. Will you come with me? It'll be tough, but people need to know.'

'I can't.' The words shot out of my mouth too fast, it sounded like fear. 'I need to be here. If the siege ends, if things change . . .' I tailed off, unsure what to say. As far as I was aware, Marian knew nothing about my situation; like all the reporters I came without any life beyond the daily occurrences at the Ragusa. 'You're right to go though. It's like you say – everyone's in Sarajevo.'

'I know I'm right,' she said coolly. 'Just like you're wrong. We're a good team, Miro, and nothing is going to happen here for weeks.'

I looked at her; she held my gaze. Nothing in it gave any hint that she was thinking about what nearly happened in the shop doorway, and yet there was a challenge in her look. Something like tension crackled between us and I found myself in some strange, contradictory no-man's-land where I was both relieved she was going and yet hugely disappointed she would no longer be here.

'I can't go, Marian, I'm sorry.' She tutted slightly, threw her cigarettes and pens into her bag and swept off the terrace, leaving me feeling both humiliated and genuinely regretful. Damir had been right – work had been a distraction from my grief, but as the weeks stretched into months it had also become something I felt proud of. If I had to be away from Dina, it was better to be doing something worthwhile, and I took pride in being part of a team that showed people the truth of what was happening in my country even if, as Marian repeatedly told me, our stories were often buried in late-night slots, or didn't make the cut at all.

'Annoyed the Iron Lady, have we?' said Stefan as I passed him on the terrace. It was his favourite nickname for Marian, based on

Britain's steely ex-Prime Minister. I laughed, but the feeling of humiliation grew, and I walked out of the hotel to try to get some space.

Almost immediately a car horn barked noisily. I kept walking,
eyes fixed on the ground. The sound came again, longer this time,
an impatient, imperious yell. I turned; across the road a JNA Jeep was
parked in the shadow of a plane tree, and as I squinted through the
sunlight the man behind the wheel lifted his hand in a half-wave. I
stiffened. *Pavle.*

I ran to the Jeep, pulled open the door and climbed in beside him.
'What are you doing here?' His face had grown thinner, shadowed by
a beard; the skin around his eyes was grey and sallow. 'Can I come
home? Is Dina with you? Is she OK?'

He raised his hand as if to bat away questions. 'I had business in
Dubrovnik today, thought I might see you.' His voice tailed off and I
clawed the torn leather seat with impatience. 'I came to tell you she's
all right. She's managing. At first everyone was worried; she didn't
go out, wouldn't see anyone. But slowly, as the warmer weather has
come, I see her sometimes in the garden. She seems . . . a little better.'

Our garden. I could see it so clearly: Dina tying the long tendrils
of the bean plants to the canes, Irina asleep in her pram beneath
the almond tree. I ground my teeth into my lower lip and clenched
my hands tighter around the seat until the tips of my fingers stung
with the pressure.

'And your brother . . .'

My stomach lurched. 'Goran?'

'He's alive. Your mother had a phone call. Tara – is that her name?
– she had a letter from him. Your father told Dina and she wanted
me to tell you.'

'Oh my God, Pavle, that's such amazing news. I thought, I
thought . . .' I stopped and swallowed.

'And you? Everyone will want to know how you're managing.
Dina, your parents, Ivo, Marjana.' He laughed, a short bitter sound.

'D'you know the irony? They all blame me. They all think it's my fault you're here.'

I dragged my thoughts away from Goran and stared at him. 'Well, whose fault is it if it isn't yours? If your fucking army wasn't in my town.'

'It's my town too. I've as much right to be there as you, as anyone.'

'Even wearing that?' I pointed at his army fatigues. 'Anyway, it's Dina I want to hear about.' I thought of the nights I had spent in the editing suite, watching endless reams of discarded footage in an attempt to drown out the grief and anxiety about what was happening to those I loved back at home. 'Does she have people around her? In the evenings too? Is she safe?'

'I would never let anything happen to her,' he said. 'She was questioned at first, they all were – your mum and dad, even your aunt and uncle. Argović threatened to imprison them all, but I think once he realized you'd gone for good and there was nothing he could do . . .' He shrugged. 'They were lucky. He can be a sadistic bastard.'

'I don't *care* about Argović. Tell me about my wife.'

'There's not much more to say. She sees a lot of Karena, I think. Occasionally I see your father with her in the garden.' He paused and looked down at his hands. 'Sometimes I go in. One evening I went around and she looked so thin and tired and there was nothing in the kitchen. So I bought some meat and *fuži* and made her a meal, sat with her while she ate it. I do it sometimes – at least then we know she eats.'

I could barely believe what I was hearing. 'You do *what*? You cook for my wife? In my house?' My heart was thumping hard against my ribcage. 'You bastard. You fucking *bastard*. Is that why you made me leave Ljeta? So when I was out of the way you could—'

'No.' Pavle turned to face me, but his eyes were utterly unreadable. 'Think that of me if you like, but do you really believe that of Dina? Whatever's happened, it's you she loves. You're all she ever thinks about, you and Irina.'

'Don't you dare speak my daughter's name.'

He was silent for a moment. 'Don't you see? We both have nothing. She's lost her family, and what do I have besides this?' He plucked at his lapel. 'We're both alone, and I think it's a kind of comfort for her to be around someone else who's lost everything. Can't you understand that?'

I looked at the man sitting next to me and realized every time I saw him he became more of an enigma; the bully who slapped Jelena, the old friend who saved me on the harbour, the familiar stranger who sat in my kitchen, alone with my wife. 'If you lay a finger on her, I'll kill you.' I felt cold suddenly, strangely calm. 'Even if she never forgives me, if she never wants me back, if you so much as touch her . . .'

'I've *told* you,' he said, his voice growing loud and tense, 'it's you she wants. Only you. She was desperate for me to get news of you when I told her I was coming here. She feels nothing for me.'

'I don't care. I don't want you setting foot in my house again. Do you hear me? I'll know. When I come back, if I find out—'

'You'd rather she sat alone then, with her thoughts? Her memories?'

Something snapped inside me and I grabbed Pavle and shoved him against the door of the Jeep, our faces so close I could feel his breath on my skin. Unexpectedly the door flew open and his body flicked backwards, legs pinned on the seat beneath mine, only my hands on his shirt stopping his head smacking on to the ground. I leaned my body on his and pulled his face up to mine. 'Leave my wife alone,' I whispered.

'Fuck you.'

I pulled my hands away and he fell backwards, legs pulling out from mine, slithering on to the street. I pushed open the other door and stepped into the sunlight, staggering away on legs that shook as I walked.

'Miro.' His voice spun down the silent street. '*Miro.*'

I turned; Pavle was standing on the ridge of the Jeep, the upper half of his body poking out above the roof. 'Got to go,' he yelled, and his voice was high and a little wild. 'Your wife'll have dinner on the table.'

I turned then, ran back towards the car, but he slithered back into the seat, started the engine and was already pulling away as I brought my arms down hard on the back windows. The wheels kicked up dust as I yelled his name and in the heat and fury of the moment I spun around and slammed my fist into the wall, sending pain shearing up from my knuckles with such force that I fell to my knees, fighting the urge to throw up in the street.

'Miro?' I looked up to see Stefan standing behind me. 'Are you all right? Your hand's bleeding.'

I wiped my other hand across my face and slowly stood up. Stefan took a handkerchief out of his pocket and I held it to my bloodied knuckles. 'Come on,' he said, his face shadowed with concern. 'I'll buy you a drink. You look like you need one.'

I followed him into the hotel, but when we entered the bar the only table with free seats was where Marian was sitting. I threw myself down and tossed back the large shot of vodka Stefan passed to me, immediately holding out my glass for another.

'You OK?' Marian looked at me curiously. 'You're going at it a bit strong, aren't you?'

I closed my eyes and in that moment an image shot through my mind, an image so painful I actually couldn't breathe. Pavle and Dina *together*, naked, his hands on her legs, her breasts, his lips on her neck, her mouth murmuring his name. I sat up straight, ran my fingers through my hair and looked at Marian.

'I've changed my mind.' The words felt unreal, even as I said them. 'About Burjska. Have you found anyone else yet?'

She shook her head.

'Then count me in. I'm coming with you.'

CHAPTER 18

I woke suddenly. According to my watch I had only been asleep an hour, yet I had had a long vivid dream, a dream of Dina, where she was crying, sitting beneath an olive tree in a clearing in the Konavle woods, a shady secret place she and I had discovered together that first perfect summer when we became lovers. I sat up in the darkness and suddenly remembered my reckless decision to go to Burjska with Marian. What would Dina think if she heard I was hundreds of miles away, involved in a conflict that wasn't even ours? Since Irina's death I had to prove I would never put anyone or anything before her. I would tell Marian I couldn't go.

It didn't even occur to me to wait to tell her in the morning, that a few hours would make no difference. I stumbled out of my room and felt my way down the inky black corridor, counting the door handles to find her room. I knocked lightly, ran my tongue around my mouth, recoiling at the taste of stale vodka and cigarette phlegm.

'Who is it?' She sounded irritated, a little anxious.

'It's me, Miro. Sorry, I know it's late. I need to talk to you.'

The door clicked open slowly and her face appeared through the gloom. She was almost unrecognizable; an old T-shirt skimmed her hips, her face was free of make-up and her normally sleek hair was tangled and messy. She looked about fifteen. Guilt shot through me.

'Do you know what time it is? What on earth do you want?'

'I'm sorry, really sorry, I can't come to Bosnia with you,' I said, rushing the words. 'I shouldn't have said I would, but something happened. I was angry and . . . a part of me really does want to come, but I just . . . I just can't.'

'You're not coming? Well, you'd better bloody come in and explain why.' She pulled the door back and I stepped into the darkness. 'This is pretty shit. One minute you say one thing, the next something different.'

She flicked on the light switch but nothing happened; I felt my way to the chair and sat down carefully. Marian sat on the bed opposite me, pulling a cardigan around her to cover her legs. 'I'm really sorry,' I said slowly. 'Something happened. It's no excuse but I – I just went a bit crazy. I know it's not fair on you. But I know you'll be—'

'Fine.' The word snapped out. 'Of course I'll be fine. It's my job, isn't it? And I'll find another cameraman and it will be . . . fine.' Her voice faded, and as I peered at her through the gloom I thought she was trying not to cry. I stared, almost in disbelief, as a tear tipped over the rim of her right eye and began to trace a line down her cheek. Marian didn't cry. Marian was the toughest woman I had ever met.

'God, I'm so sorry. I've let you down.'

'It's OK.' But her voice cracked and another tear fell, then another, until her face glistened wet in the darkness. 'I'm just tired, I guess. It would have been easier – and, well, nicer – to go with someone I know. To go with you. To not be . . .'

She didn't finish her sentence but I knew where her tears came from: the prospect of being alone in a strange, unruly town, the desperate loneliness of another bleak hotel room. Almost without realizing what I was doing I moved to sit next to her on the bed, put my arm around her, felt the warmth of her body as she lay her head on my shoulder. Silence drifted in, and in the darkness something flickered inside me; the desire I had felt in the shop doorway began to uncurl and rise. I leaned my cheek against her hair, felt her thigh against mine, bare skin visible through the gap between her cardigan and T-shirt. I wanted to lean in and kiss it. Who would ever know?

As if sensing something, Marian drew back a little and I found myself slipping my fingers under her chin, tilting her face up to mine, spurred on by some strange conviction that we were somehow apart from the real world, that all that existed was this unlit room in a broken city, in a life that I no longer recognized as mine. I kissed her, one soft kiss, and then she brought her hands up to my face and I was lost; pushing myself into her mouth, feeling her pull me back on to the bed, her fingers tearing at my jeans, my hands ripping at her T-shirt, desperate to feel every inch of her body wrapped around mine.

Something happened to me that night; it was as if I became a different man. Months of pent-up longing flooded through me and I felt the same need in Marian; kissing until our lips were sore, losing ourselves in each other's bodies with a desperation that bore a strange, frenzied passion. Afterwards we lay tangled together, hot and breathless, and as I felt her heart gradually slow, I tried to feel something – anything – about what had just taken place between us. But I felt nothing, just a numb, exhausted sort of bliss, and as the first grey tints of dawn floated in through the shutters, I slipped out of bed, silently pulled on my clothes and sat on the chair to lace up my shoes.

'You're going?' I looked up to see Marian staring at me, head propped up on her elbow, blonde hair falling into her eyes. Reality swung in, hard and fast. Jesus, what had I done?

'I think I should,' I said, trying to keep my voice steady. 'I don't think it'd do your reputation any good if people saw me sneaking out of your bedroom.' It was wrong of me to prey on her insecurities, but it worked. She ran her fingers through her tangled hair and I thought again how young she looked. Something stirred unexpectedly in my heart.

'OK,' she said, half smiling. 'I guess I'll see you later. It'll probably take me a day or two to find a replacement for you. But don't let's be weird about this, OK?'

I nodded mutely, leaned in to kiss her cheek, caught her scent – so different from Dina's that my stomach flipped over. My hands shook as I closed the door behind me, and when I got back to my room I stripped off my clothes and sat in the bath, my skin still smelling of her. It was several minutes before I realized there was no water coming from the taps. Somehow it didn't matter; I sat naked, knees hunched up, slim raised lines on my upper arms and chest where Marian had raked her nails across my skin. I stared at the cracked, grimy tiles, picturing Dina's face, the expression in her eyes when she learned I had broken just about every promise I had ever made to her. I stood up. That conversation was never going to happen. Dina could never find out. And I knew, instantly, that the only way to save my marriage was to get home to her, away from the strange, intoxicating pull I felt for Marian. Ljeta was barely forty minutes by car. Downstairs there was a bar full of war reporters. One of them would take me home.

But when it came to it, none of them would. There were fewer journalists around now. Many were in Bosnia, and those that weren't had no intention of battling through the unpredictable checkpoints and risking sniper fire just to drive me to Ljeta. But I was determined. I had lost Irina; I wasn't going to lose Dina too. If no one at the Ragusa could help, then my only option was to find Bobo; he'd got me home once, he could do it again. I set off for the hospital, hoping to find Cata was on shift, that she would be able to tell me where to find my brother-in-law.

When I turned the corner and saw the hospital I froze. For a moment I was back there, that sunny December morning when I had left my daughter in bed with my wife and come to the city to try to save her life. It struck me suddenly that throughout the subsequent catastrophic chain of events I had relinquished any sense of control. Bobo enabled me to return to Ljeta, Dina threw me out, Pavle insisted I had to return to Dubrovnik, Damir found me work. I thought back to allowing Pavle to drive me out of Ljeta and away from Dina; my compliance seemed like the action of an obedient child, or perhaps just a scared one. I had been afraid of everything then: of my grief, of Dina's fury, of the simmering resentment between my parents. Most pathetic of all, I had been scared of Pavle.

I strode towards the hospital; fear was no longer going to drive me. I had beaten it once, that day in Dubrovnik, when Marian and I stood in the shop doorway while the shells rained down, tipped over the edge from terror into a strange visceral thrill. It was like Nic said: fear was just a barrier that stopped you being what you wanted to be, or going where you wanted to go. Once you had conquered it, anything was possible. And I was going to get back home.

'I'm looking for Cata Denković,' I said, leaning on the desk in the hospital's cluttered reception area. 'Can you tell me where I'll find her? Which ward?'

'*Miro?*' I turned round and shock whistled through me. Cata looked so different, her face gaunt and almost translucent-white, eyes huge and dark. 'What are you doing here?'

'I need to talk to you about Bobo. Is there somewhere we can go?'

To my surprise her eyes reddened and she looked as if she might cry. 'Oh my God, have you seen him? Has he talked to you?'

'No. That's why I came. I need to get hold of him urgently. It's really important, Catz, I have to get back to Ljeta. Are you seeing him later?'

She shook her head. 'What? No, Bobo and I, we're not together any more. Which you'd know if you ever bloody came to see me.'

I reddened. During my time in the city I had only seen Cata once, preferring to stay among strangers who knew nothing of my life in Ljeta. 'I'm sorry, Catz, really, but I have to see him. You must know where he is.'

'Didn't you hear me? We've split up.'

'But I need his help.'

'Help? You want that man's help?' She looked at me for a moment and then slowly slipped off the cardigan she was wearing. Purple marks formed matching rings around her upper arms.

'Our last row,' she said wearily. 'Don't look so appalled – I survived. But he hurt me. And not just physically. The war's changed him. He was always tough, you know that, but underneath there was a gentleness that only I saw, that I loved. But it's gone. All gone. The war, all this . . . horror. It's stamped it out.'

I pulled her into me, holding her tightly, trying not to think about what this meant, that without Bobo there was little chance I could get home. 'Are you OK, sweetheart? Are you . . .'

'I miss him,' she said, her voice muffled by my coat. Her body shook a little and I realized she was crying. A familiar, weary anger rolled through me: at my bullying brother-in-law, at the exhausted woman in my arms, at the war and what it was doing to all of us.

'I'm so sorry, Catz. But maybe it's for the best? If this is what he's capable of . . .'

She drew back a little, looked up at me. 'I know. I know you're right but . . .' Her lip wobbled, and for a moment she looked like the small girl I had first met on the harbour, a lifetime ago in a different world. 'Anyway, why are you trying to get home now? I thought it was too risky? Everyone is saying the siege will be over soon. Can't you hold on for another week or two? It might not even be that long.'

I smoothed her hair down and kissed her cheek. 'I just have to. It's time. But, look, are you OK?'

She shook her head. 'I really loved him, you know? We used to talk about what we'd do after the war; he'd open a law practice, and after a year or two he'd be able to support me while I trained to be a doctor. He really wanted that for me. But it's been so long now and things are so *hard*. He just became so angry, always drinking. I used to say that at least we had each other, that love was what mattered. But he said I was stupid and unrealistic and couldn't I see that love wasn't enough? Hatred and violence are stronger than love, he'd say. Hatred will always win.'

Cata's words came back to me as I lay in bed that night, forcing myself to relive the hours I had spent with Marian, to face up to what I had done. Just the memory of touching her skin made my body stir with excitement; a need for comfort had quickly become something wild and uncontrolled, a desire that surpassed anything Dina had ever provoked in me. And she had been unfazed by the force with which I kissed her, pushed me back on to the pillows, held me inside her, and when I rose up to meet her we wrapped our bodies around each other so tightly that I genuinely couldn't tell where her skin ended and mine began.

It was a relief when dawn broke and I could plunge myself back into work. That day and the next I managed to avoid Marian – the translator for the CNN team had just become a father and Eric Douglas, their burly news reporter, had reluctantly agreed to let him spend a couple of days at home with his new son. I happily stepped into his shoes, leaving the Ragusa early and returning straight to my room when I got back. But on the third day the translator was back, and I was hiding out in the editing suite when a heavy French accent announced that Nic was back at the Ragusa.

'Got a strong stomach?' he asked, shoving me out of my seat and slipping a tape into the machine. I noticed his hands shook a little.

'Where have you been?' I asked, as an image of rolling hills and a cluster of small farmhouses appeared on the screen.

'The Balsac valley. Looks idyllic, doesn't it? Keep watching.'

Nic's footage was almost unbearable to watch; skeletal men in fenced-in compounds, a picturesque farm where the barn held unimaginable horrors, bodies stacked on bodies, slowly decomposing. He said nothing as I watched, but I noticed that at times his eyes were averted from the screen, staring down at his hands. When the tape finished, we sat in silence; both of us knew little of his footage would make it on to the air. It was simply too gruesome to show.

'I need a drink,' he growled. I looked at my watch; it was just before six, and I knew Marian was usually quite disciplined about not allowing herself a drink before seven. I calculated I could have a quick beer with Nic and be back up to my room before there was any chance of her appearing in the bar.

'Just a quick one,' I said. 'Can't keep up with you guys. I need a night off.'

'Fuck off,' said Nic, and his voice was harsh. 'After what I've seen, I need to get out of my head. And you're going to keep me company.'

There was never any arguing with Nic. By seven o'clock he had drunk half a bottle of vodka, by half past he had switched to coffee and cigarettes. 'Got to keep myself presentable for the Iron Lady,' he said.

'Are you talking about me?' I turned round to see Marian standing behind us.

'Ah, Mademoiselle Wiseman.' Nic pulled up a chair and tipped what was left of the vodka into a glass, pushing it across the table. 'Off to Burjska, I hear. Well, you'd better get drunk and stay drunk; you don't want to take that place sober.'

'Off tomorrow,' she said, slipping into the chair beside Nic. She lifted the glass to her lips and smiled at me as our eyes connected. A small thrill shot up my spine. I was aware suddenly of the redness of her lips, the triangle of skin visible between her shirt lapels. I had kissed her there three nights ago, brushed my lips up her neck, held her wrists against the pillow while I slid into her, hard and fast. I looked away as the memory washed over me; when I glanced up her eyes were still on my face and I knew her thoughts were in exactly the same place as mine.

We both knew what was going to happen. The night drifted on, blurred by vodka, cigarette smoke and loud, sardonic laughter, and when she began to say her goodbyes I rose as if it had been agreed between us and waited for her at the top of the stairs, barely able to breathe at the thought of stripping off her clothes and kissing the soft, smooth skin that lay beneath.

I slept well that night, the curve of her body already familiar to me. And when I woke next morning and saw the peace in her sleeping face, I remembered that she was leaving and she was scared and I began to kiss her gently, to make love to her without alcohol or the same desperate need, to let her know how I felt, that we had genuinely shared a strange and wonderful moment in our lives.

'I'm not good at goodbyes,' she said later, as we walked down the corridor. 'So let's not. Who knows – perhaps there'll be a night in Sarajevo, Belgrade – even London.'

'Perhaps.' I smiled, but I couldn't meet her eyes. If there was any hope for me and Dina, I knew I could never see Marian again. 'With the crazy life you lead, who knows?' I tried to laugh but there was genuine sadness in her face and as we stepped into the lift and the doors closed, I bent down to kiss her. It was a last kiss, a goodbye that moved from her cheek to her lips, that made me drop my bag and slip my arms around her, deaf to the sound of the doors opening and the footsteps of other people entering the lift.

'Miro?' The voice was unmistakable. Panic ripped through me; my hands fell from Marian's body. '*Miro?*'

It couldn't be happening. But it was. Bobo.

CHAPTER 19

'Bobo? What are you doing here?'

'I saw Cata,' he said. I waited for him to say something more, but he simply stared at me, his eyes cold with fury. Marian looked at me expectantly, but my mouth wouldn't seem to work.

'Marian Wiseman,' she said, holding out her hand. Her crisp British voice echoed across the lobby; was I imagining it or had people turned to look? She smiled the cool, professional smile she had used on murderers and dictators and terrorists. 'I'm sorry, I don't know . . .'

'I can't believe he hasn't mentioned me,' he said, and the false jollity in his tone chilled me. 'I'm Dina's brother. Dina – his wife?'

Marian didn't blink. 'Of course,' she said smoothly. 'Well, I'm sure you two must have a lot to catch up on so I'll leave you to it. Miro –' she looked at me, her features utterly unreadable – 'thanks again for all your hard work.' And suddenly she was gone, slipping away between the neat figures of the UN staff and out on to the terrace beyond.

'Outside.' The word hissed out of Bobo's lips, and I followed him through the lobby, my heart starting to race. When we were through the revolving doors he pulled out his cigarettes, offered me the packet, and as I looked down to take one I felt something rigid and heavy smack into the side of my face, fell backwards on to the floor, pain searing my cheek.

'You fucking little *shit*.' I tried to bring my knees up but Bobo was too quick and I doubled up in agony as his foot connected with my stomach. 'Is *that* what you're doing in Dubrovnik? Is that what you were doing when your daughter was dying? Fucking some foreign *whore*?'

His anger seemed to overwhelm him and he spun away from me; I pulled myself up against the wall, my body creasing with pain. 'How can you say that?' I wheezed. 'I came to Dubrovnik because Irina was sick, for the medicine she needed. You know what happened. I didn't want to leave Dina, I was desperate to stay with her, you must know that.'

'I'm not sure I do. Five months you've been in this city – you haven't even tried to get home, and now I've found out why.'

'Because I can't *get* home,' I yelled. 'I'm fucking working for her because her cameraman got shot at the Ljeta checkpoint.'

'Don't you mean you're fucking her because you're working for her? Don't tell me that wasn't what it looked like. Don't treat me like I'm stupid. You're fucking her, aren't you, that uptight fucking Brit?' I said nothing, tried to meet Bobo's gaze while my mind worked frantically; could I lie, *should* I lie?

'Tell me the truth,' he shouted, as his boot connected with my knee. The pain rippled up and down my leg.

'Once,' I yelled. 'Just once.' His face darkened and I closed my eyes, readying myself for the next onslaught. It didn't come. A short bark of surprise shot into the air and I squinted up to see Bobo totter backwards and fall on to the floor.

'Pick on someone your own size.' The French accent was unmistakable; Nic, at least a foot shorter than Bobo, had felled him with one swift kick.

I felt thick hands on my arms and slowly staggered to my feet. Nic pointed to where Bobo lay squirming on the floor. 'Toecap to bollocks,' he said, grinning. 'Quickest way to take a man down.'

'I'll tell her,' Bobo spluttered, his face contorted with pain. 'I'll fucking *tell her*.'

'And ruin her life?' I leaned against Nic; I felt like I had been hit by a truck. 'Like you've ruined Cata's?' Her face swung into my mind; cheeks stained with tears, arms ringed with bruises. I swung back my good leg and watched, almost unconsciously, as it connected with Bobo's guts. He groaned, something fired in my brain, a release, it felt *good* to hurt him. I moved to kick him again, but Nic laid a hand on my arm. 'Leave him. You've made your point. Come on.'

'Your marriage is over,' taunted Bobo, as we walked away.

'Ignore him,' said Nic, as I limped into the hotel. The lift doors closed and I slumped against the dirty panelling.

'Sorry. He's . . .'

'No business of mine. Just need to get you fixed up.'

I sank gratefully on to the bed in his room while he busied himself in his suitcase; a bottle of TCP, gauze bandages and a box of aspirin landed on the blanket beside me. Without turning around, he spoke: 'I don't need to know anything about all this. Keeps it simple. You're a friend, he's an arsehole. You help your friends, right?'

'I've done something stupid,' I said, peering at myself in the cracked mirror and dabbing at the blood caked around my nose and jaw. 'I need to get home, Nic, back to Ljeta. I need to get there before Bobo does. Will you take me? I know the risks. I've got some money; I'll pay you.'

'I can't.'

'Nic, please. You're my last hope.'

'I didn't say I won't. I said I can't. There's no fuel, Miro. The Jeep's empty and no one's going anywhere. I've tried all my contacts, but it looks as if we're all stuck here, at least for a couple of days.'

I sank back on to the bed. 'But I have to get back. I have to.'

'Look, if I can't get any petrol, that thug won't be able to either. And when there is some to be got hold of, I'll get it first. And then I'll take you to Ljeta.'

'You will?'

He grinned. 'Always up for a little jaunt, *mon ami*. You've been a real help to me in this city and you work hard. My turn to repay the favour.'

It was three days before Nic managed to lay his hands on any fuel. The normally mild May sun burned down with the ferocity of an August heatwave, leaving the city airless and seemingly bereft of life. The hours ticked by and I lay in my room, reliving the moment Bobo had seen us in the lift, a monotonous ache drilling into my body from my knee and jaw. Occasionally I would allow Dina's face to float into my mind, imagine the look in her eyes when I told her what I'd done. And when the pain got really bad I drifted back to being in bed with Marian, only she was Dina, and I was Pavle and that was the deepest agony of all.

When Nic finally knocked on my door to tell me the Jeep was ready and we could go to Ljeta, I didn't know whether to feel excited or terrified.

'I've got to say goodbye to Damir,' I said, wincing as I swung my bag on to my shoulder. 'Give me a minute.'

I found him in the editing room, and his face clouded as I told him that I was going back to Ljeta, and Nic was taking me.

'You're leaving with that maniac?' Damir lit a cigarette and shook his head. 'What the hell's going on? I've barely seen you this last week, now I do it's obvious you've had the shit kicked out of you by someone, and then you tell me you're going back to Ljeta, in spite of the roadblocks, in spite of the fact the village will probably be free in a week or two. And, worst of all, you're going with that French arse. Are you in trouble? You know I'll help if I can.'

I shook my head. 'I'm not in trouble, at least not like you mean. But I do have to get back to Ljeta. And as for going with Nic, he's the only one who said yes when I asked.'

'That's because he's crazy. It's just another sop for his ego; he's only taking you so that he's got a fresh anecdote to tell in the bar this evening. Is that what you want? To be a walk-on part in the latest Nic Richaud production? Why can't you see through him, Miro, see him for what he really is?'

I sighed. 'I don't want to argue with you. I have to go, and I'm going with Nic. But if it wasn't for you, you and Serenja . . . you saved me. Don't be angry. Isn't there enough of that going on without you and me falling out too?'

His face softened and he lowered himself on to the edge of the desk. 'You've grown up,' he said. 'You were still a boy when you came to me, and now . . .' He held out his hand. 'Good luck. And you know there's a job here for you when all this insanity is over.'

I shook his hand and smiled into his tired, flushed face. 'Thank you.'

'And, Miro?' His grey eyes were clear and cool, still filled with the defiance that had defined him the first day we had met in his cluttered, airless office. 'When you get back to Ljeta, try to forget all this. Think of it as another life. What happened here, these months . . . none of it was real. Try to remember that. None of it was real.'

But it felt real. It felt real as I sat in the passenger seat of Nic's battered Jeep, staring down at the mix of cigarette papers, ash and sweet wrappers that oozed out of every slot and compartment. There was little traffic on the road – nothing moved between Ljeta and Dubrovnik aside from UN vehicles and military Jeeps. The first checkpoint went smoothly; Nic had flashed his credentials and a bored-looking soldier had simply waved us through without even asking to see mine. We both knew the second checkpoint would not be so easy.

'One more time,' said Nic, as he flung the Jeep into a tight bend with a huge drop to the sea below. 'Who are you?'

'I'm Joe Courić, reporter for Ljubljana TV. We're going to interview Major Argović. You know him – you've interviewed him before for TF1.'

'And where are your papers?'

'I stopped to talk to a bunch of Croatian kids and they stole my wallet with my papers in.'

Nic snorted. 'They'll love that. It's a win-win. They'll feel superior to you for being such an idiot, and to the Croatian race in general, because they're bringing up their children to be thieves.'

Damir's words flicked up in my brain; it was the perfect Nic anecdote, getting a Croatian man to tell a story against his own people to Serbian soldiers and having to laugh with them about it. I put aside any feelings of distaste; if being the butt of Nic's questionable humour was the price I had to pay to get home, I was more than willing to do it.

'Just let me do the talking,' he said easily. 'Thing is, you just can't tell what they're going to be like. Sometimes they just wave you through, like the last one, but sometimes their arses are so tight it's like they've never had a shit in their lives. So get ready, because if you fuck up we both go down, remember that.'

We turned the corner and my heart sank. At one side of the road-block, six soldiers sat around a rickety table littered with playing cards and empty bottles of Stock. At the sound of the car they rose to their feet and picked up the guns that had been lying on the ground. One of them approached, weaving slightly, clearly drunk.

Nic wound down his window. 'Evening.'

A bearded, dark-eyed face peered in at us, yanked open the door and gestured with his gun for Nic to get out of the car. 'Papers?'

He produced them from his pocket. The soldier took one look, drew himself up and spat noisily at Nic's feet.

'Fucking reporters. You write lies. Only lies. Whose deaths will you blame on us today?'

'Well, that depends on what your Major Argović tells me,' said Nic airily. 'I'm on my way to Ljeta to interview him. All the news networks are full of how you lot are about to withdraw, what a humiliation this has been, how all you've done is cast yourselves as villains in the eyes of the world. But you can't all be that stupid, right? I mean, everyone's got to be missing something, surely. So that's what I'm going to ask Argović.'

'You're going to see Major Argović?' Another soldier walked over, taller, thickset. I watched him through the car window as he smiled coolly at Nic. 'Today?'

Nic smiled back. 'That's correct. He's waiting for us.'

'Really?'

'Yes.'

An unexpected silence fell. My fingers gripped the door handle, sliding greasily against the metal. This was not going well. Whether Nic was deliberately ignoring the signals or just oblivious to them, I couldn't tell. But I could see from the triumphant look on the soldier's face that he knew he had Nic in a corner.

'I'm sorry to tell you that Major Argović—'

'*Nikolić.*' I was out of the car before he could finish his sentence, walking around to Nic, pushing him roughly. 'Nikolić, you idiot.' Nic looked at me, bemused. 'Fucking foreigners,' I said to the soldier in Serbo-Croat. 'Lump us all together, no bloody idea who's who. Lord it around thinking they know everything – they know fuck all. *Idiot.*' I shoved Nic again, raised my arms in a display of frustration at his stupidity. 'Pavle Nikolić, remember? Argović is the man in charge, but he turned us down, gave us Nikolić to talk to instead.'

'Oh right, of course,' Nic caught up suddenly. 'Because he was going to be in . . .'

'Belgrade,' interjected one of the other soldiers helpfully.

'Exactly,' I said, lapsing back into Serbo-Croat. 'Listen, we're going to miss our time with Nikolić if we're not careful. Now Nic here might be a stupid Frog, but he usually has a treat or two in the back of his car.' The older soldier followed me as I wrenched open the boot and pulled back the tarpaulin to reveal a battered cardboard box with six gleaming Johnnie Walker Red bottle tops clearly visible. The soldier's eyes glistened. I leaned in to pull out a bottle, but he pushed me aside and grabbed the entire box, holding it greedily to his body. He barked something to the other soldiers and they got up slowly and began to move the barricade.

'Get in the car,' I muttered to Nic. 'Enjoy,' I said to the soldiers, but they no longer had any interest in us, already passing the first bottle between them, faces lit up like children with sweets. Nic put his foot to the accelerator, and only as we pulled away did I realize my heart was beating so fast I could barely breathe.

'Six bottles?' yelled Nic, when we were out of sight of the checkpoint. '*Six fucking bottles?*'

'You're damn right, six fucking bottles. You're lucky that's all it cost you. You were going down, man, *we* were going down. If I hadn't—'

'I had it under control,' Nic barked, swerving to avoid part of a wall that had crumbled into the road. 'You took your time to step in though – almost thought you'd blown it.'

'*I'd* blown it?' I looked at Nic and he glanced at me, raising his eyebrows and grinning ruefully. In spite of myself I began to laugh and he joined in, until both of us were giggling like schoolboys, fuelled by adrenalin and exhilaration and sheer bloody relief.

'Feels good, doesn't it?' he said gleefully. 'Like you stepped beyond the person you thought you were. You did well, Miro, I've got to hand it to you. We're a good team, you and I. I'd work with you any time.'

Pleasure rippled down my spine. 'Thanks.'

'So where's good? To let you out?'

I pointed to a rutted track that led between two houses. 'I can run it from there.' The engine ground slowly to a halt and I dragged my bag off the back seat.

'Thank you.'

Nic held up his hand. 'Get going,' he said roughly. '*Bonne chance*, Miro.'

Before he had finished speaking I was off and running, darting through the olive grove that backed on to our cottage, barely able to believe I could see our back gate, the tall spines of the bean canes peeking over the top of the wall. The house was in darkness and I gently tried the back door; it was unlocked, a habit Dina had grown up with and was unwilling to break.

I should have felt overjoyed to be home, but instead my first thought was how forlorn it seemed, orderly and neat, but without any signs of life. The living room was devoid of the fresh flowers Dina had always loved, the jars of dried herbs and rice stood dusty and unopened on the side. I stopped suddenly; there on the draining board: two plates, two forks, two mugs, a meal shared. Pavle's words flicked up in my mind: *Your wife will have dinner on the table.* I began to feel slightly sick.

The blood thumped in my ears as I climbed the stairs to our bedroom, but when I pushed open the door everything looked the same; our bed, bare but for a pale pink sheet, pillows smooth and untouched on my side, slightly squashed on hers. I sat for a moment, let my fingers drift across the sheet, but almost immediately a sound stopped my hand from moving. Downstairs the front door clicked, creaked slightly as it opened and shut. Footsteps fell on to the wooden boards, the soft swish of a coat dropped on to a chair, water whistled through the kitchen tap. And then came the soft creak of her feet on the stairs; I could almost feel her presence growing closer to me.

'Miro.'

'Hello, Dina.' I stared at her, almost in disbelief. Her gorgeous face was pale and drawn, her body seemed to have shrunk, the cotton dress hung limply from her shoulders. But her dark hair was still thick and glossy, pulled into a plait that hung down her back and reminded me of the hot schoolroom and the sunlit days of our adolescence, when I knew I loved her even before I knew her name.

'You're *here*,' she whispered. 'But what happened? Your face . . .'

She bent down and touched my bruised jaw; I wrapped my hand around hers and laid my finger to her lips. Her eyes blurred with tears as I slowly reached behind her, slipped the band from the plait and shook her hair loose across her shoulders. I bent in to kiss her neck, slip the straps of her dress from her shoulders and my skin fired up as she slid her hands around my waist, pulling my T-shirt up over my chest, her lips suddenly on mine, so soft, so familiar. Somehow we found ourselves on the bed and at first everything felt gloriously, wonderfully the same and then something shifted; my kisses grew frenzied and hard, her hands were tearing at my jeans, and suddenly I was inside her and everything that had happened seemed to roar out of me and she cried out as her body rose up to meet mine, over and over, her hands in my hair, thighs tight around my waist. I felt a wave of pleasure rip through me, so intense I thought I might drown in it, and then it was over and we lay together, hot and sticky, both beyond speech, neither of us entirely sure what had just happened.

'Oh, my love,' she murmured, when our breathing had slowed and I had pulled her to me, her hair tumbling across my chest. 'How is it that you're here?'

I tilted her face up to mine and felt a lurch of guilt as I remembered holding Marian in my arms; for a moment it was as if the floor had opened up and I could see down below, into a wriggling morass of burning streets and dead bodies and a blonde-haired woman who wrapped her body around mine. None of it was real. Wasn't that what Damir said? I tried to drag my mind away and looked down into her wonderfully familiar face, gently traced the cluster of freckles scattered across her nose.

'I can't quite believe I'm here.'

'But how did you get here? Why now?'

I took her face in mine and tried to find the words I knew I had to say. If Bobo hadn't told her – and it seemed he hadn't – I knew it was just a matter of time. As soon as he could get back to Ljeta he would make sure Dina knew what he had seen at the Ragusa. I had to tell her now; I tried to form the words in my mind: I slept with someone else, it didn't mean anything, it wasn't *anything*. But I knew it would ruin everything. I looked into her warm hazel eyes, and my heart swelled with love and relief at holding her in my arms again. I couldn't do it, not now, not *yet*.

'I just had to see you. I couldn't bear it any longer. And there was this crazy journalist coming to interview Argović and he reckoned he could get me through the checkpoints. None of the other reporters would even consider it, although I kept asking.'

'It just seems strange now, after so long.'

Something stirred inside me at the question. 'Aren't you pleased to see me?'

'I think I've proved that already,' she said, and there was something in her voice, a slight edge I didn't recognize. Her face softened and for a moment I thought she was going to cry. 'It doesn't matter anyway, how you got here or why you're here. All that matters is that you're home, with me. Just kiss me, kiss me again, Miro. Kiss me like you've never been away.'

CHAPTER 20

'I wish it could always be like this.'

'I know.'

'It's like being children again. Just our secret.'

'But I love you more now. More than before I went away. You kept me sane, Dina. You were the only thing that kept me sane.'

'And you, me,' she said, lifting her head slightly and dropping gentle kisses on my chest. 'When it got bad, when the pain of missing her . . . I told myself how much worse it must be for you, how alone and afraid you must feel. I told myself if you could bear it, in that desperate city, surrounded by strangers, then I could. I would do it for you if I couldn't do it for myself.'

Not for the first time, guilt twisted through my system. Dina's impression of my time in Dubrovnik was not wholly accurate; I had explained about working at the Ragusa, but elected not to mention the long drunken nights in the bar, the forays out into Bosnia where the strange mixture of fear and adrenalin made me feel more alive than I had ever felt before. But I knew she was holding back too; Pavle was never mentioned, and aside from giving me a long, sad letter from Cvita, she seemed oddly unwilling to talk of my family. Occasional anxieties crept into my head, but they dissipated swiftly, melted by Dina's kisses, the dishes she brought up from the kitchen, the feeling of her smooth skin, warm against mine, in the long baths we took each afternoon.

Two weeks passed and we saw no one but each other. I didn't leave the house, barely went downstairs for fear of someone seeing me through the window. Occasionally I heard Karena's voice; once I flinched when I recognized Pavle's clipped tones, twisting up through the window from the garden. I didn't mention I had heard him, and Dina said nothing, and I pushed the incident to a shady corner of my mind where I stored the memories of my time in Dubrovnik, and hoped there would never come a time when I had to reveal what lay hidden in the darkness.

When change came, we had little time to prepare. Dina came home one afternoon to find me in the bath, and as she slipped off her clothes and slid into the water, I could see something had happened.

'No one has seen Pavle for two days,' she said, tucking her legs around mine. 'Karena overheard two of the soldiers talking about a retreat from Dubrovnik. If that happens, surely they'll have to go from here as well. The siege may be over soon, my love, can you imagine?'

The water cooled against my skin. Once the soldiers went, there was nothing to stop Bobo from returning to Ljeta, no way to stop reality from crashing into the secret world Dina and I had created for ourselves. 'Are you sure? Maybe Pavle has just been sent away somewhere. And even if Dubrovnik falls, it doesn't mean Ljeta will necessarily follow.'

'Don't you want us to be free?' she asked, frowning. 'After all these months of living and not really living, to have our village back, to be in control again? I know you haven't been here, but . . .'

She seemed oddly angry. I leaned forward and kissed her. 'Of course I want that. I just don't want you to get too excited about something that might not happen.'

'It's going to happen, I can feel it. Oh, Miro, how wonderful to be free again. All of this, the months we were apart, we can pretend it didn't happen; it will be like none of it was real. Wouldn't that be wonderful? If none of this had been real?'

I wondered for the thousandth time if she knew what had happened between Marian and me. Sometimes she said things I didn't quite understand, the same slight edge in her voice I had heard the first day I came back. I knew there was a meaning that lay beneath the actual words, but I didn't know how to unravel it, wasn't sure I even wanted to. At times I imagined Bobo telling her what he had seen, the slow, creeping shock spreading across her face. Had she simply decided to set what he told her aside, to box it up and put it away as I had tried to do? Or was it time spent with Pavle that made her seem a little different to me? We made love with a passion we had never shared before I had gone to Dubrovnik. Had she changed at another man's touch?

It was only a matter of hours before her prediction that the siege would end came true. She woke me from sleep, hissing my name from where she stood by the open window.

'*Look*, Miro. Get out of bed, come here. They're going. *Look*.'

I stumbled out of bed and peered over her shoulder. Sure enough, a military truck was rumbling up the road with two neat lines of soldiers sitting ramrod straight in the back, moonlight glinting off their guns. None of them moved. Seconds later a second truck ground past carrying another similar group of men.

'They're fleeing,' I whispered. 'Christ, Dina, you were right. It's over. It's really over.'

She kissed me then and we made love on the soft pink sheets, tenderly this time, her eyes locked on to mine, both of us knowing that with the departure of the soldiers, the secret, intimate world we had created would inevitably break apart. Somewhere, beneath the relief and joy at the liberation of my village, I felt a small, hard nub of dread. I wasn't sure the real world was a place I wanted to return to.

When I woke in the morning Dina had already gone, returning

with the news that all of the troops had indeed fled; the police station was empty and people were waking up to the strange feeling of being masters of their own destiny again.

'Barely anyone saw them leave,' she said, pouring coffee and beaming excitedly at me. 'Tomas heard the trucks start up – he said they left in almost total silence apart from Argović, barking at them to move quickly. Obviously they just wanted to disappear as fast as possible. Cowards. And no sign of Pavle anywhere.'

'Good,' I growled. 'Good riddance.' An expression crossed her face, the one I couldn't read, didn't want to. I sipped my coffee. 'I guess we'd better go and see my parents. Coming?'

To my surprise Dina shook her head. 'I won't. But you go. Of course you must let them know you're here, and safe.'

'You won't come?'

'No. I . . . Look, it's you they'll want to see. They'll all be overjoyed. Let them have you to themselves.'

'OK.' Something wasn't right, Dina's eyes were hard and cold. 'But Mother's bound to want to make lunch. I'll come back and pick you up later?'

'No.' The word snapped out of her. 'No, Miro, I'm sorry. I can't.'

'Are you OK? Has something happened?'

She looked at me, clasping and unclasping her hands. 'No, nothing . . . but, well, things have been difficult. Ljeta became a different place over the last few months. People whom I thought I could trust, who I thought trusted me . . .'

'Trusted you about what?'

'Look –' she paused and I could see she was choosing her words carefully – 'I know how much you love your mother. I'd never do anything to come between you and her. Of course you must go, I completely understand that. But I can't come with you.'

'But why? I don't understand. And why are you telling me this now?'

She shrugged. 'I didn't want to spoil the time we had together. I knew the real world would come knocking soon enough.'

'But why won't you come?'

'Because I won't be welcome,' she snapped. 'And if you want to know why, you'll have to ask your mother.'

It was Marjana, sweeping the cobbles outside the restaurant, who saw me first. As my footsteps drew nearer she glanced up and before I could speak she had drawn me into her with a little cry of delight. I was glad she couldn't see my face. I was stunned by the change in her; her broad, comfortable body had shrunk; her ruddy, smiling face was gaunt and drawn. And yet the same lavender scent seeped off her skin, soothing me with its familiarity.

'Baby boy, you're home. You're *home*. Come in, come in. When did you get here? Jada, Petar, look who's home!'

For a moment, none of us spoke. For the first time in my life my parents looked *old*, and they stared at me as if they couldn't believe what they were seeing. The four of us stood in the dim light of the kitchen, surrounded by the mundanities of everyday life – saucepans and coffee pots and odd bits of washing-up on the draining board – trying to cope with emotions that were anything but everyday. And then suddenly the spell broke, my mother hugged me to her and I heard my father mutter, 'Thank God. Oh, thank God,' as he lay his hand on my shoulder.

'It's OK,' I said, tightening my arms around my mother. 'I'm home. I'm fine.'

'Oh, my child,' she whispered, 'what have you been through?'

'Put him down, Jada.' There was humour in Pa's voice but it was choked, thick with emotion. 'You'll crush the life out of him. There's not much of him as it is.'

'We're so blessed,' said Marjana. 'Thank God. Now we know all three of you are safe.'

'Goran? You've had news? Where is he? Is he . . . ?'

'On TV,' said Mother, smudging away tears with the tips of her fingers and smiling. 'It was incredible – we were just watching the news – it was somewhere near Sarajevo – and then Ivo cried out, "Goran, it's Goran!" And there he was, standing in a group of soldiers. He looked the same. Just the same.'

'Your mother screamed out loud,' said Marjana, laughing. 'She—'

'But where's Ivo?'

'Ivo's in here,' croaked a voice from the next room, and I turned to look at Pa, whose smile had faded.

'He's not been well,' he said quietly, as a burst of coughing echoed through the wall. 'These last months . . .' His voice tailed away and I followed him into what had once been the restaurant but was now a ramshackle lounge. Only one lamp was on, and I barely recognized the hunched, silver-haired figure sitting in the armchair with a blanket over his knees.

'Come and give your uncle a hug,' he said gruffly. I wrapped my arms around his body and he leaned into me, gingerly, as if it hurt him to do so. His skin felt papery against mine, scented with the strange, sweet smell of a body that had already begun to decay.

'It was a heart attack,' Pa said later, as we strolled along the harbour while Mother and Marjana prepared *lònac* for my homecoming lunch. 'I didn't want to tell you the moment you got through the door, but Mesić said it was pretty major. He just couldn't bear what was happening to Ljeta. He and your mother, they just got angrier and angrier as the weeks went past. Ivo started to drink too much – every night he'd rant about the war and the occupation, and then your mother would join in, about how it was Pavle's fault that you'd been banished from your home and . . .'

'And how you'd been wrong not to stop me going?'

He nodded and his shoulders sagged a little. 'I still think I was right. Hiding out for two weeks is one thing, but month after month, it wouldn't have been possible. Things have happened here, it got much tougher as time went on. Restrictions, curfews – that was one of the things that made your uncle so angry.'

'Fucking Pavle,' I muttered. Pa looked at me, his expression unreadable. 'Is it his fault Ivo had a heart attack?'

'Indirectly, I suppose, but really Ivo just couldn't deal with the realities of occupation. The curfew used to drive him crazy; this is my village, he'd say, and I'll walk around it whenever I please. The evening it happened was, oh, early April and it was warm, really unseasonably hot. Ivo decided to go for a walk, but he'd barely reached the harbour before Pavle collared him and ordered him home. Ivo refused. Pavle threatened him with a gun, but he still wouldn't turn back.'

'What happened?' The two words hung in the air, heavy with meaning. It was a question I wanted to ask over and over. What happened with Mother and Dina, with you and Mother? *What happened with Dina and Pavle?*

'He fired between his feet – deliberately, so as not to injure him. It was enough to make Ivo come home, but when he walked through the door he was raging, berating himself for not standing his ground. He became angrier and angrier and then suddenly he clutched at his arm, complained of a terrible pain, and within seconds he'd collapsed.'

'Oh, Pa.'

'It was a massive shock, for all of us. It's taking him a long time to recover, to get back to his old self.' He stopped walking suddenly, laid his hand on my arm. 'And you? I know what you said in there,' he nodded towards the pension, 'losing yourself in work, staying with Damir at the Ragusa. But how did you manage, for money, for—'

'I will tell you,' I said slowly, 'but not now, not today. Right now all of that . . . it's too *different*. It's almost like it happened to someone else. Remember when Goran came back from Krno? It took him days before he could even begin to tell us what had happened to him, and now I understand why. I don't know that I can really describe what it was like, how I lived. And honestly, I'm not sure how much you need to know. I got through it and I'm back and I belong in this world, not that one. I'm much more concerned with what's been going on here. Like Mother and Dina – what's happened between them? Dina wouldn't come with me, and Mother didn't even ask how she was.'

Pa turned away and looked out across the sea to where the islands shimmered in the haze. Silence drifted in, dense and uncomfortable. 'Pa?'

'You should talk to Dina,' he said eventually. 'It's her place to—'

'She won't tell me. And I don't want to have to ask Mother – she's so happy I'm back. I don't want to ruin things, but I need to know what's been going on.'

Pa began to walk again and I fell in step, finding myself slightly irritated at the slowness of his pace as we left the harbour and began to walk between the pine trees. 'Look, I don't know what's true or not, and I've only got your mother's side of things. I don't necessarily agree with what she says, but the fact is, well, from quite a while ago there was talk. About Dina.'

'What *about* Dina? For Christ's sake, Pa, just tell me.'

'About her and Pavle. People thought . . . He was seen coming and going from your house, sometimes after dark. There was gossip – Ljeta changed while you were away, people had nothing to do, not enough to occupy their minds. Other people's lives – for some they became their main focus of interest.'

'But surely Dina knew what was being said?'

'She did. But she changed once you left; after losing the baby it was like nothing mattered to her any more. I know they're talking, Petar, she said to me once, when I went round to see if she was OK. I know what people are saying and I don't care. And I think that was exactly it. She just didn't care about anything.'

'But you didn't believe it.'

'None of us did at first. And I still don't think there's any truth in it. But your mother . . . they had a big row about, well, she became obsessed with not being able to visit Irina's grave. It was something she wanted to do for you as well as for her, but because Irina was buried somewhere up in Konavle and not in the churchyard, it wasn't possible. The way she tells it, she said to Dina that she didn't understand how she managed to get up into Konavle with all the troops everywhere and –' he took a deep breath – 'Dina told your mother that Pavle took her. That he drove her up into the woods and . . .'

I closed my eyes. 'Don't.'

I felt Pa's hand on my arm. 'It was just too much for her, Miro. She couldn't bear that it was him, at her granddaughter's burial.'

'*My daughter's burial.*' I could barely get the words out.

'Yes. I know.'

'And so that proved they were having an affair?'

Pa shook his head. 'Your mother asked her, straight out. You know what's she's like. And Dina refused to answer. She just told her to leave. They haven't spoken since.'

'But that doesn't . . . I mean . . .' I looked at Pa, trying to find some semblance of truth in his familiar, kindly face. 'Do you think it too then? Does everyone?'

'I don't,' he said firmly. 'And what does it matter what anyone else thinks? All that matters is what's true. You need to go home and talk to her.'

'But what if it is true?' I shouted. 'He came to see me, Pa, he came to see me in Dubrovnik. Did you know that?'

'Of course we knew – we were desperate for news of you. But that just made your mother more angry. She accused Dina of sending her lover to find out how you were.'

'That doesn't sound like Mother.'

'She's changed,' said Pa sadly. 'The war's changed all of us, but your mother, it's like she's retreated into herself. After what happened to her as a child, what she saw, she needed to be able to believe that was all behind us. That's why Knin was so important to her, Serbs and Croats living together; in some way it proved the struggle had been worth it. To have it all explode again . . . she's angry. Looking for someone to blame. Often it's me. But Dina's got caught up in it too.'

'Oh, Pa. Are you all right?'

He looked at me then, my wise, kindly father and in his eyes there was such sadness that I felt the old anger rise up in me, an ache of fury for the damage the war had wreaked. 'I'm alive and well,' he said. 'And so are my children. That's more than many others can say.'

Lunch passed off awkwardly, with all of us aware that however much we talked there was far more we weren't saying. I smiled at the most recent pictures of Cvita's children, read Tara's latest letter where she talked of meeting Goran in Split, and how – apart from being thinner and sporting a dark beard – he seemed amazingly unchanged. I wondered how honest she was being, but as I joined in with the slightly hollow laughter and talk of what Ivo would do when he was fully fit again, I realized truth had become a currency everyone was wary about dealing in. As I walked home, I noticed how different Ljeta looked to the village I had left behind six months earlier. The shop windows on the harbour front were smudged with grime and dust, the flower beds outside the *slastičarna* that Mij had always tended so lovingly were full of withered brown plants, ugly against the soil. Slogans had been sprayed on walls – *Serbs go home* – and a strange, bitter silence seeped through the streets like mist. Even the birds seemed muted and the cats ran silently in the shadows, bodies low to the floor.

In spite of the soldiers' retreat, Pavle was still a presence. He was Ivo's rackety cough, the sorrowful look in my father's eyes, the anger and distrust that had soured the relationship between Dina and Mother. I stopped outside my house and made a silent promise that I would not let him destroy my marriage; whatever had happened between them couldn't be any worse than my affair with Marian. I was in no position to judge.

'So?' Dina was in her gardening clothes, grubby jeans, a scarf around her head. My heart ached a little. 'How were they?'

'They were fine. Overjoyed that I was safely back, as you'd imagine. But they all looked so old. And as for Ivo . . .'

'I know. I'm so sorry, he's such a sweet man. When we heard what had happened, when I heard—'

'We? Who's we?' The words snapped out of me, harsh and fast.

'Your mother told you then.'

'Told me what?'

'Don't be a child, Miro. We both know what she's been saying about me.'

'Actually it was Pa that told me. Mother didn't mention your name.'

'I bet she didn't.'

'Dina . . .' I was at a loss for words, she seemed so *angry*. 'I don't understand all this. You used to be so close. How will things be if you two don't speak? She loved you like a daughter.'

'*No*. No, she didn't. No mother would have failed a daughter as she did me. I lost my child, lost my husband. And what she accused me of, that she could even think . . .'

'But you didn't deny –' I broke off, but it was too late.

'So you *did* speak to her.'

'No, I told you, I talked to Pa. I made him tell me what she suspected. I know you would never have done anything, I know . . .' I sat down at the table and looked up at her. 'I just don't understand why when Mother asked you, why you wouldn't tell her it wasn't true.'

'Why the hell should I have to deny it?' she snapped, banging the table with her hand. 'How could anyone think I could betray you? Is that what you think?'

'No, of course not.' But I knew I didn't sound convincing. No one – including me – would ever have thought me capable of betraying Dina, and yet I had, in the worst possible way. Suddenly it occurred to me that maybe this was my punishment – not the guilt, but the knowledge that it was possible to sleep with Marian and still come home and make love to my wife as if it had never happened. If I was guilty of such treachery, how could I know she wasn't capable of the same thing?

'You think I did it, don't you? Or at the very least you're not sure.'

'No. I don't know. I don't know what to think.' I leaned across the table and wrapped my fingers around her cold hands. 'We've had two weeks together and you didn't tell me any of this. I thought everything was the same, maybe even better, and now I find out that beneath the surface everything's different. I don't know what to think – can't you understand? Why are you so angry?'

'If you don't know what to think, then ask me. I'll never lie to you.'

'I don't want to ask you. I don't need to.'

'I think you do. I think there's a part of you that's dying to ask; did I sleep with Pavle? Did I take him into our bed?' There was something frantic in her tone, almost manic, as if she was pushing for something, for some kind of climax. 'Ask me. You want to, don't you?'

I saw him suddenly, in the Jeep beside me in Dubrovnik; almost immediately another image flicked up, the one that made my stomach churn, Dina and Pavle as Marian and me, bodies wrapped around each other, kissing with the intensity I had never experienced in her arms until I returned a fortnight ago.

'Yes,' I muttered. 'Yes, I do want to know.'

She lifted her chin, her eyes locked coolly on to my face. 'Then. Ask. Me.'

I took a breath, felt my heart stir, couldn't bring myself to say his name. 'Have you been unfaithful, my love?'

For a moment an expression flitted across her face that looked strangely like relief. 'No,' she whispered. 'I have never been unfaithful.' Her fingers tightened around my hands. 'But you have. Haven't you?'

CHAPTER 21

It was colder than it should have been, out in the pine woods. Summer mornings normally started balmy with the dawn, a translucent mauve light creeping across the sea, while the highest peaks of the mountains that linked Ljeta to Dubrovnik glimmered gold as the sun began to make its ascent. Some mornings, when Irina woke early, I would walk her down to the harbour and we would wait together for the first hint of light to seep over the ridge. 'A new day,' I would whisper. 'What adventures will it hold?'

I no longer thought a new day would bring adventures. Instead each dawn seemed to bring new heartbreak, new revelations about those I loved and no longer seemed to know. When I had finally told Dina the truth about Marian there had been no angry scene; instead she listened silently, tears rolling down her face, hands tucked beneath her legs, body locked against any entreaties from me. She had asked no questions, offered no comment, simply brought me a pillow and sheet from our bedroom and disappeared upstairs without a word, the door clicking sharply behind her.

Sleep had proved elusive, and at first light I was out on the harbour, walking towards the pine woods, trying to process what had happened. Was my marriage over? Why had Dina pretended for so long she didn't know? Why hadn't I told her when I first had the chance? I was so lost in thought that it wasn't until I heard my name echoing through the silence that I realized Cata was sitting on the seat I had just walked past.

'Catz?'

She waved her fingers at me and smiled ruefully. As I drew closer to her I realized she was wearing a pair of her father's old pyjamas with a cardigan over the top, her usually neat hair was pulled back into a messy ponytail and her face was grey with tiredness. 'What are you doing here?' I said, hugging her. 'When did you get back?'

'Yesterday. I came as soon as I heard Ljeta was free. Bobo had told me about what happened to Dad. I wanted to come and see him, but Mum said not to risk it, to stay in Dubrovnik. Have you seen him, Miro? God knows, I'm used to being around people who are sick but he just . . . he looks so *ill*.'

I sat down next to her and slipped an arm around her shoulders. 'I know. They all look so old. I feel like I've been away for years. All those months I longed to get back and now . . . everything's a mess.'

'Oh, love,' she said, and I knew instantly that she knew everything, that Bobo had told her what he had seen. 'I'm so sorry. How are things with Dina?'

I shrugged. 'How do you think? That fucking evil brother of hers . . . sorry, but he is. I know you'll say I destroyed my own marriage, but it was nothing, it meant nothing. There was no need for Dina ever to know. What did he think he was going to achieve by telling her?'

'Don't give him that much credit,' she said, bitterly. 'Bobo doesn't think, not any more. He just hurtles about like a tank, fuelled up on anger and vitriol, hell-bent on destroying anything he comes into contact with. I've realized a lot about him since I saw you that time at the hospital. And one of the most important things is how weak he is. It takes a lot to maintain strength or integrity . . . or hope in a situation like we've been in. It's much easier to cave in and just make everything bloody and dark. That's where he is. He doesn't care about anyone or anything.'

'And you? How are you?'

'I'm OK.' She sighed deeply and pressed her fingers to her eyes and I realized she was close to tears. 'But I've made a decision. I'm moving away, Miro. To Zagreb. A friend of mine's parents have a flat that's empty and I'm going to rent it. I've got a transfer to the hospital there. After everything that's happened, I've got to get away. I can't come back to Ljeta, I'd go crazy, and I can't stay in Dubrovnik; everywhere I go makes me think of *him*.'

I pulled back a little and looked into her face. The shadows beneath her eyes were almost purple. 'Wow. That's a pretty major decision. How did your mum take it?'

'We had a huge row last night. It was supposed to be a homecoming, but it turned into a terrible scene. How could I abandon Dad? Didn't I care how ill he was? What did I think running away would achieve?' A tear tipped over on to her cheek and I smoothed it away with my thumb. 'They don't understand, do they? And I don't know how to make them . . . Christ, the things I had to do in Dubrovnik – I've seen more operations, amputations . . . sometimes I have nightmares where I'm drowning in all the blood I saw. But they don't want to hear that from me, and I don't want them to know – and that just leaves a huge gap, doesn't it, a huge bloody gap. Even if the tourists do come back to Ljeta, I can't make breakfasts and clean rooms and open beers at sunset again. There has to be something more. I've got to *do* something more.'

I shifted a little on my seat. Cata's words made me uncomfortable because something in them rang true for me too. After the first wave of joy at my reunion with Dina had started to fade, I began to remember the limitations of my life in Ljeta, the small monotonies that grew to irritate me, the relief of getting on the boat to Dubrovnik and the sweltering, buzzing offices of Zagreb TV.

'I know,' I said hesitantly. 'It's like . . . every day meant something there, didn't it? It was grim, but I felt so *alive*. I don't think I've ever felt more alive.'

'Ironic, since we were all so bloody close to death all the time.'

'But you know what I mean.'

'Honestly? I'm not entirely sure I do. I barely saw anything besides my flat and the hospital. But you, being out in it, filming, and all those people you met, that woman—'

'Don't. It wasn't anything.'

'Then sort it out with Dina. There are worse things than sleeping with someone else, I should know. And she loves you so much. Don't fuck it up. And don't . . .'

'Don't what?'

'Look, don't take this the wrong way, but don't get carried away with all that war-correspondent stuff. Those people, they're not *normal*. That life isn't for you. Don't be—'

'I'm not stupid,' I said, feeling more than a little humiliated. I thought of Nic. 'I didn't even like most of them really.'

'Then go home. Go home and try to make things right.'

I kissed her cheek. 'And you too. Make your mum understand, and if you need me to come and back you up, just call, OK?' I began to walk away when I stopped. 'Cata?' She looked up. 'If . . . if I can't make things right, if Dina won't forgive me, can I come with you to Zagreb?'

'It won't come to that.'

'No, I know. But just, if it does . . . can I come?'

She smiled and nodded, and as I walked away a fresh wave of guilt washed over me, as if in some way I had just betrayed my wife all over again.

Dina was sitting in the garden when I got home. I hadn't expected her to smile when she saw me, but she did – a sad, wistful little smile that made my heart twist. I sat down beside her in the sunshine and we began to talk, haltingly at first, her about her growing friendship with Pavle and me about my time at the Ragusa and the strange characters with whom I shared my days. Instead of the sanitized snippets we had shared in our first weeks back together, we began to talk of our separate realities; her daily horror of having to wake each morning to an empty house, bereft of Irina's laughter and the sound of my breathing in the bed beside her; the terrible destruction I saw and the constant unpredictability of life in a city under siege.

'I can't bear you've done this,' she said, her eyes blurry with tears. 'I think of you, with her.'

'Don't,' I said, taking her hands in mine. 'Imagining things like that, that's what I did when Pavle came to see me in Dubrovnik. It drives you crazy. Don't do it, don't imagine it. It happened once.' I tried to ignore the twist of guilt at my dishonesty. 'It meant nothing.'

'But you worked with her for months.'

'Yes, but that was all before anything happened. She left a day or two after we . . . I didn't see her again.'

'But if she hadn't gone?'

I took a deep breath and tried to convince myself what I was about to say was the truth. 'It was a drunken mistake. It meant nothing. And I'll never see her again. I'm so, so sorry.'

'I'm sorry too, sorry that Pavle was there when I . . . when Irina . . .' Her face crumpled and I drew her to me. 'I just knew that was where she had to be, and he was the only one who could get up into Konavle.'

I laid a finger to her lips. 'Take me there,' I whispered. 'Let's go. Let's go now, please. You can't imagine what it's like not to know where she is.'

'I don't know if we can get there,' she said slowly. 'I haven't been into Konavle since Pavle used to—'

'Please. Let's not mention his name again. No Pavle. Just you and me.'

'And no journalist bitch.' The bitterness in her voice filled me with self-loathing; I had put that note there, that harsh, angry tone. It had never existed before.

'Let's just try.'

She looked at me. 'Yes, let's try,' she said, and a part of me wondered what she meant; let's try and forget your infidelity, let's try and recover from the death of our daughter, let's try and ignore the fact that our marriage suddenly seems to have four people in it rather than two.

We were barely out of Ljeta before the scale of the destruction wreaked on Konavle became apparent. Greying empty fields stretched either side of the road, dotted with burnt-out cottages and scorched, decapitated trees. Silence hung across the valley like winter mist. I drove slowly, feeling the car jolt across potholes and shattered stretches of road, steering to avoid rotting carcases of sheep and goats and piles of crumbling rubble.

'All these lives,' Dina whispered. 'Decades to build them, centuries even. Blown apart in one night.' She pointed and I turned the car left, driving slowly into the small town of Sipili. 'Can you believe this is where we used to dance? I loved those Sunday mornings so much – getting into my costume, driving up with Karena and Sara; the first moment when we stepped into the middle of the square and the music began. It was so wonderful, to be part of something that celebrated all that I loved most. Do you remember how beautiful it was?'

'Of course. I used to beg Mother to let me off clearing breakfast, just so I could come and watch you dance.' I could still picture it so clearly: the women, clad in scarlet, twirling their partners around the square, the smell of spiced *sremska* twisting up from the nearby stalls, Dina taking visitors by the hand and leading them into the dancing, all of us laughing as they tried and failed to follow the steps. We pulled up in the main square and I stared through the windscreen. It seemed impossible that anything good had ever happened here. The town was completely destroyed, blackened gutted houses leeching the detritus of abandoned lives across silent streets.

'It reminds me of Dubrovnik,' I said slowly. 'All this destruction . . . and the air, it has the same . . .' I stopped and looked at Dina, realizing I didn't want her to understand the sickly, cloying scent of decay that hung all around us. Konavle reeked of death, of decomposing bodies and animal corpses left to rot in the sun. It took me back to some of what I had seen on trips into Bosnia and I felt thankful Dina hadn't witnessed what had happened here and would never fully understand the horrors I had seen.

'Miro?' I turned and her face was stained with tears. 'There's nothing more, is there? You have told me everything? Because I do want us to get through this, but there can't be any more lies.'

'There's nothing more.' I ignored the now-familiar twinge of guilt and slipped my fingers under her chin, kissing her gently. 'And I'm more sorry than you'll ever know.'

She nodded. 'Let's go on.'

I reversed the car slowly and she pointed to the entrance to a road that led up to the hills, but we had only driven a few hundred metres before the way was blocked by a burnt-out van. I reversed and turned up another side street, but the road was equally impassable, scattered with huge chunks of debris and a wall that had crumbled into the street.

'There's no other way up,' said Dina, in a small voice.

'Can we walk?'

'It's too far. Too hot. And there might be mines. I'm not sure it's safe.'

There was nothing for it but to turn the car around. Neither of us spoke, but as I nursed the car along the uneven streets I couldn't avoid feeling there was something horribly symbolic in not being able to reach Irina's grave.

'We'll get there,' she said, reading my thoughts. 'Maybe tomorrow we'll go early and get as far as we can and then walk. I'll get you there, I promise.'

But we didn't go back into Konavle the next day, or the one after that. The summer weather finally broke and thick grey clouds rolled in, glowering down on all of us as we tried to piece together the scattered fragments of our lives. Dina let me stay in the house, even in our bed, but there was no intimacy between us. Life became a series of unspoken conversations. She and I didn't mention Marian or Pavle; more worryingly we didn't talk about Irina. Mother and I kept Dina out of our conversations, and when all of us gathered to put Cata on the bus to Zagreb, no one mentioned that Marjana remained at the back of the group and refused to hug her daughter goodbye.

Somehow the sense of euphoria we were all waiting for – the relief of liberation, our sudden reclamation of freedom – never came. 'It's like a permanent wake,' I said to Damir, as we sat at a table in one of the few cafes that had reopened in Dubrovnik. 'All anyone does is talk. They sit for hours, outside the pension, in the cafes, just talking about what happened. But what really happened to them? Compared to what we saw in Dubrovnik and in Bosnia, life in Ljeta was like a school picnic.'

Damir shook his head. 'That's hardly fair. They're grieving for the lives they had, for a time before they knew what they know now. Why are you so impatient with them? And all those refugees from Konavle, they suffered far worse than many people here. Everyone needs time to grieve, including you and Dina. How are the two of you?'

It was a question I didn't want to answer. I had come to Dubrovnik at Dina's insistence to tell Damir I wouldn't be coming back to Zagreb TV for the next few weeks at least. No amount of insisting that it was a job, and I couldn't just come and go as I pleased, made any difference. As Dina saw it, our lives had been smashed apart and we needed time to put them together again, a process that would not be helped by me running off to Dubrovnik every day, back to the world that had almost destroyed us in the first place.

'Difficult,' I said slowly. 'On the surface OK, but underneath ... Jesus, Damir, it's a mess. I know you know what happened here, with Marian. Dina knows too, but the irony is the whole bloody village thinks she did the same thing with one of the soldiers. Everyone thinks I'm the injured party and she's the guilty one. She won't deny it because she doesn't see why she should; my mother won't speak to her, we're living like bloody brother and sister and now she's insisting that I tell you I can't come back to work for weeks because we have to put things right at home.'

Damir leaned across the table and laid a hand on my arm. 'Miro, she's right. Of course she's right. Everyone needs time to get over what's happened, and for what it's worth, I don't think you've even started. Why don't you and Dina go away for a bit? Go and stay with your sister – isn't she up in Istria now? Or what about that friend of yours, Tara? Isn't she on some island somewhere? Getting away from here would do you both the power of good.'

'You don't understand. Dina wouldn't go away in a million years, not now – she's already involved in all sorts of meetings and trips into Konavle to see what can be salvaged.'

'Keeping busy is good,' he said firmly. 'You know that's always been my philosophy. But you both need time to mourn, together. Losing Irina was a tragedy, a real tragedy, and instead of being able to grieve you found yourself in a completely different world, surrounded by people who live a very particular way of life.'

'But what if I *liked* that way of life? What if it made me feel, I don't know, worthwhile? All the years I've watched my brother, first in the police, then in the army, really doing something that mattered. And that's how I felt those months at the Ragusa, out on the road with Marian.'

'And you can have that again. Not like it was – thank God – but there'll be work here when you're ready to come back. Right now you need to be with your wife and family, and you're so lucky that you have the opportunity to do that. Why isn't that enough for you? What is it that you're scared of?'

'I don't know,' I said honestly, but I couldn't get Damir's question out of my mind as I sat on the boat home. I knew, deep down, that my grief for Irina lay buried and unprocessed, but what Damir had recognized in me was something I could barely admit to myself. He was right, I *was* afraid, and as the rooftops of Ljeta slowly drifted into view, I realized the fear was of my own life, the one that I had lived before the war came. I was afraid it would no longer be enough.

CHAPTER 22

As the days grew shorter, and the winter sun cast a gentler light across the shell-shocked streets of my village, things slowly began to change. It was as if Ljeta was waking up; shops reopened, houses were painted, and up in Konavle work began on trying to make at least some of the villages habitable again. A man was sent from the government to establish the scale of the rebuild operation, and after much discussion Dina was chosen to drive him around and try to explain how the region had looked before the invasion. When she came back each evening, flushed and excited with plans for the rebirth of the region she loved so much, it was the happiest I had seen her since Irina died.

But while Dina flourished, I felt increasingly marooned. Everyone I had been closest to had gone: Cata to Zagreb, Josip to Germany, Pavle disappeared for good. 'It's so bloody ironic,' I said to Mother, as we sat over coffee one morning. 'All those months I was so desperate to get back here, and now I'm here all I seem to want to do is get away.'

'You need to go back to work,' she said. 'Just tell Dina – she can't stop you. I just don't understand why you do as she says all the time.'

'Because she's had a dreadful time and I want to make her happy,' I snapped. 'You don't understand how things are.'

Mother's lips pressed into a tight line, but I knew exactly what she was thinking. I had lost count of the times I had insisted nothing had happened between Dina and Pavle, but each time she would nod and pat my arm and say, 'If that's what you want to believe then I quite understand.' Pa would shake his head and exchange glances with Ivo, and Mother would tut and tell them that she wasn't blind and if Pa had something to say perhaps he should say it out loud. I knew, deep down, that I should come clean about what had really happened, admit that I had been the unfaithful one, not Dina, but just the thought of the disbelief on my mother's face, the disappointment on my father's, kept me from telling them the truth.

'I just thought I'd warn you,' Pa said, appearing in the kitchen in dirty, grime-clad overalls, 'that bloody brother-in-law of yours is back. Saw his car outside your house.'

'Bobo? Christ, that's all I need.' I kissed Mother on the cheek and hurried out of the pension and back along the harbour. Bobo had already done his worst, but I had little doubt that he would happily cause further trouble if he could.

To my surprise, when I opened the door he turned and shifted from foot to foot, unable to meet my gaze.

'Bobo, I'd like you to leave please.'

He cleared his throat awkwardly. 'Miro. Look, I know what you think about me. I understand . . . but I'm not here about you. It's, look, do you know where Cata is? It's like she's just disappeared off the face of the planet. I want to talk to her . . . things were said.'

'Things were said, or things were *done*?'

Bobo's face went scarlet. I watched his fingers tighten on the back of the chair. 'What happened is between us. But I want to . . . I need to, well, just talk to her.'

'Oh, between you two, is it?' The memory of Bobo's boot in my guts burned through my body. 'Like our marriage is just between Dina and me? Because it didn't seem to stop you steaming in and trying to destroy it.'

'I haven't *fucked someone else.*' The measured tone had disappeared. 'My sister had a right to know.'

'And it was my right to tell her,' I shouted.

'Then why didn't you?' Dina said, her voice high and angry. 'Why didn't you tell me? I waited and waited for those two weeks, a whole fortnight we had together with no one else to interfere . . . You could have told me then, tried to explain.'

'Clearly Bobo had already done so,' I said, unable to keep the bitterness out of my voice. 'I bet you fucking *ran* from the Ragusa to tell her, didn't you? You must have been delighted . . .'

'Don't be ridiculous,' snapped Dina. 'He thought I should know and he was *right*. Unlike you.'

'I wanted to tell you. I meant to,' I said desperately. 'But it was so perfect. I didn't want to spoil it.'

'Perfect until your mother told you I'd been sleeping with Pavle.'

'You believed *that*?' Bobo's voice was thick with scorn. 'Not everyone betrays people they love quite as easily as you.'

'It wasn't easy,' I said, looking at Dina. 'I told you, you know what happened. I saw Pavle in Dubrovnik . . . He tried to make me think something was happening between you two and I just couldn't bear it. I got really drunk and out of control and it just happened.'

'Say that again?' Bobo stared at me. 'You slept with that whore the day Pavle came to Dubrovnik?'

I squirmed. 'Yes.'

'And it was just one time, and it didn't mean anything?'

'Yes.'

'*Liar!*' Bobo roared. 'I was in Ljeta the day Pavle came to Dubrovnik – remember, Dina? It was Mother's birthday. I was here when he came back and told you he had seen Miro. I slept on the sofa that night. I didn't go back to the city until two days later. Don't you remember, you persuaded me to try and talk to Cata, and I found her at the hospital and she told me Miro was desperate to see me. So I went to the hotel and, well, there you were. With *her.*'

Dina stared at me, her face taut with anger. 'So you slept with her the night Pavle came to the city. And then my brother saw you kissing her in the lift three days later. Tell me again, how many times did you have sex with her?'

I looked at both of them, my heart racing. Bobo's mouth curled into a triumphant half-smile that was totally devoid of warmth. 'Come on, Miro. Tell the truth now. If you know what that is.'

'Bobo, get out. This has nothing to do with you.' The contained fury in Dina's tone made my heart sink. Even Bobo recognized it, picked up his coat and slowly walked out of the house.

'So?'

I took a deep breath. 'It happened once more. Just once. She was going away; everyone was drunk.'

'Oh, and that makes it OK does it? Being drunk?'

'*No,*' I protested. 'But I don't know what else you want me to say. I slept with her twice, it meant nothing, I was drunk. It's . . . it's that kind of world. I just lost myself.'

'When we were up in Sipili, I said no more lies. I *asked* you was there anything else.'

'This isn't anything else. This is nothing but trouble, stirred up by your brother.'

'Don't blame him,' she shouted. 'Don't blame him for your transgressions. You did this. You've ruined everything.'

'Christ, Dina, don't you ever stop?' The words were out of my mouth before I had even realized I was going to say them. 'I'm sorry. I've said I'm sorry a thousand times and I mean it. I've done what you ask, not gone back to a job I love. You have to get over this.'

'And if I can't?'

'Then I'll go. I'll go to Zagreb and stay with Cata. I can't live like this any more.'

She stared at me for a moment, shock written across her face. 'You'd go to Zagreb? Is that what you've been planning? To be with *her*?'

'Who? *Her*? Of course not, don't be stupid. But if you can't forgive me . . .'

'You'll run away again?'

'What do you mean, again?'

'Like Dubrovnik, when you left me here alone to grieve for our daughter?'

I stared at her. 'You can't think, I mean you can't . . . I didn't have any choice, you *know* that. If I'd stayed, I would have been arrested, *you'd* have been arrested. Pavle made that perfectly clear. I was desperate not to go. I went because it protected *you*.'

'Bobo would have found a way to stay,' she said, and there was an edge of spite in her voice. 'Goran wouldn't have gone either.'

'Well, maybe you should have fucking married him then,' I yelled. 'Or maybe you should have fucked Pavle and then we'd be equal and you could get off the moral high ground and stop making me feel like shit all the time.'

'Well, maybe you should go to *fucking* Zagreb,' she said, imitating the way I swore with icy precision. 'You've brought no happiness back to this house, or to me. You've lied to me over and over, destroyed my trust, hurt me more than you can know, and I didn't think that was possible after Irina.'

'Well, maybe I should go then. If I'm making you so unhappy.'

She deflated suddenly, ran her fingers through her hair, and when she looked at me there was real devastation in her face. 'Yes,' she whispered, 'I think perhaps you should.'

The next few days felt like a bad dream. I began to put plans in place to move to Zagreb; talking to Damir about whom I should contact for work, asking Cata about staying with her, looking at bus times. At every step I told myself that it wasn't going to happen, that this was just some elaborate game Dina and I were playing, that sooner or later she would ask me to stay, or I would tell her that I didn't want to go. I found myself missing Goran desperately, sure that somehow he would have stopped the situation escalating, forced us to come together and talk. But without him the conversation didn't happen; it was as if an invisible wall had grown up between us, and neither of us knew how to scale it. I slept on the sofa, unwilling to let my parents know had bad things were, and for three days we circled each other like strangers and I struggled desperately to think of the words that would pull us back from the abyss.

On the fourth day, Dina appeared in the kitchen with her overnight bag packed. 'I'm going away for a few days,' she said wearily. 'Back to Morsać. Some of the houses there are still habitable, and Mother says there are workmen ready to start clearing. I want to be there when that happens.'

'How long will you be gone?'

'When are you going to Zagreb?'

'Dina, *please*.'

She sat down carefully, keeping her distance. 'Miro, tell me one thing, and don't lie this time. If that *woman* hadn't been going away, would you have carried on sleeping with her? Did it really mean nothing?'

I looked at my wife and knew that if I lied to her now, whatever came after would be worthless. Truth was the only thing left, and I sat forward in my chair and put my head in my hands. 'Honestly? I don't know. It didn't mean nothing, but it only meant something . . . in that world. It was like I wasn't me any more; I lost who I was. And I thought I'd lost you too.'

'But you hadn't,' she said, and the unspoken words hung in the air: '*But you have now.*'

'Don't go.' Panic began to rise up inside me. Christ, this was really happening, she was going, she was leaving me. 'Please, Dina, don't do this.'

'It's already done,' she said, and I realized she was crying too. 'It's too much, Miro. I can't take any more.'

'It's Irina, isn't it,' I said bitterly. 'You never forgave me for that.'

She looked at me, her beautiful hazel eyes blurred with tears. 'I have tried,' she whispered.

'But it wasn't my fault.'

'Perhaps. But this is. And I just can't forgive you again.'

Within twenty-four hours I was on the bus out of Ljeta. No one came to see me off. Mother and Pa were horrified I was leaving; *giving up*, Pa called it, *running away*, according to Mother. I hadn't even bothered to try to make them understand, still too shocked by the fact that my marriage appeared to be over. Nothing mattered apart from getting out of the village and finding my way as quickly as possible back to a world that enveloped me so completely I could forget the pain of my daughter and now the loss of Dina.

'They're just hurt,' Cata said, as we walked through the busy streets from Zagreb bus terminal back to her flat. 'They want everything to go back to the way it was – for their generation that's the way it works; they want to pretend it all never happened. But we can't do that, can we? I don't want to go back. It's like we were all living in some sort of childish dream.'

I nodded. 'It doesn't seem real now, does it? I try to picture Ljeta as it was, with tourists and water taxis and those two brothers that used to come and play the *tamburitza* and sing every night. D'you remember? It's like some kind of fairy story. Like we all just made it up.'

She unlocked the door and I followed her into a dimly lit hallway. 'So what will you do? Try and get some work for Zagreb TV?'

I shook my head. 'I want to go to Bosnia – that's where the story is. Sarajevo maybe.'

She raised her eyebrows. 'Are you crazy? You won't get in for a start. The Serbs will never let a Croat through the checkpoints, no matter who you're working for. And it's too bloody dangerous.'

'I don't care. Christ, Cata, I've lost my daughter, now my wife . . . I've got to do *something*. I was good in Dubrovnik, I know what I'm doing with a camera, maybe I can help.'

'But there are enough journalists out there already, the city's teeming with them.'

'I don't *care*,' I said again, bitterly. 'Don't you understand? I've got nothing left; I'm like them, those poor fuckers in Sarajevo; I understand what it is to lose everything. I can't be in Ljeta, or even Dubrovnik, where people go to work and come home to their husbands or wives or children and eat their meals and sleep easy in their beds. I had that and I lost it. I fucked it up and that's in my head all the time, from the moment I wake up till the moment I go to sleep, and I've got to go somewhere I can't hear it or I'll just go fucking crazy.'

'You still love her, don't you?'

'So much. She's like a part of me.'

'Then go back to Ljeta. What are you doing here? Go home, tell her how you feel, try and put things back together.'

'I *can't*. Not yet at any rate. She's too angry, and I don't blame her. Everyone's angry there; it's like people pushed down their emotions for so long during the siege, now everything's come to the surface. Mother's endlessly sniping at Pa, she and Dina don't speak, your mum is angry at the world because of your dad.'

'And because of me.'

'You've done the right thing,' I laid my hand on top of hers. 'And this is right for me. I'm not that person any more, I don't fit there. I don't know where I fit any more. The only thing that makes sense of this whole bloody, god-awful situation we're in is to work. To get out there, in among it, where life is really happening.'

'I don't know about life happening,' she said, sadly. 'Sounds to me like you've got a bloody death wish.'

Zagreb suited my cousin. Once I had settled into her tiny flat, stowed my bag behind the sofa and smiled wistfully at the pictures of Ljeta on the wall in the kitchen, she took me out and showed me the life she had built in the city: the chic, glass-fronted cafe that served her coffee and fresh pastries each morning, her favourite walk through Maksimir Park, the battered trams that carried her back and forth from the hospital. She lived in an old part of the city, where elegant townhouses looked out through towering plane trees and it was so utterly different in every way from Ljeta that I managed to box up the pain of my broken marriage and store it away, in the same dark corner where I kept the memories of my daughter.

Work proved easy to come by, although Cata was right, getting to Sarajevo seemed an impossibility. A Foreign Press Bureau had been set up at the Novi Hotel and within days I had work as an interpreter, driving back and forth up to Slavonia and into the Krajina, where the war was still ongoing and there was no sign of the kind of withdrawal by the Serbs that had brought peace to the south of the country. Each morning as we set off I told myself this was the day I would find Goran; that if I was going to run across him anywhere it would be the Krajina, the area where his own personal war began. It was a ridiculous hope, but I clung to it through the long days with the German crew and in the hotel bar later, when I drank their vodka and listened to their stories, and it almost felt like I was back at the Ragusa, with a marriage to go home to and a life that wanted me.

Christmas came and went and I didn't go home with Cata. I

couldn't face the disappointment in Mother's face, the rejection in Dina's. I had written to her twice, asking how she was, but there had been no response. Snow fell and I felt constantly chilled; as the old year slipped away and the first days of 1993 drifted by, I felt a sense of going nowhere, my mood as grey as the thick, dense clouds that hung above the city. The RTL crew had taken off to Bosnia and, apologetically, told me they couldn't take me with them. I spent my days hanging out in the Foreign Press Bureau, doing snippets of translation and hoping someone I knew from Dubrovnik would pass through. When I heard that three journalists had been injured in Sarajevo, one of them a blonde English woman, my heart leaped at the thought of it being Marian, at the possibility she would be airlifted out to Zagreb hospital.

'Claire someone,' Cata said, when I asked her casually whether any journalists had been admitted to the hospital that day. 'Nasty leg injury, but it could have been a lot worse. I'm so glad you're not there, Miro. One of the guys brought in today said reporters were being picked off by snipers like target practice. He was quite a character, said when he got back to the city he was going to paint over the word "press" on his car with "Shoot me, I'm immortal". He thought they might have more respect for that.'

I looked up; something about the attitude sounded familiar. 'Did you get the guy's name?'

'Yes, but I've forgotten it. He was French though. Phenomenally lucky – he'd taken a bit of shrapnel in his shoulder. An inch to the left and it would have hit his jugular. I told him he was incredibly fortunate and he just laughed. "God and I have a deal," he said. I thought he was a bit cracked.'

Nic Richaud. Here, in Zagreb. My only possible ticket to Sarajevo. 'So his injuries weren't serious?'

She shook her head. 'Not really. We patched him up. He should have stayed in overnight but he wouldn't hear of it. I expect he'll be on the next flight back to Sarajevo. Crazy.' She looked up at me. 'You going somewhere?'

'I know him,' I said. 'He's the guy that got me back to Ljeta. I need to see him.' I pulled on my coat, scarf and gloves and bent in to kiss Cata. 'Have a hot bath – you look done in. Don't wait up.'

CHAPTER 23

The flight banked sharply and I looked across at Nic, who grinned and stuck his thumb up. 'The old team back together, eh, Miro? Couldn't believe it when you walked into the Novi. Always hoped we'd work together again. You're about the only fucker I've met who's as crazy as me.'

I smiled and tried to tell myself it was a compliment. Out of the window, the pockmarked rooftops of Sarajevo were juddering into view and I tried to mentally catch up with myself. Three days ago I had been sitting in Cata's flat, the prospect of another day at the Foreign Press Bureau filling me with despair. Once I had found Nic at the Novi Hotel, it had taken all of ten minutes before he suggested I go back to Sarajevo with him, totally unfazed by the risks of taking a Croatian national through Serbian checkpoints. I agreed instantly.

'Get ready,' he said. 'The airport is under constant sniper fire; it's one of the most dangerous areas in the city. Put this on –' he threw across a flak jacket. 'And before you say I'm not wearing one, that's my decision. I know how this place works. You don't.'

Within seconds of the plane door creaking open, adrenalin was pulsing through my body. The ice-cold air hit my face with a smack and my ears rang to the sound of tracer fire as we raced across the tarmac, my heart thudding in time with my feet. Nic pointed to an armoured car; a man got out as we approached, threw him the keys.

He caught them with one hand and hurled himself into the driver's seat in one seamless manoeuvre. I pulled the handle on the passenger side; it clicked but nothing happened. Sniper shots clapping in my ears, I pulled again. 'Door's fucked,' Nic shouted, 'bullet or something in the mechanism. Slide in through the window.'

I dived in head first, ending up a sprawling mess on the back seat. The man in the passenger seat roared with laughter as the car screamed away, Nic fiddling with the tape recorder while he drove. Within seconds, the roaring guitars of *Tri Lopovi* were booming out of the tinny speakers; I rubbed the back of my head where I had connected with the opposite door and sat up feeling dizzy and disorientated.

'Welcome to Sarajevo,' said Nic. 'Like my theme tune? Nino, what are this lot called again?'

'*Tri Lopovi*,' yelled the man in the passenger seat. 'Three thieves.'

Nic nodded, smacking the steering wheel in time to the thumping drums. I listened to the song: *No bullet, no knife, no threat, no weapon, nothing can hurt me if I have your love . . .* Just as I was wondering if he knew what the lyrics meant, he surprised me by singing along in English. 'Nino translated it for me,' he bellowed, grinning into the rear-view mirror. 'He reckons they wrote it with me in mind. Now, if I time this right, those three *lopovis* will be singing their last *I'm gonna live forever* just as we pull up in the car park at the hotel. Nice touch, eh? Play it every time. If I lose this tape, I'm fucked.'

I was surprised. War reporters were a superstitious bunch, most had their own rituals they believed would keep them safe, but Nic had always sneered at such things when we were in Dubrovnik. Perhaps Sarajevo had changed him. As I peered out of the window into the gathering gloom I could see why: the destruction was on a scale that far outstripped anything I had seen before. Every building seemed to be damaged, great gashes in the brickwork, windows blown out, street lamps twisted and bent like drooping flowers.

Black-eyed traffic lights ignored us as we roared down the empty road, burnt-out cars rusted on street corners like rotting metallic cadavers and in the air there was the reek of human decay, the one I recognized in Konavle, that I first smelt in Dubrovnik.

'Two minutes and we'll be at the hotel,' said Nic, his eyes fixed on the road. 'You might want to hold on to something. I like the underground car park, but you have to take the road down at a bit of a lick as the snipers love it. Most of the hacks leave their cars out front, which is why they're all riddled with bullet holes. Ready?'

I grabbed the handle in the passenger door as Nic shot past the front of the Sarajevo Hotel and flung the car around a tight downward bend. Sniper fire rang out and I shrank down in my seat. He laughed contemptuously. 'You'll get used to it.' The car juddered to a halt and I realized my fingers were wrapped so tightly around the handle I had red welts on my palm. 'When you get out of the car, stay close to the wall, and if I say run, run. The guy up on that building over there lives to try and take us out. There's one around the other side too, so never, *never* use the front door. And don't use the lift either, although there's rarely any power for it to work. There's a sniper who's got a direct line of sight into it from a building opposite. Juergen from RTL found that out to his cost a few weeks back.'

The hotel lobby was dark apart from a few candles; behind reception, a gaunt young woman with huge violet eyes broke into a smile as we approached. 'Nicolas,' she said, leaning forward to kiss him on both cheeks, 'you're back. What do you have for me?'

Nic pulled out a wedge of deutschmarks and laid them on the desk. From his trouser pockets he produced two bars of chocolate, a tube of toothpaste and a floral-wrapped bar of soap. Her face lit up as if he had given her a diamond necklace.

'Is your brother still up for a meet?'

The woman nodded, her fingers tearing at the chocolate, snapping off one chunk and biting into it carefully. She savoured it, rolling it around her mouth, a look of ecstasy on her face. 'I'll save the other half for Ilena,' she said. It took me a moment to realize she meant the other half of the chunk, rather than the bar.

'Marta's brother's in the Bosnian army, such as it is,' Nic told me, after I had dumped my bag in a small dark room that held nothing but a bed and a wooden table with a half-burnt candle on a saucer. 'He can take us right up to the front line, the one in the city. They're so close to the Serbs they can smell their farts. Might give you a day or two to get used to things first though.'

'Looks like it takes a bit of getting used to,' I said, following him out of my room and through the door opposite. Nic's room was bigger, but no less bare. A half-finished bottle of Johnnie Walker stood on the table next to a battered cassette player; he flicked the switch and the strains of Miles Davis seeped into the smoke-filled air.

'You're not wrong there,' he said. 'The question is, young Miro, are you ready for it? Because I don't do this city like half of these lazy fuckers who never leave the hotel, file their live reports from the roof and make like heroes. We're getting in amongst it, going where angels fear to tread. Or maybe we're the angels, eh?' He passed the bottle of whisky and I took a long slug, remembering happily its seemingly magical ability to dissipate the anxiety and guilt that flickered permanently in my mind.

'Hardly angels. But what's the point of being here if you don't get stuck in? That's why I came. To really get the stories told.'

He looked at me curiously. 'I have been wondering. Didn't you have a life you were keen to get back to? Didn't I run a couple of checkpoints and lose six bottles of whisky because you were so desperate to go home?'

'Things didn't work out,' I said shortly, my fingers massaging the gold metal disc that hung around my neck. 'And I'm here for the same reason everyone is: because what's happening is beyond shocking and the world needs to know about it.'

He laughed a sharp bark that was devoid of humour. 'Still such an innocent, aren't you? The world does know. That's not the problem. It's making the world *care* that's the tricky part. And don't believe for a moment that everyone is here for such noble reasons as you.' I tried to ignore the slightly mocking tone that had crept into his voice. 'Some want to play the hero, others are voyeurs, some simply have a death wish. There are junkies and travellers looking to save their souls, fantasists and sadists who've washed up here because it's the latest, biggest fight. We've all got a reason. Even the Iron Lady is on some mission to prove she can live up to her father's legacy.'

'Marian's here?' I said it too quickly. Nic knew it; he missed nothing.

'She's in and out. She went east a couple of days ago with a UN convoy – Goražde, I think. The question is, my Croatian friend, which are you? Hero or voyeur?'

'None of the above,' I said firmly. 'I just needed a new start.'

'Well, you've chosen a strange place to do it. Sarajevo is a city in its death throes. It's an ending, not a beginning.'

Two weeks passed before Marta made good on her promise to introduce us to her brother, a fortnight that seemed long enough for a season to turn. Sarajevo was nothing like I had imagined, more desperate, more belligerent, more chaotic than it was possible to comprehend. Nic gave me a crash course in the city: the hospitals, the stinking morgue, the orphanages where silent children stared up from grimy cots, their eyes dark and clouded. I remembered how to film injured bodies, focusing in on haunted faces, rather than severed limbs, shielding those who watched our footage in the comfort of their own homes from the horror we saw on a daily basis.

There was one family in particular Nic had befriended, and he would pop in most days, always with something for them, a packet of cigarettes, some gum, half of whatever the Sarajevo Hotel had managed to give us for breakfast. There was a daughter, Suzanna, around fifteen, who drifted in and out of the lounge exuding teenage boredom. She laughed at Nic's jokes, teased him about his clothes, and it was obvious she reminded him of the girl in Geneva, the one he took ice-skating and knew he had lost to another man.

'You want chips?' she asked me, one afternoon when we were sitting around the table in their neat lounge. 'Mum's just put some on.'

'Chips? Really?'

I looked up as a tired-eyed woman with greying hair brought a steaming bowl of food into the room. Something in the way she moved reminded me of Mother and I missed her suddenly, felt a stab of guilt that I had not been in touch since I had left for Zagreb.

'Try,' Suzanna said, nodding towards the bowl. I picked up a chip and ate it; it tasted of flour and dust and had a strange, sour tang. 'She makes them from flour, cornmeal and yeast. They're better to look at than to eat, but there's nothing else today.'

Food itself was a story in Sarajevo; random items found their way into people's houses from a variety of sources. Three days ago we had visited Suzanna and supper had been a pigeon her father had shot, tiny mouthfuls for all of them, cooked on the fire they fuelled with broken bits of furniture and old window frames they found on the street, dodging sniper fire to scavenge what they could. Once, she told us proudly, they had eaten foie gras, smuggled off the UN base and exchanged for a pair of Suzanna's brother's shoes that no longer fitted. Some days there was no food at all.

By the morning Marta's brother was due to pick us up from the hotel, I felt I'd got the measure of the city. I'd learned fast which roads to avoid, the shortcuts that could be taken through deserted shops, even the hierarchy of reporters who met in the bar each night. There were cliques: the British and Americans, the Germans and a couple of Scandinavians, whose blonde beauty seemed almost inappropriate against such a backdrop of destruction. Nic belonged to all and none; some dismissed him as a lunatic, others as a pleasingly diverting presence. No one questioned his bravery.

'Are you Nicolas?' A tall, gaunt man appeared at our table just as we were finishing the last of the undrinkable coffee.

'Marta's brother?'

He nodded. 'Danić. You are just two?' His English was halting and so thickly-accented I could barely understand him.

Nic gestured to me and I shook Danić's hand, his fingers clutching mine so tightly I almost gasped. We followed him outside, and before I had even closed the door of his battered Fiat we were moving, flying through the empty streets, speed the greatest protection we could have. 'We don't go up Igman,' he said, referring to the mountain south-west of the city, where the Bosnian army was holding on to its last route out to the rest of the country. 'Everyone knows about that, huh? But people should see how it is here, right in the city. So crazy. The Chetniks are not fifty metres from us. If I spit, it lands on their skin.'

My skin began to prickle as we drove into a quarter of the city I hadn't been to before. Hollow-eyed buildings stared down at streets spattered with dried blood, pavement corners blurred by dirty grey hummocks of snow that stubbornly refused to melt. No one was visible and yet the occasional flash and flat bangs of sniper fire proved the area was anything but empty.

'First I show you something.' We followed him down some steps into the basement of a building that had lost its upper two floors. He opened a door and a roomful of children turned round. 'School,' he said. 'There are many like this in the city. They're learning English, so that when they're older they can leave and find new lives.'

'Is it OK to film here?'

'Yes. But fast.'

The children began to clamour around Nic, and he nodded at me as I focused on their faces. 'Please carry on,' he said to the teacher, and she resumed, repeating sentences in Serbo-Croat and then English.

'*Pour ces enfants la guerre n'arrête pas l'éducation,*' said Nic, looking impassively into the lens. '*Chaque matin . . .*' His words were interrupted by a huge blast that shook the building. Some of the children began to scream. Another explosion hit just seconds later, closer this time; a light spray of dust and rubble rained on to the makeshift wooden desks.

'We get out *now!*' shouted Danić. 'Building not safe.'

The teacher barked an order at the children and they all rose to their feet apart from one small boy who stayed frozen in his seat, wide eyes swivelling with fear. Danić lifted him out of his chair and led the way out of the room; we followed, the children between us, trying to soothe them, help them stay calm. Another shell fell, even closer, and one small girl locked her arms around my leg. I shifted my camera to my other hand and scooped her up, almost toppling backwards as she wrapped herself around my neck. 'Keep down, keep *down,*' ordered Danić, as we ran low behind a row of burnt-out cars. 'Under bridge,' he yelled, pointing to a dark space beneath the road. 'Safe there.'

'*Mika!*' screamed the teacher, and I turned to see one of the children had begun to run in the opposite direction, back across the wasteground and into the street. 'Mika come back!' The child turned, and as he did he fell, his body twisting in the dirt. Sniper fire rang out; a sudden explosion. '*Mama,*' he was calling; '*Mama . . .*' and suddenly my mind threw up images: the girl in the alley, Tara lying bleeding into the dusty grass, and anger and disbelief surged through me. Not again, *not again.* Almost without realizing what I was doing I thrust the girl into Danić's arms and began to run into the open space, Nic's shouts echoing behind me. The boy had his hand extended; *Mama,* he called again and suddenly I was back there, back in Dubrovnik, before that in Knin, my heart kicking violently in my chest. Gravel scraped along my arms as I swept him out of the road, warm blood oozing through my shirt from the wound on his leg. But his eyes were open, his fingers clung to my arms, and as I hurtled back I knew we would make it, that he would be safe, that I could outrun them, out-dodge them, that this was why I had come. I leaped down the steps and almost threw him into the arms of his teacher. The street rang to the sound of frustrated sniper fire.

Danić looked at me. 'You're brave.'

I shook my head, breathing hard, a grin spreading across my face. 'Not brave,' I panted. 'I just couldn't let him lie there.'

'You could have been killed,' said Nic.

'But I wasn't, was I?' I ran my fingers through my hair and felt a rush of triumph at saving the boy's life. I wanted to laugh at the snipers, run back into the street and taunt them that they could open fire and I would dance around their bullets.

'Not this time,' he said, and the familiar sardonic smile spread across his face. 'I think it's called beginner's luck.'

But if it was luck, it extended long past the point when I was a beginner in the city. By the time the last of the winter snows melted away I was an established figure at the Sarajevo Hotel, the 'crazy Croat' who would always go further, stay longer, hang on for that extra minute to get the perfect shot. Some said I was brave, others stupid, and I knew there were those who said even less complimentary things when I wasn't around to hear. I didn't care. For the first time in a long while I had some respect for myself, for the way I spent my days. The risks I took were worth it for the stories we brought back: the lost children of Sarajevo, the orphans and the street kids, bewildered faces staring up at me, believing I could help. 'You're more of a lunatic than me,' Nic would say, when I returned from streets that no one else would walk down. 'Just doing my job,' I'd say, unable to admit what we both knew – that I took such risks because of my baby girl who I hadn't been able to save, and because I had nothing left to lose.

I had long given up any hope of seeing Marian. Rumours flew

constantly as to her whereabouts, in Goražde, in the Krajina, back in the Gulf, on leave in London. When I walked into the dimly lit bar one chilly May evening, I didn't even see her sitting two tables across from Nic until he pointed her out.

'The Iron Lady's back,' he said, grinning. 'Aren't you going to go and say hello?'

My stomach twisted sharply. I looked across, recognizing the sleek blonde hair, the pristine white shirt; she laughed suddenly, sliding her fingers through her hair. 'I'm sure she'll spot us before long,' I said, trying to ignore the shivers of desire rippling across my skin. 'Did you watch the footage back? Any interest from TF1?'

'They loved it,' he said, smiling. 'To be right up on the mountain, in among the soldiers . . . that mountain is key to this whole shitfight. Can't believe you got so close to the action.'

'*Besmrtnost*,' I said, raising my glass and grinning.

'*Besmrtnost*.'

As I drained the whisky I felt a hand on my shoulder. 'Hello, trouble.' I looked up to see Marian smiling down at me. 'Fancy seeing you here.'

'Marian,' I said, standing up to kiss her. Close up, she looked different; her face was thinner, dark shadows under her eyes. 'I knew you'd turn up sooner or later. How are you? Got time to drink some of Nic's whisky?'

'Always.'

Nic leaned back on his chair and reached behind him for an empty glass from the bar. He winked at her, poured three shots and handed them to us.

'What are we drinking to?' she asked.

'*Besmrtnost*,' I said. 'Immortality.'

'*No bullet, no knife, no threat, no weapon . . .*' chanted Nick.

'*You're gonna live forever.*' I pointed at him and grinned.

She didn't smile. 'That bloody song. So you boys are still hell-bent on out-manoeuvring death? Think I'll drink to something else, thanks very much. Peace, maybe? A ceasefire?'

'Oh, lighten up, Marian,' Nic growled. 'Don't be so bloody prissy.'

'Fuck off, Nicolas.'

'Isn't this just like old times?' I said. 'You know you adore each other really.'

But it wasn't like old times. There was something different about Marian, something darker and quieter, and I didn't need to look in her eyes to know we would end up together that night, that she needed something from me, even if I didn't quite know what.

'Look at it,' she whispered, when we were back in my room. I had kissed her when the door closed behind us, but she had pulled away and walked across to the grimy window, staring through the dirty plastic sheet that had been taped across the window frame. 'This used to be an amazing, vibrant city. Look at it now. Cowed. Devastated. How many dead, Miro, how many do you think? Ten thousand? Twenty? How many more to come?' I slipped my arms around her waist, my body growing warm with desire at the familiar scent of her skin. She turned slightly and I kissed her neck, felt her lips against mine. The strange, intoxicating passion she provoked in me began to build, and I pushed her back roughly on to the bed.

'No,' she said, turning her head away. 'Not like that, not this time. I don't want to fuck, Miro, I want you to make love to me, I want to feel something. Can you do that? Can you make me feel something?'

Something stirred in me, fear almost, that what she craved was the opposite of what I was searching for. I wanted to lose myself in her body the way I lost myself on the streets, when there was nothing but impulse and instinct and no time for thought or reasoning or any sort of sense. If I ever felt anything real it was grief; for Irina, for Dina, for the life I had lost and left so far behind. I kept it at bay in the days and most of my whisky-soaked evenings, but sometimes in the cold, still hours of the morning the demons came and I longed for my wife with such ferocity that my body physically ached.

'Of course,' I whispered, but a slight sense of unease began to ripple up my spine. I slipped my hands inside her shirt, her body begin to writhe, but every time our lips touched her eyes were on my face and I couldn't look away, felt as though I was falling in to her.

'You're so very lovely,' she whispered, and at the gentle touch of her lips and hands, everything I had built began to crumble. With each kiss another piece of me fell away until I felt utterly exposed, and as she wrapped her body around mine I couldn't keep myself together any longer, buried my face in her neck, and instead of pleasure at her touch all I could feel was grief and loss and disbelief, at where we found ourselves, who we had become, all that had happened.

We came together, our eyes locked on each other's faces, and afterwards, as we lay in the inky silence, I realized she was sobbing.

'Don't cry, darling –' but my voice broke on the words and I could feel my lips trembling.

'Why not?' Her voice was little more than a whisper but she sounded broken; my heart caught at the sound. 'Why the fuck not?'

'Because I can't . . .' I stopped. She bent in to kiss me. and the gentleness of her touch was too much, something broke inside me and suddenly my mind was filled with everything, everyone: Dina, Tara, Mika, the girl in the alley, my baby daughter in her unseen grave. 'I can't bear it, Marian.' She tightened her arms around me and I gave in, began to sob, my body shaking in her arms. 'I just can't fucking bear it.'

CHAPTER 24

I woke to someone banging on my door. Marian had gone and I pulled on the jeans that lay in a tangled heap on the floor and staggered to open it. A man I vaguely recognized stood in the corridor looking awkward.

'Are you Miro? Miro Denković?'

I nodded. 'Who wants to know?'

'I'm Juergen Mueller. RTL. Look, I've just got back from Zagreb, been in hospital there. I've got a message for you from one of the nurses. Cata. She said she was your cousin?'

'Is she OK?'

'She's fine. But, well, I'm sorry but I've got some bad news. Her father – your uncle? He passed away two days ago. Heart attack apparently. She said you'd want to know. Said you were close.'

Ivo. I suddenly saw him so clearly, remembered the first day I had seen him on the harbour in Ljeta: the affable giant in the neat grey shirt with buttons that strained to meet across his bulk. My chest tightened. 'Yes. We were. Thank you for finding me.'

'She said the funeral will be next week. Said she hopes to see you there. I said that getting in and out of Sarajevo is a nightmare, but . . .'

'I'll find a way. I need to be there.'

'Right,' he said, a little awkwardly. 'Well, I came on a UN flight last night – they were talking of one going out to Split in a couple of days' time. Maybe you could get on that?'

'Thanks.'

'Right,' he said again. 'Well, sorry.'

He turned and walked away and I clicked the door shut and sank down on the bed. Ljeta. It was almost too much to take in: Mother and Pa, Cvita, Cata, Marjana, *Dina*. At the thought of seeing her my heart leaped, but even as I pictured her face I could still smell the scent of Marian's skin on my body. How long was it since the day I had got on the bus? Seven, eight months? Time seemed meaningless in Sarajevo, each day a new beginning, a chance at life or death; the outside world meant nothing. Going back terrified me, yet I couldn't miss Ivo's funeral. He had changed my life, and if this was my last chance to honour him I was going to be there, whatever it took.

It turned out getting a flight out was the least of my problems. 'You can't just piss off when you want to,' Nic said, when I told him I would be gone for a few days. 'You're fucking working, man. I need you here. Who was he, what did you say, your uncle? That's not exactly a close relation, is it? You'll be saying you want to go home because your pet cat's snuffed it next.'

I stared at him. I rarely saw this side of Nic; when I did it was a nasty reminder that there were aspects of his character that were seriously unpleasant. 'Nic, we were close. And I'm not asking you *if* I can go, I'm telling you that I *am* going. You'll have no problem finding a replacement for a few days; Drago's good, or Bojan. You're always going on about the endless freelance fuckers hanging around with nothing to do.'

'Well, you've obviously made your mind up,' he said coldly. 'So go on then, fuck off. I'm sure you have to ponce around and pack, or do something equally pathetic.'

'I'll be back in four or five days if the flights work out.'

He waved a hand at me dismissively and stalked off, shrugging melodramatically at Marian as he passed her on the way into the bar. 'Are you OK?' she said. 'Juergen told me about your uncle. You were close?'

I nodded, awkwardness rising up in me at the memory of the previous night. 'Nic's furious.'

'Of course he's furious. He doesn't understand, because he doesn't care about anyone but himself. You're going back for the funeral? Juergen said you were going to try and get on the Split flight the day after tomorrow?'

'If there's space. I'll pick a car up from somewhere and drive down. I'm not sure when the funeral is exactly, but hopefully I'll make it in time.'

She smiled. 'It'll be good for you to go home, I think. See your family, remember the world outside this one.'

'Is there a world outside this one?'

She took my hands in hers and looked at me with the same intensity I had seen in her eyes last night. 'Yes, sweetheart,' she said, 'and it's a much healthier, saner place than here. I know this might sound odd, particularly after last night, but, Miro, try not to come back.'

'What?'

'When you go home . . . You don't have to be here, you know? It's a choice. And I'm not sure it's the right choice for you. I'm not sure you belong here.'

'It wasn't a choice,' I said, and to my horror I could feel my voice cracking a little. 'I had nowhere else to go.'

'Well, you're going somewhere else now,' she said firmly. 'Try and stay there. That's your life, not this one. Try and stay in it if you can.'

I thought about her words as we bounced up through the clouds out of the city, and they rang in my head as I drove through the streets of Split and out into the moonlit countryside. I wanted to believe that I would get back to Ljeta and Dina would welcome me with open arms, Damir would take me back at Zagreb TV and the

village streets would be filled with mothers doing their shopping and
tourists taking photographs, rather than mute and cowed. Instead I
felt increasingly anxious; it had been impossible to let anyone know
I was coming, and I wasn't convinced Mother and Pa had forgiven
me for disappearing to Zagreb. One thought, more than any other,
kept playing in my mind: would Goran be there?

Dawn was just beginning to rise as I drove into the village, the
sky a pale mauve-orange. I pulled up outside our house and stared
at the untended garden, rotting plants, windows shrouded in curtains. The key stuck a little in the lock and I leaned on the door
to push it open, collecting up the letters that scattered across the
floorboards. In among the bills I recognized my own handwriting;
the two letters I had written to Dina, crumpled and unopened.
There was no reason to linger; the house was bare and unkempt
and I couldn't leave it quickly enough. The warm May sun broke
over the mountains as I turned the corner on to the harbour, and
as I looked along the cobbles I could make out a solitary figure,
hunched over a table with his back to me.

'Pa.' He didn't move, sat at the table in the soft dawn light, polishing a stack of cutlery. He took one knife at a time, sliding the tea
towel up and down, before placing it neatly in a line next to the
others. '*Pa.*'

He turned and stood up. 'Miro? Is that you?' As I walked towards
him I saw he was smiling, his face alight with pleasure. 'Son. You
made it. Cata said she knew you'd try.'

'Pa. It's so good to see you.' I put my arms around him; his body
felt stooped and frail. 'I'm so sorry about Ivo.'

'I can't tell you what it means you're here. What it would have
meant to him.'

'He was such a good man. I had to come.'

He nodded. 'Cvita's come all the way down from Istria, bless her,
left the children with Branko. Only your brother won't be here. God

knows where he is, we haven't had any news for weeks, but you have to hope.'

'Tara hasn't heard from him?'

He shook his head. 'But you're here. Your mother will be over the moon. She's been so worried about you.'

Guilt twisted in my stomach. I tried to push it away. 'What happened? Was it another heart attack?'

'Yes. We were out walking in the woods when he suddenly complained of pain in his arm. We'd been talking about the pension, possibly fitting a new kitchen for the restaurant, making all sorts of plans. And then his face . . . it was like a kind of spasm. He grabbed my arm and just sort of slid down my body to the floor. I knew before I felt his pulse he was dead.'

'Oh, Pa,' I said. 'To see it happen . . .'

'It helps, strangely enough. That I was with him. To know his last moments, to know he didn't suffer. He was my big brother – you know what that's like, Miro; I know you know because of Goran. And what more could I want for him? The sun was shining, we were out in the fresh air, the town he loved was coming back to life and he was planning his part in that.' He paused, leaned on the back of the chair and stared out to the sea. 'God, I'm going to miss him.'

'I know.' I smiled. 'You had Ivo, I have Goran. I know how you feel.'

'But we must wake your mother up,' he said briskly, 'and Marjana too. You've no idea how good it is to see you, to have you back.'

'One thing,' I said, as we walked towards the restaurant, 'I've been to the house. It's all locked up. Where's Dina? Have you seen her?'

'Not for months. She's moved back to Morsać, we never see her. I only knew she'd closed up the house because Karena told me she'd helped her. I hope she'll come today. Ivo was tremendously fond of her.'

'She loved him too,' I said. 'She'll be there, I'm sure. But will Mother be civil?'

His face darkened. 'She'd bloody well better be. I'm not having one of her petty feuds ruining my chance to say goodbye to my brother.'

But at first it seemed I was wrong. We walked into the church in silence, Pa with his arm around Marjana, Mother holding Cata's hand. Cvita and I slipped into the pew beside them and I turned to watch the other mourners file in, desperately hoping to see Dina among them. I felt oddly disconnected from what was happening. In Sarajevo people went out to get water and didn't come back – a friend of Marta's got shot in the face through his bathroom window while shaving. Death had become an everyday occurrence, and I had almost forgotten how to treat it with the reverence it deserved.

'What a turnout,' whispered Pa, his face lit up with pride. Behind us, the church was overflowing with people, squeezing on to pews, standing in the corners. I turned to look and just as I did Dina walked in, her head covered in a black lace scarf. She must have felt my eyes on her because she looked across; her face didn't move, but she raised her hand and moved her fingers in a small, silent greeting.

'She came,' I whispered. Pa glanced around and smiled.

'I knew she would. You must talk to her afterwards. Try and sort things out.'

'I know. If I've learned anything these last few months ... life's short, isn't it? Love is all that matters.'

As the mass began, I couldn't help but turn to snatch another glance at Dina. Her head was bowed and I thought how small she looked, my beautiful girl in among the farmers and fishermen, all of whom had been friends with Ivo. Pa spoke of his brother with such wistful love that tears glinted in the eyes of even the flintiest villagers. And as we carried the coffin out, Dina looked over and smiled at me and I thought my heart would burst.

'She came then,' Mother said to me as we walked slowly through the graveyard.

'Of course she did. She loved Ivo, you know that. It was right that she came.'

'I don't know.'

But I wasn't listening. Out of the corner of my eye I could see Dina had cut off from the group and was walking away from the village. I laid a hand on my father's arm. 'I'll be there soon,' I said, 'but I have to . . .'

He followed my gaze and nodded. I turned away and began to follow Dina's route out through the side gate, on to the harbour and up into the woods. I wanted to call her name, but somehow I didn't quite dare; just as I was finally about to speak, she stopped and turned around.

'Miro. I knew it was you.'

'Are you going? Won't you come to the restaurant?'

She shook her head. 'You know I can't. I came to pay my respects to Ivo. But nothing's changed. Have you been to the house?'

I nodded.

'Then you know I've moved back to Morsać permanently.'

'I didn't know that. Why didn't you tell me? Why didn't anyone tell me? I've been writing to you, Dina. I didn't understand why you didn't respond.'

'I never got the letters,' she said flatly.

'I know. I found them on the mat. But look, that doesn't matter.' I took a breath, grabbed hold of her hand; it lay limp and cold in mine. 'What matters is I love you. I love you so much. And I want us to try again, I'll come back from Zagreb, you come back from Morsać. We'll open up the house and start again, can't we do that?'

She looked at me, her eyes wide. 'But I thought . . . Miro, I know you're upset about Ivo, but you can't just come back and expect to be able to put everything back together. We tried, but it didn't work, did it? Too much had happened, too much that the other one didn't know, and couldn't understand.'

'But it's fading – everything's fading, isn't it? In time it'll all be forgotten and we can go back to how we were. I won't go back to Zagreb TV, I'll work at the pension; tourists will start coming again.'

She shook her head. 'It won't work, you know that won't work. You say that now, when you're exhausted from Sarajevo and upset about Ivo, but within weeks you'd be bored and frustrated.'

I stared at her. 'Come on, Dina, this is what you wanted. I'm saying I'll give it to you, everything you wanted, just for another chance. Why won't you say yes?'

She pulled her hands out of mine and looked away. A cold twist of fear began to curl around my heart. 'What's the matter? Has something happened? Is there something I don't know about?'

She pointed to the seat and I sank on to it, my heart thudding. She sat next to me and I looked at the slim gold band on her left hand, gleaming in the sunlight. 'This is difficult,' she said slowly. 'Look, Miro, I'm so sorry. The truth is, well, the fact is I'm . . .'

'Oh my God, is there someone else? You're involved with someone. Who? Who is it? Not Pavle?'

'Don't be ridiculous.' She looked down at her hands. 'It's Anton. Remember? The man from the government who came to look at the rebuild project in Konavle? He relocated here full-time a few months ago and—'

'A few months ago? Jesus Christ, Dina, I'd hardly left.'

'At least you *had* left,' she said, and her voice was thin and cool. 'At least we had separated in some way. Anyway, are you seriously telling me that you're not sleeping with that . . . *woman* in Zagreb or Sarajevo or wherever the hell you're living?'

Memories of the strange, intense night with Marian flooded into my mind. I said nothing, felt Dina's body tense next to mine.

'You see? You come here, trying to persuade me to try again, and all the time you're sleeping with another woman. What's the plan? Keep her sweet until you know whether I'll say yes or not? Or are you hoping to keep us both on the go?'

'Don't be *stupid*,' I snapped, anger welling up in me. 'I've slept with her once, just once.'

'Christ, don't start that again,' she said, her voice rising to meet mine. 'Once, twice, who knows – who *bloody cares*? This is exactly what I don't want. I can't bear any more arguing and fighting. I'm with Anton now. You just have to deal with it, like I had to deal with her.'

'So what are you saying?' I said, trying to speak calmly. 'You want a divorce?'

It was Dina's turn to look shocked. 'No. Yes. I don't know. Oh, just leave me alone, Miro, go back to Sarajevo or wherever you've come from. Haven't we caused each other enough pain?'

But the shock in her eyes at the mention of divorce was enough to give me a glimmer of hope. 'Just answer me one question and then I'll go.'

'One question?'

'Just one. But tell me honestly, Dina, do you still love me? Because I love you. I love you so much.'

She turned and looked at me, her face streaked with tears. For a moment I thought she was going to put her arms around me, but then suddenly she stood up, dragged a hand across her face and tried to smile. 'I do love you. I always will. But it's not enough, is it?'

I watched her walk away from me, hope ebbing with every footstep, feeling as though I had lost her all over again. Only respect for Ivo stopped me heading for the car and driving away; instead I dragged myself to the gathering on the harbour and tried to avoid Cvita's anxious glances as I threw back a large glass of Stock and lit a cigarette.

'How did it go?' she said, after I had shaken hands with half the village and smiled and nodded while they all told me what I already knew, what a wise and generous man my uncle was. Cata stood beside her, her eyes pink and sore.

'I tried everything. I told her I'd come back, give it all up, Zagreb TV – everything. I'd work in the pension again.'

'You can't be serious,' said Cata. 'We both said we could never go back to how it was.'

'I'd have tried,' I said bitterly. 'Maybe I'm being unrealistic – that's what she said. That I'd get bored and frustrated. But that wasn't the real reason, it was just an excuse. She's seeing someone else. She's with someone else.'

'Really?' Cata's eyebrows lifted in surprise. 'Who?'

'Some guy from the government who came down to work on the rebuilding in Konavle. Whatever I do, whatever I offer, it's just not enough. She can't forgive me ... for Marian. Or she won't.'

Cvita put an arm around my shoulders. 'Well, she's a fool,' she said. 'And a sanctimonious one at that.'

'Who is?'

I turned to see Mother frowning at the three of us. I looked at my sister, willing her not to speak, but tact was never one of her strongest points.

'Dina's seeing someone – that man from Zagreb. Miro's just talked to her.'

'Well, good,' said Mother firmly. 'Now perhaps you can move on.'

'Good? *Good?*'

Cata nudged me; people were starting to look.

'Yes,' said Mother in a low tone. 'Good because maybe you can put it all behind you. She's not here any more, she's moved on with her life, the house is empty. You can come back and get on with yours.'

'Mother, I am getting on with mine, in Zagreb, in Sarajevo.'

'But you only went because of her,' she hissed. 'Because of what she did.'

I brought my fist down on the table; everyone was looking now but I didn't care. 'I went because of *you*,' I shouted. 'Because you made it impossible for us. She did *nothing*, do you hear me? Nothing. It was me. Your precious son. *I* slept with someone else, I had an affair with a woman while I was in Dubrovnik. Not Dina, me. And she tried to forgive me, she tried, but there was so much hatred and distrust in this village, so much distrust of *her*, that we never had a chance. I broke up our marriage, I destroyed everything. But I couldn't have done it without your help. So, are you happy now? Well, are you?'

CHAPTER 25

The journey back to Zagreb was more than a little uncomfortable. Cata had refused to speak on the drive back to Split, and her face remained set and closed as we boarded the bus to the capital.

'I'm sorry,' I said, as she threw herself into the seat next to mine. 'I know I shouldn't have said—'

'No, you shouldn't,' she hissed. 'It was a funeral, for God's sake. My father's funeral. What's wrong with you?'

'I don't know. I don't know what's happening to me. I just get so angry, and what Dina told me, I just couldn't believe it. But I know it's no excuse. I really am so sorry. And so sorry for what I said to Mother too; I didn't mean it.'

'It's that bloody place, it's ruining you,' she said. 'I suppose you're going back?'

'Sarajevo? First thing tomorrow. There's a Saudi aid flight going in, leaves about seven. Marian knows one of the pilots.'

'Her again.' She looked at me, but I said nothing. There was nothing to say.

When we reached the flat Cata disappeared into her room without a word. I began to unpack, pulling out the letters I had picked up at the house. As I glanced through them, I realized that I recognized the handwriting on one of the envelopes. I tore it open and read the first words I had heard from Josip in years: how sorry he was to hear about Irina, that he was in Germany but planning to come back to Croatia soon and hoped that we could find a way to meet.

I threw the letter away. Josip was just another part of the past, and by the time I was on the flight to Sarajevo I had forgotten he had even written. To my surprise Nic was waiting for me at the airport. 'Got to look after you, those other fuckers are beyond useless,' he growled as we shot down the main street, *Tri Lopovi* booming out of the tinny speakers.

It was a relief to be back. Nic didn't ask about the funeral, talking instead of a story that was breaking around the city, that the British and German governments had announced a plan to airlift some of the worst-injured children to hospitals in Berlin and London.

'It's a fucking publicity stunt, nothing more,' he said, wrenching the gear stick with both hands. 'And it's obscene, like playing God. They can't take *all* the children, so how are they going to choose who to take and who to leave behind? And who gave them the power to offer life to some and condemn others to death?'

'Are you going to cover the story?'

'Damn right. But I'm not interested in footage of brave English doctors carrying injured children to shiny planes. We're going to talk to those they pass over, those who don't have the right kind of injuries, who aren't endearing enough. Who the hell do these people think they are? More to the point, how stupid do they think we are – like we won't realize it's just a way to make it look like they're doing something, in a way that'll play well in their media. The Iron Lady's already at the hospital; the BBC's all over it.'

'I can't believe she approves.'

'Doesn't matter if she does or doesn't. She'll have to take the "heroic Brits in daring airlift" line. She won't have a choice.'

Nic drove to one of the hospitals we visited regularly, but when we arrived the air of chaos far outstripped what we were used to. Film crews were jostling in the hallways. Occasionally a man in a white coat would walk through carrying a child and they would burst into life, calling out questions, flashes of light, clawing at the figures that walked behind, sometimes a mother, sometimes both parents, their faces a mix of joy, bewilderment and fear.

He barged through and I followed, my mind racing to catch up; who was giving permission for the children to be flown out? Who was making the decisions? Were the parents going too? I heard Nic haranguing one of the local doctors with the same questions, and as their voices grew louder I glanced around the makeshift ward and suddenly realized the child in the furthest cot was Mika, the boy from the school group who had run out into the road. I walked over to the bed and a woman sitting next to him looked up at me, her face brightening.

'Have they changed their minds?' she said. 'Will they take him after all?'

'I'm sorry. I don't know. I'm not with them. But I met your son some weeks ago. We were filming in his school and he ran away.'

'Was it you?' She stood up and walked around the bed to stand in front of me. 'Are you the man that ran after him? That took him to safety?'

I nodded. She took her hands in mine and kissed them; I tried to smile but my chest was tight. 'Thank you,' she whispered. 'You saved my son.'

'But he's ill?'

'His kidneys are failing. They don't know why. They can't do anything to stop them. He needs dialysis, a transplant.'

'But they can do that in London. Why didn't they take him?'

'The doctor said . . .' Her face twitched and tears brimmed in her eyes. She gripped the bed and her body visibly tightened. 'He was very kind, he examined him thoroughly, but he said . . . they told me he said that they couldn't take him because he needs a transplant.

They couldn't give an organ to a Bosnian child that a British child might need. He said he was very sorry.'

I looked at Mika, his sweet, young face asleep on the pillow. I remembered him running, the speed with which his thin legs carried him across the wasteground. Anger began to build, the anger that had made me shout at my mother, and I wrapped my fingers around the metal back of the chair and took a deep breath. 'This can't be allowed to happen,' I said. 'They can't just leave him here to die. I'll talk to someone, see what can be done.'

As we drove back to the Sarajevo Hotel under the beating August sun, I found it impossible to get Mika's face out of my mind. Somehow this was more upsetting than anything else I had witnessed since I had first come to the city. I had become used to the random nature of death; there was something oddly fair in the fact that everyone was equally at risk the moment they stepped outside. But what was happening at the hospital seemed utterly macabre; some magically whisked out of death's grasp, others condemned to it.

'TF1 had better run that interview,' I said to Nic as we walked into the lobby. 'People need to know what's really going on here, the truth behind all these staged heroics.'

'I need a drink,' he said, and I followed him into the bar. Marian was there already, sitting with Juergen and his crew from RTL, an open bottle of vodka on the table. I threw myself down next to her and she looked up at me with eyes that were already slightly blurred with alcohol.

'Nice work by your heroic British doctors today,' I said sarcastically. 'Nothing like a bit of playing God to make you feel special.'

'You came back then,' she said slowly. 'Now why in God's name would you do that? Why are you *here*, Miro? Christ almighty, don't you want to stay alive?'

'Nothing's going to happen to me. *Besmrtnost* – remember? And while things are happening in this city like they were today, I'm not going anywhere.'

'Oh, get off your high horse,' she snapped. 'OK, so they couldn't take all the children, but they took some – isn't that better than nothing? Those children will have a chance of life, rather than dying in this shitty, godforsaken hellhole. How the fuck can you not want that for them? What's wrong with you?'

'Blimey, Marian, what's wrong with *you*?' Juergen and the two men he was with had already moved to another table. Sarajevo was stressful enough without people kicking off in the bar.

'I'm sorry,' she said. 'It's just, I'm so *sick* of this bloody city. This bloody war. I'm tired of trying to tell who's right from who's wrong; you know what, if some doctors want to help save some children's lives, then that's *right* in my book. Everything else is so blurred, so bloody confused – I go up to Goražde and I see what the Serbs are doing to the Bosnians, and then I go south and I see the hell the Bosnian Croats are imposing. I talk to the mothers of Serbian soldiers, and their heartbreak is just as real and heartfelt as that of mothers of soldiers from your country. It's all a nightmare and I'm sick of it. There's no *cause*. Or too many causes. It's just one huge, bloody unending mess. D'you know what I think? The only way this is going to be resolved is when everyone's dead.'

I said nothing and we sat in silence, both of us watching the stub of a candle flicker on the table in front of us. Marian's words shocked me; she had always seemed so unassailable, so sure. I didn't want her composure to crack; somehow it seemed indelibly linked to mine. When I took her to bed that night I held her to me, feeling her body slowly relax, her breathing regular on my chest, hoping a few hours of not being alone would soothe the fears that had started to dominate her.

The night stretched out long and dark and I barely slept. I couldn't get Mika's face out of my head, and by the time I was sitting in the lobby, drinking what passed for coffee, I had made up my mind. If Mika stayed in the hospital he was going to die, and I couldn't let that happen. But when I told Nic that I wanted to go back, that I wanted to film Mika's mother, to make the footage so harrowing that it would emotionally blackmail the British government into doing something, he simply laughed.

'That story's over,' he said brusquely. 'Christ, TF1 didn't even use our footage. When I asked them why, they just laughed. A feel-good story from Sarajevo, why wouldn't they use that? Why show the negative side? All they wanted was Alain's straight airlift piece; ours was a non-starter. Made me look a complete idiot, and I'm not having that again. Anyway, I've got wind of something else: Juergen's talking about going down to the south-east, near the border with your lot. Apparently seven shades of hell is breaking loose down there. I thought we might go check it out before he does.'

I stared at Nic. 'Didn't you hear me? That boy is going to die unless we do something. If we get down there, make it really raw, talk to the mother—'

'For fuck's sake, Miro, that's not our job. We're here to observe and report; we can't go blundering in like that. And anyway, what's so special about this one kid? Who's playing God now, choosing a child to save while others die? Hundreds of them are going to die, hundreds already have. He's just one more.'

'Christ, you're cold. Doesn't anything touch you? What if it was your daughter? What if it was Claire?'

He smiled grimly and shook his head. 'You still don't get it, do you? That's another world, *she's* part of another world. This is work, Miro, and you're right, while I'm working *nothing* touches me; no bullet, no knife, no threat, no weapon. I'm here to tell the stories, not create them or change them, or play any part in them. And neither should you. I don't know what you're searching for – absolution? Adoration?'

'My own humanity,' I said stiffly. 'When did you lose yours?'

'Marian, tell the boy he's nuts,' Nic said, and I realized she was standing behind me. She looked immaculate. No one would have guessed she had been asleep in my arms an hour earlier.

'What are you two bickering about now?' The weariness in her voice was palpable. 'Can't you go and race each other up Sniper Alley or something? Isn't that what you do for kicks?'

'He wants to go back to the hospital,' Nic said witheringly. 'That boy the doctors didn't take, the one who needs the transplant – Miro here reckons it's a great story. He seems to think if we go down there and shoot a few frames your government'll send a private jet just to shepherd the child and his mum to London. I've told him the story's over, it's done. But he won't listen.'

'Come with me,' I said. 'Marian, please. I know how you feel, but what's happened to Mika and his mother is wrong, one-hundred-per-cent wrong, and we have a chance to show that. What a story; while the other Brit news crews have all been celebrating your government's largesse, you can show the other side of it. That story isn't over, Marian, because it hasn't been told in your country. Not yet.'

'I admire what you're trying to do, Miro,' she said slowly, 'but today it's Mika, tomorrow there'll be another child. You can't save them all, you can't make this some sort of *crusade*. It won't help you. It won't take away what you lost.'

'This has nothing to do with that.' I suddenly heard Irina's soft, sweet chuckle, felt her minuscule palm against my cheek. 'This is not about me.'

'Oh, this is so about you,' said Nic.

'Marian, please. You know I'm right – this is a great story. No one else is telling it . . . this is what we do, isn't it? What we *should* do?'

She looked at me and then at Nic. Something unspoken passed between them and with a muttered 'for fuck's sake' he took the car keys out of his pocket and slid them across the table. 'Have her back in two hours,' he said. 'I want to make some calls about Postić anyway, find out what's going on down there. But bloody well be careful. She's a temperamental bitch, and if you force her too fast she'll conk out altogether.' He winked at Marian. 'Oh, and the car's a bit tricky too.'

The drive to the hospital did not go smoothly; the car lurched and spat down the streets, screeching angrily when I tried to change gear, constantly threatening to cut out completely. By the time we reached the hospital both of us were silent and tense and I led Marian through the grim, dimly lit corridors until we reached the ward where I had talked to Mika and his mother.

'That's not him,' I said, as we walked towards the bed. Panic started to rise. 'That's not Mika.'

Marian touched the arm of a nurse standing by the next bed. 'The boy who was here yesterday, his name was Mika. Do you know where he is?'

She shook her head. 'Sorry. I came in this morning and the bed was empty. This boy has just come in.'

'Did he die?'

'I don't know. I'm sorry.' She looked at her curiously. 'Did you know the family?'

'I knew the family,' I shouted. 'I came back to help them. Someone must know what happened, who can I ask? Who can tell me?'

'You'll have to come back later. We're all a new shift right now.'

'But how is this possible? There was a boy here yesterday, in this bed, his kidneys were packing up and the British doctors wouldn't take him – and his mother, she held my hands, she thanked me for saving his life. And now he's going to die anyway? Why didn't I just leave him to the snipers, Christ, it would have been kinder and quicker.'

The boy in the bed where Mika had lain began to cry. 'You're scaring him,' said the nurse crossly. 'I'm going to have to ask you to leave. Now.'

I felt Marian's hand in the small of my back, and as I looked at the boy in the bed, his lower lip shuddering with fear, I felt ashamed. 'I'm sorry,' I said. 'I'm just upset.'

'Then take it somewhere else,' said the nurse. 'There's no time to be upset here.'

I followed Marian out of the hospital, but my anger hadn't dissipated, just transmuted into some strange, bitter fury that seemed to fizz around my body and make my head spin slightly.

'I don't even know where they live,' I said, as we climbed back into the car. 'Nic's going to have a field day with this.'

I wrenched the car into gear and we began to judder back towards the hotel. Sniper fire spat in the air above us but neither of us flinched, numb to the threat. I sped up, wrenched the car into fourth gear, took a corner too fast, throwing Marian against the door.

'Jesus, slow down.'

Her words just made me angrier, and I slammed my foot harder on the accelerator. Something fired in the engine, and instead of climbing, the speedometer began to drop. Frantically I pushed my foot to the floor, pumping at the pedal, but there was no traction, nothing bit; I stared in horror as the needle fell further and the car gradually slowed to a dead stop. I looked at Marian. We were around one kilometre from the hotel, on one of the most dangerous streets in the world. Armoured or not, in the car we were sitting ducks.

'Fuck.'

'Fuck.' Marian looked at me and I could see real, cold fear on her face. For the first time I realized that with the disappearance of her conviction in the job she was doing, her faith in her own immunity had gone too.

'Get out of the car and keep down. The snipers are on the other side of the street so you'll be safe. I'll slide across to your side and then we'll take it nice and fast, and before you know it we'll be back at the hotel drinking Nic's whisky.'

She nodded mutely and I watched as she carefully opened the passenger door and slid slowly to the ground. Shots rang out and I flattened myself across her seat. For a moment I couldn't move, mesmerized by a dribble of spit that was slowly dripping from my mouth on to the cracked dirty leather. I inched forward, slithering out of the car, hands on the gravel road, walking myself slowly forward, legs slithering down behind me. Marian had her back to the car, eyes wide, knees pulled into her chest. She looked terrified.

'We're going to have to run for it,' I said. She nodded. I raised my hand to her face and gently tilted it towards me. 'Marian, it's going to be fine. We go from here to that car, see? And then behind that broken wall. Keep low, keep moving.'

She nodded. My heart was racing, my skin prickling with fear, but I felt fired up. This was when I truly came alive, when I knew death was lurking around the corner waiting for me and I was going to outwit it, outrun it. I leaned in towards her, kissed her hard, feeling the same bolt of desire that had first hit in the dusty doorway in Dubrovnik, hoping it offered some sort of reassurance that I would get her back in one piece.

'You don't miss a chance, do you?' The flash of humour reassured me. I pulled her up from behind the car and we were away, sunlight bright in our faces, dust kicking up as we ran. In the distance shells roared and bullets squealed above our heads and I felt invincible, just in-fucking-vincible.

We reached the car and crouched down; she looked at me, breathing fast. 'We're going to make it, aren't we? That's got to be the worst of it.' I nodded. Of course we were going to make it, this was what I did best: risking it all and coming through unscathed, laughing at those who tried to take me down.

We dashed from doorway to doorway, dodging, sheltering, waiting for a lull in the firing before crossing the street. The hotel was in sight, squat and scarred at the end of the street. 'NOW,' I shouted, and I felt the soft skin of Marian's hand in mine as we left the safety of the doorway. Suddenly the air was filled with a thousand different noises; gunfire and explosions and crying and in among them all I heard a woman scream and I threw myself at Marian and the force of my body against hers propelled us to the ground behind a wall of shell-blasted bricks. We lay there for a moment, her limbs pinned beneath mine, her hair against my cheek. 'Marian? Are you OK?'

She didn't move. 'I think so. Yes. I think I'm OK. Are you?'

'Yes.' I began to raise myself up on my hands and knees, keeping my body below the level of the bricks. 'Nothing damaged ... oh *shit.*' A wide scarlet mark had spread across the creased grey cotton of my shirt. I rubbed my hand across my abdomen but there was no pain, not even a twinge. And then I looked down at Marian and my stomach turned over at the sight of a matching patch of scarlet, leeching its way across her lower back.

'Miro?'

I couldn't speak.

'Miro? I don't think ... I can't move. Have I ... ?'

I flung myself on the ground next to her and looked at her face, right cheek pressed against the filthy street, blue eyes blurred with fear and shock. 'It's all right,' I said, as calmly as I could. 'You've been hit, but I think it's just a surface wound.'

'Oh.' Her voice was small and I suddenly saw the young girl again, the one who had sat beside me on the bed at the Ragusa, whom I desperately wanted to take care of. 'Is it bad?'

'I'm going to take a look. It's going to hurt, but I have to do it, OK?' She didn't speak as I pulled up her blouse and almost retched at the sludge of blood and skin that lay beneath it. I ripped off my shirt and pressed it to the wound; an involuntary wail of pain slipped out of her mouth. Bullets whizzed above our heads and I tried to think; we were so close to the hotel now, I could run there, find a medic ... but as the scarlet stain spread through the balled-up shirt

I was holding against Marian's skin, I knew she didn't have much time. But if I tried to carry her, I'd be much slower. Both of us could end up getting killed.

'Miro? Don't leave me.' I lay back down beside her, keeping one hand pressed hard against the wound in her back. Her face was wet with tears but her expression hadn't changed; she lay frozen on the street, her blue eyes staring out at me. 'Please. I don't want to die on this street alone. Please, if this is . . . Please stay with me.'

I sucked in my breath, trying to slow my pounding heart. 'You're not going to die, Marian. Not while I'm here. But I'm going to have to pick you up. And it's going to hurt. But you've got to keep your eyes open, do you understand, you must stay awake. It'll only be a few seconds and then we'll be at the hotel and it will all be OK, I promise. But you're going to have to be brave. Do you understand me?'

She closed her eyes and I could see she was drifting. 'Marian, speak to me. You have to stay awake.'

Her eyelids flickered. 'OK, Miro. Yes . . . awake.'

'I'm going to sing, OK? I'm going to sing that bloody song of Nic's, and each time I stop you're going to sing the word, or say it, or just fucking breathe it at me, but we're going to sing it all the way back to the hotel and you're going to be fine. You and me.'

'OK.'

'OK. So I'm going to have to slide my arms underneath you and I'm going to try and keep your back as flat as possible. It's going to hurt. Concentrate on the song. *No bullet, no . . .*' I snaked my hands under her body, gravel scraping at my skin.

'*Knife.*' The word flew out of her in a mangled scream.

'*No threat, no . . .*'

'*Weapon . . .*' We were up now and I was moving, her body was limp and heavy and all I could look at was the hotel, growing closer, so nearly there, so close, so close. '*Nothing can hurt me if I have your . . .*'

'*Love . . .*'

'*I'm gonna live forever, baby . . .*' The words were tumbling out of me as I ran and I no longer knew if Marian was singing or answering and everything blurred and the doors loomed closer and my arms screamed at the weight of her body. 'Sing, Marian, FUCKING SING.'

'*I'm gonna live forever,*' the words were whispered, disappeared into the air as soon as she had spoken them, but they were hers, she was still conscious, and that knowledge powered me across the street and through the doors of the Sarajevo Hotel.

'Medic, medic, I need a medic!' I yelled. Within seconds people were out of their chairs, crowding around me; an accented voice rose above the others, telling them to get back, to give him room. I fell back against the wall, my chest heaving, as a blond-haired man knelt down beside Marian.

'What's her name?' He looked up at me, his fingers pressing on her neck. 'Her *name*?'

'Marian,' I wheezed. 'Is she . . . is she . . . ?'

'Marian –' the man's voice was clear and strong – 'can you hear me? You're safe now. I'm going to take care of you. If you can hear me, can you squeeze my hand a little? Marian? Can you hear me?'

CHAPTER 26

'Marian?'

She stirred and opened her eyes, a slow smile spreading across her face. 'Miro.' She lifted a hand and waved it vaguely. 'Sit down. It's lovely to see you. You came before, didn't you?'

I nodded. In truth I had spent most of the last three days at Marian's bedside in the cramped room in the hospital, staring at her clear, unblemished face. She looked so well, so unharmed, that it seemed impossible she was so seriously injured.

'I'm going home,' she said, her voice a little stronger. 'They're medevacing me out tonight.'

'Are you sure? Are you sure you're OK to be moved?'

'That's what they say. Blood pressure, heart rate, all that sort of thing, all fine. It's just the area where the bullet hit.'

'But that's fantastic news. God, what a relief. You'll be . . .' I stopped. Tears were running down Marian's cheeks.

'It's not. It's really not. My back is agony, but that'll pass – at least I can feel it. But my legs . . .' She reached out and wrapped her fingers around my wrist. 'It's like they're not there.'

My stomach turned over. 'Oh, sweetheart,' I said, pulling a tissue out of my pocket and leaning in to smooth away the tears. I wished she would stop crying. It made me want to break things, smash things up. 'I'm sure it's just shock or bruised nerve endings. What do the doctors say?'

'They won't say anything,' she said, and her face crumpled like a child's. 'Just that the bullet entered at the base of my spine and that it's done some damage, but it's too soon to tell how much and how permanent. But I know. It's my body and I know.'

'Marian, you don't. You don't know anything right now.'

'But it was always going to happen, don't you see? It's inevitable with the life we lead. I just thought it'd never happen to me.'

'And it wouldn't have done if I hadn't made you go to see Mika that day. This is my fault.'

She tightened her fingers on my arm. 'Don't. You know no one can ever make me do something I don't want to do. If you say this is your fault, then it's my fault your marriage broke up. Christ, we haven't been very good for each other, have we?'

'You've kept me sane. I don't know where I'd be if it wasn't for you.'

'Probably not here,' she said, twisting her head slightly. 'Prop me up a bit. There's something I need to say to you.'

I slipped a pillow behind her head and she looked up at me, her expression serious. 'Miro, I want you to promise me something.'

'Anything.'

'I want you to leave Sarajevo. Go home. Go home to your wife. And before you say anything, I know things aren't good between you. But you don't belong here, you never really have. It's not that you're not good at what you do, you're brilliant. But this isn't your war any more, and your country, your village, it's starting afresh. You should be there, where there's a future. There's no future for you here.'

I bit my lip and tried to think what to say. 'You know I can't do that. This is my life, whether you approve of it or not.'

'It's not that I don't approve,' she said. 'I just don't want it for you. All this immortality stuff with Nic, he knows the game, he's made his deal. You don't, and sooner or later something is going to happen, it just *will*, and then it will be too late and whatever it is will have changed you, or injured you, or killed you. And I really don't want that for you. You're such a kind, sweet man and you've so tried to look after me, the only man I've ever met in this world to do that.'

Something stirred in my heart at her words and I felt my eyes sting. 'Marian, I'm so touched but . . .'

'*Please*,' she shifted slightly and her face spasmed with pain. 'Please, Miro. Promise me you'll leave Sarajevo. Get work in Zagreb if you really can't go home. But if I just know . . . if I can be back in England and know you're safe, that I actually did one thing that had a positive influence on your life. Please? It would make such a difference to me.'

I felt a stab of annoyance at the familiar sense of someone else controlling my life, yet part of me knew that it was down to me that she had been running on the street that day, and if I could give her any peace of mind, I should. 'OK.' I tried to tell myself if I broke the promise it wouldn't matter, she would never know. But the old part of me, the Ljeta boy who was brought up to always tell the truth, knew that once I'd given her my word I couldn't go back on it. 'OK. When I've found a replacement for Nic, I'll go back to Zagreb. If it'll help you. But you have to do something for me in return.'

She raised her eyebrows. 'I do?'

'No more talk of being . . .' I couldn't say the word *paralysed* '. . . of knowing more about your injuries than the doctors do. I want you to think positive, to be positive.'

'Dear Miro.' A tear slid down her cheek. 'All right, I'll try to be positive. But thank you for your promise; you've no idea how much peace that'll bring me. And now, I'm sorry, I'm so tired. I don't mean to be rude.'

I realized suddenly that I would probably never see Marian again. She would go home to England and had already made it clear she wouldn't be returning to Bosnia. I thought about saying, 'We must keep in touch,' but somehow the words seemed inappropriate. We had seen and shared too much.

I stood slowly, and she looked up at me and smiled, a real smile, and in that instant I saw all the versions I had known of her: cool and unassailable in front of the camera, flirting in the bar, naked in my arms, sharing a depth of passion and intimacy with me I had never experienced with any woman before. I laid my palm against her cheek, looked into her eyes and kissed her as softly as I could, trying to tell her everything she had been to me and all that it meant.

'Be happy,' she whispered.

'You too,' I said, turning away before she could see the tears in my eyes.

But I couldn't leave without knowing the truth. In the corridor I recognized one of the doctors who had been with Marian when I had visited on a previous day; as he walked towards me I laid a hand on his arm, my heart thudding.

'Can you tell me what the prognosis is for Ms Wiseman?'

'Are you a friend?'

'We're close.'

'Good. She's going to need her friends. Such a tragedy.'

I felt the muscles in my neck tighten; my fingers shrank into tight, tense fists. 'What do you mean?'

His glance moved away from my face and he shifted a little from foot to foot. 'Mr . . . ?'

'Denković.'

'Mr Denković, Ms Wiseman has sustained a severe spinal injury to the cauda equina. Although it's impossible to be one-hundred-per-cent sure at this stage, with this kind of damage, well, I'm afraid it's extremely unlikely she'll ever walk again.'

I stared at him. 'But she said you couldn't tell, didn't know . . .'

He spread his hands apart. 'Why tell her now?' he said simply. 'She's already terrified, thousands of miles from home, in a badly equipped hospital in a war zone. The flight home will be traumatic enough. This kind of news is incredibly hard to take in and accept.

We made the decision that it would be better if she was told in England. I'm so sorry.'

'Fuck, man, that's shit.' Nic's response to the news about Marian was predictably eloquent. 'She all right?'

'Of course she's not bloody all right,' I said, lifting the glass of vodka to my lips and knocking it straight back. 'She knows what's happened, even if they're not telling her. And it's my bloody fault, Nic. She's never going to walk again and it's my bloody fault.'

Nic slammed his glass on the table and glared at me. 'Stop. Stop that right now. You can't do guilt in this game. People make their own decisions; every risk is your own. Don't make this about you. No one ever made Marian do anything she didn't want to – she's a tough girl, she'll survive. It's gonna take more than a few jacked-up Serbs to—'

'She's *paralysed*!' I yelled. 'Didn't you hear me? A few jacked-up Serbs did for her pretty good as it happens. And you couldn't even find the time to go and see her.'

'And what good would it have done if I had? D'you think she'd want me there, feeling all sorry for her, reminding her that she just got unlucky? We'd both know that it could have been me, but it wasn't. It'd just have made her angry.'

'You can tell yourself that if it makes you feel better, but that's not how it felt to me.'

'Of course it wouldn't have felt like that to you – you're not the same as us. She and I have got drunk and shared time in some of the most godforsaken places in the world. We know the rules. You only play this game as long as you're fit for it. Once you're scared or weak or injured, there's no place for you, no one wants to see anyone in that kind of state, because it's a reminder of what can happen to any of us.'

'Apart from you, right? The immortal Nic Richaud.' He raised an eyebrow at the palpable sarcasm in my voice. 'It's never going to happen to you.'

'Dead right. And d'you know why? Because I'm too fucking important. God keeps an eye on me cos I'm the only guy crazy enough to get the stories from places where He won't go. Godforsaken places – my speciality. He forsakes them, I go in. That's the deal we have. That's how I won my immortality.'

It was at times like this I had serious doubts about Nic's sanity. 'You're full of shit.'

He raised an eyebrow. 'Oh really? That'll be why you and I are going down to Postić tomorrow then.'

'Are you crazy? No one can get into Postić, it's completely surrounded. No one even knows quite what's going on there.'

'You're wrong,' he said. 'Juergen met some bloke who's desperate to get a TV crew in there and says he has the means to do it. According to this guy, there's a mule convoy that goes in and out at night carrying weapons and supplies. Sounds like something out of Ernest Hemingway. The town's encircled, the northern side has been taken by the Croats, and they're forcing all the Bosnians into the southern side of the city. Half the time when they walk across into the Muslim quarter, the Croats just shoot them down. They're using kids for target practice. It's inhuman what's going on down there, just beyond belief. Juergen's too chicken-shit to go, but you and I are going to tell the world what's happening. We're going to sell this footage to CNN and the BBC, and if this doesn't get those cowardly fucking politicos to do something then I'm going to retire to Hawaii and make grass skirts for a living, because what's the fucking point?'

'I'm not coming,' I said. 'I promised Marian.'

'Oh yes, you fucking are. You left my bloody car on the most dangerous road in the bloody city. Do you know how much I had to pay to get it back? Fucking Danić could retire to the sodding Caribbean, the stack of deutschmarks I had to give him and his boys.

The windows are all shot out, it's basically just a crate on wheels, but those fuckers at TF1 still won't stump up for a new one. So you owe me. I need someone along who knows what they're doing, who isn't going to get jumpy and fuck it up. I'm going to be banging on your door at 6 a.m. tomorrow and you'd better answer it. We're going to win awards for this.'

Before I could answer, he threw back his chair and stalked out of the bar. I poured the dregs from the whisky bottle into my glass and downed it. I felt odd. I lit a cigarette but it just added to the whirring in my brain. I thought of Marian lying in the hospital bed, and then I tried to imagine what tomorrow would bring, the journey to a new city I didn't know or understand. It made me realize how familiar Sarajevo had become, in spite of the dangers. In Postić we would know nothing, and that made us hugely vulnerable.

Sleep evaded me that night; noises that normally wouldn't have registered made me jump and shudder. I tried to reason with myself; it was just fear, I had to get over it as I'd done before, ride out the waves of anxiety to the great expanse of freedom and opportunity that lay beyond. But my demons spun ever greater terrors: injuries, paralysis, darkness – I thought of the pain of seeing Marian lying there, and suddenly it was as if a wall fell away; how could I risk putting Dina through that? Or Mother, or Pa? My mind was crowded with the faces of those I loved: Cvita, with her arms around her children, Goran's wide laconic smile, Cata's neat doll-like bob. I remembered the sick feeling of guilt and sadness I felt as a child every time I saw Tara limp towards me, or slip her injured hand into her pocket. What was I thinking? What had I been *doing*?

I sat up, grabbed a notepad and began to write, one letter to my mother, another to Dina, only to be opened in the event of my death, telling them that I loved them, that I was sorry, trying to make them understand all they had given me and why I had never really thanked them properly before. When I had finished, I reached around my neck and unclasped the St Christopher, slipping it into the envelope with Dina's letter.

When dawn broke I rose, almost unconsciously pulled on my clothes and checked my camera. I felt like a man on the morning of his execution. Death and I were long-time adversaries, but suddenly it felt as if the game had changed and I no longer knew the rules.

'*Ready?*' bellowed Nic through the door, hammering on it with his fist. I picked up my camera and put the letters in the top of the bag I was leaving at the hotel, trying not to think about Mother and Dina opening the envelopes and reading the farewells they contained.

The journey to the mountains that surrounded Postić was almost laughably straightforward. While I had been sitting in hospital with Marian, Nic had somehow managed to obtain the necessary papers from both the Bosnian government and the Serbian army to get us through the checkpoints we had to cross in order to leave the city. On the seats behind me, next to my camera, a generator and a huge box containing Nic's satellite phone, lay a pile of oddly disparate objects: a white envelope oozing deutschmarks, ration packs, bottles of water, packets of chocolate, toothbrushes, biscuits, sachets of shampoo. I knew the boot held a crate of beer and another box containing six bottles of Johnnie Walker. I couldn't bring myself to ask Nic where he got it all from.

'See?' he said, as the city's broken landscapes began to ebb away, replaced by open fields and lush rolling hills. 'God's on our side. I tell you, Miro, unless the UN come storming in while we're there, we're going to become legends for this story.'

'If we don't get killed,' I muttered.

Nic looked at me. 'The only thing that's going to get us killed is if you've lost your nerve. I know what happened to Marian was shocking, I understand it's the first time something like that has happened to someone you're . . . close to. I know you feel responsible.

But you can't let it throw you. You have to put her out of your mind. Put what happened right out of your mind.'

But the image of Marian lying in the hospital was the only thing I could think of as the car ground on, through sunlit valleys where children played in the fields and villagers stood and gossiped on doorsteps as if there wasn't a genocidal war taking place just a few miles away. Such pockets of normalcy were one of the oddest things about the Bosnian conflict; one village might be relatively unaffected by the war, while the next had suffered total cleansing. We drove all day, the appalling state of the roads and the unreliable nature of the car making the journey torturously slow.

'Jirińce,' said Nic, pointing to a sign and swinging the car off the main road. 'That's where we'll find Dino, the guy Juergen met. He's a bit crazy apparently, but he's our man.'

I said nothing as the car juddered forward. Houses began to rise up on either side of us, dilapidated and crumbling, more through age than from the destruction wreaked by Serbian guns. Nic pulled up outside a dimly lit bar and leaned over to the back seat, lifting a wedge of deutschmarks out of the envelope. We both clambered out of the car and I watched as he opened the boot and pulled out a bottle of Scotch. My body felt stiff and sweaty after the hours in the car and my mouth was dry.

'Stay here,' Nic said, and disappeared off down the street. I lit a cigarette and noticed my hands were shaking.

He was back within minutes, minus the whisky and the money. 'Turns out Dino's a big whisky drinker,' he said, grinning. 'We're going in at first light. Reckons it'll take the best part of the day. Going to get some kip. You want the back seat?'

Before I could answer, Nic had got back into the Jeep, lifted a blanket from the back and settled himself in. I stood on the street and lit another cigarette, trying desperately to think. Nic could work a camera – maybe he could go on without me and I could take the car back to Sarajevo. If we left it out here, the odds were we would never see it again – didn't it make more sense for him to go on and me to go back? I stood in the dark, beneath the milky-white gaze of the Bosnian moon, and I could almost taste the fear in my mouth: metallic, ashy, like a sour cigarette. An image of Dina floated into my mind, Mother, Cvita; the look on their faces at Ivo's funeral. What was I *doing*?

The fear bit harder. Snores were already echoing through from the front seat; I pulled open the boot and took one of the bottles of Scotch. One long swig and the fear began to recede, a second and my hands stopped shaking. By the time I had drunk a third, a fourth, the idea of sleep was becoming a possibility. I clambered into the car, tipped the bottle back again and let the warm glow of the alcohol blur the horrors I knew tomorrow would bring.

CHAPTER 27

The next day it soon became clear that drinking half a bottle of whisky was the worst possible thing I could have done. There was nothing to eat, and as our car crept along behind Dino's battered Jeep, I felt horribly sick. When the walk began things got worse; the stench from the horses and the men who rode them curdled my stomach. As we began to climb the rocky path that led over the mountain and down into Postić my head swam, and I drank so much water that the other men started to complain I hadn't left enough for them.

'What's wrong with you?' muttered Nic, as we scrambled up a rocky section of the path. I watched the donkey ahead staggering beneath the weight of our satellite phone; I knew exactly how it felt. 'Christ, you need to get it together. They're taking us because they think we're professional reporters. You look like the work experience boy on a Sunday-school outing. Fucking shape up.'

Fortunately as the route grew steeper all of Nic's energies had to be concentrated on the walk, rather than on berating me. The mountains reminded me of Knin: grey-hued and joyless, dotted with faded green scrub and patches of scree. We walked slowly; the trail was littered with tree roots and sudden drops and I kept my eyes on the ground, trying not to think of the miles of unkempt path twisting ahead of us. The sun was unrelenting; my boots began to rub, clothes clung to my skin and when we finally reached a stream

I plunged into it, ducked my head under the water and let the cool liquid pour down my throat, not caring whether it was polluted.

It took eight hours of walking to reach the outskirts of Postić, and by the time Dino pointed out three battered military vehicles on a road below us, waiting to transport us into the town, I was beyond speech. We scrambled down the last slope but there was no respite at the bottom; Nic and I loaded the camera, phone and provisions on to one of the trucks, while Dino's men humped guns and boxes of ammunition. As we drove towards Postić, shelling and gunfire began to split the air that had been so blissfully unbroken up in the mountains.

'Just think about where you're going to put all the awards we're going to win,' said Nic, grinning at me as we jolted along, wedged into a corner so tightly the metal edge of the bench bit into my thigh.

I didn't smile back. The collapsed streets and crumbling buildings created a wearying sense of déjà-vu: another city on the brink of destruction, its population slowly being annihilated. 'Nice to see your lot can put on a show just as gruesome as the Serbs,' said Nic. 'You know the American networks won't go near this story because they reckon it's too complicated to explain that in this area of town, the Croats are the bad guys. Much easier just to stick to the version where the Serbs are guilty of everything. But it's your lot who are up to the genocidal tricks down here, isn't it? Kind of ironic you're here to be filming them, eh, Miro? Don't s'pect this footage will find itself on Zagreb TV.'

'You're such a stupid fucker,' I said, trying to control the anger his words provoked in me. 'If you're trying to get a rise out of me, it's not going to work. I'm as disgusted as you by what the Croats – Bosnian Croats, mind – are doing in this part of the country, so if you're expecting me to argue, forget it. Just remember these aren't my countrymen. That's all.'

'Well your army's here. Thousands of 'em. Tuđman knows full

well what's happening in this part of Bosnia. He's funding it. Don't try and absolve your lot.'

I was on my feet before I knew it, grabbing Nic's collar, pushing his head back against the metallic wall of the truck. 'Don't call them *my lot*, all right? What's going on here, it's nothing to do with me, or my country. They're animals, just like the Serbs. Stop trying to wind me up.'

Nic's eyes rested on my face, cool and grey, vague amusement flickering across his features. 'All right, Miro,' he said quietly. 'Just having a bit of fun. Sit down, there's a good boy. None of us has got the energy for a fight.'

I took my hands off Nic's shirt but kept my eyes on his face. Suddenly the fear had gone; my anger had tipped me over the edge and I knew I was free of it.

Postić challenged me in ways I could never have begun to imagine. In Sarajevo, the air was filled with fear, but also belligerence, defiance, a determination to survive no matter what. In Postić, there was just terror. It clung to the walls, punctured the air with a continuous mix of gunfire, shouting and occasional high-pitched wails that made my skin prickle. We'd set up camp on the floor of the old PTT building, in the Bosnian southern half of the city, and from the rooftop we could film the bewildered straggle of people crossing from the Croat side: elderly women in housecoats and slippers, mothers carrying children who screamed and wept, whole families moving in huddles, arms around each other. Every so often one of them would be carrying something that told me a little about the life they had left behind; a dark-haired girl clutching a pair of pink shiny ballet shoes, a small boy letting a dog's lead dribble out of his hand. One old woman, tottering between the stacks of rubble, clutched a picture frame to her chest. I wondered who was in the photograph: a dead husband, a son in the army, a once-happy family now ravaged by the conflict that had rained misery and fear into her life. I zoomed my lens on to these tiny snippets of lives left behind, trying not see the desperation in their faces, telling myself I was a reporter, not a voyeur.

And all the time I couldn't deny the creeping sense of horror that these crimes were being inflicted not by the Serbian army but by forces that shared their name with mine. I found myself adrift, angry and bewildered. No one seemed to be in the right any more, everyone was wrong and I no longer knew why I was there, or what I was doing.

'Good news,' Nic said excitedly, as I sat up on the roof on the third morning, smoking a cigarette and wondering idly how much it would hurt if I just walked to the edge and kept on going. 'We're going into the northern sector. Your lot have given us permission.'

'They're not my lot,' I said mechanically.

'All right then. The Bosnian Croat army have given permission for us to film in their half of the city. Is that better? It's going be a crapshoot – they're just going to show us what they want us to see, probably boy fucking soldiers holding hands with Bosnian grandmas and leading them politely over the line with cups of tea and sympathy – but you may be able to get something more interesting when they're not looking. Ready?'

'Yep.'

'Christ. Can you spark up?'

'Nope.'

'If this is still about Marian—'

'Oh, just shut the fuck up,' I said. 'Let's go. You want me to shoot some footage of my lot abusing the crap out of innocent civilians, right? Let's go do it then, and cut the bullshit.'

Nic raised his eyebrows but said nothing and I followed him out of the building. The crossing point into northern Postić was a short walk away and I lagged behind as he flashed his press card at a grey-haired soldier in grimy fatigues who gestured to a door behind him. Once inside, my heart sank at the sight of three men sat around a table, a bottle of *slivovitz* in front of them. It was a tradition Nic referred to as '*slivovitz* hour', when the local commanders drank with a reporter, to size them up and decide how far they could be trusted. In the areas around Sarajevo it had been an integral part of getting into the villages and valleys, and I had lost count of the afternoons I'd spent trying to avoid drinking the shots Nic and the local commanders were throwing back, so I could still focus the camera properly when we finally got to film.

'If you're going to be here for a bit I'm going to do a recce,' I murmured to Nic.

He nodded. 'My cameraman wants to take a look around while we talk,' he said to the oldest of the three men. 'Is that OK?'

The soldier looked at me and my skin crawled; there was something about his eyes, they were unmoving, utterly blank. It made me wonder what they had seen.

'You go at your own risk,' he said. 'I can't guarantee your safety, but if you wish to walk we've nothing to hide. Obviously you'll leave your equipment here, until we're ready to take you to the sites we have in mind.'

'Be back in an hour,' muttered Nic. 'Otherwise this could go on all day.'

I nodded and walked out of the building, relieved to be away from the soldier's dead-eyed stare. I began to walk, helmet tight on my head, flak jacket chafing under my arms, moving swiftly yet with no particular aim. I wondered what on earth the Bosnian Croats thought we could film here that would show them as anything but appallingly violent aggressors. I knew what Nic's trick would be, that he would try to re-nose the footage and use it to undercut their claims.

I turned a corner and stopped in horror at the scene that was unfolding before me. Unlike the previous roads that had lain empty and silent, this street was dotted with people. An elderly couple were lurching along, the man bleeding from one eye, the woman dabbing at his face with her scarf, weeping and raising her hands to the sky, calling to a God who clearly wasn't listening. Every house was in some sort of disarray; soldiers striding in and out, women weeping on the street, children scooped up by parents as they ran out of their front doors. As I realized what I was seeing my skin felt cold; *etničko čišćenje* – ethnic cleansing – happening right before my eyes; men, women and children torn from the houses in which they had built their lives, fallen in love, raised their babies, grown old. I stared in horror as a young woman was dragged screaming and struggling from her house by two burly soldiers. They shoved her through the gate, laughing, and she fell face down on to the road. At the next house, another soldier was coming out, dragging a man by his hair. I was just about to look away when something stopped me.

The soldier shoved the man heavily and he fell into the street. I was mesmerized, frozen to the spot. It couldn't be right, what I was seeing, it just wasn't possible. The man crawled across to his wife, scooped her up from the road, cradled her in his arms, screaming obscenities at the soldier, who just laughed. But as he turned to walk away, the man kicked him hard in the leg. There was a bark of pain and the soldier spun around, pulled a gun and shot the man in the foot. Screams ricocheted up the street, the soldier laughed, nausea catapulted into my system, holy Christ, it couldn't be! Not here, not like this, not after all this time.

'GORAN?' I yelled his name, unable to stop myself, willing it not to be him, desperate for him to draw closer and have a different face, neater features; let this thug not be my brother, not the one constant in my life, the one thing I still believed in after everything else had been destroyed. 'Goran?'

He looked over, stared and then began to jump up and down and wave. As he walked towards me my heart grew tight; '*Moj brate*,' he called back. 'My brother.'

It was him. As he drew nearer I realized I couldn't speak to him, if I did it would make it real; that he was part of this, this *cleansing*, and I turned and began to run, tripping on the uneven streets, desperate to get away, to not see what I had seen.

'*MIRO*.' His voice chased down the street after me, my stomach lurched and I quickened my pace back towards the military building, willing Goran to give up. But he was too fast, his footsteps grew closer and then his hand was on my arm, dragging me to a stop, dust spinning up beneath my feet.

'Miro, wait. What the fuck are you doing here? How did you get here . . . ? Christ.'

'What are *you* doing?' I shouted. 'What are *you* doing here? What was that I just saw, that man, you fucking *shot* him?'

He stared at me for a moment and I felt a sense of utter disbelief that I was looking into my brother's face. He looked exactly the same. 'What? *What?* That man? Fuck that, Miro, you're here. Christ, it's been so long.' He went to throw his arms around me and I backed away. 'What? What is it?'

'Are you a part of this?' My whole body was trembling. 'This *cleansing? Etničko čišćenje*, Goran, don't you remember? The horror? The Krajina? You told me. And now this is what you do?'

He stared at me. 'Don't – don't you dare – *judge* me. Who the fuck are you to judge? What are you doing here anyway? You've never picked up a gun for your country in your life.'

'But this isn't your country.'

'It will be. I'm fighting for Croatia, for a new Croatia. I always have been. What are you fighting for, Miro, behind your camera, hidden away behind a lens? What I've done, all I have done, makes me a soldier. What does standing by and watching everything make you?'

'You're wrong.' My skin began to ripple with anger, my face felt flushed and sweaty. 'I've been everywhere you've been, seen everything you've seen, and d'you know what I've realized? That after we've lost everything – and we have lost *everything* – all that's left is our own humanity. When did you lose yours? When did you become one of them?'

He said nothing for a moment, and there was sudden static tension in the air, a tangible sense of a shift from a time before to a time afterwards, when nothing would ever be the same again. 'Don't *ever* say that to me,' he spat, and it broke the spell and I hurled myself at him with such force I knocked him off his feet and we were rolling on the ground just as we had done as children, only this time the punches were real and the anger flooding through me was threatening any sense of control I had left.

'You fucking bastard,' I forced him on to his back, slamming my fist into his face. 'You were all I ever wanted to be, you were all I had left.' He grunted in pain and something in me was released; it felt good, I wanted to hurt him more. I punched him again and again, raining down blows on his body, for the man he had shot, for Marian, for Nic's endless bloody taunts, for Dina's new boyfriend, for Ivo, for the whole fucking, bastard, cunting war that had detonated something in me, and in thousands, millions of others, turning us from people who loved and were loved, into those who fought and maimed and killed and shot old men and laughed while they did it.

Goran's body was in a tight ball, but I kept hitting and kicking. There was blood now, everywhere, on my hands, his clothes, people were shouting, but I couldn't stop, didn't want to, and then suddenly someone's hands were on my body, dragging me away. 'I think you've fucking killed him,' said a man standing behind me, and I stared down at my brother, inert and lifeless on the floor.

'Christ, it's the UN,' someone said, and I looked up to see white trucks rumbling up Postić's broken main street.

I turned back to see two soldiers bent over my brother, one with fingers around his wrist, the other propping open his eyelids. Then I noticed there was a man standing near them, and as I looked more closely I realized it was Nic. His face was hidden behind my camera, but when he lowered it he was smiling, a strangely triumphant expression on his face. And I knew suddenly, beyond any doubt, that he had been there the whole time, that while I punched and kicked and beat my brother, he had stood to one side and filmed it all.

PART THREE

August 1993–May 1995

CHAPTER 28

'Oh, Miro.'

'Don't. Don't say anything. I can't . . . I'm sorry, I shouldn't have told you.'

I watched as Cata stood up and walked to the kitchen drawer, taking out a box of cigarettes and a lighter. I had never seen her smoke before. She put one to her lips and lit it, steadied herself against the cooker. 'Goran, of all people.'

'I know.' I stretched out my hand and she passed the cigarettes to me. I couldn't meet her eyes. 'It just . . . something happened. That place, Postić, it was like hell, a real hell on earth. People say that, don't they? Sarajevo, Srebrenica, Mostar – all their own separate hells. But Postić was something else.'

'Why on earth were you there?'

'It just sort of happened. I'd been with Marian, just found out she was . . . how bad her injuries were. She'd made me promise to leave Sarajevo, said if I didn't get out sooner or later something bad would happen. In the end I agreed, I didn't feel I had much choice, but then Nic said I had to go to Postić with him. In some twisted way it almost felt funny; I was doing what she asked, leaving Sarajevo, but going somewhere *more* dangerous. It was all so fucked up, Catz. And Nic, I don't know, I didn't know how to say no to him. The night before we left I was terrified, I knew it was a stupid idea. But what I feared was getting injured or shot. Not something like this.'

'And then to see Goran . . . it must have been such a shock. I mean, of all people.'

I was back in Postić suddenly, watching Goran's eyes flick open when the soldiers gently tried to move him; a gaze locked on to me from a face that was already beginning to bruise and swell. 'I'd dreamed of it so often, lost count of the times I'd caught sight of someone and thought it was him: army fatigues, dark hair, right height. And then he'd turn around and I'd feel so awfully, horribly disappointed. I thought I might turn a corner in Sarajevo and there he'd be. But to suddenly see him, like *that*. It was like, there he was at last . . . but I desperately didn't want it to be him, couldn't bear that he was a part of what was happening.'

She nodded slowly. 'That's why I can't understand, you've always loved him so much. To hurt him like that . . .'

I put my head in my hands. 'I didn't mean to, but once I started I couldn't stop. It was terrifying, Catz, I've never been out of control like that before.'

She walked across the room and slipped her arms around my shoulders. 'Your brother is the toughest man I've ever met. He'll recover from this. It'll take time but you both will.'

'Will we?' I lifted the cigarette to my lips; my head was spinning. 'I bloody left him, just walked away. Left everything behind.'

'You were in shock.'

'I should have stayed, should at least have tried to find out where they took him, if he was going to be OK. But then I realized that Nic . . . he'd just stood there, filmed it all. He was supposed to be my friend. I knew he was hard, I knew he didn't really care about anything, but we'd worked together for years. It was just a story to him, a great story, brother against brother. What if they show the footage? What if Mother sees it? Christ, how will I explain it to her? How . . . ?'

'He won't do anything with it,' she said soothingly. 'And even if he did, they'd never show it on Croatian TV. No one will ever have to know, no one but you and Goran.'

'I hope you're right.' I closed my eyes and Nic was in front of me, grinning triumphantly, the walls echoing to the sound of trucks rumbling up the street. 'Never thought I'd be grateful for the UN.' I tried to laugh but it caught in my throat. 'If that convoy hadn't turned up, if I hadn't got that lift back to Sarajevo, Christ knows what would have happened to me. I really, honestly, don't know.'

There was a pause and I realized Cata was crying. 'I'm so tired of it all,' she said, her voice cracking with emotion. 'Everyone I love is hurt or damaged. Please tell me you're not going back, Miro. Not again.'

'Not this time.'

'Will you go home? Back to Ljeta?'

I shook my head. 'I can't face it. I know I should see Mother, try to talk to Dina, but I just don't have it in me.'

'So where then?'

I reached into my pocket and pushed a white envelope across the table. 'I found this letter when I got home. It's from Josip. He wrote before, but I never replied. Go on, read it.'

I watched as she picked up the first sheet and skimmed it, her eyes widening as she read Josip's words; that he was back in Croatia, living with his parents on the island of Tršt, that he had made money in Germany and was planning to open a restaurant the following summer.

'I've heard that you're in Zagreb now, working as a cameraman – I can't imagine what that must be like, but I hope you're safe and enjoying it – if that's the right word.' Cata laid down the sheet and picked up the next, raising her eyebrows at me. 'Maybe if you get a few days off you could come down to Tršt – it would be great to see you. Or come for longer – I could do with a partner in crime, and you were a pretty good waiter as I remember. You're going to visit?'

I nodded. 'More than a visit. I spoke to him this morning; he wasn't joking about the waiter thing.'

'Weird. History repeats itself.'

I smiled, remembering the small kitchen in Knin; Pa's face as he read out Uncle Ivo's words. 'Well, let's wait and see. You know Josip – I might get there and find out it's all a complete fantasy. But I need somewhere to go, and he sounds, I don't know, lonely, I suppose. It'll be so good to see him.'

'When will you go?'

I reached across and took back the sheets of paper, slipping them back into the envelope. 'As soon as I can,' I said. 'No offence, Catz, you've been great. But the sooner I get out of Zagreb, the better.'

It wasn't until I reached Split's chaotic port that I realized how much I had missed the sea. I had barely seen the water in the few hours I had been back for Ivo's funeral, but I was suddenly struck by the clear, golden light that painted the container ships and rusting ferries, the vast swathe of glittering, undulating blue that stretched out to the horizon. I stood on the deck as we pulled away from the mainland and tried to persuade myself I was leaving it all behind: my failed marriage, the loss of my daughter, the broken relationship with my brother. As the sea swung in around the hull of the ferry I told myself it was a chance for a new start; that perhaps in Tršt, with my oldest friend, I could work out who I was actually supposed to be.

It was almost two years since Josip had disappeared, and somehow I expected the intervening time to have changed him. But as I walked off the boat and saw the tall, rangy figure leaning against a battered white Fiat it was as if we had seen each other just last week: the same long shorts hung to below his knees, the T-shirt was one he used to wear in Ljeta.

'Miro.' He threw his arms around me but I could see from the expression on his face that I was not as unchanged as he was. I had lost weight, hadn't slept properly in weeks and my face still held fading evidence of the fight with Goran. The last time Josip had seen me I had been a married father with a successful job. Now I felt like a refugee.

'Christ, you've looked prettier.' He drew back. 'No need to ask how things have been.'

A flash of resentment passed through me at all that Josip had avoided by leaving when he did. He must have sensed what I was thinking, because he coughed a little awkwardly and put out a hand to take one of my bags.

'Weighs a ton. What have you got in there?'

'Cameras,' I said briefly. 'Didn't think I was actually going to risk going into business with you, did you? Thought I'd start up a little photography studio.' He stared at me for a minute, unsure what to make of this. 'I'm kidding,' I said, laughing at the confusion on his face. 'Believe me, if I never pick up a camera again, it'll be too soon. Just brought them out of habit, I suppose.'

His face broke into the wide, lazy smile that had been such a part of my childhood. 'Come on then, get in,' he said, opening the boot. 'Ma and Pa are dying to see you; it's so amazing you're here. I never actually thought you'd come.'

'My diary was suddenly empty,' I said, trying to keep my voice light. There was a packet of cigarettes on the dashboard. I took two out, passed one to Josip as the engine spluttered into life.

'So, you look like complete shit. Been tough?'

'Yup.'

'Wanna talk about it?'

'No.'

I looked at him and he winked. 'Fine by me. Anyway, a couple of weeks here and you'll be a different person. The beer's cheap, the girls are friendly, the sea's warm. What more could a couple of village boys want?'

I laughed and wound down the window as we drove away from the tiny port, the grey bulk of the ferry standing out against the ripple of hills that stretched away from the sea. Josip edged the car down narrow streets lined with low-slung stone houses. Pots of geraniums sat on windowsills and elderly men in flat caps sat together on rusty benches, soft wisps of cigarette smoke rising as they talked. Before long the town melted away and the road began to climb; to the right the sea glimmered in the evening light, to the left the hills glowed a vivid mauve colour.

'Smell it?' He grimaced. 'Lavender. It's the island's trademark. Believe me, you'll be sick of it before long; they put it in everything.'

'It's nice. Reminds me of Aunt Marjana.'

'How is she – and your parents? They OK?'

Something twisted inside me; I didn't want to think about Ljeta. 'Yeah, I think so.' I gestured out of the window. 'This is all very rural and lovely. Feels like you've retired.'

'Are you kidding? Tršt used to be the hottest place on the whole coast. Cocktail bars, posh hotels, everyone came sailing across from Split on their yachts. Wait till you see the old town, it's still got all the old Venetian buildings, it's just stunning. It's quiet now, but it'll be one of the first places tourists come back to. Thought we'd pop in on the way back, take a look at the restaurant.'

'You're up and running already?'

'God no.' He braked sharply to avoid a clutch of goats lurching on to the road and I thought of the streets in Sarajevo: burnt-out cars, crumbling houses, decomposing bodies. 'I've just taken the lease on a space. It's right on the piazza. I thought we'd call it the Dalmatia, cook all those recipes we used to love as kids.'

He pulled up to the kerb and I followed him through a tangle of shady alleys that opened out on to a wide sunlit square paved with gleaming marble slabs. It reminded me of Dubrovnik. Elegant Venetian villas lined three sides, studded with wrought-iron balconies and tiled roofs that glinted a rich, rusty red in the sunlight. The ground floors were mostly given over to shops or restaurants, all closed up, with dusty windows and faded signs. The fourth side of the piazza opened out on to the sea, with a wide promenade curving away out of sight and a handful of boats shifting silently on the sparkling water.

I spun around slowly on my feet, trying to take it in. 'This is astonishing. It's like the war never happened.'

'It didn't here,' he said. 'Not really. The island was blockaded, but Serbian forces never set foot in the place. The biggest factor has been the refugees, hundreds from Vukovar and now Bosnians. All the hotels are full, but not with tourists.'

'Isn't this a bit of a strange time to be starting up a business?'

'Well, I'm not rushing at it.' He grinned lazily. 'I figure we can take the winter, hang out – you look like you could do with a whole lot of doing nothing. But I want to be the first new place to open on the island. Christ knows I didn't do anything while the war was actually happening – we both know what a fucking coward I was – but I'd like to be a part of what comes next, do something positive to help move this place on. Look at this piazza – it's dead. If we can bring just one corner to life, with food and drink and music, isn't that a positive sign for the future?'

I looked at Josip as he pulled a bunch of keys from his pocket and envied him all the things he didn't know and hadn't seen, the childish air of enthusiasm he had never lost. I was so used to being around people who were grief-stricken or haunted or terrified that instead of resenting my old friend's easy optimism, I found it joyful. He pushed open the door and we walked into an empty room; piles of unopened post stacked on a windowsill, a clutch of wicker chairs piled precariously in one corner, in another a dusty cash register sat next to two candle stubs.

'You've got to use your imagination. There's a kitchen and bath-room out the back and three good-sized rooms above. We're going to have to start from scratch in the kitchen, but the bedrooms are in pretty good nick; coat of paint and we could move in.'

'This is quite an undertaking,' I said, 'but I've got some money saved too. I'd like . . .'

He held up his hand. 'This isn't about money. I did well in Munich, but if you want to invest that's fine. We can talk about it sometime. We'll sort everything out in time.'

The months that followed were – if not happy – certainly the calmest since I lost Irina. Josip's parents welcomed me in like a long-lost son; Bulat kept me supplied with cold beers each evening while Ruža took it upon herself to redress the physical effects the war had wreaked on my body. Each morning I came down to a table piled with eggs and rolls and batches of crispy *sremska*; at lunchtime she would appear at the restaurant with flasks of soup and thick sandwiches stuffed with warm meatballs, or tangy cheese and *pršut* from the farm that lay up the road from their house. At night the four of us would sit around the table in their cluttered kitchen and discuss plans for the Dalmatia: where to buy furniture, what recipes to use, who to talk to on the island to source the best wine and shellfish.

'Maybe you ought to scale it down a little, boys,' Bulat said one night, when we were planning a trip to the mainland to buy the furniture we needed. 'There's no sign of the refugees going home, and with everything that's going on in Bosnia . . .'

I shuddered inwardly. While my days were busy enough to distract me from what was going on in the rest of what had once been my country, at night my mind roamed through all that I had seen, as if in some desperate attempt to lay my ghosts to rest. My dreams were peopled by those I had left behind: the girl in the alley, Marian lying bleeding on the street in Sarajevo, Tara in Knin, Goran battered and bloodied in Postić. Sometimes Dina appeared, in a house that was ours and yet oddly different, Pavle beside her, or Anton, the man who had taken my place in her life. Sometimes she was in the garden with Irina, and they were the worst dreams of all.

'All the more reason to have a hell of a party when we open,' said Josip, glancing at me. 'Maybe we'll simplify the menu a bit, make it more of a cafe at first. But people want to feel better, they want to move on. I know you think it's too soon, Dad, but I'm right, aren't I, Miro?'

I nodded, even though I wasn't sure. People wanted to feel better, there was no doubt about that, but no one seemed to know how to move on, myself included. 'I think it'll be really good for the town,' I said slowly. 'Someone has to be first, and if we keep it simple – pastries and cakes and just a couple of dishes each day – we should be able to cover our costs.'

Josip leaped to his feet. 'Exactly. Come on then, let's go and measure up. Don't worry, Pa, really. It's going to be amazing.'

But as we walked out into the night he turned to me, concern etched on his face. 'Do you think he's right? Do you think people will come? You know much better than I do; I wasn't here, I didn't . . .' He ran his fingers through his hair. 'I've got this dread that people will say, "That bloody man – he disappeared off when things got tough and now he's just back to make money." But it isn't that, it really isn't.'

'I know,' I said. 'But no one knows about that here and even if they did, no one would think that.'

'Oh come on, even you do a bit. The stories you've told me, these months working on the restaurant: being in Sarajevo and Dubrovnik, what you saw and experienced—'

'And what good did it do me? It nearly broke me, Josip, it nearly sent me crazy. If it wasn't for you, for all this, God knows where I'd be.' He unlocked the door to the restaurant and I followed him inside. 'Do you remember when Ljeta was first occupied? You were so angry and you were talking about how we should go up to Konavle and fight, and Mother said, "Don't wish for it." Remember?'

He nodded.

'Well, I'm saying it to you now. Don't wish you'd been there, or that you'd seen what I saw. It wasn't honourable or brave or even bloody worthwhile. Everyone was bad and everything was twisted and if you didn't see that, if you didn't have to witness it, then be thankful.'

Josip laid a hand on my arm. 'Are you OK? You haven't been yourself the last couple of days.'

I said nothing, ducked behind the bar and retrieved two dusty glasses and a bottle of Stock. I laid them on the counter and felt in my pocket for a letter I had been carrying around since it had arrived two days before.

'This came.' I poured the Stock into the glasses and knocked mine back in one.

Josip peered at the long slim envelope. 'What is it?'

My throat tightened and I poured myself more brandy. 'It's from Dina. She wants a divorce.'

It was dawn by the time Josip and I finally left the restaurant, our heads fogged up with brandy and dozens of cigarettes. Somehow Dina's letter had unlocked the last of our secrets and we had talked through the night, Josip telling me how he had escaped from Ljeta, the bribes he had paid, the terrifying trip from Dubrovnik to Korčula, hidden beneath blankets in the ferry captain's cabin. And in return I told him the truth about Marian, the lies I had told Dina, the terrible anger that had built up inside me and which I had finally vented on Goran's body. And when we stumbled out into the pale pink dawn I found that I felt better, as if some of what I had been carrying around for months had finally lifted.

'You'll sign the papers?' he asked, as we walked back to his parents' house.

I nodded. 'She's made a new life. I've got to want that for her, haven't I? To be happy? Christ knows I hurt her so badly.'

'But everything was twisted and crazy, you've said so yourself. Maybe you should go there, try and persuade her. I know you still love her.'

'Of course I do. I'll always love her. But that's why I can't go back. I've already had her tell me once she's replaced me with another man. I can't hear it again.'

Josip went to speak but I held up my hand and he pressed his lips together and nodded silently. There was nothing more to say. In some odd way it was a relief; I could finally stop the endless debate in my head as to whether I should go back to Ljeta and try to talk to Dina. It was too late, she had made her decision. She had made a decision for both of us.

I signed the papers, sent them back and boxed up all thoughts of my old life, throwing myself into preparations for the opening of the Dalmatia. There was something hugely pleasurable in building something new out of the ashes of the old, and slowly the restaurant took shape: simple wooden chairs and tables, whitewashed walls with large, bright canvases Josip had bought from a local artist. By the time the late-spring sunshine was starting to warm the wide marble stones of the piazza, we were ready to open – candles flickering in tall metal lanterns, bar fully stocked, glasses gleaming and ready to be filled.

'Shall we do it?' Josip stood by the door, keys in hand. Outside, small clusters of people had begun to gather, lured by the promise of free wine and food from the small posters we had taped up around the town.

I nodded. 'Let's.'

He slipped the key into the lock, clicked it and pulled the door towards him. 'I declare the Dalmatia well and truly open,' he said, grinning at me. 'Pour us a cold beer each – it's going to be a busy night.'

He wasn't wrong. Within minutes the tables on the piazza were full and I found myself running back and forth to the kitchen with trays of mussels *buzara*, bowls of salad and heaped baskets of bread from the town's bakery. Before long it was clear that Josip and I couldn't cope with the demand, and his parents stepped in, Bulat opening bottles of beer and pouring wine, Ruža slicing more bread and cutting slabs of cake and wrapping them in napkins because we had already run out of plates.

'Quite a night,' Josip yelled as he raced past me, carrying handfuls of empty glasses. 'Dad's tuning up his *tamburitza*. People want to dance. Isn't it fantastic?'

I nodded, grinning as he bounced up and down behind the bar. 'Let's stop for a minute,' I said, passing him a beer. 'Look at what you've done, Josip. This is amazing.'

We stood in the doorway of the Dalmatia and looked across the busy tables to the piazza beyond. Someone had moved two of the big candles so part of the square was lit up; Josip's father was playing the *tamburitza*, someone else had a tambourine, another a guitar. The town was no longer silent or hushed; the piazza rang to the sound of feet clicking on the stone slabs, women laughing, glasses chinked together in toasts to the future. And then I saw them, a woman and a small girl, dancing together, hands interlinked, both of them giggling as they moved.

Josip followed my gaze and I felt his hand on my arm. 'You OK? . . . Miro?'

I swallowed hard, turned and smiled. 'Yes. I'm OK. Tonight is about the future, isn't it? Not the past.'

Josip raised his beer. 'To the future then. A new life.'

I clinked my bottle against his. 'Yes. A new life.'

CHAPTER 29

'We've run out *again*?' Josip stood in the doorway of the restaurant, wiping his hands on his apron, the bandana around his head slightly askew.

I nodded. 'The cupboard is bare, as they say. We've got one portion of lònac left, and a slightly dog-eared slice of kolači. We're going to have to close the kitchen – just do drinks for the rest of the day.'

'You know what we need?'

'A holiday?'

'More staff. Where's that list of names? Time to spread a little of our good fortune, Miro. I'm off to the Adriatica.'

I watched him pull off his apron and walk out into the boiling August sunshine. In the three months since we had opened, the restaurant had gone from strength to strength, helped by our decision to keep things simple and costs low. After the frenzy of interest around our opening, things had quietened a little, but on the weekends a handful of yachts would appear from Split, disgorging couples who seemed to have missed the war entirely and had deep enough pockets for long lunches and wine-fuelled dinners. On weekday evenings the local fishermen would tie up their boats and walk across the piazza for cold beer and a plate of bread and cheese, and when anyone on the island had a birthday or a celebration, the Dalmatia was where they came. Some of our most frequent visitors were the refugees still housed in the Adriatica, a sprawling hotel complex on the other side of the harbour. Some asked for free food, but most came in search of work, and we divided up what shifts we had and gave them to as many as we could.

'Busy again?' I looked up as Ruža staggered into the restaurant, her face hidden behind a stack of plastic boxes. 'Brought you some more *kolači*; people will always eat cake. You short on anything else?'

'Everything,' I said, taking the boxes and giving her a kiss. Something twisted slightly and I thought of my mother, of the wistful tone in the letters she sent. 'It's been crazy.'

'That's what I like to hear,' she said, beaming. 'Oh, and while I remember –' she rummaged around in the huge tapestry bag she always carried with her – 'there's some post for you. It's still coming to the house. Haven't you told people you've moved?'

I shook my head. Although it was weeks since Josip and I had taken up residence in the rooms above the restaurant, somehow we often ended up back at his parents' for meals, and baths where the hot water could actually be relied on. 'Sorry. I will, next time I write.' I looked down at the letters she had passed me and raised my eyebrows. 'This is from Cvita. I haven't heard from her in ages.'

It felt strange to see my sister's handwriting and I smiled as her voice rose up from the page, telling me she was well, how the kids were doing at school, that she had been in Ljeta in the summer, staying with Mother and Pa. It wasn't until right at the end that the surprise came; she was visiting them again in October and intended to come via Tršt and stay for a couple of days.

'Good news?'

'She's coming to visit,' I said, feeling slightly nonplussed. 'It's lovely, but ... God, I haven't seen her since my uncle's funeral, eighteen months ago. I'm not sure I'll know what to say.'

'Don't be silly,' said Ruža briskly. 'She's your sister. And presumably she's bringing the kids – what are they six, sevenish? You won't be able to get a word in edgeways with those two buzzing around.'

'You're right. It'll be lovely, won't it? Family's family after all.'

But as the week of Cvita's arrival drew closer I felt increasingly uneasy, obsessing over whether she was in touch with Goran, and what he would have told her. And would she bring news of Dina? Was she coming to try to persuade me to go home? On the evening I drove to the port, I realized I wasn't sure how old my niece and nephew were, and felt far from convinced they would even recognize me. Yet the second they walked off the ferry, my sister loaded down with bags, a small boy and girl spinning around her legs, all my fears disappeared and I pushed through the crowd of waiting people towards her.

'Hello, stranger,' she said, and when she kissed me the feel of her skin against mine reminded me of Mother. 'How long has it been? Let me look at you.' She drew back and I looked into her sweet, open face, reassuringly unchanged. 'God, you look different – I'm so relieved. Cata said when she last saw you . . .'

'Don't.' I bent down to kiss the children and picked up her bags. 'That was another life – one I try not to think about. Anyway, you've come to see my life *now*, haven't you? To report back to Mother and Pa?' I grinned to let her know I was teasing and she slipped an arm around me as the kids scrambled into the back of Josip's battered Fiat. As we drove she wound down the window and sniffed the air. 'Lavender,' she said, and I smiled, knowing exactly what her next words would be. 'This whole island smells like Aunt Marjana.'

Within hours of Cvita being in Tršt, I realized how much I missed my family. Introductions were made, wine poured, hugs exchanged between Josip and my sister. We ate well that night: crispy squid, tiny shrimps, glasses of crisp, cold Pošip, and when the children grew drowsy we simply drew the chairs together, gently lay them down and placed blankets over their weary bodies.

'So how are you *really*?' she said, sipping her wine and looking at me carefully. 'After everything that's happened, are you happy here? In *exile*?'

I had forgotten Cvita's tendency to become a little melodramatic when she had had too much wine and I leaned over to refill her coffee cup. 'It's a good life. Better than many people have right now. Am I happy?' I stared up at the sky for a moment and felt Irina's soft fingers against my cheek. 'I miss a lot of things. But I'm not unhappy.'

'You miss . . .'

'Everyone. Dina. Irina. Mother and Pa. Goran.' As I said his name, an expression flitted across her face and my stomach lurched. 'Have you seen him?'

'Yes. He came to stay with us for a few weeks last year, after –' she broke off.

I closed my eyes. 'You know then.'

'Yes. He came to us when . . . when he had been discharged from hospital. He just turned up again, like he did with you in Ljeta. Said he couldn't go to Mother and Pa. And when he told me what happened, I could understand why.'

'Oh God,' I put my head in my hands. 'Christ, Cvita, what must you think of me? What does *he* think of me? Does he hate me?'

'Of course he doesn't.' She wrapped her fingers around mine and gently pulled my hands away from my face. 'Darling, what happened – I know, I know all of it. Goran talked and talked those weeks; it was like everything he'd never said throughout his whole life just came pouring out. He told me things he'd done, what he'd come to believe, the lies he told himself to justify what he had become. And he told me that it all collapsed, everything just fell apart, the moment he saw you in Postić.'

'It was like a dream,' I said quietly. 'A nightmare. I so desperately wanted to see him, and then when I did, I couldn't believe it really *was* him.'

'He said exactly the same thing, like it was some miracle to see you there, something really wonderful – and then it became awful, that the expression in your face, how you looked at him . . . it was as if he could see himself through your eyes.'

'I was so shocked, Cvita, so horrified. And so *angry*. I actually think I could have killed him.'

'You're not as tough as you think,' she said, smiling. 'And he had a great nurse. After the first few days he asked me to ring Tara, of all people, said that he tried to write to her at least every couple of weeks, and if she didn't hear she'd worry. I didn't even know they were still in touch. When I told her what happened, she was on the first ferry back to Split – I couldn't stop her. She came and stayed until he was completely well again.'

'Tara?'

She nodded. 'It was very sweet actually. He let her fuss around him far more than anything I could ever get away with.'

'Did he tell her? That it was me?'

She shook her head. 'I don't think anyone knows except me. And, honestly, the real tragedy in all this is that you two aren't in touch. You ask me if he hates you, he was worried that's how you felt – but you both hate yourselves, you for what you did and him for what he had become. He loves you, just as he always did – and it's obvious how much you miss him. Won't you write? You know Goran – for all that he can talk, he has his pride. It must be you that writes first.'

'I wouldn't know what to say. Maybe too much has happened for things ever to be how they were. But what you've said, I will think about it. And I'm so glad you told me.'

I expected her to smile, but instead she looked sad and tired. 'What is it? Is there something else about Goran? Something you're not telling me?'

'Not about Goran. But there is something – I just don't know if now's the time. Maybe tomorrow.'

'No, come on, I want to know it all now, whatever it is. You being here, it's about the present and the future. But first we have to clear away the past. So let's do it all tonight. What else is there? What do you need to tell me?'

She leaned across the table and took her hands in mine. 'Sweetheart, it's Dina.'

'Oh my God what, *what*? Is she OK?'

'Oh, yes, she's OK.' There was a slight hint of contempt in my sister's voice. 'You know Anton, the man who came down from Zagreb? He was overseeing the government's rebuilding programme or something.'

'Yes, yes, I know about him. She's seeing him.'

'That's it, she's not just seeing him. Not any more. They got married, Miro. Last week. That's partly why I'm here – I didn't want you to hear it by letter or over the phone. I wanted to—'

'This all looks a bit serious.' We both jumped and I watched as Josip threw himself into the vacant chair and topped up his wine glass. He looked from me to Cvita and back again. 'Sorry, am I interrupting something?'

Cvita looked at me. 'I was just . . .'

'Dina got married,' I said, forcing the words out.

Josip let out a long, low whistle, reached into his pocket for his cigarettes, lit two and passed one to me. My hand trembled as I raised it to my lips.

'Well, she's not one to let the grass grow, is she? Miro, I'm so sorry.'

I tried not to let Cvita's news spoil our time together, and when the children were around I managed to put thoughts of Dina to the back of my mind. We took a boat to the Igleňi islands and I watched, mesmerized, as the two of them ran along the small jetty and launched themselves into the water.

'I remember you doing that.' Cvita nodded at them and smiled.

'You and Josip and . . .' Her voice tailed off and she shifted awkwardly on her towel.

'Pavle. It's OK. He was such a part of our lives, even after the occupation. Sometimes I even miss him a little – feels strange just to be Josip and me. I don't suppose he'll ever go back to Ljeta.'

'And you?' She waved as Emilja ran back into the sea. 'When will you go back?'

'Don't ask me that. Not now. How can I?'

'But Dina's not there. She doesn't live in Ljeta any more; you wouldn't run into her. What about Mother? She misses you so much, and neither her nor Pa are getting any younger.'

'Look at them.' I pointed to the kids, splashing each other and giggling as they rolled in the shallow waters that crept up and down the sand. 'We were like that once, remember? How do I unknow it all, Cvita? Everything I saw and did, Irina, Dina . . . Here I don't have to remember; all I am is Josip's friend who appeared on the ferry a year ago. No backstory, no past, no affair, no daughter. It's easy.'

'It's not living though, is it?' she said. 'Not really. You've got to lay the past to rest; otherwise how can you move on? And don't tell me you have. There's no woman, is there? Not since, what was her name, that reporter?'

'I leave all that to Josip,' I said, trying to lighten the atmosphere. 'He's the master.'

'Some things don't change.' She smiled, and I watched as her children came bounding towards her. 'But you can't live the rest of your life alone. If you do, well, the war has won, hasn't it? It's made a victim of you for life. Don't let that happen to you, honey. You deserve to be happy as much as anyone.'

I thought about her words as we walked back from the beach, and they came to me again as I waved her off on the ferry the following morning. Part of me knew she was right, and spurred on by the knowledge of Dina's marriage, I began to let Josip introduce me to some of the local girls he knew. As the weeks rolled past I relearned how to flirt and kiss, sometimes taking the girl back to my small room above the restaurant, slipping off her clothes and exploring her body with an enthusiasm that was only as deep as the amount of whisky I had drunk. On the surface it looked fun, but underneath lay a creeping sense of loneliness, unlocked by the few days I had spent with my sister and her children, a glimpse into a world I still longed to be part of.

Christmas came and went and we were so busy at the Dalmatia that I had little time to think of Ljeta. On New Year's Eve we threw a party, and it felt as if half the island came to drink *travarica* and usher in the bright new days of 1995. But the optimism proved misplaced; within weeks all anyone could talk about was the sudden upsurge of tensions on the mainland, with Tuđman and Milošević up to their old tricks as they tussled for land that both believed belonged to them. When I had first come to Tršt I had avoided watching the TV news or reading the papers; everything was too raw, too reminiscent of the strange world I had left behind. But as the months had passed I had begun to reconnect, found myself inwardly criticizing badly shot footage or grainy images in the newspaper. One afternoon, when the restaurant was quiet, I pulled out a box from under my bed, took out my camera and began to clean the lens. For the first time since Postić, I found myself wanting to take pictures again.

As winter turned to spring, I began to borrow Josip's car and drive into the countryside to try to capture the crisp, clear light that spread across the purple-hued hills, throwing shadows around the crumbling farm cottages and long neat lines of cypress trees. I rediscovered the joy of framing a perfect moment, the split second when a shaft of sunlight flickered through the branches of an olive tree and picked out the slim fronds of lavender dancing in the breeze. There was nowhere to get my films developed on Tršt, and so I would store them up and catch the ferry to Split every couple of weeks to buy fresh stock and pore over the images I had taken. Josip never minded me taking time out from the restaurant, and I used my trips to the mainland to bring back spices and cold meats and cheeses we couldn't find on the island.

'That's quite a haul,' he said, when I appeared in the restaurant one Saturday, laden down with bags of soft pink hams, chunks of parmesan and bunches of fresh thyme and oregano. 'Get your pics done?'

I nodded, setting the bags down in the kitchen and pulling a beer from the fridge.

'Just as well you're back. Someone's been asking for you. A woman. And a rather sexy one at that.'

'What?' I leaned out of the kitchen to find him grinning at me, eyebrows raised. 'Who was she?'

'You can ask her yourself, she's sitting outside. British, judging by the accent.'

Christ, Marian. It couldn't be. 'What does she look like?'

'Dark hair, slim, tall. Big camera, notebook on the table. Looks like a journalist.'

'Dark hair?' Josip nodded, reading my thoughts. I picked up the glass of wine he'd poured along with my beer and walked out on to the piazza, intrigued. I saw her immediately; head bent over the table, writing furiously on a large dog-eared notepad; as I drew nearer she looked up, her face hidden behind wide dark sunglasses.

'Hi. I'm Miro. My colleague says you were asking about me?'

She slid the glasses on to the top of her head and I found myself looking into wide brown eyes the colour of cedar wood. Her hair was drawn back into a ponytail and she looked cool and chic in a black v-necked top and cream linen trousers.

'Well, hello.' She smiled and stood up; I noticed her body was slim and toned, lightly tanned. Something stirred in me, surprising me. 'Kate Leeson – pleased to meet you.' She extended a hand and I shook it, feeling oddly formal. 'Will you join me?'

I sat down. 'So . . . ?'

'I'm sorry, this must be quite weird. I'm guessing it's not every day you get some strange British woman turn up and start asking about you.'

I winced slightly, tried to turn it into a smile.

'Oh Christ – did you think I was Marian?'

'You know Marian?'

'Of course, that's why I'm here. Well, not why, but how . . . God, I'm sorry, I always do this. Just because I know the whole story in my head there's no reason why you should. Hopeless.' She grinned and I found myself smiling back; she was a beguiling mix of chaotic, confident and utterly direct. 'It was Marian who suggested I get in touch with you.'

'Are you a reporter?'

She shook her head and slid a business card across the table. 'Not exactly. I make documentaries. I'm here researching a film for the BBC about the war, about how life is here, everyday life. It's been going on so long now, nearly five years. I want to find out how people are living, those that have been displaced, those that have stayed put, Croats in Serbian areas, Serbs still living in Croatia. Try to disentangle things a bit, make some sort of sense of it for people at home.'

'Well, good luck with that,' I said, trying to keep my voice light. 'Most of us can't make any sense of it and we live here. But I'm not sure you're really in the right place. There are some refugees you could talk to up at the hotels –' I pointed – 'but you're better off in Zadar or Dubrovnik, or ideally up in the Krajina, if you can get there.'

'I'm trying to get up to Knin, but there's all sorts going on up there again right now,' she said pleasantly, and I knew instantly I had underestimated her. 'And this is a stop en route to Zadar. But the thing is, my film isn't really going to be about the places where things happened. It's more about the stories of people who were involved, their experiences. Your war, and the one going on in Bosnia, have displaced hundreds of thousands of people, all now having to build new lives from the bottom up. It seems to me that war explodes everything, and when things fall back to earth nothing and no one is in quite the same place. Literally in some ways, metaphorically in others. And I'm exploring what that means, you know, in everyday life.'

She smiled again and something flickered inside me. I recognized it instantly: desire. But something more too, her words echoed the thoughts I had been having over the preceding weeks. 'You're right about the displacement. Neither Josip – he's my colleague, the one you met – or I are from here originally. But why are you so interested? I thought most people in your country didn't give a damn about what happened here.'

'Ouch.' She raised her eyebrows. 'Harsh but not unfair, I guess. But I have some history with your country. I used to come on holiday to Dubrovnik as a child – when the war happened I'd watch the news reports, and because Marian was a friend I felt even more closely linked to it. It seemed incredible that places I knew were being bombed and blown up, and I used to wonder what happened to the people I knew. And I'm just appalled we've done so little to help.'

'You'll find a lot of sympathy with that view. But . . .' I saw Marian suddenly, her face pressed against the dirty road in Sarajevo, blue eyes staring at me, terrified and hurt. 'How is Marian? Did she, I mean . . .'

Kate reached into her bag and brought out a photograph, passing it to me. I took a deep breath, but she looked exactly the same: neat blonde bob, crisp white shirt, pristine jeans. The only difference was that she was seated in a gleaming silver wheelchair.

'Oh.' Guilt flooded through my system. 'So she . . .'

'She's really well, she's doing brilliantly. One of the reasons she wanted me to find you – aside from the fact that apparently you're a very talented cameraman and I should employ you for my film – is that she wanted you to know she's got out. She works in radio now for the BBC, does programmes on disability and women's issues. And she's writing a book about Croatia. She said she wanted me to find out if you kept your promise, although she wouldn't tell me what it was. Did you?'

I looked around, at the wide, sunlit piazza, the sea shimmering in the distance. 'Yes,' I said, smiling. 'I did keep my promise . . . eventually. She wanted me to get out too, and I did. I'm so pleased that she's doing all right. She's . . . very special.'

'Well, she said the same about you. And she also said you'd be a great person to talk to about the war and how it affected people, said that you'd seen it from all sides. I wondered if I could buy you dinner and maybe we could talk a bit?'

I shifted uncomfortably. 'Look, I don't want to be rude, but I don't know that I can help really. I mean, I can tell you some things that happened and maybe suggest some good places for you to go. But I don't know, I mean, talking about my own—'

'Of course, of course.' Kate held her hands up and blushed slightly. 'God, I can quite see that you might not want to go unearthing everything for someone you've just met. The last thing I want to do is pry. I'd just be interested in your perspective on things – it doesn't have to be personal.'

I looked into her tanned, open face and let my gaze drift over her slim, brown shoulders. 'OK then, dinner. I'm not sure how much help I'll be, but dinner sounds lovely.'

There was something perfect about that first dinner with Kate. The evening stretched lazily into night, the first stars appeared in a sky that was still rose pink and a warm breeze blew around us, bringing wafts of lavender scent down from the hills. Josip brought us *pohane sardele* and *crni rižoto* and we ate the sardines with our fingers and I laughed out loud at the expression on her face when he explained the *rižoto* was coloured with squid ink. Kate insisted he join us and together we drew her a picture of our childhood so vivid that I could almost smell the pine trees and see the sun bouncing off the harbour wall.

'So your parents ran a pension?' she asked. 'And you worked there?'

'From when I was quite little. I used to run out the breakfasts before I went to school, much to Josip's envy.'

'Envy?' He grinned. 'I used to *dream* about doing your job. Can you imagine, at the age of ten, eleven, whatever we were, all those tourist girls in their skimpy dresses and tops? Me and Pavle used to think it was completely wasted on him though; he never spoke to any of them.'

'Pavle?'

Josip and I exchanged a look, each waiting for the other to speak.

'He was . . . a friend of ours,' I said eventually. 'But he was, well, he was Serb, and it made things difficult.'

Kate picked up the change in atmosphere instantly. 'So do you think tourism will come back to . . . is it Ljeta?'

'I hope so. It'll take time, but we're getting a few visitors, so hopefully the same is happening there. We're a tiny country, tourism is what supports us. We've got to get them to come back.'

She yawned suddenly, covering her mouth with her hand. She looked like a little girl and it reminded me of Marian, sitting on the bed in the darkness in the battered remains of the Ragusa.

'You're tired. And it's late. I'm so sorry – I'm afraid all Josip and I have done is take you on an extended stroll down our very own memory lane. Probably not quite what you had in mind.'

'It's been lovely,' she said, standing up. 'But I'd love to talk some more, Miro, if you don't mind. I've got some things to do in the day tomorrow but—'

'I'll be here,' I said, feeling an unexpected twist of anticipation in my stomach. 'Come along any time and I'll try and help you with what you want to know. Whatever that is.'

She smiled and nodded. 'Goodnight then. And thank you both for the dinner. It was delicious.'

I watched her as she walked away, a scarf thrown across her bare shoulders, bag slapping against her hip. She moved with a graceful confidence that reminded me of Marian, but it was softer, somehow sexier. I was mesmerized.

'Nice girl.' I turned to see Josip collecting the candles and salt and pepper mills from each of the tables. 'Very nice girl.'

'Shut up,' I said, smiling.

'I think she's a bit taken with you.'

'Well, that's not going to last,' I said, unsnapping the pegs from each of the tables and pulling off the covers. 'So, Miro, what did you do in the war? Well, my daughter died, I cheated on my wife and I nearly killed my brother. As stories go, it's hardly a crowd-pleaser is it?'

Josip put the candles on the bar and sat back on one of the stools. 'Christ, Miro, are you ever going to forgive yourself? I thought you'd got over things a bit, that Cvita had talked some sense into you. Yes, bad things happened, but, bloody hell, it was a war. It's not like you went and shagged someone else when everything was peachy with you and Dina. And as for Goran . . .'

'Don't.'

'Didn't Cvita say that he wanted to hear from you?'

'It's not that simple. I hurt them both so much, in different ways – what am I going to say to them? I don't *know* how to make it better, don't you understand? And anyway, why should they forgive me? I let them both down, disappointed them.'

'Oh, right – an ex-wife who remarried within minutes of her divorce coming through and a brother who committed war crimes.'

'Fuck off. What the fuck gives you the right?'

Josip stood up. 'Because I'm your friend and it's the truth. You're no more guilty than any of us; we've all fucked up, if that's how you want to look at it. We've all done things we'd never have done if it wasn't for the war, Christ, I still feel like a bloody deserter. But at least I'm getting on with my life. You need to sort yours out, man. It's not that I'm not glad to have you here, working with me, but you're just treading water really, aren't you? Some time sooner or later you're going to have to start living again.'

CHAPTER 30

'*Besmrtnost.*'

'"*Besmrtnost?*" What's that?'

I looked at Kate and thought how ironic it was that she had come to Tršt to try to unearth the past, while I had come to bury it.

'It means immortality. It's what Nic and I used to drink to in Sarajevo.' I lit a cigarette and felt my skin prickle at the memory of him holding my camera, filming every second of my fight with Goran. 'He was . . .'

'I met him once; you don't have to tell me. I can't see you two getting on at all – I never understood why Marian liked him. He came to see her when she was in hospital in England, did you know that? They're still in touch. I think he's in Chechnya now.'

'That figures. "Where God forsakes, I go in." That's what he used to say. Reckoned he'd done a deal with God to ensure his immortality.'

'And you? What had you done to be . . . *besmrtnost?*'

I smiled at her pronunciation of the word, but it faded as memories of Sarajevo flooded back. 'Nothing. I just . . . I guess I just didn't care. It was so bloody ironic; I became quite infamous in Sarajevo – the risk-taker, the one who would go furthest to get the story. They all thought I was brave – or crazy. I might have been the second, but I certainly wasn't the first. I'd lost my daughter, my marriage, it made me reckless – just stupid. It took what happened with Marian to make me see how incredibly selfish I was being – when I saw her in hospital, I realized what it would do to my family if something like that happened to me. And then . . . and then I just couldn't do the job any more.'

'So you came here?'

'No, I . . . Nic and I ended up going to Postić.' Kate raised her eyebrows. 'I know. It was the most horrific place I'd ever been and suddenly all the confidence, or arrogance, or whatever it was that kept me safe in Sarajevo completely disappeared. Nic had this theory about fear; he'd say it was like a barrier you had to scramble over, and once you were past it you had infinite freedom to do anything, go anywhere. I used to think he was right, but now I think fear's there for a reason. Go beyond it and in some ways you're out of control, beyond the realms of reasonable life.'

'But that's war, isn't it? Beyond the realms of reasonable life?'

I looked down at the table, moved my knife and fork, smoothed the cover, fighting back the images that were flooding into my brain; little Mika on the street in Sarajevo, Marian underneath me on the road, her blood leeching on to my clothes. 'Can we walk?'

'I'm sorry,' she said, as we strolled down to the promenade that stretched along beside the sea. 'You're upset. I've no right to do that. I don't mean to . . .'

Almost without realizing, I took her hand, felt her fingers tighten around mine. I stared straight ahead, our feet hitting the marble slabs in perfect time.

'The thing is . . .' I stopped, oddly aware that I was about to say things to Kate that I had never actually formed as thoughts before. 'It's almost like . . . I kind of feel war has always been a presence in my life. When I was a very little boy –' I paused for a moment, shuddered slightly at the memory – 'my best friend stepped on a landmine. She was lucky; it took off half her foot and a finger but she survived. I was with her, but escaped with just a few scratches and bruises.'

'Oh my God. You saw it happen?'

I nodded. 'I pretended I didn't. It was like I didn't have the words for what I'd seen. We moved away soon after it happened – it changed all our lives. I had a great childhood in Ljeta, but I used to have nightmares and I'd think about it all the time, although I never really told anyone. I always felt it had been my fault, felt guilty that Tara got hurt and not me; everything was all mixed up, the way things are when you're a kid. When things started going wrong in Serbia and people started to say there might be a war, I felt weirdly drawn towards it, like I had to be part of it. I had an idyllic life in Ljeta, could have just helped run my dad's pension, lived with Dina and our daughter, but it wasn't enough. It was like what happened with Tara was a glimpse of something . . . I don't know. For whatever reason, I couldn't sit by and not be involved.'

'And so you became a cameraman. Not a soldier?'

'Not brave enough,' I said simply. 'And for me . . . it was about telling people what was happening, making sure people *knew*. Tara got hurt because no one ever talked about anything; it's like there was all this bad stuff everywhere in Knin, and yet people pretended not to know. That started to happen down in Ljeta too; when fighting broke out up in the mountains, people would say, "Oh, it won't come here – let's just get on with life as normal." And I tried to be like that for a while, but I just couldn't . . . it was like, I don't know, maybe I was trying to atone for something.' I shrugged and smiled at her. 'I'm sorry. I'm sure you don't want to know all this stuff.'

'If you want to tell me, then I do,' she said. 'And your friend? What happened to her?'

'We sort of lost touch a few years ago – she moved to quite a remote island when the war started, and then when my daughter died and I moved to Zagreb . . . life changed so much. She's still in touch with my brother, I think, but he – I mean, me and him – well . . .' The words caught in my throat as I remembered his bruised face, blood seeping from his nose and lips.

Her fingers tightened around my hand. 'Forgive me, but this is . . . it's all still so *raw* for you, isn't it? When you talk, it sounds as if it all happened yesterday.'

'I suppose so. I just don't usually talk about any of it, not even with Josip.'

'And your family?'

'I haven't been back to Ljeta for almost two years.' A wave of exhaustion swept through me; I looked at Kate and longed for her to understand that although part of me wanted to tell her everything, another part wished there was nothing to say, that the stories she wanted to hear belonged to someone else. I felt overwhelmed suddenly, began to scrabble in my mind for the words to form an excuse, to walk away, when I felt something soft against my face and I realized it was Kate's hand, and she was going to kiss me.

'You're awake.'

'And you're gorgeous.' I pulled her body to mine and felt the same rush of warmth that had surged through me out on the promenade the previous evening. Her kiss had led to another, then another, and there had been no need to ask, no question to answer, and I had led her back to the restaurant and up to my small room and we had slowly undressed each other in the moonlight, and when I slipped inside her I didn't recognize how I felt, couldn't think of the word, and then I realized, it felt *right*. She was *right*.

'I don't normally . . .' She stopped and a flicker of embarrassment passed across her face. She propped herself up on an elbow and looked straight at me. 'This isn't my usual style. I don't, I mean . . .'

'It's really not mine either. After everything.'

She pressed a finger to my lips and smiled.

'No more sad stories, not today. I'm sorry – I feel like I overstepped the mark last night. It's just, what you were saying, your family, how you haven't seen them . . . that's so exactly what I want my film to be about. Your whole country must be made of hundreds of thousands of people like you; separated from their loved ones, grieving for those they've lost.'

'Even when they're still alive.'

'That must be strangest of all.' She looked at me and I could tell she was fighting the urge to ask questions.

I kissed her. 'Yes.'

'Yes, what?'

'Yes, I do miss my family. I do want to see them. It's just . . . the problem is that war changes you. Everyone. It shows you sides of people, sides of yourself, that you can't ever forget. And then somehow you've lost the version of them that you used to know.'

'And you don't think you can get that back? Your friend – what was his name? Pavle? If you saw him now, would you still be angry?'

His face appeared in my mind; not the gaunt, haunted features of the soldier I had come to know in recent years, but the boy from the past, mischievous and kind. 'Maybe. I don't know. I was beyond angry with my brother too, and now . . . I just miss him.'

'But you still love him?'

'Of course.' I remembered Bobo suddenly. 'It's funny, my ex-brother-in-law, who was a complete bastard, once said that hate was much stronger than love. That hate would always win. I didn't know what to think at the time, everything was so crazy, but now I think maybe he's wrong. I just wish, I wish we could all be the people we were before the war came. But it's not possible.'

'Maybe it's about going forward, rather than back,' she said, 'Wars change everything, we both know that, but people survive and rebuild their lives and your brother is still your brother, your family still your family. You've survived such a dreadful time, all of you. Isn't it now about creating new lives, new ways of being?'

I tried to smile. 'What do you think I'm doing here?'

Before she could answer I kissed her again, desperate not to have to talk any more. She sensed the conversation was over, slipped her arms around me and somehow the day disappeared in a haze of kissing and talking and exploring her warm, elegant body. I only left the room to pile a plate with cold meats and cheeses, fresh tomatoes and slices of bread and take the cold beers that Josip passed me, a huge knowing smile on his face.

The next morning we finally made it down on to the piazza and swam in the cool, clear water that lapped the town's small beach. I didn't ask how long she was staying, didn't want to break the spell, and we lay on the sand and I let my fingers drift up and down her damp salty skin. The hours floated by and when the sun began to drop and the air grew cooler we dusted the sand from each other's bodies and began to walk back slowly to the restaurant.

'MIRO.' Josip's voice echoed across the piazza. '*Miro.*' I looked up and realized he was running towards us, waving his hand. 'Miro, thank God you're back – I didn't know where you were.'

'We were just on the beach.' I slipped my arm around Kate's shoulder; her salt-stiff hair tickled my skin. 'Everything OK?'

'Yes . . . no, look, I don't know. Your dad telephoned a few minutes ago. He . . . he sounded odd. He said you need to call him straight away – I asked him if everything was OK, but he said he needed to speak to you. He said it was important.'

A twist of anxiety burrowed its way into my stomach. Pa never called. On the rare occasions I rang Mother, he and I would have a brief conversation, but the phone made him awkward, almost monosyllabic.

'I won't be long,' I said to Kate. 'Are you OK out here for a bit?'

She smiled and nodded, and I walked into the restaurant, picked up the receiver and dialled the number. 'Pa?'

'Miro, thank God.' His voice sounded thin and sharp.

'Pa, are you OK? Josip said to call. Is everything all right?'

There was a pause. 'No, son. Everything isn't all right. You need to come home. It's your mother. She's not well.'

'What do you mean, not well?'

'I mean . . . she's ill, Miro. Seriously ill. You need to come and see her.'

His voice broke and I stared out the window, on to the piazza to where Josip and Kate were sitting chatting. I had been with them just minutes ago, everything had been normal, the three of us together. Now suddenly I was separate from them, somewhere new and unexpected. I couldn't think.

'Miro? Are you there?'

I swallowed hard. 'Yes, I'm here. But, I mean, how ill? Of course I'll come, but for God's sake, Pa, what's going on?'

There was silence and then a noise, a kind of choking gulp. 'I'm so sorry.' His voice was little more than a whisper. 'It's cancer. She's got cancer. You need to come. Now. Can you do that?'

I watched my reflection nodding in the glass of the window.

'Miro? Can you do that?'

'Sorry. Yes, of course. There's no ferry today, but tomorrow, I'll come.'

'I'm so glad. We'll see you . . .'

'Pa?' The words were forcing their way out of my mouth even as I desperately didn't want to say them. 'She's going to get better though, isn't she? I mean, she'll be all right?'

There was a sharp intake of breath at the other end of the phone. 'There's nothing they can do, son. You need to understand. You're coming to say goodbye.'

None of it made sense. I stood unmoving, my hand clamped around the receiver, nails digging into the circles on the dial. I felt utterly bewildered. How could my mother suddenly be so ill? Why had no one told me before? Did Goran know? Cvita? I stared at the phone, longing to call my father back, to make him tell me it wasn't true, it was all some hideous mistake.

'Miro?' Kate pushed the door open and raised her eyebrows at me. 'Is everything all right?'

I shook my head, staring past her, out on to the piazza. I had been sitting out there. My mother had been alive and well. Only she wasn't. It was just that I didn't know.

'Miro?'

I turned my face towards her. 'It's my mum. She's got cancer.'

'Oh God, I'm so sorry.'

'I've got to go back. Back to Ljeta.'

'Of course. Of course you do. Today? Can I do anything? Help you pack?'

'I don't know.' I pulled a bottle of Stock from the shelf, sloshed some into a glass and gulped it back. It didn't help. 'I can't believe it. I don't understand.'

'How long since you've seen her?'

'It must be, um . . .' I could hardly bring myself to say it. 'It's about two years.'

'Oh, sweetheart. Are you close?'

'We were. Are. But we had a falling out the last time I saw her. It was my uncle's funeral and things were said, things about Dina. She . . .' I stopped, suddenly pictured my mother, the expression on her face; bewildered, hurt. That was what I had left her with, for two long years. 'I always thought there'd be time, you know? That we would make it up in the future.'

'But you can do that now.'

'She's *dying*. It's too late. It's like everything, it's too late.'

'Don't say that.' She came towards me and laid her fingers on my arm. 'It's never too late.'

'Oh God, what you don't know!' I said, anger flooding my system. 'Of course it's too late. You want to know what war does to people, well, here it is, in glorious Technicolor, happening right in front of you. You want to know what it's like for those of us living through a war? *This* is what it's like; people get sick and injured and die, and even if you think you can put things back together, you can't; everything is changed and broken and all you can do is live with the mess. It's not easy for me to go back; there's so many bad memories in that village, so much hurt. It's not as simple as just chucking some clothes in a bag and driving off.'

She looked at me in astonishment. 'Surely it's exactly that simple. If your mum is . . . well, you've got no time to waste. I know it'll be hard, but maybe this is a chance, like you were saying this morning, to try and put some of those things behind you.'

'You don't understand,' I said, gulping back more brandy; this time I felt the alcohol hit.

'You're right, I don't,' she said calmly. 'I can't know what you've been through, but I can see this is a chance to make things right, isn't it? To make up with your mum, to see your brother, maybe to make some peace with your ex-wife? You haven't actually lost them, not really, not yet.'

'Don't tell me what I have and haven't lost,' I said, slamming my glass down on the bar. 'You've no idea what you're talking about. I lost everything, *everything*: my daughter, my wife, my brother, my home – my faith in my own country. Now it's my mother's turn. Why do you think I live here on this bloody perfect island, drinking cocktails with silly girls and running a fucking cafe? Because there's nothing to lose here, nothing of any real worth. Don't you dare stand there and lecture me. I'm not some fucking subject in your film; this is my *life*.'

Kate stood up and her eyes flashed with anger. 'Silly girls, eh? Well, perhaps you're right. Perhaps I am silly, because I truly believed you were a good man that bad things had happened to. I really respected you when I first met you, thought you'd made a new start after a really terrible time in your life, moved on, become someone new. You tell me this is all about creating a new life, but actually it's just running away; everything is just . . . buried, not gone. And now you're yelling at me because you've been forced to face up to what you've been running from all this time? Well, I'm sorry about your mum, Miro, I truly am. But I'm glad I found out in time what you're really like.'

By the time the moon rose above the harbour I felt as if I had lived the longest day of my life, and yet I was still no closer to understanding the enormity of what my father had told me. I had packed a bag, blindly throwing socks and T-shirts on top of each other until Josip had poked his head around the door and gently suggested I'd probably put in enough. He pushed a brandy glass into my hand and I sat on the bed, watching while he assembled toiletries and clean jeans and all the things my numbed brain had forgotten I would need.

'There's one more thing you need to sort out before tomorrow,' he said, when the bag was zipped up and we were downstairs sitting at the bar, the 'closed' sign firmly in place on the door.

I looked at him. 'I know. I behaved like an idiot. And I was rude. *And* hurtful. No wonder she stormed off.'

'Just go and see her,' he said calmly. 'You'd had such a shock, it's inevitable you were going to have some sort of reaction. It's just unfortunate she caught it. Even if you never see her again, you should leave things on a better note.'

'I don't want to never see her again.'

'All the more reason to go and sort it out. It's either that, or finish this –' he waved the bottle of Stock at me. 'I know which would be better for you.'

I nodded, pushed back my chair and began to walk across the piazza, trying to get my thoughts into some order. There was nothing to be done about my father's news, not until tomorrow; all I could do now was attempt to set things straight before I left. I ran my fingers through my hair and struggled to think what I could possibly say to Kate. An apology would probably be a good starting point.

'Miro?'

I looked along the street and realized Kate was sitting in the garden of the small pension where she was staying. A dim pool of light above her head picked out the notepad in front of her, covered in lines of neat handwriting. As she leaned forward I could see her face more clearly, eyes a little guarded and unsure.

'Are you working?'

She nodded. 'Just making some notes. Plans. I never make an itinerary before I come on a trip like this. People talk to me and they suggest things and I go where the trail leads. It's better that way. Leaves you open to, well, anything.'

I sat down. 'Kate, I'm so sorry.'

She held up her hand. 'No, I'm sorry. It wasn't my place to say any of those things, particularly after you'd got such dreadful news.'

'It's just such a shock. And just as . . . I mean, we were just starting to spend some time together.'

'I know.' She smiled, her eyes softened a little. 'We had a nice time, didn't we?'

'Yes. It's been a long time since I've felt any of that. Honestly, I didn't know if I still could.'

'It *was* lovely.'

'Was? Does it have to be was?'

She sat back a little and looked at me. 'Miro, what are you saying?'

'I don't know,' I said honestly. 'Just . . . I don't want to say goodbye to you right now. I've got to go tomorrow, back to Ljeta and face things, face the past. And actually that's OK, it's time. But I'd like to think there's maybe a way to go forward too.'

'How do you know you won't find that in Ljeta?'

'Maybe I will. But all I know is that I don't want to say goodbye for good. You're here, aren't you? For a few weeks? Researching?'

'I'm moving around. But the Foreign Press Bureau in Zagreb can usually find me. You know it?'

The irony wasn't lost on me. 'Oh yes, I know it. And would you want me to find you?'

She smiled. 'Yes, I think I would. But you've got a lot of other things to think about right now, Miro. A lot to cope with in the next few days and weeks. Let's not make any promises. Whatever happens, it's been lovely.'

'Can I sit with you for a while? Not talk, just sit. You can work . . .'

She nodded and I laid a hand on her arm, and let my fingers drift up and down her wrist. The air was sweet with lavender, and up in the apple tree at the end of the garden a cicada kept time with the distant lapping of the sea. The town was silent, and it felt as if no one was awake but Kate and me, two familiar strangers on a moonlit street, each a long way from home.

CHAPTER 31

'Welcome to your new home, my boy. You're going to be so happy here.'

Ivo's words came back to me as I parked Josip's car and walked down on to Ljeta's small harbour. The journey had been straightforward but long; the morning drive across the hills to the ferry port, the slow drift across the sea, a strange sense of being drawn inexorably home as the landscapes became more familiar and the thick grey walls of Dubrovnik began to shimmer in the distance.

When I finally arrived in Ljeta, the sun was just starting to slip below the horizon, flooding the sky lavender pink, the two small Krpani islands floating like displaced purple hills above the sea. Almost twenty years since I had first set foot on the cobbled waterfront, and now Ivo slept in the graveyard behind the pine woods and I would never again come back to find my mother in the kitchen, stirring huge silver pans of *rižoto* or *buzara* sauce. I tried not to think of Dina, but she was everywhere: on the road down into the village where silvery green saplings had replaced the decapitated trees, in the newly painted *slastičarna*, on the cobbles with Irina, lifting her up into the sunshine, waving to me as I filmed them with the camera Mark and Sarah had given me.

As I turned the corner, I realized how much had changed since I had been away. When I had come back for Ivo's funeral the village

had barely started to recover from the trauma of occupation: shopfronts boarded up, rotted boats in the harbour, the streets still
strangely hushed. Now, two years on, the village looked almost as
I remembered it from my childhood: tables on the cobbles, black-
boards offering *crni rižoto* and mussels *buzara*. Only a few of the seats
were taken, but there was music coming from the tinny speakers
above Tomas's cafe, and I could see Mij behind the silver canisters
of brightly coloured gelato, handing cones to schoolchildren who
giggled with delight as they walked out of the ice cream parlour.

'Welcome home, Miro.' I spun round and found Aunt Marjana
standing behind me, her figure less gaunt than before, cloaked in a
bright floral dress. 'Aren't you a sight for sore eyes?' Before I could
speak, her arms were around me and I found myself drawn in, her
lavender-scented skin warm against mine.

'Aunt Marjana,' I said, smiling at the delight on her face. 'You
never change.'

'Well, you do,' she said, standing back and beaming in approval.
'You looked like a ghost the last time I saw you, and now look, my
handsome nephew is back.' She tucked her arm into mine and I let
her guide me along the cobbles. 'And how are you? Is life on Tršt
agreeing with you? How's that Josip – still one for the ladies?'

I laughed. 'He's the same. Wonderfully the same actually. The
restaurant's doing well and it's a good life. We think business will
be even better this summer.'

'Shall we sit?' We were outside Tomas's cafe and I smiled and
waved as he came out into the dusky air.

'*Miro*. My God. How long has it been?' I shook his hand, felt the
familiar sense of guilt spread through me.

'Two years or so. The last time was . . .' I looked across at Marjana.

'I know – it was for Ivo's funeral,' she said quietly. 'It's OK. It's
true what they say – time heals.'

'Does it?'

She patted my hand. 'To a degree. Shall we have a drink? I know you want to see your mother, but she was sleeping when I left and she's quite peaceful at the moment. You must have so many questions. I'll answer everything I can, better than your father . . . He's being wonderful, but it's so hard for him. Cvita's with him now.'

'And Goran?'

'Tomorrow.' She looked at me for a moment, touched my cheek with her fingers. 'All of you back together. If only . . . if only it was in happier circumstances.' Her voice faded and I saw there were tears in her eyes. I closed my hand over hers; I knew that for all their bickering, she and my mother had become like sisters over the years.

'We're going to open the restaurant again this summer,' she said, straightening her back and smiling. 'Your parents and I had great plans for this year; everyone's desperate to start making some money again. And some of our visitors are very loyal. Mark and Sarah have written, they're coming out in a couple of weeks. And did you know Cata is coming back? She's going to run the place. Unless you want to help?'

I shook my head. 'I don't think so. But that's great news about Cata. The last letter or two I've had from her gave the impression she'd tired of Zagreb. And there was some man.'

'There's always a man with my daughter,' she said, laughing. 'That's why I need her back here so I can keep an eye on her, introduce her to a nice village boy.'

'And Pa? Does he still work? He always used to love it so, sitting with the tourists.'

'He does,' she says. 'He's a bit slower on his feet now, we all are. Not that I was ever the quickest, if I'm honest. I know it used to drive your mother crazy, my tendency to sit in a deckchair while she was cooking up those great vats of spaghetti sauce and *rižoto*.'

I laughed, but there was a tightness around my chest. Tomas poured the wine and I lit a cigarette as memories washed over me, sunlit mornings with Mother placing boiled eggs into the blue china eggcups and scolding me for being slow to bring the bread and coffee.

'They were such good times. We had no idea how lucky we were, did we?'

Marjana took a sip of her wine and her eyes went a little misty. 'No, I don't think we did. Not at the time. None of us realized it could all be taken away from us, that those days would only last a few precious years.'

'They felt precious to you too?'

'So precious. It was our own business, the first time we really had any money, we answered to no one but ourselves. It wasn't perfect of course – in high summer that kitchen could feel like an oven. But at the end of the night the four of us would sit together, your mother drying the cutlery, Ivo counting the takings, your father singing to himself as he stacked the chairs. I used to look at us all sometimes and think, This is perfect, really perfect. And even when the war started in Slavonia, I never really believed it would come here, that we could lose everything.'

'Is that how you feel? Like you've lost everything?'

She thought for a moment. 'Sometimes. I miss Ivo every day. Every morning, even now, I wake up and for a second it's OK, life is normal and I don't remember. And then it swings in: there's no warm body in the bed next to me, no one to pour coffee for, no one to giggle with. Because we always found something to laugh at, even when things got really dark. He wasn't scared of being silly, you see, that was what was so marvellous about him.'

Tears had begun to stream down her face and I bit my lip hard. 'But you have Cata.'

'Yes. Yes, I do. And it's fantastic that she's coming back. A new generation, a new start. Will you really not come back too? You and she could run it together; Ivo's daughter, Petar's son – how wonderful would that be?'

'I wish I could,' I said. 'It does sound wonderful in some ways, but I just can't, and it's not even about Dina any more. It's about me. What I saw, what I did in Sarajevo . . . for a long time afterwards I thought it was just about me being crazy, running away from my grief for Irina and losing Dina. And some of it was, but recently, I don't know, I've realized that part of it was right for me. I enjoyed what I was doing. It was dangerous and hard and it took me months of being on Tršt before I felt even remotely normal again. But I'm good behind a camera and I'm good at being somewhere unfamiliar and making sense of it. I can't do that here. I can't be that person here.'

'And are you that person on Tršt?'

'Not yet. But I think, like everyone, it's taken me some time to understand what happened to me and why I did the things I did. I've started taking pictures again – who knows, perhaps I'll go back to it in some way.'

'You sound like you've done a lot of thinking.'

'Quite the opposite – I blocked everything out for a long time, couldn't bear to engage with it all, didn't know where to start. But just lately I've started to talk about things a bit.'

'Time,' she said. 'It's what you need.'

'And people. Sometimes you meet someone.'

She raised her eyebrows. 'You've met someone?'

I thought of Kate, how peaceful it had felt sitting beside her in the moonlit garden the previous night. 'I don't know yet. Maybe. Anyway, that's not something I can think about right now.' I tipped the last of my wine back and steeled myself for the conversation both of us had been dreading. 'So, is it really true, what Pa said? Is there nothing they can do? Why didn't he tell me before now?'

Marjana pulled a tissue from her bag and dabbed at her eyes. 'Silly old woman,' she said, almost to herself. 'Tears aren't going to do you any good, are they?' She straightened up and looked directly at me, her eyes blurry and pink. 'The truth is, darling, she's very poorly indeed. You know your mother, how stubborn she can be; even I didn't know how ill she was until a few weeks ago. I kept asking – she'd lost a lot of weight, her and your father kept disappearing to Dubrovnik and I knew something was up. Finally they came back one day, about a month ago, and told me. Stomach cancer. Rare for a woman. And it was a late diagnosis, she'd been ignoring pains for months. They said they could offer her a course of treatment, but it would only prolong her life for a short while and it would be pretty unpleasant while she was undergoing it.'

'Why didn't Pa tell us then? Why didn't you tell us?'

'She didn't want to worry you all. "They have their lives," she said. "They can't be here for months on end." Ironically I think she had planned to call you this weekend, but then this infection hit out of the blue. Your father came home the day before yesterday to find her collapsed on the kitchen floor. They took her straight to hospital, but apparently this is often what happens with this sort of illness. The body's immune system is just too weakened to combat the sort of infection you or I could fight off without even knowing.'

I pushed my fingers into tight fists beneath the table and tried to keep my voice steady. 'How long does she have?'

'They don't know. If she fights the infection off, then a few more weeks. If not, it could be days. That's why you needed to come, Miro. I'm so glad you're here.'

Nothing could have prepared me for how my mother had changed. Aunt Marjana had warned me that she had grown thin and weak, but I could only picture the woman I had always known: her kind, firm face, wide brown eyes, thick chestnut hair neatly pinned back, increasingly streaked with grey as the years went by. The wine we had drunk made everything feel vaguely dreamlike, and it was only when I drew up at the house and Cvita came towards me, her face raw with grief, that I finally understood the reality of what was happening.

'Thank God you're here,' she whispered, and I pulled her towards me and felt her head rest on my shoulder. 'I'm trying to stay strong for Pa, but it's so *hard*. And he's so calm.'

'Is he here?'

She shook her head. 'He's gone for a walk. I told him he needed a break. He sits by her bed all day, hour after hour, whether she's awake or asleep. But you should go up now; she was stirring. There are moments when she's lucid, although she's on quite a lot of morphine. And even if she seems asleep, talk to her, tell her that you're here. Make sure she knows, Miro. That you have come at last.'

I held Cvita tightly, felt Aunt Marjana's hand on my arm and followed her into the house and up the stairs. I stood outside the door for a moment and my heart thumped so hard that it actually hurt, fuelled by an overwhelming sense of panic that this woman I loved so was going to leave me and there was nothing I could do to stop it. I pushed open the door and my eyes stung at the sight of her in the dim light, her face turned towards me, eyes closed, unfamiliar lines around her eyes and mouth, scored like knife marks. I winced at the sight of them; they had been drawn by pain.

'Mother?' Her hand was half under the pillow and I slipped mine over the top of it. It felt strangely cold to the touch. 'Mother, it's Miro. I've come home.'

Slowly her eyelids began to flutter upwards and a small smile played around her mouth. 'Miro?' The whisper was so faint I could barely hear it. 'Miro?'

I tightened my fingers around her hand. 'Yes, darling. It's me. I'm here.'

She opened her eyes properly and relief spun through my mind; she was conscious, she had seen me, she knew that I had come. 'I'm sorry,' she said, 'to . . . worry you.'

'Shhh. You don't have to talk. And you don't have to be sorry. I'm the one that's sorry. But I'm here now. Can I talk to you a little? Tell you what your youngest has been up to?'

She smiled again and nodded, and I sat beside her bed and told her all that was good and positive about my life; the busy restaurant with Josip, the recipes she had sent me that we cooked from most nights, the sense of rebirth that was happening on Tršt, that I could see was happening in Ljeta too. And when I had run out of words, I bent in and kissed her cheek and held my face against hers and told her how much I loved her and how I had missed her and how sorry I was.

'Don't be sorry,' she whispered. 'Always . . . always proud of you. My rascal boy.' A tear rolled down her face. 'My rascal boys.'

'He's coming tomorrow,' I said, trying to keep control of myself. 'Goran. He's coming tomorrow.'

'And you're all right now? You two?'

'Yes. Yes.' I put my other hand over hers. 'We're all right now, your rascal boys. We're going to be fine.'

I dreamed of my mother that night. We walked together beneath the pine trees and she was well again, as young as she had been in Knin when I was a boy, and we talked of my childhood and the parties she and Pa threw over the years. We walked as the sun set and the first stars came out and I turned to watch the moon rise. When I turned back I saw that she was bending over an old-fashioned pram, her face wreathed in smiles, and I knew without even looking that the baby in the pram was Irina.

'Dr Mesić is here,' Cvita said when I appeared in the kitchen, bleary-eyed and more than a little unsettled by my dream.

'Is she worse?'

'No, he comes by every day. He's been amazing, Miro, so wonderful. And so good with Pa.' She poured coffee and pointed to the basket of rolls on the table.

'I'm not hungry. Do you know when Goran's getting here?'

Before she could answer there was the sound of footsteps on the stairs and Pa appeared, with Dr Mesić just behind him.

'Miro, how are you? I'm so sorry, this is such a terrible thing.'

'Doctor Mesić.' I shook his hand, trying to ignore the stabbing pain of the memory of being in his tiny consulting room, listening to him tell me that Irina had meningitis. 'How is she?'

He pressed his lips together and shook his head. 'Quite honestly, it's hard to tell. She's holding steady at the moment, but infections can be so unpredictable. I'm afraid her system is just so weak.'

'Goran's coming today.' Cvita's voice was taut.

'Well, that will be a boost, I'm sure,' he said slowly. 'And there's a chance that she may beat the infection, but even then it might only be a matter of weeks. You must all make the most of the time you have.'

'Thank you,' I said, trying to keep my voice steady. 'It's good of you to be so . . . clear. I'll see you out.'

By the time I walked back into the kitchen, Pa had disappeared back upstairs and Cvita was sitting at the table with her head in her hands.

'I need to call Branko, see how the kids are,' she said. 'And you? Why don't you go and see Dina?'

I stared at her. 'Dina? Now? I don't want to be anywhere but here.'

Cvita smiled sadly. 'You can't sit with her all day, Miro, and you heard what Mesić said; she's stable at the moment. Goran will be here soon and I think, perhaps, when he first arrives he'll need a little space. If we're all here . . . you know what he's like.'

'I have been thinking about her,' I admitted. 'I kind of don't want to see her, but I know I have to. It's constantly in the back of my mind.'

'All the better to get it out of the way then,' she said firmly. 'These next days are going to be incredibly hard. You know that. You don't want something else hanging over you.'

'But I don't even know where she lives.'

Cvita reached down for her handbag and pulled out a small leaflet. 'Here. I picked this up in Karena's shop a couple of days ago. There's a little map on it. I'm sure you can find your way.'

I stared down at the paper. 'Konavle Kitchen', it read, 'Traditional dishes made from local ingredients to my grandmother's recipes'.

'She's done it then, just like she said.'

'Done what?'

'She always said she'd open a restaurant like this. I even gave her the name, we talked about it when we were kids. She was going to cook, I'd be front of house.' I looked across at Cvita. 'Ironic, isn't it? I'm doing exactly that, hundreds of miles away. And she's got Anton to run it with now.'

'Go and see her, Miro,' she said, coming over to kiss me. 'Otherwise you're just going to keep on torturing yourself. You've got enough on your plate without that.'

I knew she was right. I picked up the car keys and drove away from my parents' house, a strange mix of anticipation and adrenalin pulsing through my system. As the car glided along the streets of Sipili I couldn't believe the change that had taken place; crumbling houses had been dismantled, streets had been repaved, trees planted. Ruined cottages still dotted the fields and hillsides, yellowing grasses sprouting from cracked walls, but there were new houses too, and scaffold-clad cottages that spoke of more renewal on its way.

I turned on to the road for Morsać, and within seconds a sign came into view: Konavle Kitchen 2 km. I followed the gravel track up to a small car park shaded by plane trees. A paved footpath led to a cluster of pretty terraces dotted with terracotta pots holding white geraniums and scarlet hibiscus. Tables were scattered across the different levels, one shaded by a canopy of vines, others in the sunlight, separated by lemon trees and potted fuchsias.

And then I saw her. She had her back to me, patiently teasing the long stems of a climbing rose through a wide wooden trellis. She wore a simple cream dress that fell below her knees, and one strap had slipped off her shoulder as she bent to tie the rose to the thin strip of wood. Her hair was pulled back in the plait she had worn since we were schoolchildren, a few loose strands blowing across her bare, tanned shoulders. I opened my mouth to call her name, but before I did she turned towards me and when I saw her face my heart seemed to swell in my chest.

'Miro.'

'Dina.' My beautiful, beautiful girl. My wife.

CHAPTER 32

'You came.' I watched her move towards me, her body as slim and lithe as it had always been.

'Yes.' I had no idea what to say. She stood in front of me and I looked into her face, searching for any sign of anger or bitterness. Instead she just smiled, a touch of shyness creeping across her features. 'You look wonderful.'

She blushed. 'Thank you. You look really well too. So much better than last time I saw you.'

I laughed. 'I've Josip's cooking to thank for that; he's quite the chef these days.'

'How is he?' she said, and her voice was full of warmth. 'I miss him, you know? Even now.'

'He's exactly the same. I don't know where I'd be without him. He kind of saved me really.'

'Maybe you saved each other.'

'Maybe.'

Neither of us spoke. It felt almost unreal, and I realized I was desperate to touch her. 'Can I . . .' but she knew, moved a little awkwardly towards me and I drew her in, felt her arms around me and my heart lurched with the realization that it was all still there, everything the same, the softness of her skin, the way her body tucked perfectly into mine.

After a moment she drew back and smiled at me, but her eyes were brimming with tears. 'I'm so sorry about your mother,' she said. 'I know we fell out, but there were a lot of happy times too before that. She loves you so much, all of you. It's a terrible thing; she's too young.'

'Thank you. It's a huge shock. But I saw her last night and she knows I'm here and that means everything.'

She slipped her arm through mine. 'Would you like a drink? Can you stay a while, or do you have to get back?'

'A drink would be lovely. I can't be hours, but a little while. Goran's arriving and he'll need some space at first.'

'How is he?' she asked, as we walked across the lawn to a table surrounded by roses on the point of coming into bloom.

'Goran? To be honest, I don't know really. OK, I think. He lives up in the Plitvice now. We don't . . . we haven't spoken for a while.'

'Really?'

'Things happened in the war. Some things are very hard to come back from. I don't . . . but it'll be good to see him. I'm hoping we can put everything behind us.'

'I hope so. It's a tragedy if you two have fallen out. Your relationship – it was so lovely.' She pointed to the table. 'Sit here and admire my garden, and I'll go and get us some coffee. You remember how it was my dream to have a place like this?'

'Of course,' I said, my voice cracking slightly. 'It's wonderful. It's exactly how you said it would be.'

She disappeared into the house and I looked around at the lush gardens, dotted with tables and wrought-iron seats. Her personality was everywhere, in the mix of colours of the flowers, all the plants flowing like water, spilling out of their beds, trickling down walls, great waves of scarlet and hot-pink blooms beneath silver-grey olive trees dotted with tiny fruit. Suddenly a small cry broke the silence; a child's wail. My heart began to thump. Dina reappeared from the house with a tray of coffee, laid it on the table and smiled. 'I'll be back in a second,' she said. 'There's someone I'd like you to meet.' She returned moments later with a tiny baby snuggled against her chest, no more than a few weeks old.

'This is Pavle,' she said, and my stomach twisted at hearing the name.

I stared at the two of them, mother and child, and it felt as if a great weight was pressing down on my heart. 'I didn't know you had a baby. I'm so . . . I'm so glad it's not a girl.' As soon as the words were out I realized how awful they sounded. 'I just mean, I'm sorry – I don't think I could bear it.'

'I do understand,' she said. 'I adore this little bundle, but he can never replace our baby girl.' Her eyes filled with tears and she gazed into the distance, to the wooded hills where she and I had first walked as teenagers, sharing fumbled touches and hot eager kisses beneath the olive trees. 'She was my first-born, Miro, yours and mine.'

'Is he a good man?' I said, abruptly. The pain was getting worse all the time and some self-destructive part of me wanted to make it as bad as possible, wanted to know about the man who shared this idyllic life with Dina, who had slipped into my place and given her a child that was strong and well. 'Are you happy?'

'Yes. And, yes.' There was a slight hesitation. 'Anton's a really good man. And he loves it here. After years in Zagreb, it's where he wants to be. When he first came I kind of bullied him into letting me get involved with the restoration of Konavle. I needed . . . something. We began to work together. I had the local knowledge, he had the power. We were a good team. I watched him fall in love with the area and it wasn't long before I realized he was falling in love with me too.'

'And you?'

'Oh, Miro. It's so difficult to explain. I know it happened so fast, so soon. But I was so lonely and I'd spent so long on my own. Pavle – he never tried anything but I knew what he wanted and sometimes I wanted it too, just for comfort, just so that I didn't have to be alone with my thoughts and memories. But I never did. And then it turned out that the whole village thought I had. They damned me for something I hadn't even done. And so when it became clear that Anton felt the same way, I was so lonely and so tired that part of me just thought, Well, if that's what people think of me, then that's what I'll do. I won't wait for Miro, or grieve for my marriage. I'll just move on.'

'You broke my heart.'

'Well, you broke mine *first*,' she said, and the baby stirred at the force of her words. She looked down, dropped a kiss on his head. 'Oh God, I don't mean that. I'm so sorry . . . That day at Ivo's funeral, I felt so terrible – it felt so *wrong* telling you I was seeing someone else. I was almost going to say I'd leave him, and then . . . and then you were sleeping with Marian again.'

I laughed, but there was no humour in it. 'You know the irony of that? All the time in Sarajevo I hadn't been sleeping with her. You were what got me through, thinking of you. I really thought we had a chance. And then Marian came back, unexpectedly, and . . .'

Dina held her hand up. 'You don't have to explain. I can't imagine what your life was like there, the pressures you were under. I used to worry about you, every night I'd pray that you were safe; even when Anton and I were together I'd watch the news obsessively, just in case I saw you, just so I could know where you were.'

'But you were so angry with me you couldn't forgive me.'

'That day, Ivo's funeral, you asked me if I still loved you? I was so close, *so* close to just putting my arms around you and begging you to stay.'

'I would have done. That was what I was offering. I *said* that.'

'I know. But I couldn't have you come back just for me; you had to want to be here for *you*. Otherwise I knew one day you'd resent me, this wouldn't be enough for you, this life. For Anton, the restaurant is enough. He's done the city living, the big job. But you, I think I'd have felt like I was restricting you in some way, and in the end I might have made you unhappy. I couldn't have borne that.'

I looked away, wondering if she was right. Kate appeared in my mind again and I wondered where she was, travelling through my country with a camera over her shoulder, sunglasses on her forehead, scribbling furiously into a notepad.

'I might put him down,' Dina said suddenly, 'and perhaps we could walk a little. Anton's in Dubrovnik this morning but his cousin is staying with us: I can leave Pavle with her for a little while. I'd like . . . it would be nice to talk more. If that's OK.'

I nodded, watched as she carried the baby into the house and reappeared minutes later, wrapping a cream shawl around her shoulders. I stood up and she slipped her arm into mine; my skin shivered slightly at her touch.

'Can you tell me – why you went to Sarajevo? How you lived there?'

'I don't know if I can,' I said truthfully. 'At the time I think I was just desperate to escape. It was like living in a different world, and that was what I needed – somewhere there was nothing to remind me of you or Irina. It was a crazy place – from the moment you woke up it was just gunfire and adrenalin and people competing to take the biggest risks. I found that weirdly comforting, because I could just get lost in it, forget everything I'd done, all the pain I'd caused.'

'Oh, Miro.' She looked up at me, her eyes soft with concern. 'Did I make you feel like this? Is this what I condemned you to?'

'No. God, no. It was my fault, all of it, and I couldn't face that. Don't you understand? That's why I went, why I just kept running – Zagreb, Sarajevo, Postić.'

'You were in *Postić*?'

'Briefly. That was where it ended. It was . . . I saw Goran there. Suddenly, completely out of the blue. He was part of, well, you know what went on there. And when I saw that, I just went crazy. It was like he was the only person left in the world I had to believe in; I'd lost you, Irina, Josip had gone, Pavle was the enemy, Mother and Pa had let you down so spectacularly, but Goran – I clung to him, the idea of him. And then to see what he had become . . .' I closed my eyes, the horror of it flooding back. 'I nearly killed him, Dina. I nearly bloody killed him.'

'Oh God,' she whispered. 'What have you been through? What did I start? If it wasn't for me . . . so often I've asked myself what right I had to throw you out of your own house that night you came back from Dubrovnik. I'd seen Mesić, he'd made it perfectly clear that even if you had got back with the medicine it would probably have done no good. But I was so angry it had to be someone's *fault*. I made it yours.'

She fell silent and we walked slowly through the woods until we came to a small clearing. I felt her fingers tighten around my arm and followed her gaze to an old olive tree that stood alone in the bright sunlight. Beneath it spread a carpet of flowers: scarlet poppies, cream lilies, pink daisies shimmering in the breeze. Dina's face was streaked with tears and I knew, without hearing her say the words, that this was where our beloved daughter lay buried, here in the Konavle earth that defined her mother, beneath the blue sky, in the shade of an olive tree.

'I brought her here the day she died,' she whispered. 'Pavle drove me – he was the only person that could get us into Konavle. We used to sit beneath this tree, didn't we? Do you remember?'

I nodded, my heart too full to speak. I thought of my daughter: her sudden, sweet giggle; how fragile she felt in my arms; the soft, snuffling noises she made as she burrowed into my neck; her tiny hand, warm against my cheek. A tear tipped over on to my face, another, then another and suddenly I was aware of Dina's hand in mine, her fingers tight against my skin.

'It should have been you. I knew there was only one place I could bear our daughter to be, and Pavle dug the grave and I planted the seeds, but it should have been you.'

'I still miss her.' I wiped my hand across my face, and suddenly the breeze dropped and everything was perfectly still. Just for a moment it felt as if I was looking at a photograph, a perfect moment in time, and I knew that all the journeys I had made since Pavle drove me away from Ljeta had been leading here, back to this peaceful, sunlit clearing where my daughter lay sleeping beneath the flowers. 'I've so longed to know where she is.'

'I'm so sorry,' Dina whispered. 'I'm so, so sorry.'

'I'm here now,' I said, and slipped an arm around her. 'We're all here at last.' I felt her body freeze for a moment and then I tilted her face up to mine and kissed her, the softness of her lips so familiar to me. For a second, a brief, blissful second, we were back in our sunlit bedroom in our tiny cottage, sheets draped around our entwined bodies, the air thick with intimacy and love. And then she gently drew away and she was smiling and crying and I knew we had kissed for the very last time.

The sun felt a little softer as we began to walk back to the restaurant, and as the gardens came into view she stopped and looked up at me. 'And you? Is there someone in your life?'

'I think so. Hope so. There hasn't been for a long time. I think, you know, I wasn't really free.'

'And now you are?'

My throat tightened. 'Yes, I think I am. I think we both are. I think that's the saddest thing of all.'

She said nothing for a moment and then smiled up at me, her face wet with tears. 'We were lucky though, weren't we? The years we were together – I look back and it all seems so idyllic. That last summer with our baby girl – those memories are perfect, aren't they? Nothing will ever be like that again. It was such an innocent time.'

'But you're happy?'

She nodded. 'It's a different kind of happiness. Maybe it's more real. But I'd never change what we had, you and me.'

'I'm so pleased you're happy,' I said. 'Pleased . . . for your son. I like that you called him Pavle.'

'You know he loved Ljeta as much as any of us,' she said slowly. 'It was terrible, what the war did to him. He was not a bad man, although he did bad things, and he'll never, never be able to come back here. I wanted to call my son Pavle so that something of him would always be here. He was a part of all our pasts.'

I looked at her for a moment, suddenly remembered that last, sunlit lunch at Tomas's before the occupation really began; Dina lifting our daughter into the air, the overwhelming rush of love I had felt for them both. 'All our pasts,' I said, slowly, my heart twisting at the memory 'You're right, we were lucky to have all that we did. She was perfect, wasn't she? Our gorgeous little girl.'

I drove away from her with a full heart, watching in the mirror as she waved goodbye, Pavle snuggled against her chest. I turned the car towards Morsać, to the tiny beach we had swum off as teenage lovers. I sat on the stones and wept, for my baby girl beneath the olive tree, for the beautiful woman who had once been mine, now happy in her life with her new son and unseen husband. My tears fell for the people we had been, the love we had shared, the life we had dreamed of, that Dina had gone on to build without me. And I wept most of all because I knew that after the long dark years of guilt and regret, what I had said was true: I was finally free to move on.

When I arrived back at my parents' house, Pa came out to meet me, his face pale and tired. 'Cvita told me where you went,' he said. 'I'm proud of you. It can't have been easy.'

'It wasn't, but it was the right thing to do. I still love her, Pa, and I think she still loves me, but we've made our peace. I think somehow after everything that's happened, it's the most we could wish for.'

'Peace is all any of us wish for,' said Pa, slipping an arm around my shoulders. 'Even that brother of yours is a quieter soul than he used to be.'

'He's here?'

'He was. He's gone down to Ljeta. I think he's hoping you'll join him in a bit. Cvita's with your mother if you want to go up.'

I nodded at Pa and climbed the stairs to the bedroom. When I opened the door it seemed that Mother was asleep, but as I drew closer she opened her eyes and smiled. 'He came,' she whispered. 'He looked so well. Made me promise . . . the wedding.'

I looked at Cvita. 'Wedding?'

She laughed. 'Oh, Mother, you never could keep a secret. Goran wanted to tell Miro himself. He's getting married.'

'What?'

My mother smiled. 'Tara,' she murmured.

She seemed to drift a little after that, and I sat with my sister and we talked a little of our house in Knin and the tiny kitchen, hoping she could hear us, that our voices would take her back to where she had been happiest, before our world grew crazy and dark. After a while she squeezed her fingers around my hand and I leaned in towards her.

'Go to him,' she whispered. 'Be with your brother. You have lots to say to each other.'

I smiled down at her. 'Yes. Lots to tell. But we'll come back and see you later. We'll come together.'

She closed her eyes and nodded; within seconds her breathing had slowed and I felt Pa's hand on my shoulder.

'He's at Tomas's place,' he said. 'Take a while. Have a beer together. And then come back, and when she wakes up we'll all be here for her. Her family, back together. It's the greatest gift we can give her now, Miro, the one thing that will truly bring her happiness.'

As I drove to the village I realized that coming back had been nothing like I imagined; life in Ljeta had changed, moved on, and it would keep changing; Cata would be running the restaurant, there would be plans for Goran's wedding, businesses coming back to life. It was different and yet the same, just as Kate had said, new lives built on the ruins of the old, and for the first time I began to feel fortunate rather than bereft, lucky that so many of those I loved had survived, that we could move on together. I walked on to the harbour front and stood, looking down the cobbles at the late-afternoon sun shimmering on to the sea, the air warm with laughter and music and the chink of glasses on tables.

And then I saw him, sat on his own outside Tomas's cafe, an open pack of Opatija on the table, legs stretched out into the sunshine. Goran. For a moment I thought of my mother, sleeping in the dimly-lit bedroom, Pa by her side, of Dina out in the garden with her husband and son, and of Kate, somewhere on the road, camera to hand, notepad on the table, and I realized that for the first time in forever my thoughts were of the future, rather than the past.

'*Moj brate*,' I murmured, and as I said the words he looked up, as if he had heard them, saw me, extended his arm in a long, languid wave. 'My brother.' I waved back, watched for a second as the slow, wide smile lit up his features. He looked the same, just the same, and I began to walk across the cobbles towards him, to sit beside my brother in the warm Croatian sun.

TIMELINE

1945 – In the post-war period, the Federal People's Republic of Yugoslavia is created by Josip Broz Tito, a communist federation of six Balkan states – Croatia, Slovenia, Serbia, Bosnia-Herzegovina, Montenegro and Macedonia – and two autonomous states: Vojvodina and Kosovo

1980 – Josip Broz Tito dies

1986 – Serbian Academy of Sciences and Arts produces memorandum claiming Kosovo and Vojvodina should be reabsorbed into Serbia

1987 – Political rising star Slobodan Milošević promises to return Kosovo to Serbia.

September 1987 – Milošević becomes leader of the Serbian Socialist Party (formerly Communists)

March 1989 – Kosovo and Vojvodina returned to Serbian control

May 1989 – Milošević is elected President of Serbia

1989 – Communist regimes collapse across Europe, creating a new hunger for democracy in Yugoslavia's six states

April–May 1990 – First free election in Croatia in 50 years takes power from the Communists and awards it to Franjo Tuđman and his fiercely nationalistic Croatian Democratic Union Party

August 1990 – Serbs put up roadblocks around the Krajina region and declare 'Serb Autonomous Areas' – later the Republic of Serb Krajina

June 1991 – Croatia and Slovenia become the first of the six states to declare independence. After a ten-day war, with few casualties, Slovenia leaves the federation. In Croatia, with swathes of territory with a high population of Serbs, war breaks out immediately

October 1991 – The JNA (Yugoslav National Army) invades Croatia, surrounding Dubrovnik. The siege lasts for eight months. By the end of 1991 almost one-third of Croatian territory is under Serb control

January 1992 – UN-sponsored ceasefire in Croatia, with UN troops in Serb-held areas, sees the JNA switch focus to Bosnia. Armed conflict continues in Croatia on a more intermittent, localized scale, until 1995

April 1992 – Bosnia-Herzegovina declares independence

April 1992 – Siege of Sarajevo begins, continuing until February 1996

May 1992 – The JNA withdraws from Dubrovnik and Bosnia

May 1992 – War breaks out in Bosnia between the newly-formed Army of Republica Srpska, the Croatian Defense Council and the Army of Republic of Bosnia and Herzegovina

July/August 1995 – Croatia launches Operation Storm to reclaim all the areas in the Republic of Serb Krajina; thousands of Serbs are forced to flee to Serb-held regions in Bosnia

December 1995 – Dayton Peace Accords bring the conflict in Bosnia to an end, with the country divided into two parts: a Muslim-Croat federation and a Serb republic

ACKNOWLEDGEMENTS

This is a novel that belongs to many people; sadly there is only space here to thank some of them. To the wonderful Laura Longrigg at MBA, whose patience, wisdom and kindness have helped make this book what it is; to Jane Wood and the Quercus team, for making the dream a reality; to Lorenc in Sarajevo, for answering all my questions with patience and honesty; to Jane Knight at *The Times*, for all her support – and for keeping me in work so I didn't actually have to starve in a garret.

But it is my friends and family who deserve my most heartfelt thanks. To Sara, chief reader, plot strategist and general Mrs P. O. Support, and to her deputy, Ali, for always making me laugh; to Roy, for something like twenty-seven years of dedication to the cause; to my esteemed writerly colleagues in the Brymore Group, Marky B and Jon, and to the whole, much-loved UKC posse; to newer writerly chums in my CB Group – particularly Theresa, Kate and Lisa; and to Hobby, who remains the best friend a girl could wish for, without ever having read a word. To my wonderful sisters, nieces and nephews and, of course, to Mark, whose inherent goodness, endless patience and tendency to bounce when excited are invaluable gifts in my life.

To everyone else – you know who you are, and thank you.

I have never forgotten that this is a book about a war, as bloody and futile and tragic as all wars. What happened in Yugoslavia, and that it was *allowed* to happen, is one of the most shameful episodes in recent history. This story is for all those, of whichever country, religion or race, who lost someone they loved. May they rest in peace.

A QUICK INTERVIEW WITH ANNABELLE THORPE

You're a seasoned journalist, but this is your first novel. What made you decide to try fiction, and how did the experience of writing *The People We Were Before* differ from writing you've done in the past?

Ironically I was writing fiction long before I became a journalist – ever since childhood. The idea was that journalism would just be a way to fund my novel-writing, but it took a long time to work out that way. Writing *The People We Were Before* was an absolute revelation; journalism is very structured, with an accent on clarity and conciseness. The freedom and length of fiction feels wonderfully liberating.

Were you at all nervous about writing male characters? Did you find it any different to writing women?

I was only nervous as to whether the characters would ring true – if they'd actually be male *enough*. Oddly, I find writing male characters easier than women – more straightforward and easier to make humorous.

What made you choose the Balkan conflict as your subject matter?

It didn't start out that way – the book was always set in Croatia, but originally I didn't particularly want to go into detail about the war – I felt it was too dark. But I did a lot of research and found it so fascinating – and also so shocking that something so awful happened in Europe so recently. It kind of drew me in and I started to feel it was something I *should* write about, so that people might gain a little understanding of what happened.

The war reporters in general, and Nic in particular, seem to have quite a flippant – one might even say callous – attitude towards the conflicts and countries they are covering. Was this informed by real-life journalists you've worked with?

Yes I think it was. Journalists do have to remain distanced because they are there to report a story, rather than become emotionally involved. The best journalists remain very clear-eyed about that. I think flippancy is a classic way to deal with traumatic and challenging situations; when I worked in newspapers I often found people would make jokes about horrifying stories. I was never particularly comfortable around that, and it's one of the reasons I wouldn't make a good foreign correspondent, although the job does appeal to me. You have to be very tough.

One of the best things about the book is the way it balances some incredible dark moments with rays of hope and humour. Did you find that balance easy to achieve?

Actually I did find that relatively easy. I'm a great believer in using humour to diffuse difficult or upsetting situations, and think that when you're dealing with quite dark situations it's essential to lighten the mood every now and then. With fiction, as with life.

Nowadays, Croatia is more famous as a holiday destination and setting for *Game of Thrones* than as the site of a civil war. Do you think it's important that we remember the atrocities, or should Croatia be allowed to move away from its past?

I don't see the two as mutually exclusive. Every country in Europe has periods of conflict and darkness in its past; Croatia's is simply more recent. I think it's very much up to individuals who live there; when you visit, some want to talk about the war, others won't mention it. It's not for me to say which is best.

Did you incorporate any of your own experiences of Croatia into the book?

Yes, particularly the early chapters. We had family holidays in Croatia – or Yugoslavia as it was then – when I was young, and Miro's early life is very much drawn from the memories of those trips.

And the quick-fire round:

Home or away?

Home. Then away. Or the other way round. Each makes the other feel more precious.

What keeps you sane?

The sea. I grew up by it and moved back to it a few years ago. Its constant movement, changing moods and infinite sense of space never fail to make me feel better.

What are you currently reading?

I'm actually researching my next novel, set in Marrakech, so I'm reading *The Caliph's House* by Tahir Shah and *A Street in Marrakech* – a fascinating book written by the wife of a US academic, who lived in the medina for a year in the 1970s.

Night in or night out?

Night out.

One thing people would be surprised to find out about you?

I'm a worrier. Not when it comes to travel – I often travel solo and never feel anxious – but about more mundane, everyday things. It's a family trait.

And finally, what is the one must-see place and one must-eat dish that any visitor to Croatia shouldn't miss out on?

I'd have to say the Plitvice Lakes, which I finally got to recently. It's a national park in inland Croatia, with huge waterfalls cascading down into lakes that have a specific mineral in them that colours them vivid blues and greens. It's an astonishingly beautiful place. And to eat – *crni rizoto* – black risotto, coloured with squid ink. It sounds revolting but it's actually delicious; salty and syrupy and a classic Croatian dish.

READING GROUP QUESTIONS

We hope you've found plenty to talk about in *The People We Were Before*. If you need to, these questions should provide a good starting point for discussion.

1. Who was your favourite character and why?
2. How much did you know about the 1990s Balkan conflict before reading this book? How has *The People We Were Before* influenced your understanding of it?
3. Do you think Miro and Dina could ever have found a way back to each other? Is it partly pride keeping them apart, or is their rift truly irreparable? If so, where do you think the end really comes?
4. Can you sympathise with Miro's decision to sleep with Marian? What did you think the consequences were going to be?
5. How far do you think some of the responsibility for Miro and Dina's split lies with the wider community, e.g. Miro's mother and Bobo?
6. Did you predict what Goran ended up doing in the war? Were you surprised by it?
7. Do you feel sympathy for Pavle? How do you think you'd have coped in a situation like his, having to treat as enemies people you grew up with?
8. What do you think of Josip's decision to leave Croatia completely? Is he a coward, or was he sensible to refuse to be sucked into the violence?
9. Which do you think Dina saw as the biggest betrayal: Miro not arriving back in time to save Irina, him sleeping with Marian, or the way that the whole village, especially his family, and even Miro himself, assumed she was sleeping with Pavle?
10. Do you think the jokes the war journalists make – like Croatia coming 'back from the brink!' again – are a reasonable response to their situation?
11. Do you think this book has a happy ending?